Praise for James A. Misko's Other Book
As All My Fathers Were

"Exhilarating"

"Incredibly entertaining...With keen commentary and descriptions of life in Nebraska, the author leaves readers contemplating the story long after its exhilarating conclusion."
—Review, *Nebraska Life*

"Unfailingly entertaining"

"An extraordinarily well written and unfailingly entertaining read from beginning to end, *As All My Fathers Were* showcases the impressive storytelling talents of novelist James A. Misko. Very highly recommended for community library General Fiction collections, *As All My Fathers Were*, it should be noted for personal reading lists that this outstanding novel is also available in a Kindle edition ($9.95)."
—Midwest Book Review

"Exciting . . . old-fashioned storytelling"

"In Jim Misko's exciting new novel, *As All My Fathers Were*, two aging brothers set out by horseback up the beautiful but endangered Platte River. Their odyssey into the heart of the contemporary American West is both harrowing and inspiring. Anyone who thinks that old-fashioned storytelling in the tradition of Lonesome Dove and Cold Mountain has gone the way of the Platte River buffalo herd must read this fine novel."
—Howard Frank Mosher   ⸻hor of *God's Kingdom*

"Illuminating"

"In this tough but tender story of two estranged brothers—and their event-filled trek down Nebraska's Platte River—Misko simultaneously paints a memorable portrait, as incisive as it is illuminating, of America's disappearing past and its increasingly conflicted future."
—Robert Masello, author of *The Romanov Cross*

"A must read"

"What is extraordinary about Jim Misko's *As All My Fathers Were* is how he makes the land, Nature, practically a main character in his stories. You can't read his novels without feeling you've been in that world, and if you haven't, you envy those who have and still are. To do this, and still hold onto tension and the excitement of good storytelling with themes that have meaning to us, makes *As All My Fathers Were* a must read for anyone who wants to breathe fresh air."
—Andrew Neiderman, author of *The Devil's Advocate*

"Remarkable"

"*As All My Fathers Were* is a refreshingly unapologetic, environmental polemic—one with living characters and a pulse. But far more remarkable than the story of two Nebraska farmers on a quest to save their land, is its author: an 80-something self-described gun-toting political conservative. Jim Misko's condemnation of modern agribusiness bares an essential truth: Nature knows no politics, and we're all in this together. Off in the distance, you can hear Edward Abbey, Rachel Carson, and the Platte River itself applauding."
—Nick Jans, author of *A Wolf Called Romeo*

"Absorbing"

"If you want to know how the Platte River works, read James A. Misko's absorbing and rambunctious tale of Seth and Richard Barrett, who must complete a journey up the river from its confluence with the Missouri to its source near North Platte, Nebraska, and back if they are to inherit the family farm. In *As All My Fathers Were*, you'll learn the natural history of this once wild river that shaped the land and those who lived near it but in the past century has been broken by energy generation and the agricultural industry. Yet as Misko's novel bears witness, the Platte still has the power to inspire the imagination and fine literature.

—Lisa Knopp, author of *What the River Carries*

"Misko at his best"

"A passion play for the New West, *As All My Fathers Were* gathers momentum the way a river grows, gathering substance with every bend and merging channel, and shines in its descriptive writing. This is Misko at his best."

—Lynn Schooler, author of *Heartbroke Bay*

"A masterpiece"

"Jim Misko has done it again. *As All My Fathers Were* is a masterpiece. This novel has everything a reader searches for in pursuit of a fine book—strong characters, brilliant dialogue, exciting plot, tension that bounces off every page, conflict, high ideals and villainy. In addition, by the end of the book, the average reader is far better educated and informed of a real-life issue of which the vast majority is uninformed."

—Stephen Maitland-Lewis, author of *Emeralds Never Fade*

Other Books by James A. Misko

FICTION

The Most Expensive Mistress in Jefferson County

The Cut of Pride

As All My Fathers Were

The Path of the Wind

NON-FICTION

Creative Financing of Real Estate

How to Finance any Real Estate any Place any Time

How to Finance any Real Estate
any Place any Time – Strategies That Work

FOR WHAT HE
COULD
BECOME

a novel

JAMES A. MISKO

Copyright © 2004 by James A. Misko

For information regarding special discounts for bulk purchases,
please contact Square One Publishers at 877-900-2665.

Cover and interior design by Frame25 Productions
Cover photo by Darryl Pederson
Endpaper maps courtesy of AT Publishing

Iditarod map the work of Thom Eley,
Mapping Solutions, Anchorage, AK.

Manufactured in the United States of America

10 9 8 7 6 5 4 3 2

Library of Congress Control Number:

ISBN 978-09640826-1-8

Misko, James A.1932 -
For What He Could Become

To Patti, Carrie,
Shannon, and Laurie

*"The important thing is this: To be able at any moment,
to sacrifice what we are for what we could become."*
—Charles du Bois

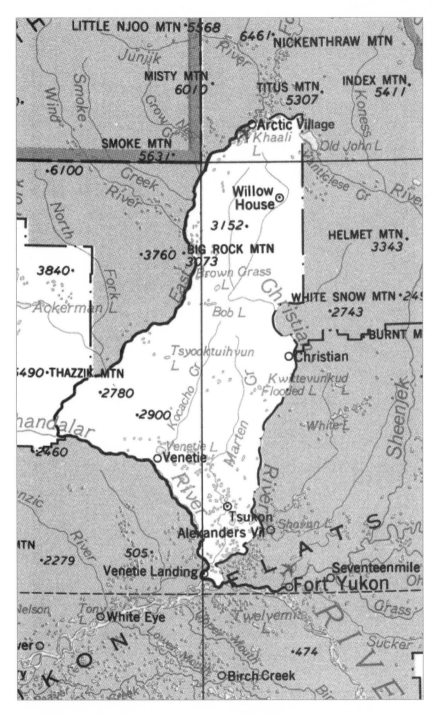

Ninety mile trail from Arctic Village to Venetie where Bill boarded
the paddle wheel steamboat to Whitehorse, Yukon Territory.

CHAPTER 1

BILL WILLIAMS NOTICED THAT there was no sound in the woods—no bird calls, no squirrel chirring. He was lying on his stomach in a rivulet of snowmelt coming out of the hills, the cold water seeping into his shirt. Water penetrated his pants, wet his thighs, and made him shiver, but he didn't move.

Upwind and 40 yards away on the side of a hill a smallish black bear was feeding in a blueberry patch, and with a bite down and a swing of its head it stripped everything into its mouth. The sound of tearing leaves and brush was close enough for Bill to hear it. He'd smelled the bear for some time, tracking it into the breeze drifting down from the hills, the smell like rotting salmon on the stream banks.

It was not a big bear. He had seen others that were much bigger in the valley across the river from Arctic Village.

Lying partway into the trail with the rifle at his shoulder, he had a clear view of the bear's hindquarters. It had taken him some time to get to that position but it had not been hard work—just slow, tedious, and wet. When he had seen bears running, they went so fast that it hadn't occurred to him how deliberately they moved when they were feeding. He could wait as he had been taught to wait. If his father were alive he would be proud to see him wait to take the animal with one well-placed shot, no big damage to meat or hide.

As his Dad had told him so many times, the trick was to sneak up on the bear from down wind. If luck was with the hunter, all he would see was the bear's hindquarters until the final moment. Done right, it would be a clean kill. Bill would be able to tan the hide and put it beneath his bedclothes to hold out the cold, or give it to Ilene.

No doubt the bear had been searching the stream banks for salmon and the sunny slopes for ripening berry patches. This diet, he guessed, was what made the bear's coat shine as if it had been oiled.

But there was something else going on. It was so quiet he thought for a moment he had gone deaf. He opened his mouth and popped his ears, straining to pick up a sound. He could feel his heart pumping, the rhythmic beat like a drum. Something was wrong.

The bear stopped chewing and lifted its head. It turned to the right, jabbed its nose in the air and sniffed. Then it lifted a front leg and swung to the left. Muscles bunched, ears twitching, it sensed something and froze. In the next instant the bear whirled around and rose up on its hind legs, jaws open, claws raking the air. The roar sprang from deep in its throat, passing over Bill with a vibration and volume that hurt his ears.

He gasped. His mind registered the picture the bear offered, but a louder roar from behind him purged any thoughts of taking a shot.

With the roar he felt the ground vibrate beneath him and turned his head in time to see a huge grizzly fill his field of vision. The bear had to be ten feet and at least 800 pounds, and it didn't see him or smell him. What it saw and smelled was the black bear, on which it focused with its pig-like eyes.

In seconds the grizzly moved from behind Bill, stepped on his leg, sprinted down the trail, and with a powerful swing of his foreleg knocked the small bear over. The bawling and roaring of the two animals deafened Bill, who jammed his hands over his ears as panic raised a sour taste in the back of his mouth. He swallowed but it wouldn't go away. He saw chunks of peat moss flung into the air and a cloud of dust rising. Through it all was the smell—a sour, dead, fish-stinky odor that stuck in his nostrils. Pieces of plants, small rocks, and earth were dropping like rain.

The black bear, forced on its back, was raking the grizzly with its claws and teeth while being pushed and pounded into the small stream. The grizzly had it by the throat and was shaking it like a dog shakes a rabbit. In seconds the battle was over, the grizzly looking down at the still form between its front legs, its nose sniffing for any remaining life. Suddenly everything was still. Bill took his hands from his ears as the peat dust settled on the ground and water bubbled around the lifeless form partially blocking its flow.

The pain in Bill's leg had not yet started—the leg was numb. Whether it was cut or broken he didn't know. But he was able to stand on it, and clutching the rifle in his right hand he half ran, half hobbled down the trail he had come up from the river.

Funny feeling—like running on a wooden leg.

He burst through an alder patch, where low-lying limbs reached for his feet, Devil's-club thorns pierced his pants and stuck in his thighs. He made no attempt to dodge them but wished he'd cut them down on his way up the trail.

The back of his neck began to itch. He imagined the bear coming on behind him faster than he could run and his heart thudded in his chest. He wanted to look back but knew he could not.

Everything he knew about bears screamed at him to climb a tree, but his feet and legs moved unattached to his mind and even as he told himself to climb, he couldn't make himself do it. He would have to stop to climb a tree, and if the bear was close, it would get him before he got high enough to be out of its reach.

His balance was threatened by his feet wind-milling out of control while a picture formed in his mind of him falling on his face, heart pounding, chest heaving, the bear standing over him. Miraculously his feet missed every root, every hole.

As he cleared the brush line, the bank of the river was in front of him. He dropped the rifle, planted one foot in the sand, and launched himself into the river, legs churning, arms thrashing, head back, gulping air as he crashed through the surface, kicking hard under water.

Underneath, water bubbled past his ears. He held his breath and swam against the current the water tearing at his clothes, pulling him downstream, slowing him down. The trapped air exploded from his lungs like a breaching whale when he broke the surface with his eyes clamped shut.

He had no idea how far he was from the bank. He gulped air and was ready to dive again when the sound of laughter drifted over the water. He tried to stand, tripped and fell, then was tumbled downstream by the current until his feet brushed across a shallow place and he stood up and shook the hair from his eyes. A quick glance at the bank showed the bear had stayed on his side of the river.

Herb Chulpach and his uncle Charlie stood on the bank, laughing. They pointed at the bear pacing back and forth upstream from the trail, sniffing the rifle. It turned and disappeared into the brush. Bill took a huge breath, then waded to the opposite bank and sat down, his head in his hands.

Herb and Charlie came over to him. They didn't speak but glanced at each other. The skin around Herb's mouth puckered up and then relaxed, and it looked to Bill like he was laughing inside. Bill didn't look at Charlie.

"Fast bear," Charlie said.

Herb snickered. The old man looked straight ahead as if he were plotting where the bear would come out next.

"Were you teaching the bear to dance?" Charlie asked.

Bill sighed. "I was hunting the bear." He wrung out his shirt.

"Hunting." Charlie nodded. "Pack on the ground. Gun on the ground. Feet in the air."

Herb pursed his lips. Both hands clasped around one knee, he rocked back and forth, a smile on his face.

"Just as I was getting ready to shoot the black bear, this grizzly made a fight with it. On its way, it stepped on my leg."

Charlie nodded, the smile fixed on his face. "Were they both male bears?"

"I didn't examine their privates." Bill held the shirt up and shook it.

"Maybe you got in the middle of their house and that old bear figured you were trespassing." Charlie snorted little bursts of air out of his hairy nostrils while Herb continued to rock back and forth. What a pair.

"Did it occur to you that I could have been killed?"

They just looked at each other. He took off his boot and rolled up his pants to look at the place where the bear had stepped on him. The claw imprints were red in the center, blue-black in between, with blood trickling out of each imprint. Charlie put his hand on the pants and pressed them down so he could see better. He looked at the muscle that was beginning to swell, touched the claw marks with his fingers.

"You're lucky," he said. "To be between two bears and get some bad meat on your leg and a cut or two. You're dumb—but lucky."

Herb rolled up on his feet in that squat he always used on wet ground and appraised Bill's leg. Head tilted back, eyes squinting, making small sounds with his mouth. At last done with the examination, he looked Bill in the eye, nodded his head several times, and sat back down on the bank.

The wet socks clung to Bill's feet and he had to work to get the boots back on, his leg pulsing and pounding now that the numbness was wearing off. He lifted the leg a few times. No serious pain. Past injuries had taught him that the real pain would come tonight or tomorrow, maybe not for two days.

His rifle and pack were on the other bank. He thought about what Herb would tell Ilene and Verda at dinner tonight, about his father and Carl and the way they had killed bear. And then he said "To hell with it," got up and sloshed back into the river, picking the shallow spots to walk over, swimming the deeper channel to the far bank.

He opened the rifle bolt, removed the cartridge, and blew down the barrel, dislodging the dirt jammed in it. He allowed himself a quick glance at the bear's tracks on the bank, then limped upriver where he could wade across and head for home. He was hungry and his leg hurt. The three-day bear hunt had lasted three hours.

CHAPTER 2

"Your dad should have stayed around longer," Charlie said. "He should have taught you better about bears. I'm not a good hunter—but your dad, he knew everything about 'em."

He swirled a stick of dried salmon in oil and fed it, dripping, into his near-toothless mouth.

"Problem was," Carl said, "you didn't get in position and shoot fast enough. A quick shot would of killed the black and scared off the griz."

Bill took another piece of dried salmon, dipped it in the oil, and popped it in his mouth.

"Well, Dad didn't stay around," he said. "He shot himself, if you recall." The salmon was tough.

"Don't talk with your mouth full," Charlie said.

"I'd of had the black bear if that griz hadn't been tracking it too."

"I'd of gotten him," Carl said. "I'd be tanning that hide in the shed right now."

Charlie nodded.

There was a cramp in Bill's chest. It tightened, making his breathing come hard. Suddenly he wanted to breathe air that wasn't tainted with sweat and dried meat and fish oil. And Carl.

"Dad's been dead eight years and all I've heard since then is how good he was and how good you are. You'd think nobody else could hunt or drive dogs or any other damn thing but you, and you learned all of it from Dad. Well, he taught me some stuff too."

Carl said, "You don't seem to have learned it very well."

Charlie frowned at the brothers and twisted his hands together.

Carl stood up. "See you later."

"Where you going?" Bill asked.

"I think Ilene's expecting me. And I want to hear what Herb told the girls about the bear hunt. Or should I call it a bear stalk?"

"Call it anything you want."

"You want me to tell Ilene anything?"

Bill lunged at Carl, who was expecting it and wrapped his arms around his chest as Bill hit him in a flying tackle. Bill pulled loose and swung his fist in a roundhouse right that just missed Carl's face. As his body followed the momentum of the swing, Carl stepped in close and drove his fist into Bill's stomach. He crumpled to the floor, gasping for breath.

Charlie was watching the action as if it were a ping-pong match. Carl stood with legs spread, fists tight, waiting to see if there would be more.

"You can't have my girl," Bill spat out. "You got everything else. You can't have her!"

"Some got it and some don't, little brother."

And he was gone.

Charlie leaned back in his chair. Bill got up off the floor and stood with one hand on the table.

"Uncle Charlie . . . I've been thinking to go to the Yukon and get me a job on that highway they're building up to Alaska. Is it okay with you I go? I've got to get out of here. It's not like you need me here."

Charlie pondered a minute. "That's a long ways—first to Venetie—that's ninety miles. How you plan to get that far?"

"I can walk. Carl did it—I can do it."

Charlie shook his head. He thought about Isaac and Chris Katongan and what they looked like when the searchers found them near Century Creek. "Too hard. I know several people didn't make it. You don't know what it's like to . . . "

"I'm not a kid anymore Uncle Charlie. Carl's not the only one who can do things. You have to let me try—I know I can do it.'"

"What would your Dad say if I lost you?" Charlie got up, walked to the window and leaned on the counter looking out. He wore a scowl visible even in the dim light. His eyes clouding, he remembered his youth. He would have walked it at seventeen—he was sure of it. Now here was Bill, just a kid, wanting to follow that trail out of the village to Fort Yukon and a life away from us. For the last eight years he had been father and mother to the boys, treating their wounds, hearing their adventures, seeing them grow, knowing they were learning what it took to be a man in this world. The mother, dead for so long now, but the father—recent enough that he could still see his face.

"There's a trail. I'll be there in two days—three at the . . . "

"You can't hunt bear! How can go all that way by yourself?"

Bill looked down.

Charlie watched him, but did not speak. The muscles in his jaw flexed. He turned to look out the window. A truck started up somewhere in the village, the distant sounds penetrating the cabin walls, nearby a dog barked. Bill heard himself swallow.

"What do you know of these things?" Charlie said. "You're just a kid. Carl had been trapping with your dad—he knew hard times. He went when your dad was alive. If he got in trouble your dad could have helped him. I can't do that. Carl's a natural athlete—strong, capable. He could go now where your dad couldn't go." Charlie shook his finger at Bill. "You can't compare yourself to Carl." He turned his head slowly and stared at the floor.

"Uncle Charlie?"

The words hung in the air until old Charlie looked at him; him standing there with his arm's spread to his side beseeching providence, the ghost of his parents, and Charlie to let him go.

"I am not a child anymore. The Old Ones live along the way and if I get in trouble they'll help me. I know where food and water is—and it's still summer. I can make it easy. How can you keep me here when there is nothing for me here? Don't I have some rights?"

"You have rights!" Charlie confirmed. He tried to sort them out in his head.

For thirty years he had been an elder; he didn't remember how to think like a youth. Carl would stay; Bill would go.

Bill stood anchored to the floor, his head back, arm's out to his side, still as a statue.

After a minute, Charlie exhaled. "I think you can go."

Whichever way Charlie decided, Bill had expected to feel something. He could go. Now. Yet he didn't know what to think or feel. The chew of salmon sat in his mouth and he wondered how he had kept it there when he was hit in the stomach.

In the morning he had a small pack with an extra shirt and socks and some food. There was a trail down the west bank of the Chandalar River to Venetie, where he could catch a boat to Fort Yukon and then down the Yukon River to where the highway was being built. Surely they would hire him—he was young, strong, and knew the country. They would need someone like that.

Herb Chulpach and his daughters Ilene and Verda were with his uncle Charlie in front of the house when he came out.

Charlie had his usual sad-eyed expression on. He would grow older here and probably die before Bill got back. Herb would probably be gone too. Ilene, he longed to see again. He thought he loved her, but he'd never told her—he didn't have much to say to a girl, and that was a hard thing to get out. He didn't have anything to offer a girl, either. What he needed now was freedom and a chance to make some money. He didn't know what either would be like but he knew he wanted both.

Bill and Herb shook hands. He wanted to hug Ilene, hold her tight to him, feel her strong body pressed against his. She looked into his eyes and stood as close to him as she could. Maybe she wanted it too—but there were all these people around. He held out his hand and she took it.

"I'll be back," he said.

"I know you will." She squeezed his hand. "I'll miss you."

"Me too . . . and I'll write you."

"Write often. Tell me what you're doing and where you are—and when you'll be back." She squeezed his hand again. "Be careful, Bill. It's a long ways."

"I'll have money too."

"That'll be good."

He was looking in her eyes when he slowly lowered her hand. They looked like they were asking for something. Whatever it was, he wanted to give it to her. But what could he give her when he was leaving?

He came to Charlie who was looking at his feet. When he raised his head he was blinking.

"I haven't been as good for you as your Dad would have been."

"You've been plenty good, Charlie."

Bill noticed that he wore the same shirt he nearly always wore, faded cotton with frayed edges at the collar and a button missing on the pocket.

"Carl thought he would be here but he might not make it, since he's fixing the fish wheel. You might catch him when you're going downriver—tell him goodbye. He's a good brother." He shifted his feet. "Bill—you don't know the hardships ahead of you."

"I think I can do it okay."

Charlie gripped Bill's hand with both of his and held onto it for a long moment. Then he dropped his hands, turned, and walked toward the shed.

It took Bill a minute to get the pack adjusted on his back, since one of the straps was broken and wouldn't tighten. He had a little trouble with it because his eyes were misty. He waved to Ilene and Verda, wiped his nose on his sleeve, and walked south out of the village toward Venetie.

CARL HAD DONE THE ninety miles in three days during the winter of 1937, and Bill figured to make it in two to three days. He might not be able to kill a bear but he could sure walk out of the village on his two feet. It seemed reasonable that he could walk to the Yukon River, get on a boat, and find work on the highway. No one from Arctic Village had ever done that, and there was no reason he couldn't be the first.

The fish wheel was up on the bank with Carl bent over the axle, his back to Bill. The river sound would cover his steps—he could sneak up on Carl, scare him for once. But when he was ten feet away Carl spun around, a fish knife in his hand.

"Gotcha!"

Bill froze.

"Saw you coming."

"Oh." Bill started breathing again.

"Is that how you got up to the bear?"

"I did better than that." Bill tried again to adjust the strap on his pack.

"Not much," Carl said.

"He didn't even know I was there."

"Well, he knew when you crapped your pants," Carl said.

"Who told you?"

"Charlie told some. Herb told some. More than likely they only got it half right. Where you going?"

Bill walked over to the fish trap and shook it. "Venetie. Gonna go work on the highway."

Carl looked at him for a moment. "You know how far it is to Venetie?"

"I know how to walk."

Carl smiled. "Ninety miles is more than a walk, little brother. Let me see what you got in your pack." He opened the flap and rummaged through. "You remember how to write?"

"Sure I do."

"Well, you write us a letter at least every six months and let us know where you are and what you're doing."

Bill nodded.

"Take care of yourself. You won't have me there to back you up or get you out of trouble."

"I'll survive without it."

Carl smiled and offered his hand. Bill took it and immediately regretted it, for in one quick motion Carl pulled him forward so fast he couldn't move his feet, and the next thing he knew he was face down in the grass, the pack riding on his head.

"Damn you, Carl."

"Don't let them do that to you out there. Now get going, you'll never get to Venetie in that position."

CHAPTER 3

THE FIRST SIX MILES were easy, although his leg hurt some towards the end. He would not have known how far he'd gone except for a note on a spruce tree blaze written in pencil that read "6 m to A. Vil" and an arrow pointing the way he'd come.

At about twelve miles he stopped alongside a feeder stream and took out the caribou jerky, smoked salmon, and some dried low bush cranberries. He scooped water from the stream with his hand, then lifted his pants leg and examined the swollen black and blue wound. The scabs were tight, and so far there was no sign of infection. Leaning against a tree, he let his eyes drift over the river that flowed in front of him, looked up at the scattered clouds in an otherwise clear sky, took a deep breath, and closed his eyes.

It was a good day to be alive.

The food tasted good and the water sparkled.

When he finished eating he started to stand up. He staggered, then regained his balance but not before he dropped the food sack at his feet.

He frowned.

He was stiff like an old man. His boots seemed too small. Dizziness disoriented him for a moment and then he straightened up and stood without weaving. He'd thought he could at least cover thirty miles a day, and here he was wearing thin at twelve miles. The damaged leg throbbed.

He marched in place until the stiffness abated, stuffed the food in his pack and started down the trail. In thirty feet he stopped, reversed direction, and went back to the creek for more water. How many times had his Dad told him to drink water to help avoid cramps and stiffness?

For the first time, ninety miles seemed like an awful distance to travel.

The stiffness went away within a mile, and he picked up the pace. The dusk moved in early along the river with tree shadows stretched across the trail and the sun over his right shoulder, his eyes adjusting to less daylight. He stopped on a level place before it was dark and built a fire.

HE AWOKE WITH THE sun in his face, determined to make it to Venetie today. He had heard of people who'd walked forty to fifty miles in a day. If he ate and drank while he walked and kept his mind focused, he could make it.

His damaged leg was swollen and tender, but so far it hadn't held him back. He decided to run part of the way.

When he tried to run the pack jumped all over his back, but when he tried a slow gait the pack more or less stayed in place. He jogged for 100 paces, then walked for 100 paces. He got bored with counting the paces and soon he was jogging until it was hard to breathe, then slowing to a walk until his breath came normal again.

After a few hours he stopped for water and jerky even though he wasn't hungry and the water tasted awful. He tried to recall what his Dad had said about eating and drinking and resting, but it wouldn't come.

At mid-morning he ate some jerky even though he wasn't hungry. In mid-afternoon he sat down on a small bank above the trail. He stared at his feet and tried to wiggle his toes, which were so tight inside the boots he couldn't tell if they were moving or not. Now he remembered what his dad had told him: "Eat before you're hungry, drink before you're thirsty, rest before you're tired."

"Well—he didn't say anything about my feet."

He got up and dipped water from the river that tasted like it came from a moose pond. He bit off a piece of jerky and tucked it between his lip and gum and let it sit there tasting like sawdust. He would chew it in a few minutes when it had softened up and then he would try and figure out why there was no good taste to anything.

A glance at the western slope told him he had several more hours of sunlight followed by several hours of arctic twilight. He didn't know if he had it in him to go further. And then there was the satisfying thought that he could just lie here until he felt like getting up and going on.

His eyes closed and then his mind shut down and his entire body relaxed into sleep.

When he awoke he started to roll over and sit upright, but there wasn't a muscle in his body that would respond. Finally he was able to slide his arms under his hips and lever himself onto his side. He lay there for several minutes, then managed to sit up.

His legs, dangling over the side of the bank, were numb. There was no mental connection with them. He squeezed and rubbed the muscles to massage the numbness out. A cramp hit, and the pain forced him to stand. He struggled. Once up, he locked his knees and stood weaving on the uneven ground.

The pain returned, and he pulled up the pants leg until it stuck on the claw wounds. He eased the crusted material away from the seeping wound, which throbbed in the cool air. Infection. He went to his pack for an extra T-shirt to wrap it with, but the shirt wasn't there. He was sure it had been there yesterday.

He started to walk in little circles, urging his body parts to work together again, his feet feeling like solid blocks. He had not gone a mile when he picked a level place to remove his boots. With some misgivings he peeled off his right sock, pulling it inside out, a brown-red stain coming into view as he stripped it off from where it seemed glued to the last two inches of his toes. There were ugly stains where the skin on the toes had swollen, then blistered and broken.

He took the boot and sock off the left foot, which was nearly as bad.

While he rubbed the foot cradled in his lap he thought about how easy it all had seemed—walk to Venetie, get on the riverboat, get to the highway job. What could be so hard about that?

He tried to eat something but the food tasted like old wood and the water like melted pond ice in the spring. He sipped a mouthful of water, then spit it out.

He closed his eyes and took a deep breath to clear his mind. He rubbed his feet until calmness settled on him, then put on his extra pair of socks and lay on his back and looked up at the sky.

BIRDS AWAKENED HIM AND for a second he didn't know where he was. He got up on his hands and knees and then stood. The blisters stung. There was a stain on the new sock and he didn't know if he should pull it loose or not. He decided to leave it there and put on his left boot. The foot wasn't so bad, but the swelling and pain from the infection were worse. He put on the right boot.

He tested his feet in both boots, lifted them up and down and noticed the clear morning with few clouds, a light breeze off the river, perfect weather for walking.

The bear leg sent tingling messages up to his groin and down to his ankles, and lagged behind the other one so that his gait was uneven. A nausea accompanied by weakness came and went.

When he cleared a bend in the trail he sat down again. He tried drinking but only got a little water down. In a few minutes he stood up and walked and thought about jogging and even made it a few yards before he fell back into a walk.

His lips hung open and he breathed through his mouth, which dried out his tongue first, then the inside of his cheeks and then his throat. His feet moved at a little over two miles an hour as he walked into the day that was beginning to warm up, the morning sunshine spilling over the low mountains and splashing a new day's color on everything.

Around midday he collapsed on a low bank and thought about his feet, which had given up the numbness and started to hurt. He had limped for some miles but he wasn't sure he wanted to know what was going on with them.

The red stain on the sock stopped him. There wasn't anything he could do about a bleeding foot. He pushed on the ball of his foot, and pain coursed through to the ankle. He felt with the tips of his fingers under the toes, around them, and on the ends. There was no feeling, and now he debated about taking the other boot off.

A chill in his chest startled him and he shivered.

'It isn't cold. Why am I cold?'

He reached around, took the blanket out of his pack and pulled it over his shoulders. After several minutes he tried another sip of water.

He yelled at the river. "It's your mind that tells your body what it can do! I'm limping but my leg isn't broken. I'm young and strong and Venetie is not the end of the earth!"

Using both hands he opened up the boot as wide as he could and jammed his

foot into it. He pulled hard on the laces and bound the foot tight. His feet could bleed on the trail or drop off, but he would not stop until he got where he was going.

BILL WALKED INTO VENETIE on the fifth day after leaving Arctic Village. He had missed the riverboat by two days, and it wouldn't be back for two weeks. Which was okay with him. The emergency medical man in Venetie needed only five minutes to determine that he was dehydrated and to start a Ringers IV in his arm. Then he called a midwife in and asked if she would be so kind as to get a pan of water, soak Bill's socks off, and clean his feet—and please ask the medic to get him some sulfa power for his damned infection.

In two weeks the feet would heal. The sulfa would take care of the infection. The bruise on his leg would fade. The claw marks would soften in the years to come, but their outline would remain for the rest of Bill's life.

CHAPTER 4

BILL WALKED OUT ONTO the deck of the *Northland Echo*, a paddle wheeler headed up the Yukon River for Dawson City. At Fork Yukon the captain had leaned one elbow on the bridge railing and looked down at him when he limped up to the gangplank.

"Can I work my passage to Whitehorse?" Bill asked him.

"Looks like you're somewhat limited in what you can do," the captain shouted down.

"My dad taught me I'm only limited by what I think I can't do."

The captain looked upriver and started to put his pipe in his mouth. Then he yelled down; "If you can cut and haul wood, it'll buy you a passage."

"I can do that," Bill said.

"Come aboard."

The captain leaned on the railing smoking his pipe, his eyes following Bill as he climbed the steel stairs to the bridge.

"My wood crew took off to work on the new highway and I'm needing wood for my return trip." He looked toward town and took several puffs on his pipe. "I'll drop you off at Forty Mile. Then I'll be back, and go to Whitehorse. Should be there in a couple of weeks. Go below and see Orville, he'll fix you up with a place to sleep." He blew the smoke away from Bill. "Where you live?"

"On this boat, I hope."

The captain smiled. "Not very damn long you don't. Pretty soon you'll be living with the gnats and mosquitoes, bucking wood twelve hours a day and wondering if I'll ever come back upriver."

Orville had "fixed him up" with a blanket thrown on a wooden frame against the bulkhead.

Now he was standing on the deck of the first paddle wheeler he had ever seen, the hard wood vibrating with the rhythmic pounding of the engines, tickling the new skin on his feet. He wondered what Ilene would think about all of this and where he might find pencil and paper to write home.

As the boat neared a group of sandbars and small islands, it slowed, shuddered, and with a grinding sound stopped and held steady against the current. Two men brought a small boat to the fore deck, slid it over the side, attached a rope to the gunnel, and rowed away.

Bill watched them work the boat to the left bank and attach the line, which itself was attached to a cable, to a large cottonwood tree twenty feet up from the bank.

When the engines came to life, the giant winch tightened the cable until it was taut to the tree. And then, like a fish being hauled in, the stern swung around and the winch on the bow of the steamer reeled in the line, dragging the boat across the sand bar.

The captain yelled down at Bill: "Get away from the bow!"

Bill moved back to mid-ship and stood in the cargo door. The boat plopped into the deeper water when it slid off the sand, the cable went slack, and the men on shore rushed to unhook it from the tree.

Two other men ran to the winch and changed the angle of the drum so it would pull the line back on in even rows. Bill ran up to help, but they ignored him as they battled to pull a pin that held the winch at an angle.

A big man handed him a steel pry bar, then bent over to pull on the pin handle with both hands. The pin kept the winch head in place, but at the wrong angle to rewind the cable. Bill stuck the bar between the winch and the iron frame to relieve the pressure on it.

"NO!" yelled the man closest to him.

He pulled back. They continued tugging at the handle. The man took the bar from Bill, stuck it through the pin handle, pried on the framework, and popped the pin loose. The winch head turned toward the tree and the cable began winding back on.

The big man with the bar turned and looked at him. "Where'd you come from?"

Bill pointed at the deck. "Right here."

"Jeysus, Mary, and Joseph, but you like to of killed us all."

"I was just trying to help."

"And just what do you think we be usin' a bar like this for, laddie? It's not strong enough or long enough to be wedging the boat up the river, now is it?"

The man was at least six feet four inches and his stomach was as flat as the river.

"Well, now, never mind. We're alive and well and none of us has a steel bar stickin' between his ribs."

He clapped Bill on the shoulder, and it felt like he'd been cuffed by a bear. A gong sounded, and Bill spun around. Someone was shouting from the doorway.

"Chow." The man's head disappeared.

Bill's stomach was growling as he made his way to the doorway. The warm strong smells of meat and potatoes and boiling coffee met him when he walked through. Every head at the long table looked up at him.

"Sure and we saved you a seat, laddie," the big man who had taken the iron bar from him said. "Move over, you lunk," he said to the fellow next to him.

Bill sat between them, his eyes level with the tops of their shoulders. He'd never seen such large men, nor had he ever seen so much food on a table. There was a constant grabbing and shoveling of food from platters onto plates and the clatter of knives, forks, and spoons clanking on the plates, plus coughing, slurping, banging, and the shuffling of feet under the bench.

The plates of the men on both sides of him were half empty already, and nobody passed him anything. He reached for the potatoes and spooned several small ones onto his plate. He couldn't reach the hamburger or the gravy, and he noticed that anyone who wanted anything either stood up and reached for it or called out for it. He half-stood in his place and reached for the meat, but he was at least a foot short.

"What d'ya want, lad?" The big man asked.

"Meat, please"

"Just holler it out, we don't have all day to get you fed and your diapers changed."

The men laughed and the big man handed him the meat. Then he gathered all the food dishes and assembled them around Bill's plate. "Eat up, lad, let's go."

Several men had finished and left the table when Bill finally got everything on his plate and started eating. Everyone was gone except the big man and the fellow on the other side of him, both of whom had finished eating and were watching him eat.

"Jeysus, Mary, and Joseph," the big man said, "the company will be only payin' you for half time. The other half you'll be eatin'."

The cook mopped the table with one hand while the other grabbed any plate, cup, or flatware, and cleared the table, leaving nothing but what Bill was using. When the cook grabbed his empty cup, Bill set his fork down and leaned back. Quick as a cat snatching a mouse, the cook reached over his shoulder and took the plate with his left hand, the flatware with his right, and the table was empty.

Bill was no longer hungry—he could make it to the next meal, and he could find some water to wash down the three bites he'd swallowed. A grin started across his face as he looked at the big man and then he laughed.

"Mighty short meal," he said.

The big man's laughter filled the room as he pulled out his pocket watch.

"Short?" he said. "Why, I could've recited the entire catechism while you were makin' a stab at eatin'." He clapped Bill on the shoulder. "Let's be getting about it," he said as he rose from his seat.

Bill followed him out and they sat on a coil of rope on the front deck.

"What's yer name lad?"

"Bill Williams."

"Where ya from?"

"Arctic Village. It's north of Fairbanks."

"Oh me god—must be a cold one up there. And what made a lad like you get on a river boat?"

"Money. I need to make some money." Bill watched fascinated as Mike braided three strands of rope with his hands while never taking his eyes off the river. "Where're you from?"

"Originally from Ireland but I've been on the river so long I think I'm from here now. Me mother named me Mike O'Leary and sent me out into the world to make a name for myself and here I am, working on riverboats since 1935, single as a priest and saving my money for a small farm in Minnesota."

Bill smiled. "Why do you want a farm?"

"Come now, a man's gotta have a piece of land, you know. A place to call home. A cow, some ducks and geese, a few sheep. It's my plan to find a woman who'll put up with me and get married before I'm too old to father a child or two." He swung his arm to take in the whole boat, "Nary a man on this tug ain't got the same dream, lad. And you?"

Bills thoughts were of Ilene. He pictured the cabin he would build, the view it would offer and exactly where the woodpile would be.

"I bargained to cut the wood for my passage to Whitehorse so I can get a job on the highway."

"You ever cut wood?"

"Cut firewood since I was just a kid."

"This is cord wood. Different sort than firewood. You gotta cut and stack it and it has to be a certain length and weight so's a man can pick it up and throw it in the firebox. Four feet long and not more than fifty to seventy pounds. How many cord did the captain ask ye for?"

"Ten to fifteen."

Mike threw the braided rope on the deck. "Jeysus, Mary, and Joseph—and you just a pup." He shook his head. "Well, no doubt about it, you've got your work cut out for you."

"How hard can it be?"

"Hard? It's not only hard, it's dirty and it's sweaty, and you're all alone there with your own cookin' and campin' to do. You'll be pullin' a cross-cut saw in your dreams every night, and there won't be any pretty girls or good food or whiskey." Mike looked him up and down. "Well, you look stout enough to get it done, lad."

Over the next two days as the *Echo* worked her way through the sandbars around Saloon Island and through the braided channel near Halfway Whirlpool, Mike went through the process with Bill of working with a cross-cut saw, setting up a rubber man, and stacking wood with the least amount of effort.

WHEN THE *ECHO* REACHED Fourtymile Creek it nosed into the bank and tied up.

Mike and Bill jumped off and walked to the cutters camp. Mike handed him the saw. "Try your hand on this log," he said.

Bill made a dozen strokes then the saw warped up in the cut.

"No, no, no, laddie. You're putting too much muscle into it. Let it glide smoothly, like makin' love to a woman. You've made love to a woman, haven't you?"

Bill shook his head.

"Jeysus, Mary and Joseph, surely there will be a place in heaven for the likes of me who have to work with virgins on the wood pile."

"Why don't you cut wood?" Bill said. "You know all about it."

"I was smart enough to leave Ireland and smart enough to get off the wood pile. You gotta be half Injun to do that work."

Bill looked at Mike and smiled. "I am."

"You kiddin' me?"

Bill shook his head.

"Half Indian and half what?"

"Half white."

"Yeah, but which white? Irish, German, Pollack?"

"Don't know."

"I'll be damned. Well, you can do the work. You find any Irishmen on the wood pile, you'll be knowin' they just got over here and ain't fit for nothin' else."

It was in the middle of the second day before Bill felt he was working the rubber man just about right. He named it "Stub," short for "Stubby." And he learned he had to put some oil on the saw blade to break it loose from the pitch that drained into the cuts; that the weight of the saw and gravity would make Stub cut through the downed logs if he didn't push it back too hard and saved his strength for the pull.

From then on he talked to Stub like he would to Carl or Charlie. He wasn't sure when he'd started talking to himself, but it was probably on the walk to Venetie. Stub found out a lot about Ilene and Carl and how things were in Arctic Village.

The woodpile grew and he was working on the second stack when he lifted up the last piece of cordwood and got a good whiff of himself. He quit early that afternoon and walked over to the eastern side of the island with a bar of soap.

That night he had corned beef hash and bread and a cup of tea brewed with Yukon River water. He heard footsteps, then saw a girl at the edge of the firelight. She was holding a dried salmon carcass.

"Hello," she said.

Bill stood up. "Hello yourself."

"I thought you might like a salmon." She handed it to him across the fire. The oily fragrance was pungent.

"You smoke it?" he said.

"I smoke some and sell it to the boat crews."

"I don't have any money."

"I brought it to you as a present."

Bill nodded. "Thank you. Here—let me get you a seat." He pulled up a chunk of log. "I'm Bill Williams."

"I'm Sarah White. My daddy's Bradford White, do you know him?"

Bill shook his head. "I'm a stranger here."

Sarah smiled. "You don't look strange."

He smiled back at her. "Could I taste it now?"

"Sure. It's yours."

"Would you like some?"

"I'd take a pinch. You got anything to drink?"

"Tea. I've got tea."

"That'd be good."

Bill washed out the cups and filled them. When he handed the cup to Sarah he couldn't get his finger out of the handle and pass her the cup at the same time. She put one of her hands on the bottom of the cup and with the other took hold of Bill's hand. A shiver went through his arm.

He found a tin plate and cut a piece of the salmon onto it.

"I can't see you very well across this fire," she said.

Bill set his tea and fish down and moved his stool around to the side. He could feel the heat in his face.

"How's this?" he said.

"I can see you now." Her smile and the firelight reflected in her eyes made him think of saying things he didn't know how to say.

"How long are you here for?" she said.

"Until the boat comes back."

"What do you do down here by yourself besides work?"

"I think. I talk a lot to Stub." He pointed to the rubber man.

"You call him Stub? Does he ever talk back?"

"Hasn't so far."

She drew her legs up and put her arms over her knees. "What do you and Stub talk about?"

"You sure ask a lot of questions."

"Well, you don't say anything, so I have to ask."

He smiled. "You're right. Let's see—what do we talk about?" He cleared his throat. "Well, we talk about how we learn things, for instance. And feelings about stuff."

"What kind of feelings?"

His pulse rate had increased and he wasn't sure where he was going with this.

"Feelings about a family, for instance. Things that happen in a family."

"Like what?"

He looked in the fire and took a deep breath.

"My mother died when I was born and my dad killed himself and I don't know how anybody in my family really feels about that. Nobody talks about it in our village." He let out the rest of his breath.

"What do they talk about if they don't talk about things like that?"

"Oh—about hunting, or like when Irem got drunk at the last dance and fell over the watermelon on the schoolhouse floor, or the plane crash at the end of the runway."

"How do you feel about it?"

"About what?"

"Your mother and father dying."

The flush had reached his neck and he unbuttoned his jacket. He couldn't look at her, but he could answer her question. "Well—I can't seem to work up any feeling about it. Sometimes I try. I stand on a hill at night and think about them, but maybe it's been too long or something, because I leave the hill feeling exactly the same as when I went out there."

When he looked up her eyes were on his, the firelight dancing in them. She reached out a hand and laid it on top of his.

"You're working too hard at it. Just think about how you feel—or don't feel—and say it. Have you ever said it to Stub?"

He shook his head.

"Why not?"

"I just never have, that's all."

She looked up at the stars, her body still, her face tilted up, and her hand on his.

"Don't you keep some stuff like that inside you?" he asked.

"I tell everything to the stars. My daddy's a minister, he travels a lot up and down the river. You talk to Stub and I talk to the stars."

"What do you tell them?"

"All sorts of things. About school, the village, boyfriends ... "

Bill looked up at the stars. "You have a boyfriend?"

"Sometimes. Right now I don't."

He smiled.

She took back her hand. "I have to go. Thanks for the tea and conversation."

Bill stood up. "Want me to walk you home?"

"I'd rather no one saw me coming back from here."

In three steps she was out of sight and the night had enveloped her so completely he wondered for a few seconds if she had really been there.

THE *NORTHLAND ECHO* BLEW its whistle before it came into view, and to Bill the sound was wonderful. He did a quick check to see how many cords of wood he had stacked up, then ran down to the bank to watch the boat come in. Mike O'Leary called out a big "Hallo, laddie" from the deck and threw a rope to him. The paddle wheel stopped, then reversed and slowed the boat until the bow nosed into the bank.

Bill had just tied the rope to a tree when Mike said, "Well, laddie, how many cords do you have for us now?"

"Twelve."

Mike gripped his biceps and squeezed. "Put on a bit of muscle?"

Bill smiled. "Thanks for the soap."

"Figured you'd be needin' it."

"You were right."

About a hundred yards down the river a man was leading a horse and wagon their way.

"How did old rubber man work?" Mike asked.

"Pretty good, once I taught him how to."

"Oh, you taught him how to work, did ya? Well, twelve cord is a fair jag. But we be needin' all there is to get the *Echo* home."

When the man got there Bill could see the horse was harnessed to a skid. The horse walked up just past the first stack of logs and stopped. Two men started loading the firewood on the skid while the man with the horse stood holding the lead rope, fanning mosquitoes and flies away from his horse's head. Then he saw Bill and beckoned him over.

Bill walked up to him. The firewood was nearly all loaded.

He had a most prominent Adams apple with gray and black hairs running all directions out of it and wore a battered felt hat with white sweat marks encircling the crown. He was tall and leaned forward from his hips. "You stay away from my son's girl," the man said in a rasping voice.

"Do I know her?" Bill said.

"Just stay away from her or you'll be sorry." His eyes glowed.

"I talked to someone last night, I didn't know she was anybody's girl. It's a free country."

"Now you know," he hissed. "Stay away from her."

Bill looked at Mike, who shook his head. "Is that what you meant by no pretty girls?" he said when he was back on the *Echo*.

"The very thing." Mike smiled. "She's a nice one, isn't she?"

"You know her?"

"Not a man on the river doesn't know Sarah White. Not a man who wouldn't take her for his own—if she was willin'."

"And?"

"Well, she's pledged to the Lord, in a way."

"What way?"

"Let's just say in a way that doesn't admit the likes of you and me."

The loading process was repeated until the twelve cords were loaded. Bill went aboard to see the captain.

"You did okay, Bill. Earned your way to Whitehorse." The captain handed him a small stack of silver dollars with a smile.

Bill hefted them up and down, the weight of them a grand feeling, then put them in his pocket.

"Thank you," he said.

The captain nodded. "You'll do okay on the highway. Keep warm this winter."

THE NORTHLAND ECHO NOSED into the dock at Whitehorse, Yukon Territory.

Mike was on shore as Bill stepped off the gangplank.

"Now look here, laddie. You'll be goin' out amongst the tough ones. Don't be afraid to ask for what you want and don't be ashamed if you don't get it. And if anyone asks, you just tell 'em Mike O'Leary from the *Northland Echo* backs you. It's been good knowin' you, Bill Williams. Wish I was goin with you." He stuck out his hand.

Bill took it. "Why don't you come with me?"

"The boat's my life and I love her like my dear mother. I couldn't let her go up and down that river without me to take care of her. Go on with ya now. Go make yer fortune."

He let go of Bill's hand.

CHAPTER 5

NEVER IN HIS LIFE had Bill seen so many people. They walked head down with a look of determination on their faces, like they knew why they were there and where they were going. Not a one of them looked approachable on the subject of where he might find a job.

The pounding of hooves on the ground broke through his thoughts. A galloping horse bolted off the road, took two more strides, fell forward on his chest, and skidded to a stop. In an instant the horse scrambled to his feet and stood with the left foreleg lifted off the ground, a length of wire ensnaring it. The wire was anchored to a nearby deck of logs.

The horse trembled, eyes wide, nostrils flared as Bill approached. He shied when Bill touched him on the neck and jerked backwards, stretching the wire until it twanged.

The horse kept up a steady pull against the wire. Bill held on to the halter with one hand and ran his other hand down the horse's leg until he could touch the wire. He pulled forward on the halter, but the horse pulled back.

He patted the horse and thought about how to get the wire off. He could feel the horse's heart pound in his neck. After a few seconds he pulled gently forward. The horse moved one back foot, then the other, then he shifted his weight and hopped forward on three legs, keeping his left foot off the ground. The wire went slack, and Bill reached down and unwound it from the horse's hock.

"Take your hands off my horse, sonny," someone said.

Bill turned around to see a man. He was gaunt and his clothing fit him like the long underwear that showed at his wrists and ankles. The clothing swelled at every joint in his body showing that they held his lean body together, from his moccasins to his nose that tilted over a great gray handlebar mustache.

"I'll take him now."

The man lifted the horse's leg to examine the hock. "Just a little burn, didn't cut through." The man looked at Bill. "Horses are valuable up in this country. You ought not try stealing a man's horse."

"I wasn't."

"Well, you didn't get far with this one. Good thing I—"

"Look here, mister, I was just minding my business when your horse tripped over that wire—ask anyone around here." He picked up his pack and went over to a man sitting on a log fence, smoking. "You saw it, didn't you?"

The man nodded.

"Well, why didn't you say something?"

"Weren't none of my business."

Bill gave himself a few seconds to calm down. Then he said, "Do you know where I can get a job here?"

The man lifted the cigarette out of his mouth and pointed with it to a log building down the road. "They're hiring locals down there for all kinds of work."

Bill took off. When he pushed the door to the log building open he saw ten to fifteen men and boys crowded around a desk. He finally got to the front.

"What can you do?" the clerk asked.

"Well, I can cut wood."

"Don't have any wood-cutting jobs. Can you walk and haul water?"

He laughed. "Sure."

"Okay. Pay's seventy-five dollars a month with board and room."

The door burst open and the horse owner stepped inside. "I need one good man. I'm paying a hundred a month plus board and room. Need someone who understands horses."

"Mr. Hanley," the clerk said, "we haven't come across anybody who knows horses yet. I'll let you know when we find someone."

"I need a man now. I start packing tomorrow and I need help today."

Nobody said anything.

"I'd like a hundred dollars a month," Bill said.

Hanley looked him up and down. "Didn't you just try to steal my horse?"

Another man stepped up. "Hanley, I saw it. This guy didn't try to steal your horse, he just unhooked the wire."

"You know anything at all about horses?" Hanley said.

"I can learn."

Hanley turned half around. "Well, come on—maybe I can teach you. Name's Peck Hanley."

"Bill Williams."

They walked down the street. "You drink?" Hanley said.

"No."

"Good. I've got a contract to move supplies and I don't need no drunk. I've got thirty horses but I don't have no help. You'll get by good here."

Bill looked at the skinny horse. His dull hair was long in patches and rubbed to the hide in others.

"Don't go judging by this swayback. Come see the rest of them."

He turned right and led Bill to a rope corral where a group of horses stood with their heads down. They had fair coats and few ribs showing, but several had peat stains up to their bellies, and their tails were a tangled mess.

"What is it you do?" Bill asked.

"We haul freight and supplies around the bogs, or through them sometimes. Ain't no equipment can get through some of these bogs. Other guys got big horses and they sink in like a tractor, but these are mountain horses and they can crawl through on a log if they hafta."

"I wanted to work on the highway," Bill said.

"Well, you will be. This is highway work, sure enough." Peck rubbed his hands together a few seconds and then said, "Look here —I'll give you $110 a month if you'll start today. We'll be on and around this highway from here to Dawson, summer and winter. Ain't no way they can build it without us hauling for them. What do you say?"

"Okay," he said.

Peck extended his hand. "Shake on it."

Bill tensed as he took the hand, but Peck didn't grip like Mike O'Leary and he didn't pump. He squeezed slightly and then dropped Bill's hand.

He had a job.

AFTER A BREAKFAST OF flapjacks, bacon, and coffee, Peck led the pack string to the clearing where the surveyors had assembled with their gear. Never one to waste daylight, he leapt off his horse and started laying out the pack tarps.

"Bill, you divide that gear into pack size. I'll pack it and then we can both put them on the horses. Be easier with both of us doing it."

The surveyors had gathered plenty of food and gear to sustain them while they surveyed and cut trail for the next ten miles. It took twenty horses to pack all their gear. Peck kept two to ride and Bill trailed the other eight horses back to the corral and threw them a little hay.

As the animals strung out on the trail, the horses left behind began to whinny. Horses were a funny lot. They'd kick and bite each other in the corral, but just let some of them leave and the others thought it was the end of their world. Eyes wide with lots of white showing around the edges, ears turned forward, necks strained and nostrils blowing in and out. They'd look in the direction the others had gone, whinny, and run around the edge of the corral to get a last look as the pack string went out of view.

The horses leaving couldn't have cared less about those left behind. Heads down, ears forward, eyes on the trail, they would bear their burden in an almost drugged attitude until something happened, then it was Katy-bar-the-door with them.

They could jump sideways so fast you couldn't stay in the saddle; they'd come to a log and decide to jump it instead of step over it, almost pitching you into the peat or against the fallen timber. Bill learned that packing with horses meant long periods of dull riding and short moments of sheer terror.

Peck stopped and surveyed the bog. It showed signs of having been recently crossed but looked mushy. On either side of the bog burned-over spruce trees huddled too close together to get a pack string through, and the ground was covered with blow-downs crisscrossed everywhere. There was no getting through there without spending half a day cutting trees. The horses stood heads down, tails swishing the flies and mosquitoes, waiting for the pull of the lead line to take them back to work.

"Don't like the looks of it!" Peck hollered back.

Bill stood up in his stirrups and looked at the bog. He knew about tundra and marshes but nothing about bogs. The first day he'd come to work, from the looks of them, he'd thought the horses swam through the bogs. Dried peat clung to their hair from their hooves to their shoulders. Peck had given him a curry comb and showed him how to scrape the animals with it and then brush their hair out. But now, standing in the stirrups, he couldn't tell if they could walk through it or if they'd have to swim.

"Try and keep 'em up on the right side!" Peck yelled. "I'm 'fraid this bog don't have no bottom in it." He spurred his horse and started the string through the lower edge of the marsh at a slow walk. Each horse craned its neck to sniff the surface wide-eyed.

In three steps Peck's horse was belly-deep in the bog and fighting the putrid mass. He leaned in the saddle and pulled the reins hard to the right. The horse stumbled, regained its feet, and tried to lunge out of the bog. It failed, then gained a footing on the bank, up to its knees in the bog. The horse stopped, its chest heaving. Peck jabbed it with his spurs. It bolted, the leap taking it clear of the soggy swamp. It shivered, the greenish-black mess dripping from its legs and belly.

Peck dismounted and walked to the edge of the bog to pick up the rope he'd dropped and coax the horses up the far right side. They were skittish and reluctant to get into it, but started moving single file, heads down, snorting, scraping their packs against the trees at the edge.

"Bill—don't let those nags beat up that equipment on those trees!"

Bill didn't know how to stop it. There was no room between the trees and the edge of the bog. The horses fought hard to stay on the bank. They snorted and threw wide-eyed glances at the green stuff bubbling around their feet, sniffing it with flared nostrils.

The first horse jumped across and dragged the second horse, which was tied to it. The next three horses reared. A tie string broke. Two turned around and pushed back against those in line who were trying to cross over bog that was tromped into a thick soup. A horse fell but quickly regained its feet and let out a snort, shaking its head and mane and danced to the side smashing the pack into the tree. A box broke and tools fell loose and crashed in a pile.

Without warning the rest of the horses broke for the edge, banging their packs on the trees, slipping and jumping over perceived threats on the ground. Suddenly Peck's horse reared, he dropped the lead line and fought to stay in the saddle. The horses snorted and bucked and took off on a dead run. Equipment banged against trees, against horses. Loud whinny's and sucking noises filled the air.

Bill sat astride his horse wide-eyed with indecision. The noise closed out all thoughts, his vision narrowed. He threw an arm over his face to ward off the flying muck and spurred his horse forward toward the end of lead rope snaking through the quagmire. .

In three jumps he was where he had last seen it. The horse was thrashing under him as he leaned out of the saddle, holding his breath, both hands reaching for the disappearing end of the rope. He felt his fingers close on it. Frigid water rammed up his sleeves and in an instant he lost his stirrup and pitched under the water.

His horse was screaming—trampling the bog. The icy liquid leaked through his clothes, tightening his chest, choking his lungs. He tried to gather his legs under him but the horses thrashing made waves that wouldn't let him settle.

On his side, under the surface, the rope tightened and the forward momentum of the horses dragged him out of the bog like a sled on water. He felt his body hit the bank and bounce onto soft peat moss. He reached for a tree in front of him—looped the end of the rope around it, then braced his palms against it. At the end of the rope the horses jerked to a stop. Bill let out a scream.

"Damned ornery no good sonsabitches!" Peck bellowed. He shot his left leg out at a horse but missed. The sight of the gloved hand between the rope and the tree told him instantly what had happened. He reached down and slowly unwound the rope. Bill shook his hand several times, then gingerly started to pull the glove off.

"Damn, damn, and more damn," Peck said. "You okay?"

Bill looked at it. "It hurts—some."

"Damned ornery no good sonsabitches. Well—you sure saved us. Those bastards could have been back to camp by now if you hadn't held on."

Bill squinted and tightened his lips. The thumb was raw, pink and green looking with little rivulets of blood starting to show where the capillaries had been severed. He shoved his glove back on while the thumb pounded like a church bell in even, steady beats. Using his right hand, he maneuvered his horse beside him and climbed into the saddle. Peck dallied the line around his saddle horn, and turned toward the trail. The others fell into place and strung out behind him, placid as could be.

By the time they got to the surveyor's camp Bill's thumb was swollen, black and blue, and leaking blood and fluid from cracks in the skin. The only guy in camp who knew anything about first aid gave a long low whistle as Bill displayed it for him.

"You're lucky it didn't get taken off," he said. "I got to bandage it."

"Damned ornery sonsabitches," Peck offered. "He saved us a lot out there by catching 'em."

Peck unloaded the equipment and repacked the horses with what little stuff was going back. By the time he was done, Bill was in so much pain he rode silent all the way back.

A MILE FROM CAMP, the engineers had built a log bridge over a stream Peck and Bill had forded on their way out that morning. The horses snorted at the smell of the fresh-cut logs and shied at the hollow sound their hooves made, but after they lowered their heads and sniffed the logs, they consented to walk over it.

"I wish they'd bridged that damned bog instead," Peck said.

When they got back to the corral and were removing the horse's saddles, three of the engineers stepped up.

"Hi," one of them said. "I'm Corporal Refines Sims Jr. from Philadelphia." He stuck out his hand.

They were the first Negroes Bill had ever seen, and while he knew it wasn't polite to stare at them, he couldn't help himself. He introduced himself, shook hands, and looked down.

"It don't rub off," Corporal Sims said, and the three of them laughed. "What you doing with these nags?"

"We pack supplies on them. Out to the surveyors." He pointed down the trail. "What do you guys do?"

Sims drew himself to attention and saluted. "Sir, we are the 93rd Combat Engineer Regiment. We been doing so much with so little for so long, we can now do the impossible with nothing in no time. We're building a road from the United States to Alaska."

The horses came up and sniffed the strangers, and Sims played with the muzzle of a horse that was licking his hand.

"The only horses I ever saw were pulling the ice wagon in Philly," Sims said.

Bill couldn't imagine an ice wagon.

"Where you from?" Sims said.

"Alaska."

"You an Eskimo?"

"I'm Indian. Athabascan."

Sims threw his head back. "Oh. We don't have any Indians in Philly."

"We don't have any Negroes in Arctic Village."

Sims grabbed the horse's lip and was playfully pulling on it while the horse tried to get his lips around his fingers.

"Can I ride one of these nags?"

"Ask the owner," Bill said, and indicated Peck.

"Aw, come on. I'll just slip up on his back and ride around inside here a couple of times. What d'ya say?"

Peck had disappeared.

"Guess it wouldn't hurt," Bill said.

Sims ducked between the corral ropes and, in a move that astounded Bill, grabbed the horse's mane in both hands and vaulted on its back. One second he was on the ground and the next he was astride the horse.

"I've seen Gene Autry do it that way," Sims said. He prodded with his heels and the horse pricked up its ears and moved faster around the corral, the other horses getting out of its way as it went around the outside loop in a slow trot. After two laps Sims threw one leg over the horse's neck while it was still on the trot and slid off, landing on both feet. He raised his arms and smiled. His companions laughed and clapped.

"I should of been a cowboy," Sims said. "Instead I drive a bulldozer for the U.S. Army." He looked at Bill. "Thank you, Bill Williams. Come on over one day and I'll give you a ride on my bulldozer."

As they walked away from the corral, Bill crawled through the ropes and grabbed the mane of the nearest horse with his good hand. He mentally pictured what he had to do to get on top of the horse with one swing. The horse started moving and he walked beside him twice around the corral, but he couldn't get a good picture in his mind of what had to happen to mount the horse in one jump. He became aware of the other horses crowding around him and felt uncomfortable getting caught between them when Peck wasn't there so he let go of the mane and dashed between the horses and under the rope. He would have to think some more about what Sims had done. That was really something.

IN THE MORNING IT was twenty degrees below zero. By noon it had stopped snowing and was thirty below. Bill walked over to the engineers' maintenance tent to see if they needed any equipment hauled by horse. His thumb was pounding like a jackhammer. Sims and a guy named Leon were working on a Studebaker 6x6, stopping every few minutes to stamp their feet and swinging their arms across their chests.

"Can't keep warm," Sims said. He had his hat flaps tied under his chin and was wearing the army-issue almost-to-the-ankles coat, but he was still shivering. "Ain't you cold?"

"No. Way you're dressed, why are you?"

"Could be because the snow's up to our butts and the temperature's about ninety below."

Bill had never been asked to solve problems for other people, nor had it ever occurred to him that he might have information they could use. But now he thought back to what his Dad and Uncle Charlie had taught him about staying warm.

"What size boot you and Leon wear?"

"I'm nine and Leon, he's a nine too."

In the equipment and supply tent that loosely functioned as a local quartermaster's warehouse, Bill found two pair of boots in size 10 and 10½. He pulled bunches of dry grass that lay beneath road equipment and lower tree limbs and took them back to the tent. The soldiers stood around watching while he filled the boots with the grass, pushing it down into the toes and up the sides. Then he shoved a sock inside and worked it into its natural position.

"Now," he said. "How many socks you got on?"

"Two pair."

"Take one off and stick your feet in there slow-like, in the other sock."

"It feels funny," Sims said, moving his foot around in the boot.

Leon tried several steps. "I don't know," he said. "This thing's too damn big."

Bill twisted the grass and fitted more into the boot.

"That's better," Leon said. "That's better. Feels like I'm walking on carpet thick enough for the king."

Bill turned to Sims. "Unbutton your coat and slip your arms out but leave the belt tight."

When Sims had done that, Bill placed a layer of grass over his back and pulled the coat up over it.

"What have you got for mittens?"

Sims showed him their issue mittens.

"You need something soft and warm on the backs of those. Maybe trade with some of the Indians around here for rabbit skins and sew them on the backs. Then you can put them to your face once in a while and warm up. You should blow your breath up by your face every so often, that'll help. And keep your parka hoods up and breathe in them." He smiled. "And if you keep working, you'll stay warmer."

There was a general groan.

"Bill," Leon asked, "how we going to keep warm at night?"

"Wrap one of those blankets around you before you get in your sleeping bag and move your cot away from the side of the tent. Put some paper and a blanket on top of the cot—if we could get some moss it would be better."

When Peck and Bill left with the pack string the next day, three of the engineers were stooped under a bulldozer pulling grass.

Bill yelled at them. "Hey—how's it going?"

They looked up. "We just shuckin' and jivin'," one said. "Got plenty of grass to pull."

They hadn't gone a hundred yards when Bill asked Peck, "What do you think they mean by shuckin' and jivin'?"

"Don't know," Peck said. "Your guess is as good as mine."

"LETTER FOR YOU," Peck said when he came back from mail call. "Looks like it went all the way through hell and half of Georgia. Has four forwarding stamps on it."

Bill, who had never received a letter before, turned the tan envelope over several times before tearing it open. It requested Bill Williams to report to Fairbanks, Alaska, for a selective service examination.

CHAPTER 6

BILL ENTERED A LINE where the recruits took off their outer clothes and moved forward in their underwear. Bill didn't wear underwear. He stood in the line naked, his clothes in a bag with a shipping tag attached to it. Several others were naked also. They all moved forward and were grabbed by one arm while a medic jabbed a needle in.

The line proceeded into the quartermaster section, where a short man with immaculate hair and a thin mustache asked him his shirt size.

"I don't know," Bill said.

The guy handed him a shirt and the line moved on.

Bill didn't have time to examine the shirt before he was in the pants line.

"Waist?"

"I don't know." Bill looked at the guy in front of him. "What size are you?"

"Thirty-two," he said.

"Thirty-two," Bill said.

The soldier handed him a pair of pants and a belt.

"Boots?"

Bill listened to guys ahead of him yelling out their shoe sizes and looked at their feet. One recruit who looked about the same size as Bill said "ten."

"Boots?"

"Ten," Bill said.

A private with pimples on his face slid the boots across the counter along with two pair of socks and a set of underwear.

The line went through a door into a large room, where the Drill Instructor was standing on a footlocker near the wall. He shouted, "Take off your underwear. Put it in the bag. Put on your beautiful OD U.S. army underwear and your beautiful OD U.S. army socks, then proceed to dress yourself if you are capable of doing that without crying for your mommy. DO NOT, I repeat, DO NOT complain, whine, bitch, moan, or cry out about the clothing or size of clothing your government has given you to wear. Put it on. If it doesn't fit we'll find a way to make it fit."

Bill felt a nudge from his side and looked around to see a large well-built man with brown skin and dark eyes stuffing his underwear in a bag.

"You Indian?" the man asked.

Bill nodded.

"What tribe?"

"Athabascan."

The man's eyes focused on the ceiling a few seconds as if trying to locate the tribe in his mind.

"I'm Shoshone," he said. "Where's Athabascan?"

"Alaska."

"I'm from Wyoming. Ever been there?"

Bill shook his head.

He had the pants up and they fit in the waist but were long in the leg. The shirt was too small. He was dressed and had his clothes in the bag when he looked at the Indian beside him again. The clothing he'd been given didn't begin to close around his chest or his waist. He put the belt around his middle and it was about four inches too short to buckle, but he smiled at Bill.

"Anybody who cannot, I repeat, CANNOT walk in the clothing they were issued stay where you are. Everyone else, right face. Forward march on the double."

Bill went out the door at a jog, his clothing bag slapping his leg, and the line went back to the barracks.

THE BUNK TO THE right of Bill was vacant, and the guy on his left was asleep already and snoring. By the time Bill had dumped his clothing bag and gotten his cot made, the Indian from Wyoming limped in and threw his clothing bag on the vacant cot. His belt wasn't fastened but the pants covered his bottom half and the shirt, although straining at all seams, was buttoned. There was a big smile on his face and his teeth were the whitest Bill had ever seen.

"They don't have boots to fit me," he said.

Bill looked at his feet. The boots had no laces in them and the man's feet bulged out of the open tongue area, the eyelets spread wide. When he sat on his bunk and removed the boots, he wiggled his toes and laughed, then stuck out his hand.

"Name's Wayne Turner."

Bill reached for it and Wayne's large hand enveloped his.

"I'm Bill Williams."

Wayne added a nod along with his big smile.

"What size boots do you need?" Bill asked.

"Twelve and a half. These are elevens."

"What're you gonna do without boots? You can't go barefoot."

"I did on the reservation."

Bill couldn't conceive of that, although he'd heard from elders about the Athabascans in Prince William Sound who went barefoot all year round. He wondered what Corporal Refines Sims Jr. would do about this. No sooner had that thought struck him than he knew what Sims would do.

"Where's the boot tight?"

Wayne pointed to the sides and toe.

"Give me one of them."

He took a pocketknife from his footlocker and cut half-moon chunks out of both sides of the boot at the widest part and at the toe area. Now they looked like high-topped sandals.

"Try that," he said.

Wayne pulled the boot on, stood up, and wiggled his toes.

"Feels good," he said.

"You put the laces in and I'll cut the other one," Bill said.

When Wayne put both boots on and laced up, he walked up and down the aisle.

"They feel good. Can't wear socks, though. Thanks."

"At least you have some foot protection. You're welcome."

IT WAS AFTER 3rd Platoon had finished mess that the DI noticed Private Wayne Turner's footwear and commented on it loudly about four inches from Wayne's nose.

"Who in the living hell said you could cut up U.S. Government property, maggot?"

Wayne looked at Bill.

"Look at me, maggot, I'm talking to you. Talk to me, maggot!"

"They didn't have any boots that fit, sir."

"I see. The United States Army Quartermaster Corps could not produce boots to fit your oversized feet, so you made your own."

"Yes, sir."

"On the ground, maggot, and give me fifty pushups, then you will remove those disgraceful shoe covers and go barefoot. Do you understand me, maggot?"

"Yes, sir."

Turner did the fifty pushups without a hitch, jumped to his feet, and removed the boots.

"Sir, what do you want me to do with them?"

"Maggot. those are not U.S. Army combat boots, they are sandals and you shall place them in your foot locker for one week to see if the leather will grow back and in the meantime you will report for all activities in your bare feet. Is that understood?"

"Yes, sir!"

LIGHTS OUT WAS AT 2200 hours. It was the first chance Bill had to talk to Wayne since the boot incident.

"Doesn't make any difference," Wayne said. "I'm used to going barefoot. Feels good."

"How'd you do those fifty pushups so fast?"

"Where I come from the elders said physical exercise was a good substitute for sex. I can do a hundred if I have to."

"Why would you want to do pushups instead of have sex?"

"I didn't. Just nobody but the ugly ones were putting out, so I did pushups."

"What's it like on your reservation?" Wayne asked.

"KNOCK IT OFF, YOU GUYS!" someone yelled.

"Talk to you in the morning," Bill whispered.

"'Night," Wayne said.

Bill pulled the blanket over his head and with a flashlight started to write.

December 8, 1942

Dear Ilene,

I'm sorry I haven't written but things have been happening fast. I made it to Venetie okay and got on a riverboat and then to the highway and got a job right away with a supply-packing outfit. But then I got drafted in the army and I'm in Fort Ord, California, going through basic training.

We're supposed to be here eight weeks then get shipped overseas. I don't know where we're going and I don't know when I can write again—they keep us real busy here.

What I wanted to ask is if you would wait for me. All the way to Venetie and on the river I thought about you and was wondering if you would write me. You can write to me at Pvt. Bill Williams, General Post Office, Fort Ord, California and it will get to me.

I suppose everybody's still laughing about my bear hunt and when I think back on it, it is kind of funny, but

I don't know of anyone ever being stepped on by a bear before. The claw marks still show on my leg.

I miss you and the village but I'm sure seeing a lot of country.

He thought about how to sign it: "Love, Bill." "With love, Bill." "Fondly yours, Bill." "Sincerely yours, Bill.'" Finally he signed it, "With love, Bill."

He tucked it under his pillow. Tomorrow after training and before the evening meal he would slip over to the post office and mail it. He figured he would just address it to Ilene Chulpach, Arctic Village, Alaska, and it would get there.

CHAPTER 7

THEY SPENT TWO YEARS in training. Groups came and left but Bill and Wayne were never in them. Finally the government activated the US 106th Infantry Division and dubbed them the Golden Lions. They took the remainder of the draftees. Two days before they shipped out, the company commander, Captain Clark, found Bill and Wayne lounging in the barracks. They stood up in unison.

"At ease," Captain Clark said. "I've got some stripes for you, Williams. Seems we need another corporal, and you're it. Think you can handle the job?"

"Yes, sir."

"Good." He glanced at Wayne's feet. "I see they found some boots for you, Turner. Take care of them, that was the only pair they got in."

They saluted and the captain walked through the barracks almost like he was doing an inspection.

"Do I have to take orders from you now?" Wayne asked Bill.

"Only on Tuesdays and Thursdays."

The division shipped for England on 20 October 1944, the plan being that they would slip across the channel and land at Le Havre, France, on December 3rd to relieve the 2nd Division on a quiet front. There they would be given an additional three weeks of combat training and be ready to support other divisions in the push to the Ruhr and into the heart of Germany.

On December 11, 1944 the division was stopped on a road in Belgium, the men soaked to the skin from their three-day ride through France and Luxembourg in open trucks. Snow began to fall, covering the mud on the ground and hanging in the trees. A disheveled three-man reconnaissance patrol materialized through the snow, their collars shoved up and buttoned against the cold.

A sergeant looked at Bill. "Who's in charge here, Corporal?"

"Captain Clark, sir."

"Know where I can find him?"

"Yes sir, he's back by those trucks." Bill pointed at a collection of trucks where men were unloading and grouping at the end of the dirt road.

"They better break up that crowd, the Jerries will drop one on them if they get the chance."

The three men walked and slid down the road in the falling snow.

Bill's men stayed where they were and stomped their feet to put off the chill and get the blood flowing in their legs. Some did deep knee bends and swung their arms.

Bill pulled out a piece of paper he'd saved since they left the troop ship, pressed the wrinkles out of it on his leg, and started a letter to Ilene.

> Somewhere in Europe.
> Date unknown.
>
> Hi Ilene,
>
> Well we landed and the war is still on. I know you probably thought once I got here it would scare them so much they'd give up, but it hasn't happened so far.
>
> We're waiting to go into our positions and we just spent three miserable days riding in trucks in the rain and snow and now we're just standing around in the mud waiting. Seems like there's a lot of time wasted in standing around waiting. Herb would do good in the army, he's such a good waiter.
>
> I just wondered if you've thought about what I said in my last letter. About waiting for me, I mean. It sure

would mean a lot to me. They'll censor this letter if I put any locations in it so you can just write me at Corporal Bill Williams, General Post Office, Fort Ord, California. Oh, yeah, they made me a corporal and I boss some people around now. Not many, but some. I miss you.

Corporal Bill Williams

He handed the letter to the company runner, who promised to get it into the mailbag that was headed to the port and to bring up the company's mail if he could find it.

One of the new men in Bill's platoon sauntered over, cleared the snow off his helmet and put it back on.

"Corporal, what's the scoop on where we going?"

"Colonel Descheneaux said we're going into the Second's positions and there's nothing to it. Their guides will be here pretty soon and take us in. We're supposed to get another three weeks of combat training." Bill looked at the kid. He wasn't even shivering. "You're not cold?"

"It gets colder than this in Omaha."

"What's your name?"

"Coric. Coric Sloboda. I came in with the last group. You probably wouldn't remember me."

"It's something I should remember."

Wayne stuck out his hand. "I'm Wayne Turner from Wyoming. You ever been there?"

"No, I never left Boy's Town after I got there."

"I've heard of that place. That's for orphans, isn't it?"

"Yeah," Coric said.

"Guess we're all orphans now," Bill said.

Coric looked down at his wet boots and twisted them in the mushy surface.

SGT. REGINALD CONNER, THE assistant platoon leader, came over and called the non-coms in for a huddle. Bill, as the acting squad leader, went to it and came back with the information.

"The guides are here from the Second, so get lined up and we'll follow them in. You have ammunition but don't load up. They say it's quiet and they don't want anything going off behind them."

"Where are we, Bill?" Wayne said.

"They tell me we're right on the Siegfried line."

"Hey, that means concrete and steel, hot showers and good food," one GI said.

"You wish," Bill said.

The men started out and slipped and slid for about a mile until they turned right across a small stream, then took a trail up a hillside to the first of the bunkers. After the platoon leader and assistant leader took the first bunker, Sgt. Connor paired the men off in either a bunker or a timber-roofed dugout. They moved further, then he pointed to a dugout and indicated Bill and Wayne were to take it.

"You guys are used to living in log houses, aren't you?" he said.

The entrance required them to slide into the opening. Bill went first, landing in two inches of water, Wayne slid in beside him.

"Crap," Wayne said as he hit the water. "Our own private swimming pool."

Bill found a knob on one of the logs forming the roof and hung his pack on it.

"Come on, let's drain this sucker."

In half an hour they had gotten the water out of the bottom and had a fire going to dry the place out.

"I was just thinking," Wayne said. "My people got out of caves and tents with smoky fires fifty years ago and here we are, right back into one."

"Yeah," Bill said. "But this time, you have a rifle instead of a bow and arrows."

"Big deal." Wayne looked out the firing slit at the front of the dugout. He squinted his eyes in the dim light and ran his hands over the top and bottom.

"Hell, those guys never got shot at."

"I'm not eager about it," Bill said.

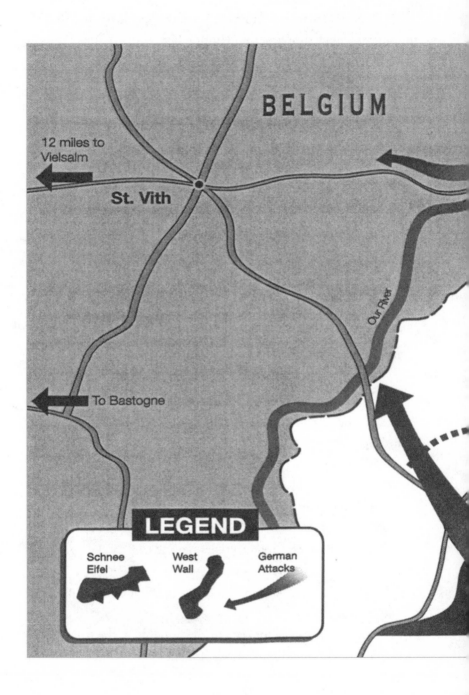

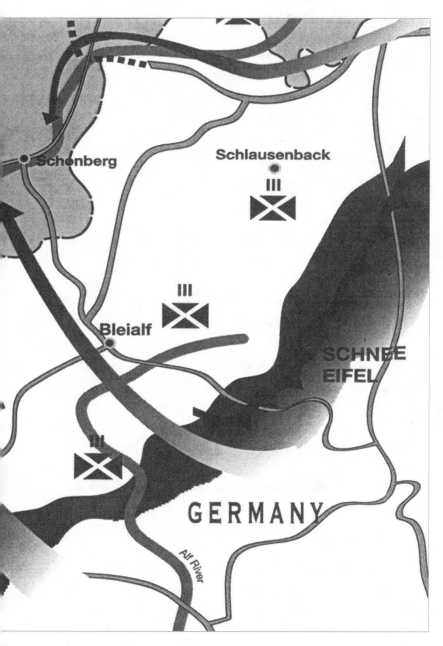

The Snow Eifel, the original push of the Battle of the Bulge
where Bill and companions escaped from German onslaught.

"Me neither. Let's go check out the area." Wayne started out of the dugout. An officer was running behind the bunkers and dugouts, stopping at each one to shout something. When he got close to Bill and Wayne he walked over to them. It was Lt. Rob Adams, a former real estate salesman from Portland, Oregon.

"Hi, guys," he whispered. "Captain Clark says its okay to load your weapons now. Don't start shooting unless you're sure you have a German target in your sights. We don't want any of our runners or the guys laying wire to get plinked."

"What position are we in?" Wayne asked.

Adams looked away a moment, as if trying to figure out how much to tell them.

"Well, we're in a horseshoe facing the German lines over there." He pointed toward a ridge. "You see those pillboxes? That's where the enemy is." He put his hands together to indicate the shape, then said, "Our company is at the back of the horseshoe."

He wiped his hands on his jacket, looked both ways, resumed his crouch position, and slipped off into the dark.

"I say we go look anyway," Wayne said.

"Okay."

Both men pulled back the bolts of their M-1 rifles and inserted a clip.

"What the hell is going on out there?" a guy said from the bunker nearby.

"Just checking out the area," Wayne said. "Going to find the outhouse."

"Well, don't walk in front of our bunker, we've got itchy trigger fingers."

"Keep your finger off the trigger," Bill said.

A light shone briefly, then blinked out, and it was silent as Bill led the way along the path where the telephone wire had been laid. With the new snow there was enough light to see across the valley where the German pillboxes were poorly concealed. It was too far to shoot with any accuracy but he could see men outlined against the ground and sky.

Bill stopped and hunched down. They had reached the curve in the horseshoe position and were walking in an oblique line toward the Germans when they heard a motor and a clanking sound. Both men scurried for cover. They listened, barely breathing, then heard the sound again. It came from the ridge behind the German defensive line.

"What do you think?" Wayne said.

"Tanks," Bill said.

"Let's go tell someone."

"Like who?"

"Like Lt. Adams, maybe."

"He's probably already heard it," Bill said.

"What if he hasn't?"

"Look. If they're tanks we'll all hear them pretty good if they're coming at us." He scuttled back to where Wayne was perched behind a tree. "Have you got a good enough feel for the territory now?"

"I've got the shivers in me timbers, that's what I've got. Let's get back to our little tepee in the ground."

"Dinner?" Wayne asked when they got back. He handed Bill a D Bar.

Bill bit off a chunk of the chocolate concentrate. He made a face and started looking around for his canteen.

"No wonder they call this stuff Hitler's Secret Weapon," he said.

"We're gonna need water tomorrow."

CHAPTER 8

ONLY CORIC AND TWO other GI's were in line when Bill and Wayne got to the food wagon the next morning. "They're gonna start serving at 0530," Coric said. "You guys want coffee?"

They headed for a coffee urn perched on the tailgate and Bill pushed down on the lever. As the coffee filled his cup he inhaled the steam, his eyes closed and a smile on his face.

The cook opened the warmer and yelled "come and get it!" Suddenly a thundering barrage of artillery shells tore into the earth, the first rounds landing behind the kitchen truck. Coric dropped his mess kit and cupped his hands over his ears.

Bill took a gulp of coffee, threw the rest on the ground, and sprinted back towards the dugout. Wayne was three feet ahead of him and dived feet-first through the hole. By the time Bill came up on his feet, Wayne had his rifle pointed out the slit.

"See anything?" Bill shouted.

"No. Maybe it's just an artillery barrage."

"Just? What did that captain say about the krauts only having two horse- drawn artillery guns out there?"

"I don't think he knew what he was talking about," Wayne said.

"They must be working those two horses overtime."

Shrapnel zinged through the air and smacked the logs with a hollow thunk. Bill put his hands over his ears and opened his mouth. It helped one minute and not the next. Wayne lay on the floor, arms covering his ears and face. The infantry would be coming after the bombardment.

Then it stopped. It was so quiet you could hear the wind that was moving the fog out of the valley. It was like the end of a lightning storm, except it didn't move off, it just stopped.

A heavy machine gun opened up to their right. It fired a few rounds, then went silent. Wayne looked out the slit.

"Holy Mother of God!"

Bill squeezed in beside him. As far as he could see there were white-clad Germans yelling and firing from the hip as they ran toward the Americans. No one from their platoon was returning fire.

"What do we do?" Wayne asked.

"How far do you think they are?"

"At least four hundred yards."

Bill looked at his rifle, then turned the elevation sight two clicks and poked the barrel out the slit, resting it on the lower log.

"You gonna shoot at them?" Wayne asked.

"Watch me." The rifle cracked, and the ejected casing hit Wayne's helmet. He ducked like he'd been shot.

"Did you get one?" he said.

"I don't know. So damn many out there I can't tell if one's down or not."

Wayne stuck his rifle out the slit. The rifle recoiled, and a German fell. They were now at 250 yards. Bill adjusted his sight, put in another clip of eight rounds, and resumed firing. His first shot took a German in the chest and spun him completely around. For a second, Bill wondered if he was dead. He watched him. He never moved again.

I wonder how old he was?

Wayne had knocked down two and now the Germans were running and weaving across the field, firing from the hip, making difficult targets but not scoring any hits. Bill shuddered, then aimed and fired just like he had been taught in basic training. He quit wondering how old they were and for the first time wondered if he would get any older.

There was a hollow "whump" and seconds later an explosion in the midst of the leading troops. The weapons platoon had found the range and dropped a few well-directed mortar rounds on the oncoming troops, the detonations throwing up smoke and flying chunks of earth that blotted out the enemy.

Somebody shouted down the roof opening, "Hang on! Keep firing! We're going to stop them here!"

The sputter of American machine guns filled the air. Between the mortar blasts they could make out the .30 and .50 caliber weapons' almost ceaseless firing.

"Maybe we oughta get out of here?" Wayne said.

Bill didn't reply.

"What do you think?"

"I don't know," Bill said. "I just don't."

"Well, I know! They could come over here and drop a grenade in this hole and blow us to kingdom come!"

Bill looked out the firing slit and could not see any upright Germans, just a lot of still forms in the field. Some of them were lying there because he, Bill Williams, had killed them.

QUIET STRETCHED OUT OVER the battlefield like the fog seeping into every bunker and dugout along the line.

"How are you for ammo?" Wayne asked.

Bill checked. "I'm okay."

"I think I should go get a couple of bandoliers and see what's happening."

"You're wanting out of here, aren't you?" Bill asked.

"You can't order me to stay here."

Wayne took two steps and was out of the dugout. Bill stayed at the slit and stared at the bodies in the field. He didn't know how many or which ones he had killed, but they had died coming to get him. He struggled to determine how he felt about that, how his family would feel if they knew he had killed people. When he conjured up a vision of his mother, she didn't say anything, just stood near the door of their house and nodded as if she understood he didn't have much choice. He couldn't bring his father up. He tried, but the image of him dead in the bedroom with the rifle against his chest caused him to fade out. He had no idea how Ilene would feel about it, or Carl, for that matter.

The sudden sound of a machine gun shook off his thoughts. Firing erupted along the front, scattered mortar rounds landed between the bunkers. As the next shell exploded, Wayne dived through the bunker opening, his rifle, helmet, and grenades crashing together when he hit the floor. The firing escalated up and down the line as he handed Bill two bandoliers of ammunition and three grenades.

Bill went back to the slit. He could see the Germans coming across the field. The regiment's mortars coughed out their rounds, the outgoing whump followed by the explosion down field.

"Sergeant says to hold," Wayne said. "Couple of guys wounded but the line's holding okay. The kitchen truck hightailed it out of here, probably back to Le Havre by now."

"Funny how I'm not very hungry. What did it look like out there?"

"Bodies all over the field. Must be a hundred—at least."

"Here they come again."

"If they don't know we're here, we might let them get closer."

"Yeah, but we only got eight shots," Bill said. "I don't like this hole. Let's go up top and fight from there."

"Too much shrapnel flying around—trees are all beat up. "

"You big chicken," Bill said. "I don't want 'em to get real close."

"How close?"

"A hundred yards."

"Okay ... at a hundred yards we move out." Wayne hooked grenades on his belt and took up his position at the slit. It was lighter now but drizzling rain, and their breath hung in the cold air inside the dugout.

There was a slight rattling sound of wood on wood. Wayne's rifle was shaking against the firing slit.

"You cold?" Bill asked.

"Hell no I'm not cold."

"You're shaking."

"So what?

The Germans fired from the hip as they advanced across the field. Occasionally a round hit the logs in front of the dugout.

"What do you think?" Wayne said.

"Start shooting—now!"

Wayne's rifle cracked, then Bill's. Two men dropped in the field.

"You shoot from the left and I'll take the right," Bill said.

He swung his rifle and took aim at a soldier coming from his right. His rifle bucked, then locked open and threw the clip into the air. He pulled another clip from his bandolier and pressed it in.

How much time had he lost—three seconds, maybe? The krauts had got further in those three seconds than ever before. How many were there out there?

"Are you squeezing your shots?" Wayne yelled. "Didn't look like you hit anybody that time!"

Bill aimed at a soldier dressed in white camouflage with crossed OD belts from his shoulders to his waist, firing from the hip as he weaved toward them. Bill counted his steps one way and then the other and shot him as he pivoted to the left, the bullet hitting him where the belts crossed. His arms jerked up, the rifle flew into the air, the helmet fell off his head, and he slammed into the ground.

"We backing 'em off?" Wayne asked.

"Can't tell."

"My God, how many are there out there?"

"Don't know," Bill said. "They're getting to the hundred-yard marker. What do you think? Should we pile out of here?"

"You're the corporal."

Bill stuffed two grenades in his pockets and jumped for the steps. Wayne was right behind him.

"Over there." Bill pointed and Wayne dashed around him and slid behind the trees.

They hugged the base of a tree. There was firing everywhere, then they saw three white-clad Germans shooting into a bunker and GI's coming out with their hands up. Bill and Wayne each fired, dropping two, and a GI shot the third.

Sergeant Conner hollered from behind a grove of busted trees: "Third Platoon—back to the CP!" then bolted to the rear.

"What's up?" Bill asked.

"Do I look like an officer?" Wayne said.

"Watch behind us. Cover me to that next grove."

"Why do you go first?"

"Okay—you go first—I'll cover you. Go!"

THE VILLAGE OF AUW had become a sore spot. Captain Clark was organizing a two-company task force to counterattack and drive the Germans back through the bottleneck.

"Who left a hole in the line?" Bill asked Sergeant Conner.

"The 14th Cavalry bugged out. The krauts are pouring through there like ants at a picnic."

"Horses and all?"

"Hell, they haven't had horses for years," Conner said.

"So what's the Third gonna do?"

"March and fight."

"My men haven't had any food today," Bill said. "How do you think they can march and fight without food?"

Sergeant Conner picked up a box of D Bars and passed them around to the men. "This will have to hold us until we get back."

"You know," Bill said, "over and over and over they told us in basic that the officers would take care of the men. So we get here and get fed D Bars for three days. Are the officers eating D bars?"

"I don't know," Conner said.

"Somebody's got some explaining to do to me," Bill said. He grabbed two D bars and turned his back on Conner.

FIFTY YARDS INTO THE attack the drizzling rain turned to snow and a wind whipped it straight into the men's faces. Their path into Aux led through forest trails, slippery with blinding snow. Wet, hungry, and tired, they emerged from the forest in mid-afternoon to face a group of houses clustered around a church on a hill. Third

Platoon led the attack, and halfway up the hill the Germans spotted them and began firing.

"Isn't this great?" Coric shouted from behind a wall. "Can't stand up, charging uphill, and the krauts looking down our throats."

Bill didn't answer. He was drawing a bead on a sniper in one of the windows. He fired and missed.

Lt. Adams hunched over then crawled up to Bill. "Gotta get back to Schlausenbach. Command post being attacked. Disengage your men and get the hell back there." He shook his head then departed.

THE FORCE DISENGAGED AND returned over the same route. As they arrived at dusk, the snowstorm abated and the men, weary from the day of run, attack, and return, dug in.

In their foxhole, which they alternated digging, Bill and Wayne ate their D Bars and contemplated how to make the hole more comfortable now that they were not being shot at.

"Let's put a roof on it and get the snow off us," Bill said.

"You think it's worth it?"

"You dig a hole in the bottom and work out the drain, I'll work on a roof."

Bill slid out, leaving his rifle facing the enemy. He returned with fir branches and an armload of dry grass.

"Put this grass in your boots. Keep your feet from freezing."

"Where'd you find it?"

"Under the trees," Bill said.

Wayne looked at him. "Some Eskimo trick?"

"Doesn't it get cold in Wyoming?"

"Just in winter."

"Winter is what we got here, Wayne."

In thirty minutes the foxhole had a roof of fir boughs, a bottom lined with boughs and dried grass, and a decent camouflage front. Except for the wet clothes and lack of food, they were going into the night in good shape.

"How're you for water?" Bill asked.

"What the hell you think? Been eating snow since we got back."

Suddenly they both stopped talking. They heard the snow crunch. They looked to their front and sides but didn't see anyone.

"Evening, men," Adams whispered from behind them.

"Judas Priest, Lieutenant, you scared the hell out of us," Wayne said.

"Sorry. Look, the Fourteenth Cav has bugged out and we're in a tight spot here. Corp is sending the Seventh Armored in tomorrow to beat these krauts back. We have to hold on till they get here. I don't know what will happen in the morning, but we bloodied them pretty good today. Just stay tight and keep your front and flanks clear. McNaulty and Krause are on your left, about twenty yards. Who's on your right?"

"Don't know, Lieutenant. Could be Coric."

"Well, don't shoot me while I go find out. You've got D Bar's?"

"That's all we got."

"We'll get the kitchen trucks back up here tonight and have a good hot breakfast." He stood up and walked behind them, disappearing into the snow and mist that was hanging on the tops of the Eifel.

"Where's my mess kit?" Bill asked.

Wayne looked in his pack. "You know what? We threw them down when the artillery started this morning."

"We're gonna be eatin' D Bars until this war's over if we don't have a mess kit."

"Quit your bitchin'. Soon as it's light, I'll go scrounge a couple and get us some water."

"You taking first watch?" Bill asked.

"Yeah—you got the grass."

Bill tried to arrange himself so wet clothing wouldn't be touching every part of him. He was only partially successful.

"Wayne," he said when he had gotten settled, "were you scared today?" He felt more comfortable asking when it was too dark to look him in the eyes.

"Twice . . . at least. Once when the artillery started this morning and again when we saw all those krauts coming straight at us. Didn't think we had enough ammunition between us to kill them all. I thought they'd run right over the top of us, shoot us in that damn hole, and leave us out there to bloat in the snow."

"Yeah. Me too."

Bill was thinking about that when he started dreaming. Sometimes he couldn't tell whether he was awake or in a dream. He didn't think he'd been asleep when Wayne nudged him.

"Your turn," Wayne whispered.

"Haven't been asleep yet."

"I never heard you snore when you're awake."

"Snore?"

"Like General Custer."

Bill rolled onto his stomach and checked his rifle. He made sure his grenades were on the lip of the foxhole where he'd left them, then said, "Who told you General Custer snored?"

"My grandpa."

In two minutes Wayne was snoring.

Bill rubbed his eyes. He stared at the night, almost wishing he could see some Germans so he'd know if they were there or not. He had never been so scared in his life. If he concentrated on seeing the soldiers coming it wasn't so scary until you saw how many of them there were. It was hard to imagine how he could shoot fast enough and accurately enough to stop them. He hadn't stopped them. The mortars had.

He heard some distant shots and saw one flare. Nothing exciting enough to wake Wayne up.

He pulled back slightly on the rifle bolt and with the tip of his finger felt the cartridge, then, reassured, slid the bolt closed and noticed for the first time how slow his movements were.

He needed to move around to avoid being solid by morning. He slid sideways out of the hole, not disturbing Wayne, and looked over the rim to see where the other foxholes were. The men would be jumpy, and he didn't relish getting shot from behind.

He decided he didn't need his rifle and left it perched on the lip of the foxhole along with the grenades. When he rolled onto the snow it was crusted and almost held him, but his elbows and toes broke through as he crawled toward a tree. His breath coming faster, he leaned against the tree and noticed it felt colder out of the foxhole. He braced his neck and head against the tree and with his arms across his chest and his heels dug into the snow raised himself off the ground.

This could work.

The exercise started slow, but after ten push-ups he had his balance and the repetitions got faster. His breath came faster too, and his stomach, which had not had any real food for three days, was aching, but he continued. When he got to fifty-five he had to stop.

"You makin' out with something out there?" a whispered voice came from a hole just beyond the tree.

Bill smiled for the first time since they'd got on the Eifel. "Yeah, you interested?"

In a minute a GI crawled out with a dusting of snow on his coat. "Where'd she go?"

"Who?"

"The girl."

"There isn't any girl. I'm trying to get warm," Bill said.

"I'm so damn cold I can't even feel half of me."

"Put your head against the tree and dig your heels in. Straighten your body out and hold it. See how many of those you can do."

The soldier looked at him and cocked his head. "How long you been this crazy?"

"Just since yesterday."

"That makes sense." He leaned his rifle against the tree, assumed the position, and tried to lift himself. Only his legs and butt came off the ground.

"How do you do that?"

"Keep working at it," Bill said. "Think of yourself as a flat board and raise your whole self at once."

He tried again. Then again. He did ten or twelve before he stopped. He was breathing hard now and whispered, "I don't think I can do this."

"Try some more." Now his helmet slipped off the tree.

A shot exploded from the side of them. The slug knocked a chunk of bark off the tree just above the GI's head.

He lay flat. "Who's shooting?"

Bill had dropped beside him. "Came from our right."

Just as the soldier reached for his rifle, another shot sprayed ice in his face.

"Don't shoot!" Bill said. He edged behind the tree. He could see Wayne's face above the lip of the their foxhole.

"Bill?"

"Yeah."

"Who's shooting?"

"Don't know. Stay down."

A voice came from the right. "Hey!"

Bill didn't recognize the voice. "Hey yourself."

"GI's?"

"Yeah," Bill said.

"What the hell you doing out there?"

"Tryin' to get warm."

"I wasn't trying to hit *you*. Didn't know what it was."

"Figure out what you're shooting at next time," Bill said.

"Damn near killed us both and I don't even know your name," the GI said. "I'm Eric Krause."

"Bill Williams."

Krause was silent for a minute, picked up a chunk of snow and threw it off to the side. "When I was a kid in Montana I always thought sleeping out in the snow would really be a neat thing to do. Now I'm out here and I'd rather be anyplace else on earth."

Bill nodded. "Well, I've slept out in the snow a lot but we were ready for it and nobody was shooting at us."

"Where'd you do that?"

"Alaska."

"My Dad always dreamed about Alaska but he never got there. He was always saying we should just pack up and go on up and see what it was like." He swung his arms around his chest a couple of times.

The GI who'd done the push-ups said, "I'm Jim Taylor. You know, I *am* warmer after doing that. And another thing . . . I feel better about tomorrow. Think it's gonna be bad?"

"I don't have any idea," Bill said. "I've been five days in this war and only two of them shooting at anybody and I don't know how it could get any worse than these last two days. I thought I'd have to draw some new underwear from the quartermaster."

Eric chuckled. "Bet there'd be a big pile of used shorts on the ground if everyone who dirtied theirs had to trade in for a new pair." Bill smiled. "You bet there would." He looked at his watch. "Time for me to go spell Wayne."

BILL SLID IN AND arranged himself to watch the slope in front of the foxhole.

"What you guys doin' out there?" Wayne asked.

"We're arranging a used shorts trade-in depot, so all the guys who've dirtied themselves can get new ones. Want to trade yours in?"

"Indian warriors don't poop their pants."

"Who taught you to lie that good?"

"My grandfather."

"The same one that heard Custer snoring?"

"That one." He was quiet for a few seconds, then he said, "Yes."

"Yes what?"

"Yes, I'd like to trade mine in."

THE FIRST SOUND BILL heard in the pre-dawn cold was Wayne trying to eat a D Bar.

"This thing's frozen like a board."

"Stick the bar under your armpit for a minute and warm it up if your old teeth can't break it."

"Why don't you worry about your own?"

"You're the one who needs help." Bill closed the top button on his coat, which had somehow popped open in the night. "What's the weather look like?"

"Foggy and colder than hell. Wind's picking up a little too. Bet the planes won't get through to help us today."

"What day do you think this is?"

Wayne thought a minute. "I think it's Sunday. Let's see . . . we came up on the eleventh, then we got hit about a week after that, then the raid on Auw . . . must be the seventeenth. Hell, I don't know—don't care, either. Just get me out of this frozen hell-hole."

A whispered voice came through the cold and fog. "Williams . . . Turner?" Sergeant Conner came up on elbows and knees, wiggling like a snake through the snow.

"Company's forming a perimeter defense. Our platoon is on the right point. First platoon on your left and second on your right. Got it?"

"Hey, Sarge, what's happening?" Wayne said.

"Krauts on both sides of us. The Seventh Armored is on its way and should be here this afternoon. We gotta hang on."

"You mean we're surrounded?" Bill said.

Sgt. Conner nodded. "Anything you need?"

"Food," Bill said. "Where's the kitchen truck?"

Sergeant Conner shook his head. "Don't know." With that, he was gone.

Wayne pulled out his bayonet and fastened it to the barrel of his M1. It slid in with a metallic click, and he wiped it on his sleeve. "I'm ready," he said, "If I don't freeze to death first."

"Or starve," Bill said.

"Or starve." Wayne started doing little pushups on his forearms and toes. "You know, I've been cold and I've been hungry, but not like this. Somehow being under orders to stay in a dangerous cold place and starve at the same time gets to me. How you can take it so calmly is beyond me. Ah, I'm gonna find some food—you watch the front."

As soon as he left, Bill pulled out of the coil he had made of himself and sprawled out so he could see in front. He tucked some of the grass between his thighs and the bottom of the foxhole. He could hear long-distance artillery and tank fire behind him and on all sides. The sky was lit up like a lightning storm, and an eerie glow wedged between the horizon and the low clouds.

The unmistakable sound of tanks drifted up from the roads that surrounded the Snow Eifel, the sound traveling uphill but its origin distorted by the trees and freezing fog. Bill had only heard the big Mark IV German tanks for two days, but after being shot at by one it was not a sound he was likely to forget.

No enemy was in his field of vision, so he rolled to one side to tie his helmet liner under his chin. He tucked his blanket in and around him, every move driving the cold deeper into his body. He tucked his hands under his armpits and coiled up again, thinking he would peek over the top every so often to assure himself there were no krauts coming up the hill.

There was a thud beside his neck. He shoved his arms in front of his eyes and covered his head.

"That warm you up?" Wayne whispered.

Bill uncovered his head and saw a box of K-rations on the grass floor.

"You son-of-a-bitch," he said. "You scared the hell out of me."

"Yeah, I know. I just got the hell scared out of me going back there and it warmed me up."

"Where'd you find K-rations?"

"The CP had some. We missed out yesterday."

"Are they frozen?"

"Like a rock."

IN TWENTY MINUTES SERGEANT Conner came by, breathless and talking fast.

"We're leaving here. No airdrops, and the Seventh isn't gonna make it. Get with Colonel Scale's Second Battalion in the center. We're gonna walk out."

They threw the stuff they didn't want to take in the hole, and grabbed their packs. Bill dashed back to the foxhole, picked up the K-ration boxes, and came running back.

"Put these in my pack, will you? Good fire-starter."

"Yeah. Like we've had a lot of fires lately."

"Maybe today we'll make one."

As they neared the command post, gunners were destroying their 57mm anti-tank cannon.

Bill shook his head. "This retreat isn't what the sergeant made out, is it?"

"I think we're in for a real fight."

They joined with other men of the 2nd Battalion and walked in a slow-moving silent group out of the valley and down the slope into the woods. Long lines of dark uniforms plodded along, heads down, looking at the feet of the soldier in front of them. They moved as a large disconnected body across the snow-covered area, all converging on the Ihrenbach stream. Occasionally a soldier threw off an overcoat as the men heated up from the first walking they had done in four days.

Colonel Descheneaux led the division on foot, which stopped every few minutes for the lead elements to search the terrain. There were no shots. A soldier slipped, his equipment banged, and everyone looked as he stumbled to maintain his balance then continued on, the sound muffled by the trees and snow. There was no food or water, but no one straggled.

By midday the 2nd Battalion was not a group. H Company was split in two, and only three squads of the four squads of 3rd Platoon were visible to Bill. Lt. Adams looked back and forth as if searching for the missing squad but he didn't go look for them nor did he send anyone to look. They would get there or not. Before dark everyone recognized that they were lost.

Bill had been all over the North Country near his home with no watch, no compass, and often with no daylight and he'd never gotten lost. Some from the village had, but they'd been drinking hooch and their natural survival instincts were dulled to the point that they hadn't known what would keep them alive and what wouldn't.

The army had spent two full weeks teaching him how to read a map and surely it must have spent more time on officers. They had maps and compasses—where was the problem? They were only a couple of miles from Schoenberg when they started, how could a whole regiment get lost in two miles? It was almost two miles from the front to the back of the columns.

As the 422nd stopped, the back of the column began to catch up.

"Did you see that fire?" a private asked.

"Which one?" Bill said.

"The kitchen trucks."

"No."

"We get no meals for three days and then they burn the trucks."

"Burned them?"

"Poured gasoline on and lit 'em up. I could feel the heat clear over to the first-aid station. Might keep our wounded from freezing for a few hours if they don't explode and kill them all."

"I saw them breaking up equipment with sledgehammers," another GI said. "Breaking cannon firing pins. Everything."

"I guess the idea is if we can't use it don't leave it for the krauts."

"I know, but it would have been good to have had a meal from them."

The ground they had halted on was frozen but had no snow cover. Some time back up on the Snow Eifel, they had walked out of the snow and Bill hadn't even noticed it.

Sgt. Reginald Conner walked up, his head bowed. When he motioned for the squad leaders to come together, he lifted his head and Bill could see wrinkles that hadn't been there a week ago and gray pods under his sunken eyes.

"All right—listen up. The Seventh Armored is stuck somewhere and as you can see, the weather's keeping the air corps from lending a hand." He mopped his dripping nose with the back of his hand. "We're going to attack Schoenberg. Make sure everyone's got full ammo and grenades. The 423rd is on our right, so don't go sending any fire that way. I know you're tired and hungry and thirsty—we all are. Let's just take this dump of a town, kick the krauts out, and have a good rest. Any questions?"

Wayne had one. "Sarge, how we gonna attack Schoenberg if we can't find it?"

Conner shook his head. "Private Turner, please do not suspect for one minute that the 422nd is lost. We're just going to charge in a different direction until we come to Schoenberg." With that he turned and walked away.

"I don't get it," Wayne said. "If we know where it is to attack it why don't we know where it is to find it now?"

"Oh, shut up, Turner," Krause said. "If you was so smart they'd make you a captain."

"I don't want to be a captain," Wayne said. "They don't get paid enough to do this. Friggin' officers—can't even find their way in the country. Does every officer need a road with a sign on it to know where he's going?"

"Back off, Wayne," Bill said.

"Okay, okay. But they're not likely to ask you or me to find it for them."

A patrol came out of the woods and reported to Colonel Descheneaux. A few minutes later the word came down that they were to go to the Auw road, stop, and form up there. In the morning they would cross the road and the Ihrenbach stream and attack Schoenberg.

The battalion moved off slowly. The soldiers found it hard to stand up and get started, their numb feet insecure on the uneven, frozen ground and their legs wobbly from lack of food.

Bill had never felt so weak and tired. Something almost defied him to move his legs. Whatever it was, it directed him to stop, lie down, eat, sleep. The debate going on inside of him was non-stop and the worst of it was that he couldn't take sides. He didn't know if he wanted to stop and lie down or keep moving his feet and stay in the ranks. His thoughts drifted back to the walk from Arctic Village to Venetie. I've done that. I can do this. For the moment he moved forward, and so long as one foot followed the other he would keep the squad together until they stopped. He was afraid that if they stopped again, none of them would get up.

His platoon came out on a small rise overlooking a road that wound through a valley parallel to a stream. That had to be the Auw road and the Ihrenbach stream. The column halted and platoons spaced themselves into a defensive perimeter. Wayne turned around in front of Bill.

"Help me off with my pack, will you?"

He threw his shoulders back. Bill pulled his pack off, lost his grip and it fell to the ground. Wayne turned around and looked at him. "Need help?"

"No."

Wayne took out his entrenching shovel and put his foot to it. The ground was frozen.

"We're gonna have to blow this ground open."

The shovel hit the ground again. Nothing.

Bill looked behind him. They had just come out of the trees and were on the edge of the slope. They could see down to the bottom of the hill, across the road and to the stream. It was the right place to dig in, but if they couldn't get in the ground it wouldn't do them any good. He looked back up at the trees, then started walking off to the side towards the officers.

"Where you going?" Wayne asked.

"See the officers."

"Bring back some food."

Bill didn't answer. He was looking for Captain Clark and found him seated on a rock watching Lt. Adams trying to dig a foxhole.

"Sir. I know it's not ideal for visibility, but if we backed up into those trees, the ground wouldn't be nearly so hard and we could get some shelter as well as get holes dug."

"We're not going to be here long, corporal."

"I understand, sir, but it would save a ton of energy if we could dig our holes there. And sir, my men need sleep. And food. They need food and water. Will there be any tonight, sir?

"I don't think so, Corporal."

Captain Clark looked over at Adams, still trying to get a start on the foxhole.

"Sir, are we gonna get out of this . . . ?" Bill asked.

"You're right, corporal," he said. "Lieutenant—order the company back into the woods. Tell them to find themselves a soft spot and dig in. We'll put a couple of listening posts out here if we can ever get through this concrete."

"Yes, sir," Lt. Adams said. He picked up his shovel and pack and started around the perimeter. "Williams, you go that way. Pass the word."

Bill looked at the captain still sitting as he was when he'd come over to him, one arm resting on each knee.

"Thank you, sir."

The captain nodded.

IT WASN'T ALL THAT easy, digging in the woods. But the ground was only frozen about an inch, and once the men got a shovel through that, they pried the frozen top off and set it aside. And digging the dirt wasn't so bad until you hit a tree root. Roots, rocks, frozen soil—all enemies of the infantryman, but at least they couldn't kill you. That was left to the machine guns, the artillery, and the freezing weather. Bill wondered how many of them would come out of this alive.

They had left their wounded behind on The Eifel with several volunteer medics. And now, only a couple of miles from their last camp, they were digging in again. Bill swore that if he got out of this he would never dig another hole again, come hell or high water.

AT 0915 ON THE 19th, with the veil of fog beginning to lift from Schoenberg, the ground erupted. The first explosion lifted Bill halfway out of the foxhole and deafened him. Wayne was writhing on the bottom, arms and legs moving as he rubbed the side of his head. Blood was coming out of his ears and nose. Bill pulled himself back into the hole, forced the helmet down over his face, and covered his head with his arms. Fist-sized chunks of shrapnel sang as they flew over their heads and tore holes in the trees. Great clods of frozen earth rained down on them, but Bill thought of them as protection rather than being buried in his own foxhole. There was no talking, no looking. It was hard enough to stay in the hole, and the noise hurt their ears as much as the concussions thumped their chests.

Bill remembered the prayers he'd been taught in the village. How often had he heard them? How did they start? He couldn't remember how they started but he could see the priest standing in the cabin they had built as a church, the Episcopal cross on the door, the pulpit. He knew the words and he knew they were for times like this.

"Death and destruction lie open before the Lord – how much more the hearts of men . . . " He remembered that. After each explosion he started over. He couldn't retain what he had just thought; it was as if each explosion erased his thoughts and all of his memory and just as anything started to take form again it was removed in another concussion.

In between explosions he heard Wayne throw up. He didn't know how Wayne had enough in his stomach to throw anything up. Now the sour stomach acid smell mixed with the acrid odor of high explosives. It occurred to him that he had never had to endure much in his life—how was he going to endure this? How could anybody endure it?

As suddenly as it began, the artillery ceased. It was as still as it had been for him under the water in the river. Then, one at a time, voices became audible. Cries for help, for the corpsman, GI's stood up and shook themselves off, looked around to see who was alive and who wasn't, took in the trees, observed the torn tops and distortion of the ground around them. Some smiled that they had survived it and seemed almost giddy, as if life had been re-handed to them and their hunger and thirst and cold and fatigue were nothing at this moment. They could wipe the dirt off, shoulder their rifles, march into Schoenberg, and clean house.

Shouts came from behind them. Bill turned, and all the fight went out of him. He saw German troops in green-black uniforms coming through the trees, shooting and yelling. GI's raised their hands and some removed their helmets. The front wave of Germans passed by, GI's still kneeling in their foxholes. The second wave of troops aimed their guns at the Americans and prodded them into a group.

Wayne was still in the hole but had reversed himself and was now looking to the rear. He glanced up at Bill with a dumfounded look on his face.

Bill was stunned. How had the Germans gotten behind them? Where was the main part of the battalion? Which way to go? His mind registered questions, thoughts, but there were no answers. He had maybe fifteen seconds. Run or surrender.

He grabbed his pack in one hand and slung a strap over his shoulder.

"Let's go!"

He leapt out of the hole and ran downhill away from the Germans, who were laughing as they came through the forest. Wayne passed him before he'd made fifty yards, then Bill struck a slick place, lost his footing, and tumbled down the incline. He spread his legs and skidded to a halt, adjusted his pack, and followed Wayne towards an area with foliage and small trees.

When Bill got to the trees, Wayne pointed out the other side. As soon as Bill caught his breath he peeked out. German soldiers were walking back and forth in front of an 88mm cannon aimed at the hillside they had just come down. They were on the road to Schoenberg, but the Germans were there first and they were in place.

A tank came into view around the corner, followed by self-propelled guns and more tanks jammed nose to tail.

"That's the Seventh Armored," Wayne whispered. "They got here."

"This is gonna be a hell of a fight. Let's get out of here!"

They both looked at the tanks edging closer to the concealed 88mm. There was no shooting. The tanks got closer—and Bill saw the German cross on the side.

"They're krauts!"

Wayne went flat on the ground.

Above them they could hear shots. They looked back up the hillside, where groups of GI's had started down the hill and were moving to cross the stream and get to the forest on the other side. They were about a hundred yards down the hillside when German tanks came out of the woods to their left and started firing at them. Some GI's doubled over, and those that weren't hit ran for the bottom. German machine guns opened up on their left. As soon as they got to the stream, German tanks on the right opened up and cut them down.

While the Germans in front of them were directing their attention to the running GI's, Bill and Wayne started back up the hill toward the remnants of the 2nd Battalion. They crawled up through a small gully without attracting attention. Near the top they ran into Lt. Adams, who had put together a mixed company of survivors and was raining mortar bombs on the German vehicles. He was wounded in two places but still directing the action. At last the tank and self-propelled gunfire drove them back into the forest and into the face of the oncoming 18th Volksgrenadier.

Lt. Adams stopped and took count of his remaining men. There were 119 survivors from fifteen outfits. Wounded, surrounded, and exhausted, the 2nd Battalion was finished. Lt. Adams called a halt to the attack.

Disorganized, confused, frightened, demoralized men slumped against broken trees, their weapons cradled in their arms. Most were almost out of ammunition and all were out of hope. What they had thought was the Seventh Armored coming to rescue them had been the enemy in full strength. Now the hillside was littered with their dead, and down in the valley, scattered groups of the 423rd and 422nd were surrendering to the Germans.

BILL AND WAYNE COULD see the Command Post and first-aid station beside it and could make out the officers nodding their heads from time to time. Rumors were going from man to man. Surrender. Fight it out. Food was on the way. The Seventh Armored was at the bottom of the hill. Bill scooped up snow once they got back on top and filled a discarded canteen. He pulled out the cardboard he had packed, quickly got a small fire going, and put the canteen close to the flame. Every minute or so he shook the canteen and added more snow. Wayne, fascinated, watched him for a minute, then found an abandoned mess kit and did the same.

GI's looked over at the little operation but couldn't seem to raise themselves enough to do it. Somebody was going to bring them food and water, there was surely going to be an airdrop today.

While the snow melted Bill pulled dry grasses from around the base of the trees and replaced the grass in his boots and at his back. He put a pile by Wayne's elbow.

The officers dispersed out of the CP, each going to his own unit. Lt. Adams called what was left of the platoon together at Bill and Wayne's location. He held his hands over the clear flame and rubbed them together. Bill noticed the cuts on his dirty fingers, the broken nails.

"We're going to surrender. Break up your weapons," he said.

Bill and Wayne looked at each other in stunned silence.

"Lieutenant—can some of us break out?" Bill asked.

Lt. Adams, his face twisted with pain from two wounds, said, "I'm sorry, Corporal. The orders are to surrender." He kept his hands over the small flame for another few seconds, then straightened up and walked back to his foxhole.

"I'M NOT SURRENDERING," Bill said. "I'm not spending the rest of this war in a prison camp."

"Me either," Wayne said. "What do we have for ammo?"

Bill felt his bandolier. "Four clips."

"I have five."

Bill reached down and shook the canteen. It was almost full. He took a drink from it, then shoved more snow into it and shook it again.

"Which way?" Wayne asked.

"I don't know."

Just then the officers in the CP stood up and walked down the slope. The men, reluctant and dejected, began to file down in columns, waving a white rag stuck on top of a branch in front of them.

"This way," Bill said and moved off to the southeast away from the Schoenberg road.

CHAPTER 9

THEIR FOOTPRINTS WERE WELL defined in the snow, but Bill hoped that with all the trails and prints on that hill there would be no one who could track their movements. They passed several GI's going the other way who just looked at them, helmets off and shoulders slumped. Moving toward capture they were shuffle-footed and distanced from the events around them. Their blank eyes stared but they didn't speak. Coric watched longer than the others.

"You guys gonna stay?" he asked.

"Yeah," Bill said.

Coric put his helmet on and stepped out of the line. "Can I come with you?"

"You got a weapon?"

"I can get one."

They didn't respond but moved away from the hill and back into the forest, away from the prisoner of war camp the battalion was moving toward.

Bill could see green-black uniforms off to his left and slid behind a tree. He heard a click and turned to see an M1 aimed at him from behind a group of small firs. He pointed to his shoulder patch, and the rifle slid back into the bush.

"Over here," a voice whispered.

Bill glanced around the tree, dropped, and crawled over. Wayne and Coric had seen the Germans and sheltered behind some broken-off treetops, victims of the last artillery barrage. They too crawled over behind the brush.

There were three soldiers set up in there. They had a .30 caliber machine gun, two canisters of ammunition, and two M1's.

"You guys staying?" one of the soldiers said.

The three nodded.

"Have you seen where they're coming from?"

"Everywhere," Bill said.

He was itching between his shoulders. He didn't like the situation here. If the six of them tried to go out together, the possibility of one of them being seen was high. But he liked the cover and the machine gun. Sweat leaked under his headband, he wiped it off with his sleeve, wondering how a person could sweat when it was freezing. He checked his watch: 1605 hours. It would be dark soon. He suspected that the Germans were cold and hungry too and that they wouldn't willingly search everywhere in this forest.

He saw that the soldiers were all privates in the 106th. He outranked them, but he didn't have much experience leading men. Then he smiled.

"Mike O'Leary from the *Northland Echo* sent me to get you out of here."

"You Irish?" the machine gunner asked.

"No." Bill didn't think the light was that bad. "But I think we can get out of here, if you're willing."

They looked at each other, trying in a minute to size up their chances of going as a group or trying it on their own. Most of them shivered, not just from the cold. They could stay put or run, and they knew they had a good chance of meeting death or detention either way.

Finally the gunner looked at Bill and said, "I'll go."

His team nodded.

"We're agreed? All of us?" Bill said.

Everyone nodded.

It was as dark as it was going to get in the snow. They could see no moon or stars, yet a slight breeze stirred the treetops and caused the sweat they had generated to turn cold.

They had heard no firing and seen no Germans since they slipped through them on top of the hill, sprinting one at a time from tree to tree in the opposite direction. None of them knew where they were, but Bill was sure they had crossed back into Germany. Two of the men thought the town of Oberlascheid was nearby.

Bill spread them into a defensive perimeter, the machine gun at the highest point. Six men didn't make a big perimeter, but it was their piece of this hill and they intended to hold it against all comers. It had turned dark before Bill found a large boulder at the edge of a narrow wood. He thought about building a fire, and the chances it would be seen or smelled.

He got a small fire going against the rock and took out his canteen. "Who's got water?"

They all placed their canteens in the center. Three of the six had some water in them.

"Wayne, get these filled with snow. We'll spread the water we have around, put snow in and shake them. Couple of hours and we'll have water for everybody. The water's gonna be real cold, so keep your canteens from freezing, keep them under you or between your legs or something. In the morning we'll find some food somewhere. Every other man awake, now—and take shifts."

BILL AWOKE SEVERAL TIMES during the night and listened. Both sides seemed to be settled down for the first night in a week. Before dawn he awoke shivering and crept into the woods to relieve himself. This was the first time he had taken a moment to consider his patrol. They were all young and strong. True, they'd been without proper food and short of water for several days, which would limit their endurance, but he thought every one of them could make it, physically.

He turned his thoughts to the enemy.

If the German tanks were heading toward Schoenberg, it made sense that they were attacking and had defeated the 106th. So for Bill and his men to get to their lines, they needed to head beyond Schoenberg but stay outside the combat area.

Ammunition and food were critical. At first light he would send out several guys to take a look over the battlefield. There must be rations and unused clips of M1 ammo out there if they looked hard enough.

He came back to the perimeter unchallenged, which bothered him a little.

Before first light he called the men together near the rock.

"I didn't get your names yesterday, but now I need to know who you are and what you're good at."

He knew Coric and liked the blond kid. He seemed eager to be a part of the patrol, and Bill told him to go toward the left and search all foxholes for discarded ammo and food. Eric and John, who were trained machine gunners, were sent one straight and one to the right. They each had a musette bag and were to stay out not more than twenty minutes, ten out and ten back. Peter, who normally carried cans of ammo for the machine-gun and protected it with his M1, was to go in thirty yards and act as a listening post.

"Check the burned-out kitchen trucks if you get to them," Bill said.

Wayne looked up. "If there's anything warm there, bring it back."

Coric looked at him. "Even if it's a tire?"

"If it's warm, bring it."

Bill knelt and watched them go. They weren't like a platoon of confident victorious soldiers, but alone amongst the dead who lay as they'd fallen.

The first to get back was Coric, who'd found several partial clips but no food. They divided up the ammo. Several minutes later the other three came in.

"What're you guys doing down that far?" Bill asked.

When they opened the musette bags pieces of rations fell out, unopened cans, D Bars half eaten, a half-can of Spam.

"The whole rations must have been picked up," Peter said, "we didn't find one."

"How about the kitchen trucks?"

"There wasn't anything left there, not even a hot tire."

Wayne said, "Next war I'm volunteering for the kitchen crew, at least I'll get food."

They put the food in the center of the perimeter.

"We'll draw straws," Bill said. "Short straw gets first pick of the rations. The guy on his left gets second choice and on around. You can trade if you want to." He held up his fist with six straws in it.

Coric got the short straw. He looked at the small pile of food that had been cast off by GI's just a few hours ago and now seemed so valuable to them. He approached the pile and hesitated.

"Come on," Bill said.

He took a partially eaten D Bar and sat down. Peter was on his left and took the Spam. "I've always thrown this stuff away before."

Each of the others chose halfheartedly.

Wayne said, "Before the day's over we're gonna need more than this to get across the river and to Bastogne."

"Saddle up—let's go." Bill took point and moved in a south-westerly direction with the goal of getting to the Our River and crossing it before it got too dark. Somehow, he had to find a way they could dry out and warm up on the other side of the river or they'd freeze to death.

He kept the patrol off the main trails, and when they had to cross one he'd send Wayne and Coric to check it out, sit beside it for fifteen minutes and see if there was any activity. He figured the krauts wouldn't keep quiet for fifteen minutes when they'd overrun the hill and taken 6,000 prisoners, and if they were watching the trails, Wayne would catch sight of them. After they'd gone about two miles they stopped on battle-scarred ground overlooking the village of Schoenberg and the Our River just as the sun peeped through a low layer of clouds. Bill sent Coric and Wayne to scout for food and ammo and kept the other three to man the machine gun.

The reconnaissance was very short.

"Foxholes all over the place," Wayne said as he dumped the contents of his musette bag on the ground.

Coric was smiling as he dumped his. "The army took better care of these guys than they did us. I took ammo out of the busted rifles, and some group had piled theirs behind a rock in the bush where I stopped to take a leak."

Bill looked at the pathetic pile of discarded food.

"Not much," Wayne said.

"No," John said. "But in the land of blind men the one-eyed man is king."

Bill said, "Divide the ammo up and draw straws for the food. I think we'll be eating where it's dry and warm tonight." They all looked at him. "John, hand me your binoculars."

He took the glasses and walked toward the edge of the trees, careful to stay in the shadow of one of them. His stomach growled. He nibbled a D Bar but concentrated on the farmhouse across the river. He watched it for an hour until he was satisfied with his plan, then got up and went back to the perimeter. Three of the guys were asleep even though the afternoon's cold air was creeping down the slope.

"What's up, Corporal?" Eric asked.

"We'll sleep here until we get too cold, then head down to that farmhouse across the river. Got a feeling we can warm up there and get some food."

Eric's eyebrows went up. The others who were awake just looked at him. Bill lay down and in seconds was asleep, a habit he had picked up the last couple of years in the army. If he'd slept during the day in the village, they'd have doused him with water.

Wayne shook him awake and pointed at his watch. He stretched his legs and felt the cold in them, and as he rolled over and rose to his knees, stiffness grabbed every joint in his body. He used his rifle as a cane and levered himself upright, his right leg finally giving him the strength to stand up. Wayne was waking the others.

Bill watched them go through their waking-up modes, first realizing they were awake, then where they were, then how cold and stiff they were, then struggling to find the best way to get upright. After they had relieved themselves, they gathered around Bill at the edge of the wood.

"You see that house just across the river all by itself with the barn off to the right rear?" he said. "We could cross the bridge but

I'm sure it'll be guarded, and we'd raise a ruckus getting across. We'll wade the river down by that bend where the tall tree stands on the far bank.

"Assuming the water isn't over our heads, we'll be wet and cold, so we gotta move fast. John, you and Eric set up the machine gun facing the bridge and Peter will cover you. Wayne will take the back door and Coric the side door; I'll take the front. I don't want anybody doing any shooting unless it's to save yourself or one of us. If that happens then we'll just have to adjust to it. The idea, plain and simple, is to overpower the people in the house fast and easy, then dry out, eat, and get to Bastogne."

He let it lie for a minute. "Any questions or ideas?"

In all of his short life he had never expected that any people close to him might get killed. It just wasn't something he thought about—now he saw it as a distinct possibility. You had to think of the consequences when you were about to cross a river at night and break into a hostile house. He and Wayne had just wanted to escape, and now he found himself leading a patrol of six guys risking death. He looked at each of them, hoping someone would come up with a better plan or at least say "to hell with it" so they'd stop.

Nobody spoke.

Bill swallowed hard and hoisted his M1.

"Okay. Spread out going down this hill, and I only want to see one person moving at a time. We've got time and we don't want to screw this up."

He went ten yards, then stopped and knelt down. The visibility hadn't changed. He looked back to see that the second man hadn't started. He got into a crouch, moved another twenty-five yards and stopped. The only enemy activity was a sandbag sentry post on each side of the bridge. He moved another twenty-five yards and stopped. When he looked back he saw the patrol was well spaced.

He maneuvered around a blasted-off tree stump near the road, sat with his back to it, and waited for the others. Each sentry post had a single soldier in it, and they didn't look or act like front-line soldiers. He could hear the next man slide up behind the stump, then the next. He could also hear the faint tinkle of the machine-gun cartridge belt bumping against itself. He pulled off his muffler and handed it to John.

"Wrap that belt in this. I can hear it ten yards away."

When they were all settled Bill crawled to the bank of the road, rolled silently down, and in a crouch dashed across the road to the riverbank. He lay still and listened, then motioned the next man to follow.

Looking across the black water that rippled in the moonlight, he hesitated. He had crossed many rivers but none in winter and none whose depths he hadn't probed first. He couldn't keep his mind off the image of him plunging in over his head and drifting downriver.

When Wayne finally got there Bill could hear his heavy breathing and see the clouds of his breath. He looked into Bill's eyes, then Bill nodded and thrust one leg into the water.

The water swirled around his knee and pushed his leg downstream before his foot reached the bottom. The current ran against his legs and made little swirls of white foam as he tried to move without making a sound. Although it was over a hundred yards to the bridge and Bill doubted either of the sentries could hear them that far away, he wasn't sure.

He moved forward and felt for a purchase with his foot, which had become numb. Halfway across he dropped into a hole. The icy water seeped through his clothes and up to his ribs and encased his chest. The shock of it seized his lungs. He tried to move faster, his numb legs flailing underwater, but the next step took him in up to his neck.

Now he was having difficulty staying upright against the current, and his feet danced across the bottom. He lifted his knees and floated to avoid losing his balance and falling sideways, his feet probing for the bottom. The next step was solid, and he lifted himself out to his waist and waded to the bank.

The men behind him had watched and waited and now one walked upriver and crossed. He was worried about John and Eric with the machine gun—although they were taller than Bill, the weight of it might tip them over. Wayne had moved downstream to catch them if they had a problem. Bill tried to clench his chattering teeth. The shivers took hold, and he knew he couldn't go back into the river to save anybody. They would have to make it on their own.

Back together again on the other bank Bill split them up. Coric and Wayne separated. Bill motioned to the machine-gun crew and moved toward the door. He stopped short of the porch, observed the quiet movements of the crew setting up the gun, and saw Peter choose a position on the river bank that allowed him to see both ends of the bridge.

Bill counted to ten and turned the doorknob. The door opened and he walked in with his rifle leveled. An old man and woman looked up from the table, soup spoons poised in mid-air. Using the muzzle of his rifle, Bill motioned them to get up and move toward the back wall. Coric and Wayne came through the door and the old man raised his arms and backed into the corner, the woman next to him.

"Check the house," Bill said. "Be careful." He kept his rifle on the pair.

Wayne and Coric came back and shook their heads.

"Okay, get the others in here," Bill said.

He lifted the lid on a pot on the stove. The soup would be a good start along with the fresh loaf of bread on the table. He motioned to the couple to sit on the floor, and with legs pressed together they proceeded to slide down the wall so awkwardly that he figured they couldn't get up fast.

Wayne let the others through the back door and they huddled around the stove, glancing occasionally at the couple seated in the corner.

"What you gonna do with them?" Wayne asked.

"Keep them on the floor and out of our way for now. Did you see anything in the barn?"

"Didn't go to the barn."

"Go check and see what it's like."

Wayne rubbed his hands over the stove, then grabbed his rifle and eased himself through the back door.

"Coric, get this food divided up and see what else you can find. Peter, get that fire going." Bill noticed the man and woman looking at each other. "Wait, Peter—don't kick up the fire. Keep it alive and hot but don't throw a lot of wood in. Might be out of pattern to what they usually do this time of night."

Wayne slipped in the back door. "Nice barn. Some hay and a good view of the bridge. A milk cow and apparently they had some pigs but none there now."

"Did you find a root cellar?"

"Didn't look."

"Go check."

"I'd like to get warm," Wayne said.

Bill glared at him. "We'll save some fire for you. Go check!" He looked at the couple. "Do you speak English?"

The man looked at the woman, who said, "Ja."

"We won't hurt you if you stay still and quiet. You understand that?"

"Ja."

"We'll be gone early morning and leave you in peace, or whatever peace you can find around here."

Coric threw a few potatoes on the table. "That's all I found."

Wayne came through the back door with his arms full of cheese, butter, and some fresh milk. "Look at this."

Bill had it worked out.

"Two guys eating, two guys by the stove, two guys on lookout in the house and in the barn. We rotate. After everyone's eaten and dried we sleep, same rotation. I want to be out of here before first light."

"Where do you want the gun?" John said.

"In the barn—in the loft."

"John. You and Eric eat first. Peter and Coric next. Wayne and I'll stick the gun in the loft and take first watch." He took his coat off and hung it on the back of a chair near the stove. Then he went into the bedroom, got a blanket, wrapped it around him, grabbed the gun off the tripod, and headed for the barn.

THE TEAM STANDING WATCH woke everyone up at 0400. The old couple, covered with sacks and towels, was awake on the floor. Bill and Wayne were in the bed, clothes drying in the kitchen. Eric had managed a night on the couch and John in a chair. Peter laid out the cheese, bread, and milk, and as the others got up and dressed in dry clothes, they grabbed some to eat and some to take with them.

"Is this all you have?" Bill asked the farmer. He looked at his wife.

"Ja."

"All you've said since we got here is 'Ja'. Can you say any other English?"

She smiled. "Merry Christmas. Happy New Year. Happy birthday."

"For crying out loud. So you don't speak English?"

"Ja."

Bill shook his head. "Don't yell or move until it gets light. Understand?"

"Ja."

"Okay, men. Let's go out the back door. We're heading to Auw."

They left single file through the back door. Two guarded the corner of the house while Eric and John got the machine gun and they faded through the field going northeast, keeping the barn between them and the house.

When they were out of sight of the barn Bill turned left and they started to work their way towards Bastogne.

Wayne came up alongside Bill. "Are all you Alaskans that cunning?"

"Just the ones from my village."

It was good to have a full stomach and be dry. Now if they could find the rest of the army . . . .

BILL KEPT THE PATROL on the west side of the Our River and headed on an undefined path between St. Vith and Winterspelt. They could hear heavy weapons traffic constantly.

"Be careful with your exposure," Bill said. "One of those guys with his head out of the turret might spot you. Wayne's seen several with binoculars looking around."

There was heavy gunfire somewhere to the southwest, but they didn't have maps and didn't know where it might be coming from. Bill wasn't an officer with maps and compass or even a mental outline of the route they'd taken to get to the Snow Eifel, and he'd paid no attention to roads, towns, or directions.

Now that he thought about it he considered himself stupid. If he'd left Arctic Village he would have noted the route, location of landmarks, direction, sun travel, weather conditions, wind. But in the army he left that to officers who might or might not be with you when you needed that information.

At noon they came to a small country road and Coric was sent to see what it looked like. He reported back: "Lots of tracks on it. Heavy stuff, guns and tanks."

One by one they started across the road. Just as John set off with the machine gun over his shoulder, a German command car came around the corner faster than anyone imagined a car could travel on that one-way road. The officer in the back seat stood up and pointed at John with his swagger stick, then started pounding the driver's seat with it, yelling at the driver to stop.

The driver brought the car to a stop. The officer unholstered his pistol and started firing at John and then at Eric as they bounced from cover to cover. When the pistol locked open on empty, the car turned around and went back. Eric and John, who had managed to get the gun set up by now, had no target. They quickly disassembled the gun and tripod and headed across the field. The others came on fast.

Bill and Wayne were the last across, and Bill noticed it was getting hard to breathe as he climbed up the ditch. He had made it almost halfway across the field when he saw John and Eric setting up the gun. His eyeballs jiggled and the cold made them tear so badly that he couldn't make out what they were doing. The next moment bullets and tracers were streaming past him twenty yards to his right, and he turned his head to see where Wayne was. Wayne was even with him, even though he had started ten yards behind.

His breathing shut out other noises, until the snarl of the .30 caliber gun deafened him. He dived past it, unslung his rifle, and hit the ground rolling. The others were in a line, firing. The command car had returned with a self-propelled gun and the officer stood up in the rear seat, oblivious to the machine-gun bullets coming close to him. Bill saw bullets careening off the armor plate on the SP gun. He took a bead on the officer, held his breath, and fired. The officer fell back on the seat, wounded, but immediately sat up and pointed again with his stick.

The first cannon shot was high and wide.

"Get out of here!" Bill yelled. He led the way to the left. The riflemen followed fast, but Eric and John were a bit slower with the gun.

The Germans unlimbered the machine gun on the turret, and bullets were zinging past and splattering the ground around them as they ran. The gunner ran through a belt of ammo, and the gun stopped.

Bill looked for a place to defend. They were in a field, there was no rise to it, no trees, no walls. He came to an irrigation ditch and dove in feet first, thinking for a split second that he was going to be wet and cold again, but the ditch was empty. It provided scant cover from the gun on the road, but each man threw himself into it and prayed it was deep enough to cover him from view. Eric and John fumbled to set up the gun.

"Don't use the pod!" Bill yelled.

Eric lifted the gun off the tripod and laid it in the grass, and John loaded a belt of ammo. Each man waited, the only sound the rhythmic breathing of the man next to him.

The first cannon round went over their heads. Bill peeked over the lip of the ditch. The command car had taken refuge behind the SP gun and only its armored front faced them.

The second round exploded against the bank, deafening them all. Bill lifted his face from the dirt and looked to see that all but one man still clung to the steep side. Coric lay on his back, arms flung out over his head, his helmet off and blood coming from his leg and chest.

Shrapnel had torn him from his left thigh up and across his stomach and torso. Panic washed over Bill. He moved across the ditch and started to open Coric's coat and pants, then stopped.

The only thing he had in his aid kit was bandages, tape, and morphine. There was nothing he could do except yell for a medic, and he hadn't seen a medic for two days.

Coric turned to him, his eyes open wide, and blinked with a vacant look, the pupils small and dark.

"Can you stay?"

Bill nodded. "I can stay."

"I'm thirsty. Is there any water?"

Bill pulled his canteen out. It was partially frozen and he shook it, breaking up the thin ice. He laid Coric out straight in the ditch and covered him with his coat.

"Can you say the Twenty-third Psalm for me?"

"Coric . . . I . . . ." Bill stopped and lowered his head. "I'm not very good at this. I'm not sure I remember enough of it."

The cannon fired again, the concussion and dust penetrating every fiber of Bill's body. He ended up on top of Coric. He pulled himself off and looked at him.

Coric's eyelids were partially closed.

Bill pinched his memory. It was going back a long time to a summer when he and Carl had been baptized by the Episcopalian Minister who came upriver. He had spent a month in the village and buried several elders. Twice a day he taught bible verses.

"The Lord is my shepherd . . . " he said. " . . . I shall not want. He maketh me to lie down in green pastures . . . "

He got most of it. When he finished, Coric said, "Again."

The SP machine gun opened fire, the bullets singing off the frozen earth. Everyone clung to the bottom of the ditch.

Bill grabbed Coric's hand and squeezed hard. "The Lord is my shepherd . . . "

Coric closed his eyes and concentrated hard on taking his next breath.

Bill said, " . . . Yea though I walk through the valley of the shadow of death . . . "

Coric sucked some air between his teeth and then his face relaxed. Even as Bill went on, " . . . Surely goodness and mercy shall follow me all the days of my life," he knew he was gone.

There was another burst of machine-gun fire from the SP gun, then nothing. They waited, occasionally looking through the grass to see if anyone was coming. No one ventured from the road, and after thirty minutes they heard the armor start up. It turned around and they all watched as the command car led the SP gun back down the road.

The men drifted over to look at Coric. They had traded one for one. Coric for the German officer. And what had either side gained from the two deaths? The Germans had gone back to their unit, and five of the original six men of his patrol would move on toward the American lines. Bill figured nothing had changed except that within a quarter of an hour two men, unknown to each other, had left this life in a violent manner and without their families knowing they'd left it.

Bill hugged the bank and cried softly. It was one thing to see men killed fifty yards away in another foxhole, or see the enemy drop as they ran toward your lines, and quite another to have a friend killed ten feet from you in the same ditch.

As he drew another breath his side stung and burned. He looked down and saw blood coming out of a hole in his coat. Slowly he laid down his rifle and removed his coat. There was a jagged tear in his shirt and long underwear. Wayne saw it and scrambled over.

He opened the coat and shirt and gently pushed Bill against the bank. A small ugly piece of shrapnel had cut through Bill's coat and lodged between his lower ribs. It had torn the flesh and bruised the bones. Wayne held the tear open and glared at the wound.

He looked Bill in the eye and said, "I don't know if I should try and take it out or not."

"Leave it," Bill said. "Sprinkle some sulfa powder on it, bandage it." He closed his eyes and sucked in air through his teeth.

When Wayne finished no one seemed eager to rush out of the ditch. He reached down, picked off Coric's coat, and laid it over Bill.

"I don't want it," Bill said.

"He doesn't need it any more," Wayne said.

"I don't want it."

"Bill, we've left dead men all over this country, don't let this one cause you to make bad decisions. We need everyone thinking right to get out of here." He spread the coat over Bill. Bill turned his head, tears tracking through the caked dirt on his face.

MOST OF THE MEN noticed the silence. The war had passed them by, almost as if they were the last remnants of some forgotten force no longer relevant. Abandoned by their officers, their comrades surrendered, they were drifting around Belgium like a piece of bark on a small creek, going with the flow here, circling in a whirlpool briefly, then bouncing against the bank to flow downstream again.

Wayne urged them to eat some of the cheese and bread before they took off. They chewed at it but their jaw muscles were slow and they all bowed their heads like their helmets were too burdensome to bear.

Wayne put an arm under Bills shoulder and boosted him up. "Let's go, old warrior."

"Wayne—take point and lead us to a safe place," Bill said.

Wayne led the patrol to a corner of a field where a small triangle of woods had been left in a low spot next to a creek. It was far enough back from the road that the chances were they wouldn't be seen.

Bill organized a perimeter and waited for dark with two watching while the others slept. There would be no fire, but the extra coat and the blankets would keep them warm. Wayne filled the canteens from the creek, and they ate the bread and cheese. Then the patrol settled down with only their eyes moving.

Bill looked at them—this good group of guys that had somehow banded together. What were the chances of any five or six guys from the regiment doing this well?

When it was full dark, Wayne crawled up to Bill. "What say I make a little circle and see what we're up against?"

Bill frowned. "I don't like it. I'd like us all here if we had a problem."

"Indians were made for crawling around in the dark. I might find a way out of here without exposing the whole squad."

Bill looked up. "No moon. Don't make it long. No more than an hour."

Noise travels far on cold air, and Bill could hear farmer-type noises, lids on milk cans, animal sounds. If he just sat and relaxed he heard more sounds than if he strained to hear.

A half-hour later Wayne came in. "We're in luck," he said. "There's a German aid station in a field about half a mile from here and away from anything else. Looks like they're bringing back their wounded from the front. There aren't many able-bodied men around, mostly medical staff. They have food and med supplies. What would you say we hit them, get you taken care of, grab some food, and take off running?"

Bill looked at him and then at the men. "Think we can do it?"

Wayne nodded.

The men said nothing.

"You guys game?" Bill asked.

They looked at each other, then nodded their heads.

"Okay," Bill said. "Mount up."

He let Wayne lead the way. It seemed more like a mile to the aid station, and his wound throbbed all the way. They crawled up behind a tent that had a light inside. There was one guard near the entry and exit of the compound and one between two tents on the side of the field.

Wayne pointed and whispered, "That tent's the mess hall."

"Okay. Take Peter with you and get some chow, then we'll find a medic and get me patched up. How many krauts here?"

"Eight, maybe ten at the most," Wayne said.

Bill looked to his left. He would take Eric and John and set up the gun between the two tents in the background, where the gun could sweep the entrance and anybody who stepped out in front of the tents.

They slid silently across the frozen ground. In the dark, Eric came upon a sentry having a smoke. Before he could drop his cigarette, unsling his rifle, and shoot, Eric jammed a knife into his stomach. There was a gurgling sound and the man went down, but the knife thrust didn't kill him. Bill grabbed him, clamping his hand over his mouth, and stabbed him in the throat.

The German was squirming, the steam rising from the warm blood draining down his neck and into his tunic. Bill sawed at his throat, reaching for the artery, the man flailing his arms, banging his wristwatch on Bill's helmet. It seemed like the struggle went on forever, the noise surely heard by others. At last the German went limp. Bill fell to his hands and knees, breathing hard, and looked at the bloody knife in his hand.

Good God, what have they made of me?

Peter came back with a musette bag over his shoulder.

"Wayne's got a medic. Come on." He reached for Bill's hand, saw the blood and knife. "You okay?"

"Hell no, I'm not okay." Bill pointed at the dead German.

Peter glared at the still form. "Come on."

They entered a tent at the far right corner of the compound. Wayne had a knife against the throat of the medic, whose eyes grew wide when he saw Bill come through the flap, blood on his arm and the front of his coat. Peter tied the flap shut and knelt down to guard the entrance.

Bill removed his coat and shirt and sat on the table. Wayne grabbed hold of the medic's collar and pressed the point of his knife in his kidney, hard enough to let him know that was where the knife would enter if he didn't do the job.

The medic looked at the embedded shrapnel, then, glancing at Wayne, cautiously moved toward the tray of instruments. It took five minutes of frantic work for the medic to remove the shrapnel and bandage the wound. Bill had never seen a doctor work so quickly, but then he'd never seen anyone work with a knife at his kidney.

He put his clothes back on while Peter and Wayne taped the medic's mouth, hands, and feet and laid him on his stomach on the ground. They then pulled his feet up and ran tape around the ankles and across the forehead, pulling his body into an inverted 'C'. Bill thought that quite creative and even managed a smile as Wayne whispered several times, "Schoenberg . . . Schoenberg." The medic looked at him.

Peter untied the flap and peered out. There was no one in the area. Eric lifted the gun, John grabbed the tripod, and the patrol headed toward Schoenberg.

A quarter of a mile out of the camp, Wayne turned hard right and followed a fence line to a corner where he turned again, heading this time southwest toward Bastogne.

"Hurt?" Wayne asked Bill.

"Everything hurts."

"Here." He handed Bill some bread. "Soak this up in your mouth and it isn't half bad. I think it's pumpernickel."

He checked to see that the safety was on and that his ammo bandolier was straight, easy to get to, and wasn't resting on his wound. He took a breath to see how deep he could breathe without pain, looked around at the men, and took the lead.

They walked all night without encountering another person. Before dawn they settled into a defensive perimeter inside some short brush that offered no protection from bullets but did shield them from sight. From that position they could observe a small lane that ran generally east and west and noticed farmers using it to move livestock to fields.

At midday they heard heavy equipment coming up the road.

"Man, I hope that's ours," Wayne said.

Eric and John had set the gun up and Bill looked over it now to see if they had a good field of fire.

"What makes you think it's ours?" Eric said.

"Didn't. Just said I hoped it was."

John crawled out to get a better look, then wiggled back. "They're tanks with a white star on the turret. Gotta be ours."

They looked at Bill.

"Wayne, go take a look. I can't crawl with this rib."

Wayne took off his helmet and crawled out where John had been. He was a long time out there before he inched his way back.

"Well, they're US tanks, all right, but I don't know who's manning them. Could be krauts."

"How we gonna find out?" John asked.

Bill was thinking about that and right now he didn't have a good answer.

"Hell's fire," Peter said. "I'll take off my coat and shirt and run out to them. If they take me in I'll let you know what they are."

"Tell you what we do," Bill said. "Let's work our way to the roadside and see if we can hear them or make a more positive identification. I'm not eager to get shot by our guys or by them."

"No sense all of us going," Wayne said. "Let me sneak up there and see what I can pick up." He took off his heavy coat and laid his rifle on it.

"You're not taking your rifle?" Eric asked.

"Want to stay light on my feet," Wayne said.

Bill put out his hand and grabbed his sleeve. "Wayne. Take it real slow and easy."

"I will."

"Yeah. I just don't want to go through the rest of this war without you."

"I'll be careful."

Their eyes locked for a moment.

Finally Wayne said, "Man, you look grimy." He smiled and left. Within twenty yards Bill couldn't see him any more.

From their position Bill could see several approaches to the road, and he kept his eyes peeled for any sign of Wayne. The armored column halted, and several GI's came out of the tanks with Thompson .45's held by a strap on their shoulder. Bill saw Wayne walk out of the brush with his hands held high and saw the men frisk him. Finally Wayne put his hands down and pointed toward the patrol. Bill could see the GI's looking at them. Wayne motioned for them to come down.

Bill's face broke a smile. "Looks like we're home, guys."

Eric said, "Man, I hope this is the last time I have to break this gun down, I'm wearing this thing out just moving it."

John grabbed the tripod and the patrol started across the ground. Bill picked up Wayne's coat and rifle and trudged toward the waiting tanks.

"John, do you feel lighter?" Wayne asked.

"No."

"Eric, Peter . . . you guys feel lighter?"

"No," they said.

Bill felt like he could jump from the ground right to the top of the tank. He knew Wayne could. As they approached the tanks, Bill squared his shoulders and straightened his back. He leveled his helmet and with a rifle on each shoulder walked evenly.

"Eric, John, Peter—line up with me abreast. Let's march in there in battle line."

It wasn't really marching. The ground was frozen and uneven and they couldn't step properly, but the four men came across the last fifty yards like a military unit. They stopped next to Wayne and ten feet from the two GI's with Tommy guns. One of the GI's, a sergeant, saluted Bill.

"Welcome back, Corporal," he said. "You did a good job. Your patrol can stand down."

"Thank you, Sergeant." He handed the rifle and coat to Wayne. "My men and I are—"

"I know, Corporal. The private here was telling me where you've been and what you've been doing. We need to be moving. There's a truck back about a hundred yards. We've radioed them—they'll pick you up and you can report when we get to the line."

"Thanks, Sergeant," Bill said.

The GI's got in their tanks and the column cranked away. The noise was terrific as the vehicles went by.

The patrol climbed into the back of the truck through the canvas curtain and flopped on the benches. When their eyes adjusted to the dimness inside, they saw forms on the floor. Then they could make out boots. There were six frozen corpses tied to the front of the truck bed.

Bill removed his helmet and lowered his head. The others did the same.

"I wonder if they'll ever find Coric," Peter said.

"I doubt it," Bill said. "I couldn't even find that ditch now if I tried."

"I think I could," John said. "Wayne could."

Wayne shook his head. "Coric's better off out there than in this truck."

They were silent for some time. Finally Peter said, "What day is this, do you suppose?"

"It's Christmas Day," Wayne said. "That's what the tankers said."

"Christmas?" John said.

"Bill," Eric said, "do you get any help from prayer?"

Bill looked at him. "I have on occasion. It's been a while."

"Could you think of a prayer that would be good now?"

Bill thought back to the Episcopal bishop. It seemed so long ago, and yet it had been only a few years.

"Well," he said, "I don't know that I've ever heard one that would work for this, but I'll give it a shot." He bowed his head. "God our heavenly father, look down on us this day. Let your hand guide those on patrol and in the lines, help the wounded, and comfort the dying. Be with us now and forevermore. Amen."

He cleared his throat and swallowed, the lump staying lodged there. Feet shuffled softly on the floor of the truck bed.

"Amen," several voices chimed in.

SERGEANT ATTERLEY OPENED THE door and ushered the men into the room. They formed a straight line and came to attention.

An officer who identified himself as Lieutenant Cole went to one end of the line and, as if he were reviewing troops on the parade grounds, proceeded to walk down the line, stopping in front of each man and looking him over carefully eye-to-eye. Bill was sure he was noting the disheveled appearance, dirty weapons, and stench of the men. After he had checked each man he went to the front, spread his legs, and clasped his hands behind him in a loose parade-rest position.

Looking at Bill, he said, "You're the ranking soldier, Corporal?"

"Yes, sir."

"What happened to the rest of your outfit?"

"They surrendered, sir."

"Was that the order of the day, Corporal?" It seemed to Bill that the lieutenant put a lot of emphasis on "corporal".

"Yes, sir."

"Then why didn't you surrender, Corporal?"

"Didn't want to spend the rest of the war as a prisoner, sir."

"I see."

Lieutenant Cole released himself from the parade rest position, slapped his leg with the riding crop, and paced back and forth twice in front of the men.

"The 106th is being re-formed on the Rhine. In the meantime we'll keep you here until I can contact some officers in the 106th to verify your story. I personally think you're deserters. You will surrender your weapons and be placed under guard."

"FOLLOW ME, CORPORAL." Sergeant Atterley led the patrol through the immediate camp towards the brig, which was a barbed-wire enclosure attached to a building that reminded Bill of a chicken house he'd seen along the Yukon River. As they neared the enclosure, the sergeant veered left between two tents and toward a vehicle parking area. When they got to the last row of vehicles, he stopped.

Bill noticed they were behind a large truck and not visible from the rest of the camp.

"The lieutenant wants me to take you guys to the brig," Atterley said, "but I'm not gonna do it. There are no written orders for you, so stay on this road until you come to the field hospital. It's down the road about a mile. Check in there with Captain Rhodes. Tell him Sergeant Atterley sent you. Tell him your story. Get some medical attention for that wound, and he'll see you get back to the 106th. You guys have done your fighting."

Bill extended his hand. "Thanks, Sarge."

Sergeant Atterley shook his hand. "Get going," he said and turned and walked toward the brig, ducking behind various vehicles along the route.

Peter looked at Bill. "Think we can make it another mile?"

"Absolutely," Bill said. "My feet aren't even bloody yet."

THE 106TH WAS REFORMED and detailed to guard the Prisoner Of War Camp at Remagen on the Rhine River. At noon on May 7, 1945, Bill and Wayne were dismissed from their guard duties. It was the first warm, beautiful spring day after the worst winter anyone locally could remember. Poplars and willows were blooming, their leaves full—overpowering the stench of the camp. They got in line for mess.

His kit full of food, Bill found a seat on a table outside the mess tent. For weeks they had debated how long the Japanese would hold out after the Germans surrendered. Today the Germans had surrendered, and everyone in the camp was happy. The local war was over, and what they didn't know about the Pacific Theatre would fill a truck. Some said they would all be sent over there until the Japs surrendered. Some said they would be sent home as fast as the troop ships could take them. Let the Brits and the Frenchies guard the krauts. They were going home.

"What now for you?" Wayne said, taking the seat next to Bill.

Bill turned and looked at him. It had come to him as the war ended that Wayne had no village to go home to. The reservation was no village. The tribal life there had fallen apart long ago, and everybody knew how squalid it was. He didn't know how he felt about leaving Wayne. He lifted his glass.

"First – I'm going back to the village. Gonna see what Ilene thinks of my letters and wear my uniform down the only street in town. Then, I don't know what. Use the GI bill to go to school, find a job, learn how to make money."

Wayne snorted. "For hell's sake, there's nothing in your village—like there's nothing on the reservation."

Bill thought of fish wheels and duck hunts and caribou coming through the hills in a herd that stretched for miles. He could see the caribou coming into the village in the winter and hear the dogs barking at them and the old people laughing. He could close his eyes and smell his grandma's fresh bannock and taste the dried black meat they dipped in seal oil they got from trading with the coast Eskimos.

"Ilene's in the village. I'm gonna visit, relax, count my money and figure out how to get ten thousand dollars and a house then ask her to marry me."

CHAPTER 10

THE FLIGHT FROM FAIRBANKS to Arctic Village took less time than Bill remembered. It was the speed of everything that had happened that threw him off. The train, then the boat, then another train, and now this flimsy airplane that drifted through the clouds following the Chandalar River and was about to land on the tiny dirt strip.

As the pilot circled the landing strip, he banked the plane and Bill could see the trail he had taken from the river on the day of his bear hunt. The memory did nothing for him. Too much had happened since that day.

He couldn't even remember now the names of the dead in his platoon, and at the time he'd been sure he would never forget them. He could remember those in his squad, but he'd lost the platoon guys somewhere between the Bulge and his mustering out. They weren't close friends, just guys who were trying to stay alive like him and hadn't made it.

He could close his eyes and see some of them on the battle-field, but mostly he didn't, because when they died he was totally engaged in staying alive and keeping the Germans away from his position. He hadn't had time to look around.

The pilot flared the plane and touched the wheels down on the dirt strip. No one knew Bill was coming home, so he didn't expect anyone to be there. A pickup was waiting at the far corner of the field, and the pilot brought the plane to a stop near it.

The pickup driver got out and walked over to them.

"Hi, Bill—you probably don't remember me, but I'm Jack Gould."

"You old enough to drive now?"

Jack laughed and nodded. "Let me help you with your stuff."

"Here, you can carry my duffel. That's it."

"You didn't bring anything else?"

He'd just wanted to get out of the army and come home. He hadn't thought about bringing souvenirs, presents, things he could have gotten when he mustered out and boarded the train for Seattle.

The pilot tossed a mailbag into the back of the pickup and set a bag of groceries in the front seat. Jack handed him the outgoing mailbag.

"See you next week." The pilot threw the mailbag in and climbed in the seat. "See if someone can't fill in that marmot hole about halfway down the runway before I come back, okay?"

"That ain't a marmot hole," Jack said. "That's where Ted Sheeley's digging for gold."

The pilot shook his head. "Tell him he's messing with government property and I'll kick his ass when I come back if that hole isn't filled in, gold or no gold."

Jack waved and turned to Bill. "I'd like to see that pilot find Ted Sheeley, let alone kick his ass."

Bill tried to place Ted Sheeley but couldn't. They got in the pickup and drove down the one-track road into the village. Bill had a strange feeling from looking at the village as they approached that everyone in it was dead except for Jack and him. He didn't see anyone moving around on the streets or near the houses; he found the feeling hard to shake.

They rounded the corner and entered the main street. He could see people it relaxed him. Jack stopped the pickup in front of the general store, flung open the driver's door, and picked up the groceries. "Would you grab the mail?"

Bill lifted the mailbag. He walked into the general store and placed the mailbag on the floor by the desk that served as the cash register, credit counter, pencil and paper collector, and magazine stack.

"Why—hello Bill," Irem said. "You look good in that uniform."

"Thanks, Irem. If you're not too busy running the store could you tell me where Ilene is?"

"Uh—you seen Carl yet?"

"No. Just got in on the plane."

Irem's eyes darted to the window then back to Bill. "I think Carl's out on the river. Ilene could be over to Herb's place."

"Thanks." A warm feeling enveloped Bill as he walked toward Herb's cabin. Nothing in town was very far. He stopped on the porch, unsure of whether to knock. The door opened.

"Ilene . . . ?" he said.

She looked at him with an expression he couldn't read. She was prettier than he remembered. Still slim, slightly shorter than him, and beautiful hair around a face that was serene and perfect. The blend of Russian and Athabascan blood had benefited her in all ways. Slim like the Russians but with the Indian dark eyes and black hair, she was an outstanding child of a mixed marriage.

"Bill? You're back!" She stammered. "How've you been?"

"Okay," he said. "Right now, I'm great."

"You're heavier."

"Yeah, I suppose I am. You're prettier."

"Have you seen Carl?" Ilene rolled up a sack and put it under her arm. Her eyes cut to the door and back.

"No, I just got in on the plane."

She took a deep breath, let it out . . . "Bill . . . ."

"I'm so glad to see you, Ilene. You don't know how much I missed you. Sitting in the fox holes, guarding the prisoners . . . I thought about you day after day. There's so much I've got to tell you, and—"

"Bill, stop—please just stop." She lowered her head. Her breathing was uneven, shaky. She lifted her eyes, the tears gathering in her lower lids. "Carl and I got married—"

He felt a roaring in his ears. At first he couldn't speak, and when he did, his voice sounded far away.

"Ilene . . . y-you didn't ever write. You—."

"I had nowhere to write—no address. And I didn't hear from you."

He half turned not knowing whether to walk or stay. Then he spun and held up three fingers. "I wrote you three letters."

Slowly she shook her head. "Bill, I didn't get any letters from you. Ever."

Bill bit his lip and stared at the floor. He raised his eyes to hers.

"Well—I wrote them. Every one of them asked you to wait for me." The anger in his chest fought with the urge to grab her and hold her and put his face into her long hair.

She shook her head from side to side, tears spilling down her cheeks. "I didn't know."

His throat hurt. He couldn't hear anything for the ringing in his ears. He began to rock back and forth wanting the ringing to stop, for his mouth to open and say something that would make the world right again. It had been three years and despite what he had done, where he had been, he was here now standing in front of her and nothing would come out.

He looked around for his duffel bag, scrapping his feet on the bare floor. The silence was desperate and in it his thoughts bounced around in his brain not knowing whether to attack or retreat, yell or cry, demand or beg.

"Ilene—I love you. I've loved you since high school. I wanted you to have my children. To grow old with you. I want to look out at the sun set and feel you with me and see you in the morning when I awake."

She wiped the tears touching her lips. Bill watched her. She was perfectly still but her image was blurred and his voice sounded to him like it was coming through a fog, distant and willowy.

She shook her head. "There is no way—nothing." She took two steps. "It can't happen."

His jaw muscles tightened and he swallowed hard. Through his mind flashed the image of he and Wayne having lunch on VE day, describing their plans and dreams. How he was going back to the village, separation pay in hand, and a proposal to Ilene on his lips. Wayne had been right. There was nothing for him in the village anymore. Bill shouldered his duffel bag.

"Do you want to come stay with us?" Ilene said.

He shook his head. "I don't think that's a good idea."

"We have room in our house . . . your dad built . . . . I'll ask Carl and see if—"

"And just what do you think that would be like for me? To see you every day, living with Carl, smiling and moving around the cabin and doing everything with him I thought we might do together someday—no Ilene." He felt the rush of blood in his face. "I'll stay with Herb or Charlie."

She touched his arm. "Bill . . . I'm sorry."

BILL HEADED BACK TO the general store.

"You gonna need anything?" the storekeeper said. "You need any credit?"

"Not now, Irem. I've got my mustering-out pay."

"Well, you need anything, we're here. Good to see you back. You gonna stay, you think?"

"Don't know, I just got here. Irem, do you recall seeing any letters I wrote to Ilene over the last three years? You'd have put them in the box, wouldn't you?"

Irem leaned on the counter, his lean body angled at the waist while he thought. "Yeah, I do, come to think about it. Couple of them were in pretty poor shape, but you could read the address all right."

"Do you recall her picking them up?"

"No. Carl always gets the mail."

Bill walked out the door and looked up and down the street. A narrow dirt street with partially buried log houses dug in along both sides. The small building that passed for a church when the visiting priest came by in the winter on dog sled and in the summer by boat or plane. The school that doubled for a community hall—where, it was rumored, the first telephone would be placed. It looked a lot different from the villages in Belgium and Germany and France and England, but not one bit different from the way it had looked when he left it.

At Charlie's house he knocked on the door as if he thought he might be waking someone from a nap. There was no response. He pushed the door open and saw Charlie reading at a table. As light entered the room from the door, Charlie turned his upper body and peered over his glasses.

"Hello, Charlie."

For several seconds Charlie just stared hard at the figure standing in his doorway.

"Bill? Come over here and let me see you." He put down his magazine. "My God, my God, it's you sure enough and dressed in a government uniform. They give that to you to keep?"

"Well, sure, Charlie. I fought for them for three years, they gave me clothes and food and some money. Still got the clothes and money."

Charlie tested the material of Bill's jacket between his thumb and fingers, "This gonna keep you warm up here?"

"There's a coat comes with it and that sure does. Kept me alive in Belgium."

"Where's that?"

"Europe. Where I was fighting the war."

"Oh." He took his glasses off, carefully folded them and put them on the table. "We heard some stories about that. Well . . . you're here now. Now you can start your life again. Find a girl, get married, have some kids. There's a lot of opportunity here now. Furs are up, and they're looking for workers on some of the mines over east."

Bill nodded. "Any chance of staying with you here, Charlie?"

Charlie looked around. It was dark inside and the air carried the mixed scents of old man's clothes and cooking oil that had gotten too hot. He waved his arm around the room like he was showing off a hotel suite,

"You can share this with me. I'm a little deaf and I snore, but I can cook good. What can you do?"

"Well now," Bill said, "I can cook K-rations over tree bark at twenty below, shoot a machine gun without burning up the barrel, crawl under a barbed-wire fence in the mud with my head down. What else do I need to know?"

Charlie laughed. "They taught you some really good stuff."

CARL BURST THROUGH THE door. Bill was emptying his duffel bag on the bunk in the corner, and it took Carl a second to spot him.

"Hey, little brother." He extended his hand.

"Hi. Carl." Bill thought he might be tugged off-balance, so he stuck out his hand and mentally braced himself. Carl grabbed his hand and instead of pulling, shoved him backwards and toppled him on the bed.

"Well, you may be older and stronger, but they didn't teach you any smarts, did they?"

"Maybe they did."

Carl looked at him. "You look bigger—are you bigger?"

"Guess I am."

"How much?"

"A couple of inches and twenty pounds."

"Come here – sit down. Where'd Charlie go?"

"He left to go find you."

"Well, tell me all about it out there. Start at the beginning. You were supposed to write every three months – you didn't do that. Now you gotta tell me what it was like."

"What happened to the letters?"

Carl spread his hands a partial smile on his face. "Those weren't letters to your family telling us how you were. They were from a teenage kid trying to stir up old love memories."

"You had no right to keep them from her." Bill bunched his fists.

"I had every right. She was my girl and she didn't need to be confused by your ramblings."

"Did you read them?"

"I burned them." Carl's eyes narrowed. "You left here, not me."

"What's that have to do with it?"

"Everything. I asked her to marry me and she said yes and that was that." He leaned back in his chair and looked straight in Bill's eyes.

Bill took a deep breath. "I learned a lot of things in the army. I could drive your nose into your brain or break your leg with one move—but brothers don't do that to brothers. Brothers also don't steal a brother's girl. You *stole* my letters to Ilene and didn't give me a chance. You didn't give her a chance—to choose—to decide for herself. I fought a war so people could have some freedom but you don't even let her have the freedom to read my letters. You had to cheat—burn the letters, pretend I was gone for good. You took her choice away from her because you thought she might choose me. You're a no good lousy son-of-a-bitch and I hate you for it. I thought she was waiting for me—and all the while, she's married to you and not giving me a thought."

Carl stood up and Bill saw that he had now grown taller and heavier than Carl. Despite that, he flinched inside.

"I'm sorry. I'm sorry for what I did," Carl said. "I'll give you a free swing at me."

"Jesus, Carl! I've killed guys. I can't fight you anymore."

"Just take a swing."

"No. I'm not going to do it."

Carl sat down on the edge of the bed and shook his head. "I can see from your point—"

"You can't see anything from my point of view. You can't get there from here."

Carl spread his hands. "What can I do?"

"Do? What can you do? Hell—I don't know Carl. I don't know." Everything was there—the energy, the desire, the knowledge. Hit the soft spot under his chin, follow that with a punch to the solar plexus and it's all over. He could picture himself standing over Carl, looking down at him as he gagged and writhed on the ground. What good would it do? It wouldn't nullify a marriage—or give him Ilene—or restart his life. He was right—there were some things brothers didn't do to brothers. This had to be one of them.

"It doesn't surprise me, you know."

Bill struggled out of his thoughts. "What?" he said.

"That we both love the same girl."

THEY TALKED UP TO dinnertime with Bill telling about the AlCan Highway, life in the army, combat missions, like a reporter might give in a radio report. He didn't mention the names of his army buddies or the towns they fought through or the escape. By the time he'd covered most of the three years he'd been gone, he was hungry.

"Do you think Charlie's coming back with any food?" he said.

"You're coming over to our place. Ilene and Verda are making dinner for all of us. You can meet Rusty."

"Who's Rusty?"

"Verda's husband. He's from Fort Yukon—you'll like him."

Bill doubted it. Verda was the girl he'd liked best, except for Ilene, and now she was married too.

THERE WERE SEVEN PLATES on the table. Herb and Charlie sat at opposite ends, Carl and Ilene on one side, Verda and Rusty on the other, and Bill, the seventh plate, on a corner between Carl and Charlie, the space so tight he had to hold the silverware he wasn't using in the hand he wasn't eating with.

There were a lot of questions asked about what Bill had done, where he'd gone, whom he'd seen. He had never talked so much in his life, and by the end of the meal felt empty, depleted of stories, like he'd told everything he knew and was now free to fill that void with new experiences.

After dinner he got a chance to talk with Herb whom he assumed was living alone now that Verda had moved out.

"You okay, Herb?"

"Can't complain."

"What have you been doing?"

"Working some. Trap a little. Fish a little. Make do."

Carl came over and clapped Bill on the shoulder. "Herb here has himself a lodger—paying rent and helping out. Highest-priced room in town."

"Who?" Bill asked.

"Crazy Ted Sheeley," Carl said. "That guy is gonna dig up the whole town looking for gold. And he smells like a ram in rut. I think when he kills a sheep he rolls in the guts, don't you?"

Herb nodded.

"Is that the guy who dug the hole out on the runway?" Bill asked.

"That's him. He thinks a glacier flattened out that place and left gold behind just under the gravel top. You'll meet him."

"I met a lot of crazy people in the army. Why do I have to meet him?"

"'Cause he's here," Carl said.

During the talk that followed, Bill felt like he was seated in the street and the others had left the door open so he could hear but had gone on with their lives, just letting him look in and overhear their conversation.

BACK AT CHARLIE'S PLACE he flopped on the bed, hands behind his head, eyes closed. The door burst open to admit Carl. With him was a man who walked at an angled stance and had on a fox-head hat that blended with his beard.

Carl said, "This is Ted Sheeley. I told him about you on the way over here."

"Evening," Ted said. "You're in the army?"

"Not any more."

"They teach you how to dig foxholes?"

Bill nodded.

"Good. I need someone to help me dig. Give you shares."

"What do you mean?"

"Shares. You know—shares of what we find. I can't dig enough by myself. We'll find lots of gold, it's all over this place. You ever see any?"

"I don't believe so."

Sheeley was only inches from Bill's face, and for a minute he didn't move because it reminded him of the drill instructors at camp. Then he realized he didn't have to put up with that and stepped back.

"I know there's gold in that air strip. You see, a glacier flattened that out when it melted hundreds of years ago and left the gold real close to the surface. The marmots have been digging in it and I've panned gold out of their leavings. You get me?"

Bill nodded.

"Well, what d'ya say? Are you in?"

Bill just looked at him.

"I need help," Sheeley said. "You ain't got no work and here you are, young and strong. I got an extra set of digging tools. What d'ya say?"

"I say no for right now. I'll think about it, but I just got out of the army and I don't want to go to work right now. Maybe later."

Sheeley looked at Carl, then back to Bill. "Fer crying out loud, ain't there nobody in this village wants to work?" He turned and walked out.

Carl had a smile on his face and Bill started laughing.

"Told you he was crazy," Carl said.

"He always like that?" Bill said.

"No—sometimes worse."

"He found any gold?"

"Nobody knows. Claims to—but nobody knows. Sure is good to have you back. Gonna stay?"

Bill shrugged his shoulders. "I was planning on it, but with everybody married and all . . . I don't know."

"There's other girls. Some of those younger ones grew up while you were out defending the country."

"Like who?"

"You'll see them. They'll be the ones whose sweaters stick out in places they didn't when you left."

They laughed. Bill felt a closeness to Carl he hadn't felt in many years. It was good to have a brother.

THE MAIL PLANE BUZZED the village, before it flew off to land at the strip. Bill jumped in the pickup with Jack Gould to go meet the plane. As they drove near the river, he saw a quick flash through the trees.

"Did you see that?" Bill said.

"Probably Ted Sheeley. He runs when he hears the plane."

"Do you think he's found any gold?"

"Some say he has and some say he hasn't," Jack said. "I ain't seen any."

"How's he pay Herb rent and buy groceries?"

"He paid Irem a bunch of money when he first got here and told him to let him know when he'd used it up. I guess he did the same with Herb."

The pilot had shut down the plane and stood with the mailbag in his hand when they pulled up beside him.

"I saw that bastard running through the trees," he said. "Next time I'm gonna gun him down from the air." He tossed the mail into the pickup. "He's made three new holes since last week. Doesn't anyone here have any control over that guy?"

Jack said, "Ain't nobody has control over Ted Sheeley."

The pilot hitched up his Levi's. "Anybody goin out?"

"No," Jack said.

"Any outgoing mail?"

"No."

"My gawd—almost wreck my plane and kill myself coming in here to dump a load of twelve letters and a package from L.L. Bean. Listen. If you see this bastard, you tell him I'm bringing a shovel with me next time and I'm gonna fill in every one of those damn holes and then I'm gonna come looking for him and I'm gonna beat his stupid head in with it. Got that?"

"I'll mention it to him if I see him."

The pilot got into the airplane and slammed the door. In just seconds he was taxiing down the runway, blowing sand and leaves in their faces. When he got to the other end of the runway he turned around and goosed it, lifted up over the holes, did a circle and dove low over the trail by the river. He wouldn't find Ted that way. Ted was hidden in a bunch of driftwood twenty feet up the bank of the river.

After the plane was gone, Ted came running back to the airstrip before they got the pickup moving.

"What'd he say?" Sheeley asked.

Jack cut the pickup engine and leaned out the window. "He said he was gonna bring back a shovel and fill the holes and then come looking for you to beat on you with it."

Sheeley said, "I need to get my gold out of there before he comes back, then." He turned to Bill. "You feel like working yet?"

"No. I need some time off."

"Dammit—I gotta get somebody to help me." He jumped into the air with both feet and landed looking down the runway. "You help me two days and I'll pay you a hundred dollars."

"What do you want me to do?"

"You just help me dig this runway, and we'll be over and done before that arrogant bastard sets his plane down here again."

He had penetrating eyes, and Bill found it hard to think when they bored in on him that way.

"Okay".

"Good. I got another shovel over in the bushes. I'll be right back."

Jack looked at Bill sideways but didn't say anything..

"Well, it won't hurt me to do some work. And I could use the hundred bucks."

BILL DUG IN THE runway area but off the main wheel tracks. He was down about three feet and stacking up the soil for Ted to run through his separator, a device he claimed would separate gold from other minerals and soil. The machine was about four feet tall and had two handles that were operated by human power, each in the opposite direction at the same time.

They worked through the two days, and Bill didn't see any gold pile up in the catcher. Ted came to him at the end of the second day and laid it out.

"Truth to be told, there ain't much gold in the catcher. I promised you a hundred dollars for two days and I'm a man of my word. Fact is, I gave all my money to Herb for rent and Irem for a food credit and I don't have a hundred dollars to give you this minute.

"But I'll tell you, there's gold here and we're gonna find it. If you'll just stay with me another two days I'll make you a wealthy man. You'll walk out of here with a small fortune. I tell ya, it's just close to where we're standing this very minute."

Bill sighed. "When you get the hundred dollars," he said, "you can find me at Charlie's. I'll be around."

CHARLIE LOOKED UP WHEN Bill came in. "Through gold mining for the day?"

Bill peeled off his shirt and walked to the sink. "I'm through with gold mining, period."

Charlie snickered.

Ted burst into the room. "Bill, you gotta think about this again." He stopped about a foot from his face. Bill put his arm against Ted's chest and backed him off a couple of feet.

"Listen to me, Bill. Carl has found gold and we can too—it's all over the place. I got the Department of Interior geological survey bulletins, and—"

"What do you mean Carl's found gold?"

"I ain't seen it, but he didn't trap last year and he didn't fish either. He paid for chum salmon for his dog food and he lived pretty high on the hog."

"So what? Doesn't mean a thing." Ted's smell was overpowering in the cabin, something he hadn't noticed outside.

"Will you do it?" Ted said.

"When you get the hundred dollars, give it to Charlie to hold for me."

Ted turned and was out the door so fast Bill couldn't believe it. How did a big man move like that?

Bill looked at Charlie, who was staring at his feet.

"Charlie, What're you thinking?"

Charlie raised his head enough to look at Bill.

"Well, Carl didn't trap. And he didn't fish, either. He was gone lots of times for several days. Then he'd go to Fairbanks and come back, and him and Ilene live pretty good. Some people say Herb has found gold too. I don't know. Nobody knows."

BILL WOKE UP THE next morning with his mind made up. He didn't see any gold in the airstrip and he doubted Ted would find any. And he wasn't about to dig in the ground for weeks helping him look.

"Charlie," he said, "I'm going to Anchorage. Find a job. Get straightened around. I might be back, but I gotta get out of here for now. There isn't anything here for me."

"Every place is the same," Charlie said.

"No it isn't, Charlie. The village is the same because nothing has happened to change it, but other places are different."

Charlie went to the water bucket and dipped a cup of water.

"Charlie, you ever been to Anchorage?"

"I went two times."

"It was different, wasn't it?"

"Lots of people. Cars. Big buildings."

"I mean the feeling of it. The feeling is different, isn't it?"

"I don't know. I don't remember any different feeling."

Bill pulled his duffel out from under the bed and started packing his clothes. He laid out his travel clothes, his uniform, folded it just right and put it under the mattress to press it, then started for the door.

"I'm going down to the store and check out the plane schedule. Anything you need?"

Charlie shook his head.

"YOU'RE NOT GOLD DIGGIN today?" Irem said when he walked into the store.

"Gave that up, Irem. Know when the plane's coming back?"

Irem frowned, then walked over to the counter and squinted down his nose at a paper by the cash register. "Says the 24th. Is this the 23rd or the 24th?" He looked at the calendar that featured a Charles Russell painting on top and an ad for David Green Furriers across the bottom. "By golly, it's today, the 24th."

"Thanks." Bill walked out of the store and down the street to Charlie's. Charlie had not moved since he left.

"You feeling okay, Charlie?"

Charlie nodded.

"Can you talk to me, Charlie? Tell me how you're feeling?"

"I said I'm okay."

Bill finished packing. He could feel Charlie's eyes on his back, and when he finished he undressed and put those clothes in the duffel, reached under the mattress for his uniform and put it on. He set the duffel next to the door and turned to look at Charlie.

"I'm going now."

"Figured you were."

He hoisted the duffel by the handle, then looked at Charlie.

"Goodbye, Charlie."

Charlie nodded, his fingers still entwined, elbows on his knees.

When the airplane buzzed the village, Bill caught a ride with Jack up to the airstrip. The pilot jumped out, handed the mailbag to Jack, and took the village sack in his other hand.

"Who filled in the holes?" he said.

Jack and Bill looked at the runway and the holes were gone. Filled in and planted over. You could tell where they'd been, but not unless you were up close.

Jack said, "Ted Sheeley filled them in so folks wouldn't know which holes had gold and which ones didn't."

"Did he find any?"

Jack smiled. "He bought a new Stinson. He's out flying it now with an instructor from Fairbanks. Said he's gonna learn how to set it down on land and water."

Bill glanced at Jack. He caught a wink when the pilot looked back at the runway.

"Well, I'll be damned," the pilot said. "Anybody goin out?"

"Bill, here. He's going out."

"Well, okay—let's get loaded up." He grabbed Bill's duffel and put it in through the cargo door.

"Jack—I'll see you."

"Okay, Bill. Let me know what life is like in the big city. I may come join you."

"You're not old enough."

"I'll be seventeen in November."

Bill got in the right front seat and closed the door. The last thing he saw before the plane took off was the filled-in holes, every one he'd dug, small plants jammed into the loose ground on top.

CHAPTER 11

"PLEASE HAVE A SEAT," she said. "I'm Lavonne, and I've been over your application." She smiled at him, so he smiled back. "You've left a lot of areas blank, so I need to ask you some questions."

Bill nodded, then said, "Sure." He looked around the room. Framed certificates hung on one wall; a typewriter and adding machine were on a table behind her desk. On top of the steel file cabinet was a tri-fold picture frame with a guy, a baby, and Lavonne.

"Mr. Williams, have you ever done construction work before?"

"No."

"What was your military experience?"

"I was in for three years."

"I mean, what was your job description in . . . the army, is it?"

"I was a rifleman."

"I'm sorry. I don't know what a rifleman is."

"Well . . . you fire a gun at the enemy."

"I see." She looked down at his application, then looked up and smiled. "Were you good at it?"

"They made me an non-commissioned officer."

She perked up and made a notation on the application. "How long did it take you to become an officer?"

Bill had to think. Three groups of recruits had come and gone. . . .

"About a year," he said.

"You mean you just started in the army and a year later you were an officer in it?"

He started to nod but sensed that speaking was better than nodding with her. "Yes. They made me a corporal."

"Will you wait just a minute while I talk to someone about your application?"

"Yes."

Lavonne got up. When she moved past him a fragrance of warm fresh flowers wafted toward his chair. She didn't touch him when she went by, but she was oh so close. He felt himself stir.

In a minute she was back.

"Mr. Williams. We need somebody right away and even though you don't have any construction experience it appears that you're a fast learner. We could start you tomorrow at five dollars an hour. You'd be doing general construction, clean-up, and carpenters helper until you picked up the trade—then, of course, your pay and responsibility would go up. If you can learn the construction business as fast as you learned the officer business, you'll do fine. Would that work for you?"

"It sure does."

"Fine," she said. "Report in at 7:00 AM tomorrow to the North Winds Construction Company—it's the gray building next to the bridge—and ask for the job foreman. Do you have any questions?"

"No. Just thanks."

BILL FOUND A ROOMING house and paid up for two weeks, then went out and bought some work clothes at a place called Fifth Avenue Outfitters. He treated himself to a good meal and went back to his room, which had two windows facing the street, a single bed, a nightstand, and a chest of drawers with a mirror on top. He emptied the duffel into the drawers and went to bed early.

He had no trouble finding North Winds Construction the next morning. The foreman sent him to wait in a room where he was surprised to see another native sitting against the wall near the door. He looked up and smiled as Bill's eyes settled on him, revealing no bottom teeth. His face looked like he had slept on small-gauge

chicken wire all night, and smoke drifted past his eyes from a cigarette between his lips. He reached up his hand and Bill took it.

"Pull," he said. Bill pulled him upright. "Hi. George Norton."

"Bill Williams."

"Glad to meet ya, Bill Williams. Where you from?"

"Arctic Village."

"Yeah? I'm just downriver. Fort Yukon. But I left there in '38
and haven't been back." His eyes were squinted so tight that Bill
couldn't make out where the pupils were. "Come on—sit down.
We'll be on our feet all day long." He sat down with his back against
the wall.

Other workers had arrived but they stood at the other end of the
hall and occasionally looked down the hallway at Bill and George.

"What you hired for?" George said.

"I don't know. Just general stuff, I guess."

"They'll have you doing everything, that's for dang sure."
George inhaled on his cigarette, held it, then pushed it out across
his upper lip and inhaled it through his nose back into his lungs.
Then he expelled it triumphantly into the surrounding air.

"How'd you do that?" Bill said.

"Secret." He did it again. "You smoke?"

Bill shook his head.

"Well, then, I can't teach ya."

A big man in overalls came out of the office door and looked up
and down the hall. The group of men gravitated toward him. Bill
and George stood up.

"Awright, guys. We're sending you all to the job at Turnagain
Arms. Get in the green truck downstairs, I'll be right behind you.
You'll all be doing grunt labor today, so you won't need your tools.
You new guys buddy up with someone who's been here awhile and
I'll get you lined out on the job."

"Come on," George said. They filed down the stairs into the
parking lot. The sun was out and there was a slight breeze. Maybe
fifty degrees, Bill figured. It was a good day for work.

IN TWO WEEKS they barely got the framing in for the foundation. It was to have been done by Thursday noon, but it took all day Friday to finish it. At 4:30 the foreman came around handing out paychecks. He stopped at Bill.

"You do good work," he said as he handed over the envelope. "Keep it up. You like this work?"

"Yes, sir."

The foreman smiled. "'Yes, Cal' will do. Just get out of the service?"

Bill nodded.

"Well, stick around." He handed a check to George. "You did good work too, George. Keep at it. Be steady for me and show up, will ya?" He walked away.

George smiled, folded the check, and put it in his rear pocket.

"What did he mean, be steady and show up?" Bill said.

"Oh, I just don't always come to work, that's all."

"You've been here every day."

"That was because it ain't fishing season and I'm out of beer." He patted his rear pocket. "This is gonna change that. You drink?"

"No," Bill said.

"Ever try it?"

"No."

George shook his head. "How old are you?"

"Twenty."

George shook his head again. "By damn—we'll get one hung on you."

THE CHEECHAKO BAR WAS full of men, and smoke hung a third of the way down from the ceiling. The noise, the acrid smoke, the mix of heat and sweat, all were overpowering and Bill struggled to control his reaction to them. George motioned him over to the table where five people were sitting.

"This is my friend Bill Williams. Comes from Arctic Village."

Bill looked at the upturned faces. All native faces, but two were Eskimo, two Athabascan, and one a woman who was quite drunk and whose origins he couldn't make out. George didn't say their names and they didn't offer them.

"Pull up a chair," one of them said.

George found two chairs, lifted them over the seated people, and banged them down on the floor. He reached in his shirt pocket and pulled out his money.

"Boys and girls—it's payday!"

They all beamed, and when the waitress came back George threw ten dollars on the table and ordered beers all around. She brought the beers and George's change, and George grabbed her and put a dollar on her tray.

Bill figured a paycheck wouldn't last long if you did that very many times. He put his hand on the pocket where his money was, the first money he had gotten since he left the army. He didn't know how much he would need, but he had to figure that out tomorrow.

He suddenly realized that everyone at the table was looking at him.

"I told them you haven't ever drunk anything," George said. "So here's to you," and George and the others lifted their bottles to him and clinked them in the middle of the table.

Bill liked the cool sour taste.

"Well, what d'ya think?" George asked.

"Not like anything I ever tasted before."

"You'll get used to it," one of them said.

George drank eight beers. Bill finished his third. It was warm, but he didn't care. He was feeling mellow, connected with himself. The smile just stayed there while the minutes stretched out, and there was time to think and assess things. He thought about the things he had done and felt there was nothing he couldn't do now.

The good job was just the start. Soon he would have the $10,000 and be ready to find a girl and get married.

But George was becoming someone he didn't know.

"I'm going to find some food," Bill said.

"Hey, Debbie!" George yelled. "Food!"

He fumbled for another bill in his shirt pocket. The folded money all came out together, landing on the table, in his lap, on the floor. Everyone laughed and grabbed for the money. Some put it on the table in front of George, some in front of themselves, some pocketed it, one put his foot on a bill on the floor and wouldn't let George pull it up. George got out of his chair and pretended to bite the person on the leg and swiped the money back.

When George got back in his chair he started counting the money. Every time he reached a total someone either returned another bill or grabbed a bill from the pile in front of him, throwing George off. He could never come to a total that meant anything to him.

Debbie came over, and Bill and three others ordered hamburgers and onion rings. When the food came, those who hadn't ordered grabbed at the onion rings. It seemed kind of like the money game. Get an onion ring and eat it while the guy who ordered it tries to keep it for himself. Halfway through the hamburger, Debbie reached over his shoulder and grabbed the neck of the bottle he was holding.

"Empty?" She shook it, put it on her tray, and set a full one in front of him.

He tipped the cold bottle up and nudged George. "How long we gonna stay here?"

George's head was close to the table and he was talking to a woman.

"Wanna leave? By gawd, you can leave any time you want to." He glared at Bill, then turned back to the woman. She laughed and George put his arm around her and they put their heads together.

Bill stood up. "I'm leaving."

"Awright," George said. "We're coming with ya."

IT WAS DARK WHEN they left the bar. George led the way to mid-block, where they turned into the alley.

"Where we going?" Bill asked.

George didn't answer. He had his hands full holding the woman up and walking down the concave alley surface. They crossed the street. The alley was poorly lit, and the lamp was broken out on the post in the middle of the block.

When they passed the dumpster, Bill heard a shuffling noise behind them. He felt a blow on the back of his head, and then his cheek bounced on the gravel surface. He lay there, semi-conscious, trying to get up. There were hands on his body, but when he tried to move he couldn't feel anything.

The hands stopped moving on him. He wasn't uncomfortable, but his eyes were blinking in a rhythmic pattern and he couldn't control the blinks. Every time he blinked there were red shooting stars behind his eyelids; they flew from left to right, disappeared then reappeared and went across his eyelids again. He couldn't hear anything.

A flashlight shone in his face and he felt hands under his arms and legs as he was hoisted off the ground and put in a truck. The back door was swung wide and a guy held his eyelid open and shined a light in it. He was beginning to hear sounds. Voices. Then he could hear words.

"Hey. Can you hear me? Come around, now—talk to me. Can you hear me?"

Bill turned his head toward the sound. A policeman moved his light away, and Bill could see his uniform hat and strong pleasant face. He tried to smile and say something, but only the smile worked.

"I think he's coming around," the policeman said. A guy dressed in white moved around fast but didn't talk.

Bill recognized his wallet in the policeman's hand. "They took your billfold. Did it have any money in it?"

Bill nodded. He tried to recall the paycheck he had cashed and whether he had spent any. He couldn't put any figures together.

"Lift your head just a minute," the guy in white said. He stuck a bandage over his ear. "It's torn there. Could be a little sore tomorrow. Keep it dry for a day or two."

The policeman helped him sit up. "Here's my card. Call me when you figure out how much was taken from you." He brushed the wallet off with his handkerchief and handed it to Bill. "They threw it in the dumpster. Typical trick on payday."

Bill looked around. "Where's George?"

"They went to the native hospital," the guy in white said. "They were out cold. You okay or do you want to go to the hospital too?"

"Help me get off this thing."

The policeman and the paramedic each grabbed an arm and helped Bill down to street level. The revolving red lights stabbed him in the eyes and he looked away.

"Where do you live?" the policeman asked. "I can drop you off."

"I can walk."

"Sure?"

Bill nodded. He took a few steps and leaned against the light pole.

He pulled his wallet out and opened it up. The bills were gone, but they hadn't messed with his other stuff.

He shoved the wallet back in his pocket and walked toward the rooming house, staying on the sidewalks under the lights. The outside door was locked when he got there, and he rang the bell. The clerk came out of the office door wearing a bathrobe.

"Are we gonna have trouble with you?"

"I got robbed."

"More likely you got drunk and got robbed. Rent's due in a week. You gonna have it?"

Bill nodded.

He went up to his room, opened the duffel bag, and then it hit him. He had taken his settlement money with him, hidden under a flap in his wallet. He took the wallet out and peeled back the flap. Gone.

ON SUNDAY, BILL walked to the native hospital to see if George was there. He learned he'd been released Friday night along with the woman he'd come in with. He didn't have an address or phone for George, but he would see him Monday at work.

He walked by the Salvation Army Post on his way back and heard loud piano playing through the windows, some of it not in key, and an accompanying voice that was a bit off from the piano music. Bill smiled. It tickled his funny bone to hear a person push so hard for something that obviously wasn't coming together.

As he passed the open door he saw a sandwich-board sign that read:

OPEN

FREE FOOD

SERVICE AT 5:00

SONGS AND FELLOWSHIP

He had just finished reading the last line when the music stopped. On a step three feet above him was a man dressed in black pants and a white shirt stretched so tight across his stomach that the buttons were tilted halfway back through the buttonholes. He smiled at Bill.

"Brother, come on in and talk with me. I haven't got anyone to talk to, and my singing is just pitiful. Do you sing?"

Bill shook his head.

"Do you play the piano?"

"No."

"Well—you can talk. Will you come in and keep a lonely man company until the service starts?" He extended his hand. "I'm Captain Russell. I was sent here to run this dog and pony show."

Bill shook his hand and found himself being pulled up the stairs and into the chapel. Captain Russell proceeded to show him through the entire post as if he were a visiting dignitary seeking to know how his financial donations were being used.

"Ah . . . here's the kitchen."

Bill could smell the soup. It smelled better than army soup. His stomach growled and he swallowed.

"Let's see what it is." Captain Russell lifted the lid and inhaled the steam. He closed his eyes, and a smile formed on his round face. "Potato soup with ham and bacon. Fresh hot rolls. Coffee. What more could God grant to man on this earth?"

Bill didn't know if he was supposed to answer or not.

Captain Russell looked at him. "I gave you my name but I forgot to ask yours."

"Bill Williams."

Captain Russell stuck out his hand again. "Bill Williams, I am happy to make your acquaintance." He grabbed a hot roll and handed it to Bill, then took one for himself. "Will you stay for supper and the service?"

Bill thought for a moment. His stomach felt empty and the smell of the hot soup made him weak.

"Where would you be if you weren't here, at this very moment, Bill Williams?"

Bill did not respond. Where would he be? He'd been heading back to his room hungry when he stopped here.

"Come on. Stay with us for a little while. I need some help. Do you speak Athabascan, by any chance?"

Bill nodded.

"That's fortunate. I've got people who can speak Yup'ik but sometimes we need someone who can communicate in Athabascan. Some of the older ones can do so much better in their native language. Especially when they're under stress. Bless me, I'm just rattling on, aren't I, and not making much sense at that."

Bill had not heard anyone talk so much, but it was interesting to hear a person who could just keep talking, making up conversation as he went along.

"What do you say? Come in for an hour and have a bowl of good soup, some hot rolls, that hot coffee, and help me talk with some of these folks. Come on, give me a hand."

He found himself washing his hands while the captain tied an apron on him. It was white with red lettering that said: "Repent OR listen to Capt. Russell's piano."

WHEN BILL LEFT THE kitchen there were eight people standing in the other room, all but one of them native. The one was a white man who carried his arms down at his side, military style, thumbs against his seams, the clothes hanging straight down on his bony frame. To Bill it looked like the man was standing at attention.

"Hello," Bill said.

"Corporal Dinsmore, sir."

"Hello, corporal. I was in the army, the 106th Division, ever hear of us?"

"Corporal Dinsmore, sir."

Bill looked around. Captain Russell was in the other room getting the food ready, but he met Bill's eyes and smiled. Bill looked back at Dinsmore.

"I was a corporal too."

"Corporal Dinsmore, sir."

"At ease, Corporal." Bill did an about-face, leaving Dinsmore standing at attention, and walked over to Captain Russell.

"Shell shock," Russell said.

"Why isn't he in the VA hospital, then?"

"He walks away. We've taken him back a dozen times and he just walks away again. Get him to sit down, he likes the food here. He won't be a problem."

"I thought I was just going to eat and . . . "

Captain Russell turned on his heel and was gone.

He walked back over to Corporal Dinsmore and in his best command voice said, "Dinsmore. Come sit down at the table. Follow me." He marched to a one-piece wooden table with attached benches on each side. The corporal was in step behind him and seated himself at the table, hands at his sides.

Bill sat down beside him.

The other people drifted over to the table. The smell of fresh hot food mixed with the accumulated odors of a dozen homeless people. After the meal everybody filed into the chapel, sitting mostly at the back of the room. Captain Russell attacked the piano, which explained why they sat at the back. The volume was loud, the enthusiasm genuine, the notes wrong as often as not.

Corporal Dinsmore sat rigid in the seat. Eyes ahead, back straight, he seemed oblivious to all stimuli. Where would Dinsmore sleep tonight, and what would he do tomorrow?

The service began, the piano playing having provided a mere prelude to the oration Captain Russell produced from the lectern. His short sermon was based on John 3:16. Like his piano playing, it made up in volume what it may have lacked in professionalism, but there was no doubt about Russell's sincerity, belief, or commitment.

At one point, after holding the bible open to the sacred verse, he slammed it shut, then took it in one hand and pounded it over and over into the upraised palm of the other hand. On his third back swing, it flew up and out and landed behind the piano. He continued to talk while he walked back and retrieved it, returned and finished the point he was trying to make. The point was, "God gave his only son Jesus, to die for all mankind so you could be free of sin. Just ask."

When the sermon was over the people scurried out and left the door open at the front of the chapel. Corporal Dinsmore stood beside the open door. Bill walked over to him and came to attention.

"Dismissed," he said.

Dinsmore walked through the door and turned left.

"So what did you think of that, Mr. Bill Williams?" Captain Russell asked him.

Bill had a headache from the loud music and loud preaching, and he wasn't sure how he felt about any of it.

"Okay," he finally managed.

Captain Russell clapped him on the shoulder. "Feed 'em, save 'em, and send 'em out happy. God only knows where the poor buggers spend the rest of the day. We need something to capture them until they commit their souls to Christ, then send them out as soldiers of the cross."

Bill felt uneasy with Russell's hand on his shoulder.

"Did you get enough to eat?"

Bill nodded.

"Good. Come back again. It'll be good to see you often. Stay and help with the dishes, will you?"

"You ever been to the Salvation Army Post?" Bill asked George when they were on break the next day.

"Yeah. Good food. The guy that runs it is crazy, but it's good chow." George blew smoke and looked at him. "Why? You go there?"

"I was walking by yesterday and he dragged me in."

"He's good at that. Give you a hot roll and ask you to help out?"

Bill nodded.

"That's Captain Russell, saver of souls, provider of food for the hungry and a warm place in winter. He don't get many, though. It's part of the trap line."

"Trap line?"

"Yeah. Place to eat, sleep, keep warm. You gotta get to know the trap line if you want to be up with things."

"Where do you sleep?"

"Oh, I got a shack down on Fish Creek behind Lowry's house. I get it for keeping his place up and agreeing to go to his church. Ain't much, but it's home. Got a toilet and sink but no tub. Just a big room, really. You'll have to come over some time."

"You go to church?"

"Most of the time. 'Cept when I'm in the hospital or on the street somewheres and ol' man Lowry can't find me."

"You a Christian?"

George looked at him. "Hell no. Going to church is part of the bargain for the shack, that's all." He completed the slow exhale of smoke between his lips up through his mustache and inhaled through his nose, then crushed the cigarette and got up.

"Let's go to work."

CHAPTER 12

BILL AND GEORGE WERE sitting in what passed as a lounge at the Salvation Army post. It was late, and Bill's stomach was making noises he was sure other people could hear. He looked at George, who was staring out the window.

"I don't have any money," he said. "I'm gonna get kicked out of my room, and I'm sore all over—I don't know if I can work tomorrow."

George turned back to the window. "You can work when you're hurt. You don't need money, neither. You go on that trap line I told you about."

"How do I do that?"

"You eat here, you sleep in the mission, you piss in the bus station and the library. There's a hundred ways to survive in this town, and I know 'em all. You can stay at my place until ol' man Lowry finds out, then he might kick us both out—who knows?"

Captain Russell came through the back door and saw George and Bill.

"Hello, Bill. Hello, George—good to see you here again. We have a very good moose stew coming off the stove in a bit, and the rolls will be done in about fifteen minutes. Hot, steamy, sourdough rolls with lots of butter and honey. Will you stay?"

"Not if I have to listen to the sermon," George said.

"Oh, come on, George." He put his hand on George's shoulder. "It isn't that bad. You might be standing in need of salvation this very moment and don't know it. You should take some time to review your life. Are you living the life you think Christ wants you to live?"

George tried to ease out from under his grip but the captain held him tightly enough that he'd have to make a concerted effort to get loose. He did not want to twist his way out of the free food.

"I guess not," he said.

"Stay for the dinner and vespers," Russell said, finally releasing his grip on George's shoulder. "Bill, you don't look any better than you did on Sunday. What happened to you?"

"I got beat up pretty bad," Bill said.

"Where were you?"

"In the alley behind the Cheechako."

The captain shook his head. "Had you been drinking?"

Bill nodded.

"Bill. This is a slippery path—it only goes down. When you were baptized the Lord had a right to expect you to live His life, to be with Him in thought and body. You see, your body is a temple, and you need to treat it with respect. It looks like your temple has been battered within and without."

"Kind of like at the Battle of the Bulge," Bill said.

"You were there?"

"I was." He sighed. "And I survived, which is more than I seem to be doing here."

"Is that something you would care to talk about to those who gather here? It's good thing when someone shares his experiences with them, especially someone whose very life was in danger. How you got out of it, what you learned from it, and how the Lord kept you safe."

"Wayne Turner and me kept each other safe," Bill said.

The captain's eyes lit up "You know Wayne Turner?" He clapped his hands. "He was over here last week. Big Shoshone Indian lad from Wyoming?"

"That'd be him. Him and me were at the Bulge. We mustered out together."

"What a wonderful reunion coming up. Now, come on, let's go into the chapel for vespers and then we can partake of that great moose stew and rolls the Lord has provided. And Bill, could I talk you into staying after supper tonight? There's something I want to talk to you about."

AFTER EVENING VESPERS, CAPTAIN Russell guided Bill into his office.

"Bill," Captain Russell began. "God seeks people for his service all through their lives, but there is generally a special time to make himself known to you. I believe he brought you through the war and up here and to this Post. And . . . ."

"I don't think . . . "

"Let me finish, please. He has seen you exposed to danger with possible loss of your life. Did you ever pray to Him then?"

"Yes."

"Well, He heard you and now is guiding you to shed this life of weekend drinking and those friends and live the life He has wished for you. You've got to respond to this, Bill. Take control of your life. Wrest it from the devil. You have so much to offer . . . ."

"I don't have anything to offer," Bill said.

"But you do. Every human has that potential. Make the Post your home and work with me with these lost people. You are found if you just look up. Promise me you'll think hard about this."

Bill twisted in the chair, and crossed his legs.

Think hard about this? This what? Every day's hard. Hard for me—hard for them. What kind of a life is it to come in here everyday and face drunks and people with no homes, no family, no future. He's asking me to help here? If that's what he wants, I could give it a try. I could work at it.

Bill looked him in the eye. "I'll think about that. I'll try."

Captain Russell put his arm on Bill's shoulder. "Good man. Good man."

AFTER WORK THE NEXT day, Bill found George in the Salvation Army post lounge, asleep in one of the big soft chairs.

He shook him. "George?"

George opened one eye and looked at Bill, then settled his eye on the duffel slung over his shoulder.

"Kicked ya out, huh?"

Bill nodded. "I need to learn about the trap line."

"Tonight you can stay at my place, ol' man Lowry be damned. But tomorrow, you're gonna get initiated so you know how to take care of yourself."

THE NEXT DAY WAS Saturday, and they were off work. George and Bill walked to the Loussac Library, where the librarian looked at them as if they were pond scum. George paid no attention to her. He led Bill away from her desk, back into the stacks of books. It was as quiet as being inside a closet full of clothes with the door closed. There was a table near the back wall with four chairs next to a baseboard heater.

"Sit down here," George said.

Bill sat.

"Now, scooch up by that heater."

Bill slid the chair over by the wall.

"See how nice and warm that is?" George walked over to the bookshelves, chose a book, and brought it back. "You get yourself a book you like the looks of and open it, then you fold you arms like this, see, and put your head on it and go to sleep. Ain't nobody ever bothers a man sleeping here except that lady up front, and most of the time she doesn't come back here anyhow.

"Now, you gotta be up and out of here by closing time. If you come in here drunk or sick, she'll call the cops on you. Patrolman Fowler, most likely, and that ain't good news. But when it's cold and it ain't eating time or sleeping time, you can come in here and get warm. It's quiet, peaceful, and you almost can feel the thoughts of all these books floating around in the air. Do you notice that?"

"Yeah."

George pushed back his chair. "Come on, we got some other places to look at. Oh—almost forgot, bathroom's down that hall. It's okay to use it, but leave it clean. If you puke make sure you clean it up."

OUTSIDE, GEORGE HEADED TOWARDS Eighth Avenue. They stopped outside a building that looked like a church.

"This is the Anchorage Rescue Mission," George said. "They'll take anyone, but you ain't supposed to be drunk. The accommodations ain't so swell, but it's warm and dry and it don't cost nothin'. No sense going in now, but that outside door off the parking lot goes down some stairs, then you turn left and right there's a big room with easy chairs and stuff in it. If you can get an easy chair you can sleep good. Sometimes you have to fight somebody to get it, but after that it's okay.

"Now you're on your way to being an educated man. I got some money—let's go get a drink."

"Sounds good to me," Bill said.

CHAPTER 13

HE FOUND THE BOTTLE where he had stashed some of his own before. Some things never changed. The cheap vodka was a particularly good street drink, the glass pint bottle being shaped like a flask marked it easy to carry and conceal. He looked at it wondering who had drunk from it last. For a moment, he held it, looking at the liquid sloshing around in the bottle, clear, cool, inviting. He put it in his coat pocket and continued the search.

The door opened and Captain Russell stuck his head in.

"How's it coming, Bill?"

"It's ok."

"You don't sound too happy."

"I've been here. I know their hiding places. Feels like I'm stealing."

"Bill—we can't have drinking going on in the Post. This is their first step towards sobriety and a new life. Removing temptation isn't stealing. Have you found any?"

Bill shook his head and the door closed.

At the end of the hall he turned the knob and walked into the alley. Halfway down the block just past the telephone pole on the right was a parking space between two garages. It was a favorite hangout if the car wasn't there because you couldn't see inside the space unless you walked up to it. He stepped in. The car was there but he moved beside it up to the fence and slid down on the front bumper. He unscrewed the lid and lifted the bottle to his lips.

Somewhere in his life something had to have been this good. Not in the village. George had started him on it; made him see that drinking made everything all right and as the contents moved from the bottle to his stomach it became easier to see what a good day this was going to be. At first he was going to drink it all but decided to leave some for the person who would find it. Carefully he squeezed the bottle between the fence slats and the garage, another familiar hiding spot. He stood up. It took a few seconds for him to feel comfortable before he walked out.

Ha. He could walk a straight line. He followed the grass hump down the middle of the alley, swinging his arms. When he reached the sidewalk he reversed and gaining confidence now, he strode purposefully toward the end of the block. Drinking was ok for those who could handle it. George couldn't handle it—he went too far. When he drank with the others it always ended in problems. This was the way to do it. Vodka didn't leave a telltale breath either. Captain Russell wouldn't be able to smell it on him and once he got his apron on in the kitchen the cooking smells would cover everything.

There was a line at the kitchen door so he used the back entry. The cook gave him a quick glance before setting the beans down on the steam table. Bill put on an apron and was fumbling with tying the strings when he felt someone else's hands take control and tie them for him. He turned around and looked into the face of Captain Russell.

"Where'd you go?" Captain Russell said.

Bill took half a step back. "Took a quick breather."

The Captain was not smiling. "I see. Well—looks like we have a crowd today."

Bill nodded.

That wasn't so hard. A person can do responsible drinking and enjoy it. It's when it gets out of hand that others don't like it. He went to work.

AT FIRST BILL DIDN'T know where he was, but he knew he needed a drink.

He looked around. There was nobody in the corner where he was sitting. It took him a few minutes to orient himself—he was propped up on a bench in a bus station.

How the hell did I get here? I was drunk, but I've been drunk plenty of times before. This is something new.

He shook his legs. He stood up and patted his pockets, and dug into each of them. Nothing. He looked around, then shuffled out the door.

What day is this? I gotta get to work.

In twenty minutes he was at the work site, the morning air having partially revived him. The foreman stared at him from across the project as he buckled on his tool belt, but Bill kept his face down.

At noon, he checked in at the job shack.

"Missed you this morning," the construction clerk said.

"I was late," Bill said. "Sorry."

"You talk to the foreman?"

"No."

"Better do it. Be in deeper if you don't."

Bill looked at the day sheet. It was Monday. He hadn't missed a whole day, anyway.

GEORGE CAME BACK TO the job site at quitting time.

"Where you been?" Bill said.

"Had us out on another job all day. When did you get here?"

"I was late . . . ."

George squinted his eyes. "I know that. I asked when you got here?"

"About 10:30."

"Humph."

"I gotta cut down on my drinking. I woke up in the bus station this morning."

"I heard that a hundred times. So what?" George said.

"Don't remember going there—that's what."

WALKING TOWARD THE BAR, Bill vowed he'd have just one beer. Just one, then he'd walk out. And go where? Where did he want to go? Who did he want to be with? It had been hard to decide those things lately. George is all right but he's starting to push me. I'm not going to be a carpenter's helper the rest of my life. Gotta get enough money to get things back together again. Maybe cut down my expenses, work the trap line until I get enough to rent another room.

He drank half the bottle on the first drink and let out a belch. The others laughed. There it was—the change over. He was truly an interesting and funny guy to these people. He needed to have a talk with the foreman tomorrow, tell him his plans and ask for a better job.

George passed him another one. "A good drinker could of finished it," he said. "Now get it down in one tip."

BILL ARRIVED TWO HOURS late Tuesday morning. The foreman was waiting for him with his paycheck.

"Time for you to find another nursemaid," he said. "You were a good worker when you got here but I've got to be able to depend on someone."

AT NOON, GEORGE SHOWED up at the bar.

"They let you go?"

Bill nodded.

"Well—by damn, don't be so hangdog about it. There's plenty of jobs. You just need to wake up and get to work of a morning. Keep your job and your fun separated." He turned to the waitress, "Give us a beer here."

WEDNESDAY AFTERNOON BILL WAS painting a wood fence for the school district. Didn't pay much, but it gave him enough to live on. He rented a room near Merrill Field and within two weeks the sound of the airplanes didn't bother him anymore. He was able to drink in his room.

Damn funny. He put down the bottle and went to the door. He only opened it a crack and looked on the walkway. The sound was constant and he partially opened his mouth to hear better. It was a noise he couldn't place. Finally, he stepped out and looked

ANCHORAGE POLICE DEPT. REPORT

Case #60-2541
Name: Bill Williams
Date of Birth: 10/10/25

Date: 6/5/68
Location: 4th and alley at C St.
Arresting Officer: Corporal J. Striker

Officer's Narrative of Event:
Suspect was reported passed out in alley by bar patron who refused to identify himself. I responded at 1728 hrs. When I approached the suspect, he was unconscious with his mouth open and drooling from nose and mouth. I was unable to awaken him and called the Fire Dept. to check his vital signs. He awoke during inspection and was taken to the Salvation Army Corp at 8th and C St. He is well known to Major Russell who is in charge of the Corp. He appeared to be suffering from overindulgence in alcohol.

J. Stryker   6/5/68
Officer's Signature   Date

Badge No. 2515
Time: 1732 hrs

toward the airstrip and rotating on the flight apron was the first helicopter he had ever seen or heard, the long blades cutting the air with a dull whap, whap, whap. It pulled up and disappeared to the south and the quiet returned. He went back to his room and sat on the bed. His mind whirled as he looked at the bottle on the table. With shaky hands he screwed the cap on the bottle and slid it under his bed. He had gone too far. Airplanes were now rising straight up and he had seen it. They couldn't do that—his eyes lied to him. He needed some food.

The fence-painting job ended, but when winter struck they offered him a job as janitor. Construction had stopped for the winter, so he took it. He'd be ready for a good job in the spring.

FOR SEVERAL DAYS AFTER being delivered to the Salvation Army Post, Bill was sober. Captain Russell had called the school district and explained that Bill was sick and couldn't come to work but would be well in a few days. He helped out around the post then moved back to his room.

HE UPGRADED HIS DRINKING to hard liquor and chose vodka. If he was careful a bottle could last him two or three days when he was working. That was a good time for Bill Williams. He saw George fairly often at the bar, he had a place to call his own, and he had friends.

"SO THIS IS WHAT jail is like," Bill said.

"Your first time?" his cellmate said.

"Other people told me about it. What you here for?"

"Drunk. It took *you* two days to come around. How much did you have?"

Bill shook his head. "Don't remember."

"My name's Lefty. You're Indian, aren't you?"

"Half."

"Indians have a tough time with booze. I've known a lot of them."

"Now you know another one," Bill said.

"It's not like I need to know another drunk. I'm bad enough by myself."

Bill got off the bunk and walked to the door, then turned around.

"How long do they keep you here?"

ANCHORAGE POLICE DEPT. REPORT

Case #68-2577
Name: Bill Williams
Date of Birth: 10/10/25

Date: 8/15/68
Location: Alley between A & B St. 4th Ave
Arresting Officer: Sgt. J. Striker

Officer's Narrative of Event:
Bartender called from the Union Club to report a group of people gathered around dumpster in the alley between A & B Street off 4th Avenue. I responded 2110 hours to find a couple fornicating in the dumpster and others gathered around watching. Several were able to run away however, this suspect was unable to stand without support and I booked him on suspicion of overindulgence of alcohol. The fornicating couple is on a separate form. Their names are: George Norton and Lily Watcha. See Case #68-2578 and 2579.

J. Stryker   8/15/68
Officer's Signature   Date

Badge No. 2515
Time: 2215 hrs

Lefty shook his head. "About as long as they want to, but usually a day or two. How long you been drinking?"

"You mean this time?"

"Since you started?"

Bill thought back to when he first met George pulling his cigarette smoke through his mustache into his nose. That was the first week after he got to Anchorage, that would make it 1945.

"This is 1968, right?" Bill said.

Lefty nodded.

"I guess twenty-three years."

"You're holding pretty good for that long."

Bill lay down on his bunk. "Twenty-three years—what a waste."

Lefty looked at him. "You get that buzz when you drink? I mean—man, I was in trouble with booze from the minute I had my first drink. The court ordered me to go to Alcoholics Anonymous but it didn't stick. Met a lot of other drinkers—nice people, too, but they weren't in my class. I guess I was in a class by myself."

Bill closed his eyes. "What a class, huh? Yeah—I get a buzz from it. Feel right with the world. Seems like it takes that sometimes to just get through a day, doesn't it?"

"You got that right."

THERE WAS NO NEED for Bill to go back to work at the school. A replacement had been hired. His final check was enough to cover his room rent and some food for another two weeks.

CHAPTER 14

The outline of the men was cloudy and lacked color, and Bill blinked several times. Through his bleary eyes he saw that they were well dressed and were talking and laughing as they came off Fourth Avenue and headed up G Street. He pushed himself up from the concrete step he'd been sitting on and fell in behind them.

He reached out to touch one of them on the sleeve, but his fingers fell short. He increased his pace. His shoes had no laces in them and they flopped like sandals. By the time they reached the middle of the block, he came alongside the shorter of the two men.

Still talking, they didn't notice him. He was used to that. No one wanted to notice him—it was up to him to make his presence felt. That's what George said. "Let them know you're there. They'll give you something if you stay with them awhile."

He started to reach out to the man's sleeve, then changed his mind.

"Excuse me," he said.

The shorter man looked at him but continued walking.

"Could you spare a dollar for a sandwich and coffee?"

The taller man looked over at him. "You'd better go eat at Bean's. It doesn't cost anything."

"They're closed now."

Don't argue with them, George had said. Just tell them you're hungry.

"I could really use something to eat."

"Go on, now. Go down to Bean's." He looked at his watch. "They'll be open in another hour."

They headed toward an office building across the street. Bill could hear them talking.

The shorter one said, "Jeez, I didn't think they'd hit you up right on the main drag."

"That guy's been around here for a while. Sometimes he's not that bad. Looks like he has a snoot full today, though."

"What in the hell's the city going to do about this? You can't have drunks pan-handling up and down Fourth Avenue."

"Hell of a thing."

BILL LOOKED UP, CAUGHT sight of the flag waving from atop the wooden pole in the square, and determined to stand at attention and salute the flag. He tried to line himself up with it and stay straight, but he wasn't steady enough on his feet. He squared himself with a lamppost that was closer. There was less movement, but his body was still weaving. He lifted his right arm, bending it until his index finger touched his eyebrow. He held it for a moment, then swung his arm back down to his side. His eyes were moist, his heart thumping in his ear. He turned, looking for the concrete step he'd been sitting on, his legs unsteady, as if the action and movement had robbed him of any remaining energy. The step was half a block away, and he thought to go there but decided instead to go look for George.

As he rounded the corner at Fourth and D Street, George waved at him from the alley. He and a man Bill didn't know were sharing a bottle next to the dumpster. He licked his lips, feeling his coated tongue slide across them. George passed him the bottle and he took a good drink. When he swallowed, he waited for the warm glow to begin in his stomach and move into his chest and up to his head. That gentle flow of warmth that eased his mind. He felt the bottle being taken from his hand, then he smiled and found a place to sit down. The bottle was nearly full. This would be a good afternoon.

BILL AWOKE TO ODORS worse than any he'd ever smelled in his life. It was dark. What little light there was came through parted curtains on the one window in the basement room.

"Jesus . . . " he muttered, half in pain, half in prayer. He looked around. Bodies were lying everywhere; on the floor, on the couch, in the three large upholstered chairs. He listened. Snoring. Some coughing. Wheezing. He looked around. Slumped into one of the chairs was a big Eskimo he thought he knew from the Salvation Army, but the light was poor—couldn't be sure.

He turned on his elbow to see who was next to him. It was George. So they'd come in here together last night. Well, at least it was warm, and he could see the light outside, and over the awful odors of the drunken men, he could smell breakfast.

He sat up. He had pain in every part of his body, and when he closed his eyes his head swirled. Always clockwise. Sometimes the colors would change, but never the direction.

George stirred, turning his face in Bill's direction. His breath smelled worse than the room.

What could make breath smell so bad? You sucked it in and blew it out and it came back smelling like death. He turned away from George.

George Norton, Athabascan from Fort Yukon, Alaska, 56 years old, widower, father, grandfather, friend and drunk.

Bill Williams, Athabascan from Arctic Village, Alaska, 45 years old, never married, friend and drunk.

He started to lie down but it hurt too much, so he stayed seated on the concrete floor, the cold seeping through his clothing and tightening up the knots in his legs.

He tried to remember a meal where he'd sat down and eaten something. A woman? The only woman in his life had been Ilene, who hadn't really been in his life. He wondered if he could just think about dying—and die. If the spirit gave up before the body did, and you could just think yourself to death. Because what was going on with him sure wasn't living.

He heard footsteps, and then the lights popped on.

"Good morning, people," said a cheery young man in a uniform. Blond hair, big smile.

"Breakfast will be served after morning prayers. Please wash up in the bathroom at the end of the hall downstairs. And then, before you come upstairs, I'd like each of you to think about what God means in your life today. Not yesterday, not last night when you came in here, but today. For today is a new day filled with the promise of God's love and His devotion to all of you. We'll start in fifteen minutes, and all who attend morning prayers will be served a good hot breakfast. So . . . good morning and may the light of the Holy Lord Jesus shine on you forever, starting this very moment."

He didn't exactly bow, but he sort of bent from the waist, closed the curtains leading into the hall, and disappeared from the lights he had turned on.

Bill figured it was kind of like a club show. Says his piece, lights dim, curtains close, and the next player is on. The next player is supposed to be the mighty Lord Jesus. How could he shine any light on me? There're thirty guys down here and there isn't a light shining on any of them. We're all dead. Nobody in this room is alive any more. They died inside long ago, and it's just a matter of time before their shells die. By God, these shells are tough, though. Hard to kill. The heart is easy to kill but not the shell.

Bill pinched himself. He squeezed hard and twisted. It didn't hurt. He dug his fingernail into the back of his hand. He pushed hard, trying to get it to cut the skin, but it just left a groove that didn't hurt. He began to hit himself.

He couldn't feel it.

He pounded himself harder. His shoulders and chest—then his stomach. His fists were clenched and he swung his arms in circles, slamming them into his upper body.

"Damned shell!" he yelled.

George sat up and stared at him. He flung an arm over Bill's arms, but the action was weak and he got his arm thrown back at him.

Bill peeled back his jacket sleeve, jammed his left arm into his mouth, and bit into the flesh.

He felt that. He wasn't dead inside. His arm jumped, but his teeth had opened the skin and the taste of his blood soured his mouth.

"Hey! Hey!" someone yelled.

There was a commotion, but few of the men moved. They had seen the fights and the seizures and the accidents, and they would see how this one did. They looked interested but did not interfere.

Bill started to cry. It wasn't the pain of the bite, it was the pain of living. Blood ran down his arm and from the corner of his mouth. It wasn't a lot of blood, he had missed the arteries and veins, but he had gotten through the shell.

The blond soldier stepped into the room and with clear eyes and determined strides stepped over the stacked men and got to where Bill sat, blood and tears mixing in a puddle between his legs on the concrete floor. The man rested his hand on the back of Bill's neck and very slowly began massaging it in small circles.

He said, "It's not right for these men—these souls—to come here and not find a way out. Life without hope should not be denied to anyone living."

Then he bowed his head, his eyes closed. When he lifted his head and looked around him, everyone in the room was standing, heads bowed, watching him as he continued to rub Bill's neck. There was not a whisper. Not a sound except for muffled noises from the kitchen upstairs.

The soldier helped Bill up, and the two of them walked through the faded curtain that acted as a door and up the wooden stairs that had hollows worn in them from fifty years of footsteps and into the sanctuary and behind the benches with the smell of oatmeal and coffee and toast filling their nostrils and driving out the odor of the sleep-off room. There was some sunshine coming through a yellow leaded window and somehow up here it wasn't so bad.

As the captain started into the morning prayers, the blond soldier, who Bill could now see was a lieutenant, slid in beside him, poured some peroxide into a cloth, and washed Bill's torn arm. Then he held the cloth under the wound and poured some into the teeth marks. He did it until the peroxide stopped bubbling, stretched a gauze pad over the wound, and taped it down.

He must have been a corpsman. First aid—clean and simple. And he'd done it while his mouth and his heart said prayers.

The bite hurt now, but Bill smelled the food and knew he was hungrier than he was in pain. If he could stand the prayers, he could wait for the food. He hunched over—he'd learned you don't feel as hungry when your stomach is shoved together in a hunched position. He would wait this thing out, eat, and get the hell out of here.

Behind him a man was mumbling out loud, providing a running commentary after everything the captain said.

"Who's he?" Bill asked the blond lieutenant.

"Jawbones is what we call him. His real name is Joshua."

"Does he always go on like that?"

"Most of the time. He lives alone out near the park, so when he comes in he tends to talk a lot. Seems like he tries to remember what talking is all about. He's a good enough guy. Just wears on you a bit after a while."

"He's wearing on me already."

"Somehow we each have our shortcomings—wouldn't you agree?"

Bill pulled up straight. He ran the statement through his mind. It went over and over like a short looped tape replaying the same words. Then it stopped.

"My God—I'm one of them," he said aloud.

CHAPTER 15

IT WAS A GOOD enough day for Anchorage, partly cloudy but warm for fall. The leaves were turning on the birch trees, and the aspen and alder were close behind. Bill and George walked toward the graveyard.

"Reminds me of hunting season," Bill said.

"You want to go hunting?" George said. "I've got a gun."

"You got shells?"

George blew a snort out his nose. "Course I've got shells."

Bill tucked his coat around him, the buttons and zipper long ago broken, and they walked toward the shack.

First the whiskey bottle came out of the cabinet and George took several swallows, wiped the bottle rim, and handed it to Bill. Bill tipped it up, then took the gun from George. He hadn't held a pistol since the war, and he turned it over in his hand, feeling its weight and the soft clean smooth lines.

He stretched out his arm and held the gun at full length. The gun wasn't steady, but once he drank more whiskey the gun would calm down and sight correctly. He had shot "expert" in the army and he could shoot this gun.

He knew about guns and he knew about animals and he was going hunting. He hadn't hunted since he'd left the village. He didn't feel very good but he hadn't felt good for a long time, and this day was no worse than any other. If they could get some fresh meat, it could be like the old days.

"Where?" he asked George.

"Anywhere. Down behind the Burger King," George said with a loose flinging of his arm in the direction of Tudor Road.

"The guy at the gun shop said we could hunt anywhere?"

"That's what the man said."

He reached for the box of shells and opened the loading gate. The nose-heavy shells slipped into the cylinder and he moved it to the next opening, loading six rounds. He took another long pull on the bottle.

George opened the door and they stepped out into the day.

"My gawd, it's bright," Bill said. The light slammed his eyes shut. He tried to walk, but it took a minute. When he closed his eyes, he started to spin. He opened them, and they burned . . . squint . . . tears coming fast to his eyes . . . then squint just enough so you don't wobble . . . blink so you can see . . . walk to that tree and stand still for a moment.

"The moose're this way," George said. "Why you standing there?"

Bill didn't answer. He just stood at the tree, blinking.

George laughed at him. "You a big hunter with six shells in your gun and you stand there and wait for moose to come up to you?" He slid to the ground and lay there and looked up at Bill.

"At least I can stand," Bill said.

He smiled. The air was good. They'd been inside too much. Too much whiskey. He breathed in as much air as he could hold and held it as long as he could. He let it out with a gush, and when that air was gone he pushed with his insides to squeeze even more out and he could smell the bad air, the air that had been in there for the last six years. They would go hunt now and then they would cook the meat and it would feel good to do that. He walked past George on the ground and down the trail toward Burger King. George picked himself up and followed.

Following the trail, Bill felt good with the sun on his face. At the bridge over Fish Creek, they stopped. There were tracks in the mud everywhere. Moose, dogs, people, bicycles, all mixed together. Bill knelt down and felt the tracks. They were old and frozen. Then he heard George chanting down the trail. He half-turned to quiet him down and saw the moose—a cow and a young bull, looking at him over their shoulders from about sixty yards up the creek. His head seemed clear now as he pulled the pistol from his belt and held up his left hand to quiet George.

The moose, who lived with people and dogs and cars, turned their heads and bit the slim branches of the willow trees. Bill moved to the edge of the bridge and leveled the gun. It wavered.

"Damn."

He rested his hand on the guardrail, squatted, and leaned against the upright post. He aimed again. The cow lifted her head and looked up at him, unconcerned.

At the sound of the hammer cocking, the young bull threw his ears forward and stopped chewing. He turned to face Bill, who aimed between his eyes and pulled the trigger.

The explosion was deafening. Fallen spruce needles on the bridge railing flew into the air, yellow leaves dropped from the alders where the slug ripped through the bark on half a dozen trees before it stopped in a telephone pole behind the Burger King. Bill fell over backwards, dropped the gun, and clutched his ears with both hands.

The cow threw her front end to the right. Her hind feet dug into the soft bottom soil, and in one leap she was out of sight. Cow and young bull crossed Tudor Road at a full run and cleared the four lanes of traffic. From there they headed through the municipal bus parking lot and up the hill towards the radio station. Drivers slammed on their brakes, honked their horns, and somehow managed to avoid hitting either of them.

George walked over and looked down at Bill, still rolling on the ground holding his ears.

"Hunters stand up when hunting, they don't roll on the ground."

"Jaysus, Mary, and Joseph," Bill said. "What the hell kind of gun *is* that?"

" .44 magnum. Shoots good, huh?"

"Did I hit him?"

George shook his head.

Bill got to his knees and looked up the creek. His ears had a constant ring—George sounded a long ways off, but he was right beside him. At least his eyes were clear. He could see where the moose had been.

"That's not a handgun—that's a cannon. It should have wheels on it and a truck to pull it."

He reached for the bridge railing and pulled himself upright. George shuffled his feet and hummed, beating his arms to his sides in a kind of mocking dance around the gun that now rested on the frozen mud.

Bill pulled his coat around him and started back toward the shack. He could hear a siren wailing. His head hurt something awful. He hoped George had some coffee back at his place.

George began to follow, then remembered the gun, doubled back to pick it up, and stuffed it in his pocket.

The flashing red and blue lights on top of the patrol car were nothing new to Bill or George.

"Hold it!" the officer bellowed, his hand resting on the butt of his service revolver.

Bill stopped. He stood weaving. The car's exhaust made him a little nauseous, but he liked the warmth of it. George stopped beside him.

The officer nodded at George. "Your gun?"

George looked down at his pocket and saw the butt sticking out. He looked back at the officer and nodded.

"You fellows been shooting in there?"

George looked at Bill. "I wasn't shooting—he was. But he didn't hit anything except the trees." He giggled.

"We were hunting moose," Bill said. His ears were still ringing, and his voice sounded very loud to him. "There are some good moose in there. Go down by the creek, they're eating on the willows."

The officer asked George for the gun, which he unloaded and put on the dashboard of his car.

"Need you two to get in the back seat here." He opened the rear door for them, got in the front, and started to fill out a form.

It was warm and comfortable in the car. The motor and the heater were running, and Bill was soon asleep. The next thing he knew, he and George were being hauled out of the patrol car and led into the Last Frontier Guns store.

"Phil. You recognize either of these guys?" the officer said.

"Yeah." The owner pointed at George. "That one."

George smiled and nodded.

The officer laid the .44 magnum on the counter. "Tells us you said he could hunt on Fish Creek behind Burger King with this."

"I didn't tell them that. You guys know better than that."

"We do. But he doesn't."

"I told him he was in Alaska and he could hunt anywhere, but I didn't mean in town or on Fish Creek. I meant anywhere outside of town."

"Hey, Phil—it isn't what you say that's important, it's what the other guy hears, huh?"

"Aw, come on, I didn't tell him to hunt there."

"But they did, and you'd told them anywhere—what would you conclude from that?"

The officer smiled and picked up the gun. "Phil—we'll try and get Fish and Game to designate behind Burger King some kind of hunting preserve—just for local residents. Something to do with native rights. I'm sure with your backing we can pull it off."

"Oh BS," Phil said.

"Moose BS," the officer said.

OUTSIDE, HE TURNED TO George. "Where you guys live?"

George pointed toward the other end of Fish Creek.

"Come on, we'll drop you off. Hop in." They stopped at George's shack. "Okay," the officer said. "I'll drop back tonight on my way home and give your gun back if you're sober. Got that?"

George nodded.

"Both of you. Let me hear you say it."

George and Bill looked at each other. Bill looked at the officer and said, "We'll be sober. Huh, George?"

George said, "We'll be sober."

GEORGE OPENED THE DOOR and stood standing in the frame of light.

"What's wrong?" Bill asked.

"Muskrat Johnny's dead."

He closed the door behind him. He pulled a bottle from the sack he was carrying and placed it on the table as if he were placing a tombstone at the head of Johnny's grave.

"How?"

"Someone beat him to death. They found him this morning down by the bridge."

"Who'd do a thing like that?" Bill asked.

"Who knows?"

George sat down at the table and put his head in his hands. Inside the shack it was quiet except for a trapped fly buzzing at the window.

"Well," Bill said, "the muskrats'll be happy."

George pulled the bottle to him, ran his fingernail around the seal, uncorked it, and took two swallows. Bill wanted a drink of the whiskey but didn't feel like getting up for it. He thought about Muskrat Johnny, how much fun he was, the money he always had and shared so easily after rat season. He used to describe his muskrat hunts and how easy it was to get several thousand of the creatures. Now he was stretched out on a marble slab at the crime lab and Doc Rogers was doing an autopsy on him.

"Hand me the bottle," Bill said.

"Get it your damn self."

Bill went over to the bottle and put it to his lips.

"All you can think about is the muskrats being happy Johnny's dead?" George said.

"It was just a joke."

"Well, it ain't funny."

Bill took a drink and set the bottle down.

"Another thing," George said. "You been drinking my whiskey and living here too long. Go get your own place."

Bill stepped back.

"Go on with you. I mean it."

Bill scooped up the plastic bag off the floor. Everything he had was in there. He started for the door. Then he stopped, went back to the table, hoisted the bottle, and took a good drink. He looked directly at George, then slammed the bottle down, nodded his head, and left.

Outside, he walked toward the highway. He cut down through the park, came out on Ninth Avenue, and continued along until his steps slowed and he stopped in the middle of the block. He didn't know where he was going. He looked behind him, but nothing gave him a clue as to why he was walking in this direction. Slowly he started for the Salvation Army post.

"Good morning Bill Williams," Major Russell said as he passed through the hall on the way to his office. "I hope you don't feel as bad as you look this bright morning."

Bill barely nodded. It was warm in the lounge, so warm. He settled lower in the thick padded chair and fell asleep.

He awakened to the smell of dinner. He had not moved in the chair, and every joint in his body seemed fused together. From long practice he started with one limb at a time and straightened it, then moved it back and forth before going on to the next one. Coming out of a drunken sleep took patience. He'd seen guys try to stand up and collapse. He stuck his tongue between his lips, wetting them so he could work his face muscles. When he slept with his head on his chest, the face muscles sagged and pulled around his puffed eyes—now he stretched and grimaced to get everything back in place.

The food smelled good, and for a change he felt hungry. He went to the bathroom, dashed his face with cold water, smoothed his straight black hair, and rubbed a finger over his teeth. He took a paper towel, wet it, and rubbed at something stuck to his shirt. He took a look in the mirror, then started for the chapel.

Before he got to the door he stopped, turned around, and came back to look again into the mirror. What he saw dumfounded him. With scrutiny he could pick out some of the features of his youth. The nose was recognizable. The ears and hair he remembered. But the cheeks and eyes and forehead seemed to have been grafted on from some cadaver. He wondered if anyone from the village would recognize him. The reflection hung in his mind, and he saw it over and over as he sat through the pre-dinner service.

The service today was about Muskrat Johnny. The major went over his life and what little he knew about him but pushed the concept that he had a contribution to make and maybe his contribution was in his death. That by dying as he had, murdered, he was an example of the end result for many of those who followed his path. He ended with a prayer that each and every one within the sound of his voice today would pledge himself to a new life, taking Jesus at His word, and becoming a light in the Kingdom.

What have I done to be a light? I told Captain Russell I'd work on it—think about it. And I have. But I never opened the door. Why don't I? Don't I believe? Did the war or drinking or George take it out of me? What's so hard about believing—just do it. God—I want to believe. I want out of this life and I'm not gonna make it without your help. Help me Lord—help me.

After dinner Major Russell asked to speak with Bill in his office. Bill found the chair he waved him into hard and straight. It was not a chair for sleeping.

"What's the change on your collar?" Bill said.

"Got promoted. Newly made a major and the Post has become a Corp. Nice upgrade from the earlier days, don't you think?"

"Congratulations."

"Thank you." The Major looked off to the corner of the room. It wasn't like him to be shy about starting a conversation.

"Bill, I have a disturbing message from your brother Carl. Patrolman Pat brought it over a little bit ago. There's been a death in the village, and Carl would like to have you come home for the funeral at least, and hopefully to stay."

"Who died?"

"Your Uncle Charlie."

Bill folded but stayed in the chair. How could he have forgotten that Charlie was getting old? A thousand memories flooded back through him and he watched them one by one come into focus and fade away. The last frame stuck, of Charlie standing in the doorway of the cabin.

Bill put a hand to his face and held his head.

"What do you think, Bill. Will you do it?"

"I don't know." He shook his head. "I don't have any way of getting there." His mind was awash in the things he would need to make such a trip. He saw Charlie's face, when he and Herb had laughed at his escape from the bear and the argument the two of them had when he wanted to walk to Venetie. Old Charlie, a widower so long, straight, lean, self contained, an old time village man, a chief. How he had wanted the boys to get along. Now gone. Passed on. Deceased. Whatever they used for death now days.

"Carl said he would send money for the trip if we could find you and if you'd come back. Can I send word that you'll go?"

"I don't know. I don't have any clothes, no way to make a living there."

"Bill," Major Russell said, "we can outfit you with clothes both for the trip and when you get there. We've plenty of that stuff. And think about this . . . you aren't making a living in Anchorage."

Bill's forehead was pounding. He needed a drink, or the pounding would take over his whole head.

"Could I have a cup of coffee?"

Major Russell stood up. "Sure. Cream and sugar?"

"No. Black."

"What do we say, Bill?"

"Please."

THE BACK OF THE Stinson was fully loaded with mail and groceries. The pilot had used every available space except the right front seat. Bill crawled out of the Salvation Army Chevrolet and handed the pilot a small bag. Major Russell came around from the other side and exhaled slowly, his bulk moving like a wave. He snapped his suspenders over his shoulders and shrugged them in place. He handed Bill a white envelope.

So this was how you went back to the village. A new set of clothes, an envelope with money, and the Salvation Army seeing you out of town.

Bill stuck out his hand. The major brushed it aside and pulled him into a big hug, his stomach shoved against Bill. He held the hug longer than Bill felt comfortable about, and when they pulled apart he rubbed the back of his hand across his eye and grabbed one of Bill's hands.

"Bill. Could we pray?"

Bill lowered his head, his eyes open.

"Our Heavenly Father, we ask these things today. That you see to a safe flight for Bill and the pilot. That today the reunion of Bill and his people be filled with Your blessings. This day is the beginning of rest of Bill's life, and we pray that you will mold it in a way that will shower glory on your name and blessings in his life. Amen."

The major looked up, held Bill's hand in both of his, squeezed it and let it go, then stepped over to the car.

"Goodbye, Bill. We're counting on you," he said.

Bill nodded. A sudden tightening of his throat kept him from speaking. He climbed in the plane, buckled the seat belt, and pulled the door closed. He looked out the window. It was a clear day in Anchorage. He could see the sun beating against the rose-colored snow on Mt. McKinley and Mt. Redoubt shining across the Cook Inlet.

He took a deep breath. It felt good. He enjoyed the vibration as the pilot pushed the throttle full forward and the plane plunged down the runway and lifted into the air, a slight shudder as the wheels continued spinning after leaving the ground. He was alive. More alive than he had been in years.

"My God—I'm going home."

"What?" the pilot asked.

"Nothing," Bill said. He took another deep breath and exhaled slowly.

CHAPTER 16

THE PILOT TOUCHED DOWN close to the end of the runway.

Bill felt better on the ground, but the approach and landing had tested his innards. For a minute he didn't move. He could see a pickup approaching and he didn't know how he felt about seeing anyone. He was sober. He had decent clothes on and he was here for a funeral. He would take it one step at a time. He unlatched the seat belt and stepped out of the plane.

The pickup roared down the side of the runway and came to a sudden stop close to the pilot who was removing the baggage and mail from the plane. Bill didn't recognize the pickup, but when the driver stepped out he recognized the limp in his walk

"Hello, little brother," Carl said, extending his hand.

Bill took it and noticed that for the second time he seemed taller than Carl. "Hello yourself."

"Did you have a good flight?"

Bill nodded and picked up his light duffel bag. It held everything he owned.

The pickup was full of kids he didn't know: a whole new generation.

Carl steered the pickup down the one-way road toward the village. He lifted his left hand from time to time to brush at mosquitoes. He didn't swat them to kill them, just disturb them.

"I'm sorry about Charlie," Bill said.

Carl nodded. "Yeah—me too. I'm glad we found you. I would have hated for you to miss it."

Bill looked out the window at the scenery that hadn't changed since he was born. "Was it ok for him? I mean, no pain or . . ."

"It was ok. He was in bed a few days but nobody thought he'd die. You know—he was tough."

Bill felt his eyes clouding up. "I'll miss him."

Carl nodded. "Yeah. He's the kinda guy you miss every day even when you don't see him that often. I still think I see him sometimes."

"Really?"

"I could have sworn he was in the dog shed yesterday. I even called his name."

An unending supply dust coming up from the floorboards whirled in slow circles in the cab.

Bill brushed it off the window. "We were lucky to have been raised by him after Dad. . ."

"That's for sure," Carl said. "That's for sure."

Bill rolled down the window and took a deep breath. Grown men don't cry at thoughts, do they? He thought of Coric laying in the ditch in Belgium. He had cried then. He had cried later, after he found out Ilene had married. He didn't trust himself about crying anymore, it was becoming easier and he didn't know what to do about it.

"I guess you didn't hear about Rusty either. He was looking for a new place to go for moose. At least that is what he told Verda. He wasn't a swimmer and nobody knows how he ended up in the river. The boat wasn't swamped."

"When did that happen?" Bill said.

"Let's see . . . about nine years ago."

"I only met him that once," Bill said.

After the long flight the pickup seat was uncomfortable. Carl didn't seem to have a backlog of things to talk about and finally Bill thought to thank him for the money he had sent.

"I haven't been working. Thanks for the money."

Carl glanced over at him and took in the clothes. He nodded, "You look alright. You're gonna stay with Herb and Verda at their place. They have the room and you might find being close to Verda would be good for both of you." He had a small smile on his face— more of a crease then a smile.

So that's it. He thinks I'm going to replace Rusty. Staying with Herb and Verda will be interesting but I don't know how I'll feel about that.

Carl pulled up at the store and flung open the car door. The kids scattered and Carl put the mailbag inside the store, got back in and without closing the door took off towards Herb Chulpach's cabin. He stopped by the front door.

Verda came to the door. She was slightly bowlegged and stood against the door jam with her arms across her chest and her right hip canted out. She wasn't smiling. Bill looked at her through the windshield and their eyes locked. Twenty-six years had intervened since they had seen each other. What would he want to tell her? Looking at her he didn't know if he felt joyful or sad.

Carl had grabbed Bill's duffel and was greeting Verda in the doorway before Bill slid from the seat and walked toward the cabin.

"Hello," she said without moving.

"Hello Verda."

It had all been arranged and Bill stepped inside.

What does a person say at a time like this? He hadn't been exposed to village life for a long time. Street life, he knew.

Before he could think of it, Verda said, "You look nice Bill. Thank you for coming."

Bill nodded. "Carl said I should come." He saw Herb half reclined in a bed against the wall. It was dark in that corner and Herb wasn't moving. Bill went over to him.

"Hello Herb."

Bill had never seen Herb when his head wasn't tilted back, his chin up, and his eyes half closed looking down over his nose and cheeks. Looking down on him in the bed he looked frail.

Herb tried to lift his head to get his eyes to look straight at Bill but gave up. He uttered some small sounds with his mouth, coughed some, wet his lips and tried again.

"Bill . . . ."

Bill kneeled down beside the bed. "How are you Herb?"

Herb's lips moved slowly, always the loose tongue and lips, his teeth long in the gums and brown from coffee. His lips opened.

"It is good for these old eyes to see you again Bill Williams." He stared at Bill. "You will stay?"

Bill nodded, not knowing if he meant to stay tonight or a week or forever. It didn't mean that much to him. He had come home for a while. He had always left before but this was a different time and who could say if he would stay or for how long.

Herb nodded and Bill stood up. Verda and Carl were standing together looking at him.

"Well . . . what?" Bill said.

Neither of them said anything and Verda moved off to the kitchen area and turned her back on the two of them. He could see her figure from behind and she was still a lean, good-looking woman, he thought. Long black hair, slim shoulders, and a very small waist. He hadn't thought about a woman for years. Whiskey tended to turn him away from the thought of women and anyhow the women he knew in Anchorage were street people like himself and while he was probably as drunk as any of them he didn't sleep with any of them. He hadn't thought about sex for a long time. Maybe the thought had a place to be nurtured and grown. At least the sight of Verda gave him a tingling feeling across his chest and shoulders. He straightened up and stood taller.

"I have to go check the fish wheel. You want to come?" Carl said.

Verda turned. "It's almost supper time, Bill. Could you do that tomorrow if you want and we can eat now that Herb's awake?"

"I'll stay here. I'm tired and hungry and this looks like a good place to cure both."

Carl turned to go. "I'll see you later tonight or in the morning."

Verda busied herself in the kitchen that consisted of a small gas range, a sink with a bucket under it to catch the water she used, and open shelves on the wall for a pantry.

She was propping Herb up with pillows and struggling with his weight when Bill eased in beside her and put his arm behind Herb's back and pushed him forward so she could get the pillows behind his back. They were very close and Bill could smell the clean healthy smell of her, the scent of her hair, and the warmth of her skin. He couldn't deny himself the pleasure of staying there just as long as he could and wondered if he had missed this in his life more than he could possibly know. Verda straightened up and bumped into him. Their eyes met and both stopped. Herb saw it. Neither acknowledged the moment and the whole thing took less time than was needed for a camera shutter to close.

Herb could feed himself, which made Bill feel that he wasn't as bad off as he at first appeared. Come to think of it, Herb had always been slow and deliberate. After Bill's encounter with the bear, Herb and Charlie had taken the better part of thirty minutes to evaluate the circumstances and make their pronouncements.

This was his first native meal in a long time. After three years of army food it had taken him six months to get used to the smell and taste of the Salvation Army food.

Bill and Verda ate in silence.

He put the pieces together in the quiet. Charlie was dead. The burial was tomorrow and everyone would be there. Now Herb was sinking lower every day and nobody seemed to know what was wrong with him but his decline was visible. Now I'm here. She doesn't know what to make of it, and frankly, neither do I.

After dinner, Herb muttered, "Get a chair,"

Bill did and as he was about to sit down Herb pointed to a small glass jar on a shelf behind him. "Get that," he said.

It was a small heavy jar. Bill tried to hand it to Herb.

"No . . . you," Herb said.

Bill unscrewed the lid and looked at the small dark colored flakes, moved them around with his finger, smelled them.

"Gold," Herb said.

"Gold?"

Herb nodded. He wagged a finger at the jar. "I found it about fifteen years ago, just after you left."

It didn't look like gold. It was heavy though.

"Do you mean you found this jar," Bill said, "or you found where the gold is and put it in this jar?"

"No . . . I found the gold. I panned it and put it in the jar."

"I didn't know you knew anything about gold," Bill said.

"There's lots you don't know. Why couldn't I know about gold?"

"You never said much of anything."

Herb worked that smile that looked like a crease in his face "You young kids, you think you knew everything anyway. What could I tell you and Carl?"

"Charlie sure tried."

"Well . . . Charlie had to try. He was your uncle and he was bound to have to try when you had no father. I figured you would find out everything anyway. I did." "You remember my bear hunt?"

"Sure."

"And you and Uncle Charlie sitting on the bank laughing at me?"

"Yes . . . and the bear on the other bank wondering whether to come in the water after you or not. See, you didn't ask anybody how to hunt a bear, you just stalked off to go hunting."

"I had heard lots of hunting stories."

"Yes . . . heard stories. But stories and hunting are different. Anybody can tell a story, a true one or one they make up. You can't hunt on stories. You need to walk in the trail of a hunter to know how to hunt." Herb coughed. "Would you get me some water, please? I haven't talked this much since you left."

Verda brought a glass of water. She lingered with her hand on Bill's shoulder.

"Did you know about this gold?" Bill asked her.

"A little."

"What do you do with it?"

"Oh," Herb chuckled after he mopped the water off his chin, "I give it to Carl to take to town and sell when he sells his."

Bill straightened up. Carl has found some gold too?

"And then what?" Bill asked.

"Then what? Why . . . we buy food and gas and clothes with the money." Herb's speech was slowed down and his voice started to crack.

Bill liked its weight. He liked Verda's hand on his shoulder too. His stomach was full, he didn't have to listen to a sermon after dinner, it was not so brightly lighted that it hurt his eyes, and a warm comfortable feeling enveloped him. "Where did you find it?"

"This place where three rivers meet near a dome. You can get there in about three days with dogs. It is easier in the winter when you can take the dogs. In the summer you have to fly out and the cost is high."

His speech, just a few minutes ago animated and high pitched, had now slowed down and dwindled in volume.

"Reach that sack there . . . " Herb pointed to the wall. "Take out that paper."

The paper had drawings and lines and circles on it.

"It is a map I made. I can't see it in this light. In the morning I will explain it to you. You and Verda can have some of the gold there. You shouldn't tell anyone. Carl knows about it but he doesn't know where it is. He has his own anyway. There are others who think I have it cause they don't know how this old one makes do with what he has."

Herb swallowed and closed his eyes, his breathing steady.

"I am tired. I haven't talked this much since Charlie was alive. Just an old man running on now, but in the morning...in the morning . . . we will look at it again and I will tell you how to read the symbols. In the morning I am always stronger. I feel better when the light is new. Don't you?"

"I guess."

Herb nodded. His eyes partially closed and his breathing became labored.

"Help me lay him down flat," Verda said.

Bill didn't know where he was supposed to sleep. He watched Verda as she cleaned up the kitchen area. She was a fine woman who moved with grace.

Wonder why she and Rusty didn't have any kids?

When she finished she stared at him, one hand holding her hair under her nose like an air filter. Then she let it drop.

"You can sleep in that room. I'll get the stuff out of there."

"I don't have anything to put in there," he said.

"Well, at least Rusty's stuff won't be in your way."

"That won't bother me, Verda." It was only the second time he had used her name since he had been back. It sounded funny to him and he wondered why he had not thought to say it before. It was a nice sounding name.

Verda didn't really clean it out she just shifted things into one corner.

Bill brought in his duffle and threw it on the floor. He removed his shoes and laid them out for quick access. Some things he had learned in the army were useful. In the morning, he would see what he could learn about Herb's gold field.

CHAPTER 17

The scream awakened Bill. It was difficult for him to determine where he was and what was happening. He pulled on his pants and shoes and parted the curtain. Verda was on her knees beside Herb's bed. His mouth was open and his arm hung down. .

"Verda?"

"He's dead."

An anxiety punched through him.

"He's dead, he's dead, he's dead . . . ."

Bill lifted his hands and put them on her shoulders. He searched for something to say but he could think of nothing. Verda was giving off little spasms that he could feel through his hands. He began to rub her shoulders and back as she swayed on her knees, sobs coming now less frequently. She pulled Herb's arm up and laid it on his chest and closed his jaw but it fell open again.

"Get something to hold his jaw closed, I don't like seeing him this way."

Bill found a washcloth in the kitchen, rolled it up and placed it between Herb's chin and his chest forcing the jaw closed.

His eyes are closed. I thought people's eyes remained open when they died? They did in the war. But those were young men killed in a moment of life. Maybe it's different when your life has run out and sneaks away from your body in the night.

Verda stood and shook silently, tears running down her face. He moved toward her and she turned into his arms and clung to him.

170

She was the first woman he had held. She felt warm and soft and her crying did not bother him. He had always been put off by crying.

While she cried Bill held her close, his eyes opening and closing as they swayed locked together. Through her hair he saw the map lying on the floor. The map to the gold with all of its lines and symbols and how to get there that was to have been told to him today. It laid there a sheet of gibberish, like a lost needle in a haystack.

He let go of Verda and picked up the map. She recognized what he had thought. "No—no." She reached for it. Bill put it in the envelope on the wall.

"We'll look at it later," he said.

Verda looked up at him, her eyes red rimmed, the sides of her nose wet with tears. He opened his arms and held her again. They stood together until she became quiet, the soundlessness becoming oppressive.

"We better find Carl and let him know," Bill said.

The gold map is a problem—I don't know if I'll ever figure it out? Would it be disrespectful to Herb if I looked at it tomorrow?

FUNERAL TIMING IN THE village was another thing he didn't know about. He knew that Charlie died last Friday and the funeral was today, the following Saturday. He would have to wait and see what happened. He had time. He hadn't done anything meaningful for years and waiting had become easy for him.

Carl walked right in, limping over to the bed where Herb lay and looked down at him. For a full minute he stood there then Verda came to him. He held her and looked at Bill over her shoulder. His eyes were moist.

"A lot of death," Carl said after a minute. "A lot of death."

He wiped his eyes with the back of his hand and started for the door.

"Bill, go over to the store and get a body bag. Tell them it is for Herb.

Verda…get his clothes out and we can dress him for the funeral. I'll go see Ernest and see if he has any caskets made up. Maybe we can get the preacher to do both burials today and we don't have to do it again. The people will be very sad."

Verda and Bill stood in the room. It was as if all life had left the room and there would be none there again. Bill was the first to move. He started for the store and the body bag.

CHAPTER 18

THREE DAYS AFTER THE funeral, Bill and Verda sat at the table with cups of coffee and the map stretched out. It wasn't like any map Bill had used in the army, no directions or landmarks or rivers. Just some symbols and lines. He turned it a quarter-turn, then another, trying to figure out what might represent anything Herb had told Verda about the gold's location, the three rivers and a dome.

Then he had an idea. "Herb was right-handed, wasn't he?"

Verda nodded.

"He probably drew this map with the notes on the right side of the lines and symbols, then. That might give us some clue. What do you suppose the lines mean?"

Verda shrugged. "Could they be trails?"

They looked at the map. Verda said, "Should we ask somebody, maybe?"

"No," Bill said. "We can't trust anyone else to look at it." Then he remembered the gold in the jar. He got it down, poured a little on the map, and looked at it.

"Didn't he say it took him three days with the dogs?"

"I don't remember," Verda said.

"I think he said three days in the winter. Think, Verda. How far do you reckon he could get in three days with those dogs, at his age?"

"I don't know. Maybe fifty to a hundred miles. Maybe."

"Did you ever see which way he took off? I mean, did he head over into the valley across the Chandalar or did he head up north?"

"I don't know, I never saw him leave from the village." She started to cry, and held her arms across her chest, rocking back and forth like her father had done as long as Bill could remember.

"We just have to figure this out." He reached over and put his arm on her shoulder. "You and I could be rich. I'm younger and stronger than Herb and I could get more gold out of that place than he did."

He folded the paper and poured the gold back into the jar.

"Bill . . . how much is that gold worth?"

Bill shrugged, then hefted the jar again. "I'd say maybe five or six ounces. You have anything in a jar with the weight on it?"

"No."

"What would they have at the store that you might need that would have the weight printed on it?"

"Maybe some jam?"

He dug in his pocket. "Take this to the store and buy something that says five to ten ounces on the label and we'll see if the gold is heavier or lighter than that."

While she was gone Bill studied the map. Herb was not a genius, so this map of his had to be fairly simple. If he could just orient it to something he knew, something that stuck out. But what did he know of the country in a 50- to 100-mile radius from the village? Nothing having three rivers and a dome. Maybe he could get a pilot to fly him in circles out from the village. That would cost money. Damn. Some people in the village had to know where the three rivers came together. If he didn't disclose why he needed the information, he might find someone to tell him. No—asking would be too risky. People were already suspicious about where Herb had gotten his money.

Verda returned with a ten-ounce jar of jelly. Bill held the gold in one hand and the jelly in the other. The jelly was heavier, but not by much.

"We have less than ten ounces," Bill said. "We have to take off for the jar. Maybe five ounces."

"I thought about this," she said. "They have a map on the wall— we can see if there is anything like what Herb said."

Wow . . . one minute she's sobbing and the next minute she's planning a frontal assault on a gold mine.

At the store, they bought foods that would last, then walked over to the map looking for three rivers that met at a dome.

THE OWNER STUCK HIS head over the counter and around the corner. "Help you find anything?"

"No thanks, Irem," Verda said.

"Nobody ever looks at that old map," he said. "Just keep it there to help hunters and hikers see where they are. Never seen a villager look at it."

His head disappeared around the corner, and Bill placed his finger on a place where three rivers came together. He looked down at Verda, who looked up at him grinning.

Bill checked the map scale. Something he'd learned in the army was going to be of use. He measured his finger on the scale, then put that finger in a straight line from Arctic Village to the three rivers spot. It looked about fifty to sixty miles. He smiled at Verda, who took hold of his arm and squeezed. Of course, he knew that what looked easy on a map could be very difficult when you were on the ground.

Back at the cabin, he went out to the shed and found an old oil barrel. Twenty minutes later he brought it inside and set it down on the floor.

"What's that?" Verda asked.

"My bear-proof food cache. You got a padlock?"

"There's one in the bottom cupboard behind the sugar sack."

Bill slipped the padlock through the hasp. "Now no bear can get my food."

"How'd you make it?"

"It's just the two ends of an oil barrel. I cut the middle out to make it smaller and put a hinge on one side and a lock on the other. With my food in it I won't have to pack it with me all day while I'm looking for gold."

"That'll work. How do we pay the pilot?"

"Give him some of the gold," he said.

"How much?"

"I'm not sure about that. Maybe ask Carl what gold's worth. Herb said he gave some to Carl to sell in town, so he must know something about it."

"Bill, we can't let on that we know anything about where the gold might be. Do you want me to ask him?"

Carl might wonder why I'm suddenly wanting to know gold prices, but he'd probably give Verda the information without question.

"It'd be better if you did it," Bill said.

Verda was out the door without another word.

IN THE CUT-DOWN barrel Bill worked out a place for everything he needed. He wouldn't have to take anything but the barrel and the pack board he'd found in the shed.

When she came back, Bill looked up. "What did Carl say?"

"Lots of nothing. He did say it could be worth more than two hundred dollars an ounce, depending on a lot of stuff, but not to sell it at the store."

"Did he know where Herb's gold site was?"

"I asked him, but if he knows he's not saying."

She took down the gold and poured some of it into his palm. "Rub it," she said. "Rub your other hand over it and just feel it."

"What am I supposed to feel?"

"Just do it for a little bit. Feel it."

Bill rubbed it. He turned his hands over and rubbed more, then smiled. "It feels warm. I like it."

"Other people are going to like it too. We just need to figure out how to do this trade with the pilot."

VERDA LEFT THE GOLD on the table and made some sandwiches of bread and smooth peanut butter. Bill preferred chunky, but Herb hadn't because it got under his lower plate, so there was a case of creamy peanut butter stored in the house.

"You know what we can do with lots of gold?" Verda asked.

"Anything we want to, I suppose."

Verda picked up the jar of gold and held it in front of his eyes. "Bill, we have something in our hands right now that won't come again in our lifetime. You haven't done too well, and I'm alone and an orphan, and—"

"You're pretty old for an orphan," Bill interrupted.

"—and neither one of us can let this chance slip by."

She stared at him, her dark eyes puffed after the two funerals, but piercing as the eyes of a hawk.

"I want to live in a house with electric lights that go on any time I want them to. And running water—hot water. We don't have a lot of years left to us. We have to make this chance work."

Bill looked at her face and wanted her dream to come true. "I'll try," he said. "I'll try real hard, Verda."

THE PLANE LEVELED OFF at 3500 feet, and Bill couldn't imagine so much country holding the three rivers and Herb's gold. It overwhelmed him to be looking over that much country.

What he had practiced for his adult years was a poor background for this work he was taking on now. He hadn't been out in the wilds since the Bulge, and then he had lots of guys around him and before that he was eighteen—over twenty-five years ago. He was going to go out where only two people knew where he was and look for some gold where he wasn't sure it was and then bring it back so he and Verda could live on it the rest of their lives. Whoopee! Who did he think he was?

What if I did find it, though? How would it feel to dip the pan into one of those rivers and come up with a bunch of gold nuggets to add to the jar? How long did it take Herb to gather that gold, and how much of it had he sold? Well, I know this, Herb found more gold than he needed to live on and had some left over. That was enough, wasn't it? I don't want to be rich—just comfortable.

"Where to?" the pilot asked.

Bill produced the map he had made from the one at the store. "Up around the Porcupine River. I need to see if there are any trails on the ground here. Could you circle over the village and then go out this way?"

"You're paying for it. I'll go where you tell me."

They flew for an hour and a half looking for three rivers and a dome. Finally the pilot said, "I don't think there's anything here like what you're looking for." Just at that moment a connecting river came into view.

"There," Bill said. "Can you land there?"

THE PILOT LANDED THE plane on a gravel bar, dodged between rocks too big to hop over, and splashed through several ponds of water. He held the tail wheel off the surface while the main gear bounced over the rocks and slowed the plane down. Every rock and rivet made a noise inside. Bill was sure the plane would come apart before it stopped.

The pilot stepped out. "This is where you want to be, huh?"

"I think so."

"I'll be back in two weeks. You got enough food and stuff to last that long?"

Bill nodded.

"Okay. See you in two weeks on this gravel bar. I should be here around the same time of day."

The plane took off and Bill lugged the barrel over to the top of the bank looking for a good campsite. His side of the river was mostly tundra, uneven and wet in the hollows, but the other side had small spruce trees and some level ground. He crossed the river without getting soaked and made camp. This would be his head-quarters for prospecting up the three rivers.

The camp was not elaborate or secure. A sheet of visqueen stretched over a center pole, the sides held down with rocks served as his tent. He threw the barrel in the back of the tent against a dwarf willow tree, then made a fire ring with river rocks close to the front of the tent. The smoke from the fire should keep the mosquitoes away. He wished he were immune to the mosquitoes like Carl—he couldn't remember a time when Carl had scratched mosquito bites.

Standing outside the tent, Bill looked up one of the three rivers. All three came out of the Brooks Range; two were clear and one had heavy glacial silt in it. The silted river might hold more prospects. There might be old evidence that Herb had been here. He must have camped somewhere, made a fire, something that would give him a clue.

He picked up the gold pan and shovel and walked along the low bank where rocks protruded from the cuts made by the river at flood stages. The bottom was covered with small to medium-sized rocks. Where the bank caved off, he put some soil and water in his pan. He had never panned before but he had seen others do it.

He swirled the dirt around the outside edge of the pan, tipped the edge a little, and let the floating dirt and debris skip out of the pan with the water. He swirled the pan again and added more water as he worked the dirt down to what he hoped would produce some color. After four pans of water there was about a tablespoon of sand on the bottom that he moved around with his finger. There was no gold. He washed the sand out, picked up, and moved further upriver.

A caribou trail where hundreds of the animals had crossed the river had broken down the bank on both sides. He knelt down and put a handful of the dirt in the pan. He added water and started the mix swirling, the water soaking into the dirt and breaking down the chunks as it circled inside the pan, some of it slopping out at each revolution. The silt wouldn't settle, but that didn't bother Bill. He knew silt was lighter than gold, and if there was any gold in the water it would go to the bottom of the pan and stay there. He got to the bottom and spread the sand with his fingers. Nothing.

He continued up the right bank and tried another half-dozen pans with no luck. Discouraged and hungry—he hadn't eaten since morning—he trudged back to his campsite, dropped the pan and shovel and headed back upstream to the gravel bar, where he had seen some driftwood. The bark had all been scraped off the wood when the water tore it from the bank and carried it down over the rocks, but it was good and dry now and hard as metal. It would burn long and hot. He gathered up an armload and headed back to camp.

It would be hard to light a fire of driftwood, but if he could get it to ignite, those peeled branches would burn all night. With some twisted dry grass and spruce bark chips full of pitch as starter, the fire sprung to life. Once it was burning he laid limbs over the fire to make a real hot spot in the middle, so hot he couldn't have put it out with a five-gallon bucket of water.

The fire was a comfort. How many times had he wanted to build a fire during the Bulge and couldn't? Freezing feet and hands and very little food twisted the soldiers' minds to not caring whether the enemy saw them or not. How rum-drum they got when, sleepless, they sat day and night in freezing foxholes and argued themselves out of building a fire. They were in woods; Bill could have built a fire in five minutes if it hadn't meant the whole squad's getting wiped out with a well-placed mortar round.

He stared at the fire until his eyes felt like they were going to burn out of their sockets and then he lay down in the tent, a supply of firewood close by, and tried to plan tomorrow. He had not planned anything before he fell asleep.

TWO DAYS HE SPENT up the Coleen River, panning for gold, looking for any signs that Herb had ever been there. He went out of his way to make trips off to the side of the river where likely campsites might have been, often several hundred yards, hoping to pick up some trace. By the end of the second day he had done nothing but make up his mind that the Coleen River was not a gold-bearing river.

The next morning he tried Boulder Creek; clear, fast-moving but rock-bottomed like the Coleen. He would leap to a rock, get a fistful of sand from under the boulder on the downside of the current, put it in the pan, and do a quick swirl of the contents. He had heard that the down-current sides of big rocks often caught and held fine gold. If he could find some color he would at least know he had the right river. Nothing.

There was one more river to chase down, Lake Creek. Tomorrow he would go up Lake Creek and see what it held.

Back in camp, he opened the lid of the barrel and looked at his remaining food. It reminded him of army rations, the same thing over and over again. He pulled out some caribou jerky and dried berries and with legs crossed in front of the small fire he dined in solitude.

He didn't mind being alone. He had spent a good deal of his life alone. The only two people he'd ever been close to were Wayne and George, and Wayne was the only friend he'd really cared about. He wondered what Wayne and George would do out here. They'd be so lost he'd have to lead them back.

He chuckled. "You guys lost?"

He hadn't spoken out loud since the pilot left.

"Hey, you guys." Then he yelled. "HEY, YOU GUYS!"

He looked around. The wild place where he was camped was vacant. If he died tonight, ravens and bears would pick him clean, then the snow would cover everything, and in the spring when the flood-water came down the canyons it would wipe everything away. There would be nothing to show that Bill Williams had ever been here.

Which was why he hadn't found any trace of Herb's camp. Tomorrow he'd go up Lake Creek and just look for gold.

AT DAWN BILL HEADED up the right bank of Lake Creek. The river had a lot of wood trash in it, and there were driftwood piles on the gravel bars. His eye fell on something that didn't look natural— he removed his backpack and hopped across rocks to get to it. It was a rusted tin can. It had been opened with a knife, not a can opener.

Would Herb have carried canned stuff? Yes—with a dog team. How long had Herb been coming out here? How long did it take a can to rust away? He looked up the river, trying to reason with it to give him more evidence that he could understand.

Then he froze. A hundred yards upstream, a female grizzly and two cubs were in the middle of the river. The sow used her front paws to dislodge rocks in the riverbed while the two cubs watched. Bill checked the wind. The cool morning air was drifting down from the mountains, putting the sow upwind from Bill. She didn't smell him. She lumbered across the river and turned downstream, her head swinging from side to side as she walked with her nose to the ground. The adrenalin pumped into his system.

She stopped. At thirty feet she swung her head back and forth, then stood up. Water dripped from her fur; the cubs piled into her hind legs. She pointed her snout in the air revealing her nursing nipples, and then she charged. . The noise of her snapping jaws carried over the tremendous pounding of the water. There were no trees to climb, nowhere to go. Bill stood stock still.

At ten feet, he gained his voice. Noise was his only chance.

He raised his arms above his head, and waved them. "Hey, bear . . . HEY!"

The sow braced all four legs and slid to a stop, her massive body splashing a wall of water that soaked him.

"BEAR! HEY, BEAR!"

Before he could get the water out of his eyes she had turned and bowled over one of the cubs. The whole family took off on a lope toward Boulder Creek. At one point she stopped and looked back at Bill, standing on the gravel bank waving a rusted tin can. She took off again, her bouncing behind the last sight he saw as she disappeared.

He lowered his arm while his heart rate started to return to normal. He hadn't seen a bear in a long time, but the last bear hunt was vivid enough in his mind to recall all of the details. He focused on the rusted tin can and noticed that his hand was shaking.

Dammit, this can could be Herb's. He shouldered his pack board and moved upriver again. Every conceivable place was searched for old camp evidence. Nothing.

Using a piece of driftwood, he pried two rocks from the bottom and dug a cup of sand into the pan, filled it with water and swirled it. There was no gold. At the mouth where the canyon walls faded back and the river spread out on the flats he tried another pan. Nothing. He kept trying. He kept getting nothing.

He had panned three rivers. He was fed up with gold hunting and the plane wouldn't be back for over a week. Disgusted, he headed back to camp.

DARK CUMULOUS CLOUDS WERE forming in the Northeast. They were grouping in the high passes, darkening as the edges rolled around the mountains. The fronts of the clouds blazed white where the setting sun bleached them, but the heavy bodies rolling into the canyon were dark gray tinged with black.

No rain had fallen since he landed. At first the ominous sky didn't bother him, and he ate his supper and got his fire ready for the night, but then the bugs became ferocious as they always did before a heavy rain and he wondered if his camp was safe if a storm hit the area. He knew fast, strong water could push trees and rocks into places they didn't belong. This camp was near the confluence of three rivers.

As the sky darkened he looked again and then kicked the fire apart, sending a thousand sparks into the night. He threw his belongings and the visqueen tent into the barrel. He had to get on the other side of the river into the high ground near the mountains or go up one of the canyons far enough and high enough to be above the water that might come. He was undecided.

Why is this so difficult? It's like battle. Decide and do it. Don't even think about it.

He grabbed the barrel by the rope, slung it over his shoulder, and headed for the other side of the Coleen. There, the dome that Herb had described, should be out of harm's way.

When he reached the top of the mound, he gathered firewood. He kindled a fire, erected a framework of branches to hold his plastic tent, and secured the sides with rocks.

Then he sat down to see what would happen. He felt like he was a spectator at some game, sitting there on his high hill watching the field below. When the sky dimmed enough that he couldn't make out individual trees on the flats, he put wood on the fire and slipped under the tent, feeling sure if the storm hit it would awaken him.

It was louder than he expected. The rocks pounded and rumbled as they roiled in the water sounding like a convoy of trucks in the dark. Whitish tips of the waves were visible as the flood roared down the cleft, driving trees and riverbank trash and rocks and churned-up earth in its bosom.

When the flood passed he tried to get back to sleep. Tried to let the comfort he felt being on the dome overshadow any decision he might have to make. Decisions could wait until daylight. .

In the morning he looked out at a complete sweep on the flats. The water was gone. It had leveled most of the small trees and shrubs, and those not leveled were half buried in debris. Boulders and logs were perched high on the bank, beached, looking dead and still. The earth had belched tons of water to cover his tracks and any traces of Herb's tracks, and if there was any gold it was now buried deeper.

His eyes wandered over the desolation below. Desolation so complete not even a bird flew over it. Whatever life had been on those flats was gone. He didn't see how anything could have survived the torrent and wondered if the sow bear and her cubs had escaped it.

In that instant he decided to walk out.

Why not? It's ninety miles—wouldn't take but a week. No trails. I went further than that when Wayne and I left Belgium, and besides that, it was winter. Plus we didn't have any food.

The plane should be back in about a week. I could be in the village by then and save a couple hundred dollars. Ninety miles divided by seven days is just a little over twelve miles a day—I'm not in great shape, but I can do that easy.

Or I could stay and wait for the plane. Could the plane still land on the gravel bar? Might I miss the one plane that is actually going to look for me in this area? It is so changed since the flash flood.

I wished I had a drink. It would calm me down and let me ease into this decision. He looked in the direction he would have to travel to get back to Arctic Village, and the decision was made.

He would walk back. There was no gold here, there was a chance the pilot couldn't even recognize the place after the flash flood, and he could save a couple hundred bucks if he got back in time to stop the plane from flying out. A gentle peace settled over him. He smiled and looked out over the devastated valley.

"Well . . . that wasn't so hard."

CHAPTER 19

BY NOON OF THE first day Bill could still see the dome. He didn't know how far he'd have to travel to be out of sight of it, but it served as a reverse beacon for him.

There was food and water in his pack. The barrel he had left on top of the dome, so there would be some trace there of Bill Williams A.F. (after the flood). He sat down on a small hummock to eat. A cramp started in his left foot, knotting hard at the instep. While he was stripping off the boot and sock, the cramp moved into his toes, curling them down so much he jumped up and hobbled around barefoot.

"Jesus Christ! Jesus Christ!"

He sat down, crossed his left foot over his thigh, and massaged the white, useless thing until it loosened and he could move the toes without further cramping. This terrain was full of hummocks with water draining through the shallow bottoms, running across a small rocky base. His boots were soaked. He hadn't determined what to do at river crossings. Whether to leave his boots on, wade across and then walk them dry or wade barefoot and risk an injury to his feet. He would decide when he reached a river. Until then he felt sure he could walk the boots dry before nightfall.

Looking ahead at the country he had to travel through it was difficult to pick a path—nothing seemed to have a trail or direct purpose to it. Caribou trails were abundant but caribou wandered, and trying to pick a dominant trail was like choosing the shortest straw in a bale of hay. He would follow one caribou trail, then switch to another when it veered in the wrong direction.

He was moving in the general direction of the village, somewhere northwest of where he stood. It was not difficult walking but it took concentration, because the hummocks required him to angle his foot between them just right or his hips and back twisted. By mid-afternoon he found a stand of trees and sat down to assess his situation. Except for the small group of trees he was sitting under, the land as far as he could see was nothing but hummocks. He drank water and ate, and looked for a spot in the distance where he might camp.

He was headed for a small island of trees and tall grasses that seemed to be a good site but found a pond between the trail and the trees. To get around it would require a half-mile of walking through hummocks; it was less than sixty yards to wade across. He pulled off his boots and socks and stepped into the pond. The ooze on the bottom squeezed up through his toes and soon he was up to his knees. By the time he made it across, he was soaked through.

There was a level spot for camp in the trees and enough dead alder wood around the edge of the pond for a brisk fire. Off to the northwest he could see more trees, but other than that, nothing but rolling hills, tundra, and a thousand small ponds with grassy edges.

He wasn't hungry, but he ate. Daily his appetite had decreased until he was beginning to wonder if he was taking in enough food to keep up his strength. Funny how hungry he'd usually been in Anchorage, doing nothing, and yet how little he was eating on this walk. The food all tasted the same, didn't matter whether he ate the salmon or caribou. The berries were greasy and tasteless but he swallowed them, feeling honor-bound to eat Verda's prepared berries and vowing to explain to her when he got back that they needed something to make them enjoyable. Sugar, maybe. Or honey.

He sat on the ground and massaged his feet. The big toe and ball of his right foot were numb. He was working on them when he heard the first howl. He took the wolves to be about a quarter-mile away and on the hill he had crossed before coming to the pond.

The cubs would be about four months old now, hunting with the adults. He could pick out the pup's vocalizing and the deeper voice of the alpha male. When he looked up a pair of eyes shone from the darkness—steady for a few seconds then gone. He sat very still, his ears straining—no sound except the crackling of the fire. The hair on the back of his neck stood up.

A series of short yelps off to his left and then they were gone.

A safe distance from the fire he stuck drove two sticks in the ground and put his socks on them to dry. Fatigue began to touch every joint in his body. Finally he lay down, the occasional wolf howl keeping sleep from him for some time.

AT THE FIRST HINT of light, he tried to sit up. He couldn't. Back, legs, shoulders so stiff he could barely move. He rolled over on his stomach and put his rear end in the air until he was on his elbows and knees, resting in that position until his body accepted the idea. Then he rolled into a sitting position and pulled first one knee and then the other up to his chest several times, finally loosening the joints to the point that he was able to stand. He ate standing up and when he'd finished bent over and tried to touch his toes.

"God, I'm stiff."

And why shouldn't I be? The most exercise I've had in years was walking to the Salvation Army Post.

The prospect of crossing the pond didn't look so good in the early morning. It's one thing to get wet just before you camp and build a fire and quite another to do it first thing in the day, knowing you're going to walk for twelve hours. He decided to walk around the pond, struck camp, and took his first steps as the sunrise painted the top of the hills pink and blushed the sky a deeper pink beneath small cottony clouds.

He looked back at the campsite. A fire ring was the only sign that he had been there. He was crazy to have thought he could find Herb's trail out here in this wilderness. He'd been too long in the city and had totally forgotten how much country there was and how insignificant a man was in it. In seven days he might leave six two-foot fire rings in an area of ninety square miles. Crazy.

Walking around the pond kept him dry but added distance. For some reason, the caribou trails converged going over a low pass and the hummocks were so beaten down by the huge herds that the morning walk was much more enjoyable.

By noon the trail ran into a narrow lake. He could see the trail on the opposite bank and saw caribou coming out of the water with their rolling gait, shaking the water from their coats, their heads close to the ground to grab a bite as they went. He could swim the lake or walk around it. If he swam he'd need to build a fire on the other side and he wasn't at all sure he could swim it with his pack. He decided to walk around.

The elevation increased on the other side of the lake and the surface changed from hummocks to hard mineral soil with outcroppings of mosses and lichen, the caribou food supply. Like a giant spider web across the tundra, trails went everywhere from the top of the hill, but it was easy for him to see the direction he needed to go. He thought he could see the Philip Smith Mountains across the Chandalar River from the village, but they looked eighty to ninety miles away.

He didn't stop for lunch but pushed to make up for the time lost walking around the water and munched as he walked. The trail was easy, there were no bugs to bother him, and all of his joints worked well. The air was clean and as he inhaled it energized him.

By God it was good to be out here feeling like this. He threw his shoulders back and walked erect, head up, his eyes focused far ahead. A deep sense of being alive and enjoying the day surfaced. This was not the same Bill Williams who'd stepped off the plane in the village.

By the time the light was fading, so was his energy. He stumbled over rocks and roots that protruded from the soft peat. He forced some water down, which helped for a couple of miles, but he knew his body had quit for the day. He should have been looking for a campsite before this.

The fact was, he'd been enjoying the day and the walk so much that his thoughts weren't on ending it but on the sheer pleasure he was getting from being alive and in the wilderness. This was where he was supposed to be, not in Anchorage. Not in a city but on the land. And gold or no gold, he was going to start a new life.

He camped with no fire, ate sparse food and laid his pack on the other side of the small rise. There were no sticks to hold the visqueen up, so he covered himself with it, hoping the insects would be baffled.

WITHOUT MOVING, BILL CONSIDERED the possibilities that had awakened him. There was no wind. He couldn't hear any sound. Yet something had startled him awake. There was some moonlight, and he rolled over on his stomach and peered into the gray night. A large dark form moved. By focusing his eyes to the side of it Bill could see it, head down, nose to the ground, not moving from that spot.

He reached his arm across the ground searching for small rocks. The bear lifted his head.

"Git! GIT!" He threw a rock at it. The bear hesitated.

"Go on—GIT!" This time he grabbed the visqueen and rattled it. The bear jumped up, cleared the ground, spun around in the air, and plunged across the valley. It chose to escape along the ridge, and Bill could see it running with the moonlight shining off its fur. He came out from under the visqueen and watched until he couldn't see the bear any longer.

"That damn bear—he knows who's boss." He was still chuckling to himself when he went back to bed. He closed his eyes, but as tired as he was, he couldn't find sleep again. Before dawn he arose. He was stiffer than he could ever remember being in his life. He lay on his back and pulled his knees up to his chin. Pain shot through his hips, knees, and ankles. He pulled his legs tight against his chest, rolled over on his stomach and arched his rear end up, then proceeded to his knees and elbows. He could picture himself getting out of bed this way and chuckled.

He didn't chuckle when he tried to stand. It took him five minutes to get to his feet and start for his pack. It wasn't over the rise where he had left it. He looked out over the tundra where bits and pieces were scattered everywhere. Nothing edible was left and the dirty clothing was shredded.

That bear—he got even with me.

HE WISHED HE HAD a fire for coffee, but that would have to wait until he got back to the village. At the end of a mile, his legs were moving at the pace he had set the previous day; at the end of two miles there was no more pain.

When he came to the river he scouted up and down the bank looking to see if the bottom was visible. It was clear but too deep and fast to judge the depth. From the alders growing along the bank he cut a seven feet stick as thick as his wrist. Then he took off his boots and socks, put the boots back on and laced them up. Jamming the stick into the bottom upstream from him, he stepped into the shallows along the bank, the current tugging at his legs. Balancing on one foot and the pole he lifted the other foot and maneuvered it on the bottom, found a crevice between two rocks and jammed his boot tight against the bigger one. The water rose over his knees and the next placement of the pole was deeper.

He looked over his shoulder—he wasn't halfway across yet. He lifted a foot. When he brought it down he was in water up to his waist. The back foot slipped, and he jammed his stick into the bottom creating a three-point stance. Cold water seeped through his clothing and around his back. His chest muscles constricted. He tried to breathe but couldn't draw a full breath. He tightened his grip on the stick and inched one foot ahead, sliding it over several rocks until he found good footing. The water was no deeper. He anchored both feet on the bottom, lifted the stick, and jammed it upstream. It didn't go in as far. Two more steps took him into shallow water.

He poured the water out of his boots, opened the laces, pulled the tongues out, and propped the boots up facing the sun. It's brightness forced his eyes closed. They felt like they had sand in them. They itched, and he rubbed them with the back of his hand. Tears ran down his cheeks. He hadn't thought about sunglasses for years, he just got by without them. In fact, he had gotten by without a lot of things, had thought he didn't want them, didn't need them. Things other people had as a matter of course. A house, a car. A family, maybe. A job.

In a patch of trees that provided firewood and tent sticks, he built a large fire. It was a white man's fire, one where you cooked on one side and froze on the other, but tonight it was a great comfort and helped make up for the lack of food and last night's cold camp. From down the valley a cool breeze swept the mosquitoes away. It was a good camp, and Bill slept straight through until dawn, when the breeze stopped, the mosquitoes started and he had to force himself through the early stages of stiffness.

The walk began easily enough, crossed the valley and moved through rolling hills with vistas that were five to ten miles long. There was not another living creature. At noon he stopped to watch five ravens swoop on an updraft, tuck their wings and dive straight for another bird, who avoided the collision at the last minute by rolling over, extending its feet, and letting out a raucous caw.

Suddenly it was over and they flew off together disappearing over the rise. He felt a pang of loneliness. Their noise and antics had been friendly, non-threatening, and he had found himself smiling at them several times. They were part of a family, a group—apart but not alone.

Now he kept an eye out for fresh water sources and drank as often as he could find it. Filling his belly with water dulled the hunger pangs.

Afternoon was the toughest. The second time he stopped to rest a cramp started in his calves. He struggled to stand up; the muscle seized, and he used both hands to massage it. The muscle was hard as stone. Each stroke of his hands felt like he was pushing on a bad bruise. He managed to hobble around in a circle while his hands squeezed up and down the muscle, feeling it harden, relax, and harden again. He could not control it and there was no cry that would suffice for the pain the leg gave him. If he had a knife or saw in his hand he would cut it off. Tears came to his eyes. Shortly after wishing his leg would drop off, the muscle relaxed like a dead fish, soft and pulpy in his hands. The pain left as quickly as it had come.

On the fifth day it occurred to him that he could drop right where he was and it wouldn't make a difference. Nobody would care. He could stop, sit down, and never get up. He imagined how Carl and Ilene and Verda would feel when they found his remains. The thought occupied him until the light faded and he found a campsite on a mound that had a small growth of blackberries glistening in the failing sunlight. He knew the effects of eating nothing but fresh blueberries and creek water but his choices were limited. At least his stomach was full. It was now the mosquito's turn.

IN THE MORNING he drank some water and started toward the village. It was lighter without the pack but every joint from his feet up to his neck had been jolted, knifed, slammed, and he had fallen like a sack of flour three times. He felt like he was ninety years old. He forced the muscles to give in to his first step, then the second, and finally developed a gait that was slow and steady. At first he could think of nothing but the pain. He tried to think about something else. Verda. He would think about Verda.

It's been thirty years since I've known her. She was fifteen when I left. Now she's forty-five—a widow. The money's gone. We're just running on old times' sake. Well . . . list her good points and see how it works out. One: she's slim. Two: she's tough. Three: she has a place to live, some dogs, a house. Four: she might not even want me, who knows?

He stumbled, then jerked up his head. He couldn't remember the last landmark he'd memorized to guide him and stopped to look back. None of it looked familiar.

He put the sun behind him and picked his path. He couldn't recall where he was with Verda's good points. Finally he let it go. His mind went blank again, and nothing could divert him from the monotony of lifting his feet and putting them down. There was a gentle rise ahead of him, and he made a mental note to stop on it and rest. He could even lie down.

No. Too hard to get up. I need to find some food.

At the top of the rise he stopped, both legs wobbly with no feeling below the ankles. Putting his right arm out for balance, he touched the ground with his hand and let his body collapse. He remained in that position for a minute, trying to isolate the muscles that had to move to get into a seated position. His breathing was slow and labored. Between breaths he straightened out on the ground and lay on it like a dead man.

"Is this the end of it?" He thought he said it out loud, but he wasn't sure. Maybe he had only thought it.

You have to find something to eat. Get some water. You're not at the end of anything. Get up.

He rolled over on his left side and propped himself on his elbows.

Eat before you're hungry, drink before you're thirsty, rest before you're tired.

It wasn't this hard in the war. How could we have walked that far with what we had? Well, he was nineteen then. He and Wayne had lived on D bars for several days, he could do it now on blueberries and creek water.

HE FELT HE WAS near to the village and that he could either push on or camp and finish up tomorrow. For the last several miles he hadn't been able to trod a decent path, his upper body seemingly detached from his lower half, leaving him to wander like a drunk over a web of caribou trails.

When he collapsed it was still daylight and he slept where he dropped. He awoke in the same position he had fallen, virtually paralyzed. For several minutes he worked to get the numbness out of each limb. He rolled to his left side and got on his hands and knees. He was unsure what else he could do and clung to that position, weaving a little. One arm supported him while he worked himself into a sitting position.

He brought his hands up looking at them, turning them over on both sides like a doctor might do. They were so swollen he couldn't see the blood vessels. His fingers would not form a fist. He held them in front of him, fascinated by the large unmoving clubs at the end of his arms.

The shivering started in his arms and shoulders, then moved to his stomach. Knowing his legs could cramp, he stood up and followed a trail across the hillside. He hurried, needing to build up body heat. It was dumb not to have prepared a camp last night, to lie out there in the cold. The heat was slow to come and he threw his arms around his body, swinging them up and down. He was close to the top of the hill. Climbing would generate body heat faster, so he cut a sharper angle and walked to the top.

There was a river passing by a village flowing south. The layout of the village looked familiar. Wait a minute. He could identify the houses and the store and the airstrip. A gasp seized his throat. Tears collected in his eyes and he fell to his knees. He was home.

For the first time since he'd left Anchorage and Major Russell, he prayed. Sobs interrupted the praying, but he continued with his head bowed, resting on his swollen hands.

"God, I thank you for getting me through this . . . " He looked out again at the village. "I'm so confused and I don't know what to do—about anything. Please help me. Guide me in my life like you did on this walk." His sobs diminished but he stayed in the bowed position for a few more moments. "Amen."

With great effort he turned one leg under him and worked his way into a sitting position. His head hung on his chest, tears dripping from his cheeks to his clothes and dribbling on his folded hands until his eyes were empty. He wiped his nose on his sleeve and looked again at the village, his thoughts a jumble in the fatigue of the past six days. With the village in sight, one goal was within reach but there was no other to take its place.

He had never seen the village from this vantage point, always before going through the valley to avoid the hills that blocked the village from sight. It looked lovely from where he sat. Everybody

from the village should have to come up here and look down at it so
they could see how it looked and how it was laid out. He estimated
the distance at five miles. He could be there before the end of the
day. He didn't want to limp into town but he had to start now, as
he was tightening up and pretty soon the pain would be too much
to avoid limping. He pushed up with his left arm, got on his hands
and knees and waited for the pain to subside. When he was stable
he started off the hill, the village in front of him.

He wondered how close he would have to get before they recognized him.

CHAPTER 20

"Get up." Carl shook his feet. "I need some ballast in the sled."

Bill turned over. "I can't walk."

"You don't need to. Just get to the sled. You can ride in the basket."

"No thanks. I think I'll stay here."

"No, you won't. You've been back three days—that's long enough." He pulled on Bill's toes. "Come on, get up. Verda has some coffee made. I'll bring the sled over closer so you won't have to hobble so far."

After Carl left, Verda poured Bill a cup of coffee and set it on the box by the bed that served as a catcher of all things. It had interlocking coffee stains on the surface and held a collection of socks, shorts, dishcloths, and rags. Bill found his socks. He couldn't bend his legs enough to pull them on, so he put the first one over his toes, then bent down and eased the sock over the blisters and onto his foot. His pants hung over the end of the bed.

"Verda. Would you hand me my pants?"

She lifted the pants off the bed frame and threw them in his lap. What's got into her?

He was testing the heat of the coffee when Carl stuck his head in the door.

"I was hoping we would do this today," he said.

Bill drank half of the coffee and set the cup down. He glanced at Verda as he left. She had her back to him.

"I FORGOT HOW FAST dogs can run," Bill said when he came back in. He threw his hat and coat on the bed. "Carl has a good team, I think."

"Is that all you think?" Verda said.

He looked at her. "What do you mean? Are you—"

"I think that's an understandable question."

Bill sat on the edge of the bed and looked between his feet. "I think lots of things. I—"

"Like what?" she said.

Bill licked his lips and looked at the window. "When I was walking back I did a lot of thinking."

She waited. He didn't offer.

"Like what?"

"A lot of my thoughts are personal, Verda."

"Did you think about the gold?"

Bill nodded.

"Did you think about whether you would make it or not?"

"Sure I did."

"Did you think about us?"

Bill's head snapped up. "What do you mean about us?"

"Well, you've been living here since you came back, do you ever think we might be together?" She was standing with her back against the stove, holding a little black wag of hair under her nose.

Bill smiled, looking at her. It warmed him to see her do that.

"What's so amusing?" she said.

"We used to tease you about that—your Hitler mustache trick."

She dropped the hair. The stew boiled over and she lifted it off the fire, the pungent smell filling the cabin.

"Open the door," she said as she stirred the contents down.

Bill opened the door. He looked up and down the street. Was this worth staying for? The rest of his life here?

"Hell's bells, Verda—that's a lot of thinking to—"

She slammed the lid on the stew and spun around. "Bill Williams, you didn't think very long about walking to Venetie and you didn't think about writing for three years or letting us know if you were dead or alive or telling us where you were in Anchorage. Carl had to make a half-dozen phone calls to find you."

For a few seconds Bill had the DI in front of his face, and he shook his head to clear the image.

"Verda, I—"

"Don't you 'Verda' me. You've been wasting your life without thinking about it. Now you're telling me it takes a lot of thinking to decide if you want to live here or not. Isn't that what you're telling me?"

She was right. He had nothing to say. He picked up his hat and coat and walked out the door.

"That's right!" she yelled after him. "That's what you do when you can't talk about it. Walk away!" He heard a cup shatter against the door. He kept walking.

As he neared the store, Ted Sheeley came out with a new shovel over his shoulder.

"They've got more of these in there. I could get you one and you could help me on the new digs. There's gold there for sure. How long you been back?"

"I came back for Charlie's funeral, then I took a trip. Actually I was looking for gold too."

"You was?"

Bill nodded.

"You find any?"

"Nope."

"See what I mean? It ain't out there." He pointed to his feet. "It's right here—I know it is. I'm so close I can smell it. What do you say I get another shovel and we go digging together?"

"Not only no, but hell no," Bill said.

"No need to bite a man's head off. I was just asking."

"I'm kind of tired of people telling me what I'm gonna do with my life."

Ted walked away.

At least that guy knows what he's doing and how every day works for him. Wonder where he gets the money to keep going?

He walked toward the dog yard behind Carl's house, thinking he might see Ilene there. The sled was there but some of the dogs were gone and so was Carl.

"Hi, Bill. Coffee?" Ilene asked.

"Where's Carl?"

She handed him the coffee. "Took the younger dogs on a training run with the car."

"Car?" Bill said.

"He rigged up an old car with no engine—he has the dogs pull it for heavy exercise. Works real good until the snow comes." She put one foot up on the fence rail. "What's Verda doing?"

"Yelling at me."

"Really?"

Bill nodded and sipped the coffee. This was the first time he'd been alone with Ilene and he wanted to touch her, just a little, somewhere. They were standing close by the fence and he let his shoulder inch over until it was touching hers. She didn't move. He glanced at her as he took another sip, but she was looking at the dogs.

"Are you going to tell me why she's yelling at you?"

"Well... she wants me to think real fast, and I need time. I need to mull things over. Every time I do something without thinking, I get in trouble."

She looked at him. "Verda want you to stay there?"

"I really don't know if she does or doesn't. I came in after enjoying a ride on the sled, and she lit into me."

Ilene took a sip of her coffee. "Did we almost get together before you left, Bill?"

Her directness startled him. "I'm not sure—I was just a kid."

"I liked you a lot. The day you said goodbye and we were standing out front of our house I thought I'd cry. And you just took off down the trail for Venetie like you were going to walk to the store. I cried every night for a week, and I waited and waited and waited for a letter from you. Nothing ever."

"You know I wrote you three letters and asked you to wait for me." He looked at her started face. "Carl burned them."

"Carl what?"

He nodded.

"He had no right to do that—what gave him . . . ."

"Ilene—he was crazy about you. He's told me so. That's why he did it."

"I could have loved you. We could have had kids, a house, a good life together. I didn't know . . . ."

"I know now. But I didn't know then. With no letters from you . . . ."

"Bill—I could have loved you as much as I love Carl."

"Well—that time is past isn't it?" He shrugged. "I'm sorry."

"That's the first time I've ever heard you say you were sorry. You're getting soft, Bill Williams."

"My feet aren't. These blisters are getting hard as cardboard."

She nudged against him with her shoulder, gently pushing him off balance. He spilled some of his coffee.

"Hey . . . "

"Hey yourself. Drink the rest of it and give me the cup."

"I'm afraid to give you Chulpach women a cup any more, Verda's thrown two of them today. One at me."

"She must have had a good reason. You want to give me one?"

"One what?"

"Reason?"

"Oh, no. Think I'll stop with just the two."

"Coward," she said.

He smiled. "Never was called that."

"No—you aren't a coward. You're many things, but not a coward." She looked up and saw the dog team coming back to the yard. "Here comes Carl. He must have worked them pretty hard, their tails are down." She took the cups and headed back into the house.

Carl was all smiles. "Damn, these dogs did fine today. And they're the young ones, too. They're gonna be a great team next year. Help me unhitch them." He pulled a rope from the car and tied it to a post. Then he took the wheel dog, led him into the yard and hooked the doghouse chain to his collar. The dog instantly rolled

on his back with all the other dogs yapping. Bill could never understand why the dogs needed to talk so much when they'd only been
separated a few hours.

They unhitched the dogs and pushed the car behind the shed.

"That's pretty good, having the dogs pull an old car," Bill said.
"It won't fit on the trails, though, will it?"

"Not many of them, but enough to train these guys," and he
motioned at the younger dogs. "Want to try it?"

"Not today."

"Tomorrow. You run the pups tomorrow. You'll like it."

The brothers stood looking at the dogs. "It's a good group," Bill
said. "But they're kind of small."

"You want them smaller, faster, with good endurance, not like
the old dogs Dad used on the trap line. These guys eat less, run
faster, can take care of themselves in the cold, and they'll run their
hearts out for you."

"How far you run them with that car climbing their tails?" Bill said.

"Oh, about two miles. We run up and down the airport a
couple of times. Works good if Ted Sheeley hasn't dug up any gold
mines lately."

"I saw him this morning," Bill said. "He was coming out of the
store with a new shovel. Wanted me to help him dig again. He ever
find anything around here?"

"Not that I know of."

"How's he live and buy stuff?"

Carl shook his head. "Beats me."

Bill took his foot off the rail and stuffed his hands in his pockets. "Carl," he said, "did you ever find any gold? You seem to be
doing pretty well trapping. Maybe better than trapping pays."

"Never had any reason to look for gold," Carl said. "Why do
you ask?"

"Just wondered. Herb had found some gold, and I thought if he
could, you sure could."

"That where you went? Looking for Herb's gold find?"

Bill nodded. "I didn't find it, though."

"He didn't get much, and it wasn't very good gold," Carl said. "He was pretty secretive about it—guess I would be too, if I knew where some was." He started toward the house. "I'll come get you in the morning for a dog run."

Bill hobbled to Verda's place. He didn't know whether he should knock or just open the door. He hesitated at the front, then knocked lightly.

"Yes?" she said.

"Okay to come in?"

"If you can walk you can come in."

He went over to the bed, keeping his eyes diverted from Verda, eased off his boots and looked at the socks. There were no stains, so he assumed the blisters were healing and not draining any more.

"Have you eaten?" Verda asked.

Bill shook his head.

She took a bowl and dipped some stew in it. Then she tore off a chunk of bread, set it in the stew, and handed the bowl to him.

He looked at her and realized he had no earthly idea what her mood was at this moment. No earthly idea how and why women reacted the way they did—or to what. He had not lived among them, didn't know their ways. No wonder they confused him.

"This is good, Verda," he said between mouthfuls.

She didn't respond. Instead she sat looking out the window over the kitchen cabinets, her legs crossed. The noise of his eating was the only sound in the cabin.

"What if we asked Carl to help find the gold?" she said suddenly.

So that was it. She was mad about his not finding the gold. He stopped chewing.

"I asked him this morning if he'd found any," he said.

"What'd he say?"

"Said he didn't have any reason to look for gold."

"And that doesn't mean he didn't find any."

"Well, so what if he did?"

"If Herb did and Carl did, then you can too. Ted Sheeley's living off something. He's probably finding some. And you saw Herb's gold."

Bill said, "Verda, I panned three rivers looking for gold. I've had it with gold hunting."

He hobbled over to the sink and put his bowl down. As he turned to go back to the bed, Verda glared at him and said, "You can wash up that dish."

No sooner had he washed the dish than she said, "You can dry it, too."

He dried it, and put it on the shelf.

"Anything else?" he said.

Her eyes twinkled like they always did when she smiled. "Oh, go lie down," she said and pulled the end of her hair under her nose. For a moment they were fifteen and seventeen again and nothing had changed.

CARL STOPPED THE TEAM outside the cabin. He had eight young dogs hooked up to the car frame.

"Send the gold prospector out," he shouted.

Verda looked at Bill. "You told him that's where you were?"

"Since I didn't find anything, I didn't think it would hurt to tell him."

Verda didn't say anything but she didn't seem mad.

Bill shook his head. There was a lot about women in general and this woman in particular that he needed to learn if he was going to include them in his life

He hobbled out to the car body. The dogs were ready to run.

"You sit in here like the driver and steer," Carl said. "You remember the commands?"

Bill nodded.

"Okay, take them out to the airport and run them at a lope down to the end once. Then stop and let them rest. Run faster on the return and stop before the riverbank. When you come into town, go slow— the dust is bad for them. Here, I'll turn them around for you."

Bill got in the seat, the only thing remaining on the inside of the old Volkswagen. Carl let loose of the lead dogs and the team took off on a sprint down the street past the store to the small hill leading to the airstrip. All the dogs but one had their tug lines tight. He whistled loud, gave a "Hey, hey!" and the slacking dog picked it up, tightened his line.

At the edge of the airstrip, Bill yelled, "Get up, get up!"

Their tongues swinging back and forth, the two lead dogs went into a strong lope. The wind whistled through the windshield opening, causing Bill to squint. The smell of the dogs, the sound of their feet hitting the ground, the cool air in his face—he could almost hear his dad telling him how to run the dogs. Near the end of the runway he applied the brakes and yelled, "Whoa, whoa!"

When the car stopped the dogs looked around at the unfamiliar man in the seat. They were panting. So was he. Nothing had excited him so much for years. He had been mad, he had been sad, he had been drunk and disorderly and slovenly and tired and scared—but not excited. His breath was coming fast and he was smiling big.

"Thanks, Dad," he said.

"Gee, gee," he said in almost reverent tones. The dogs looked back, then the lead dog made a move and the others followed. When they were lined out straight, he called, "Get up," softly, and the dogs worked into a slow lope.

The ease with which they handled this slower speed amazed Bill. He recalled that his dad had used basically three commands. Carl's dogs seemed to have at least five gears, and they were just puppies. He wanted to try the big team. This was just too much fun to be legal.

"Haw, haw!" he yelled when they reached the end of the runway where the dogs turned onto the road and picked up speed going down the slope from the airstrip to town. He braked to avoid running over the back of the wheel dogs and to cut the dust that was boiling up under his feet. Once on the road, the dogs made a beeline for the dog yard where Carl was drinking a cup of coffee. Bill could see Ilene looking out the window. He almost forgot what to do when the lead dogs stopped at Carl's feet.

"Whoa," Bill said.

Carl smiled at him. "Looks like they ran into a red light, doesn't it?"

"Well, that's good. I wasn't sure they'd ever stop."

"You have any trouble?"

"Not a bit." Bill climbed out of the car and tied the rope to the post. "God, Carl—that's the most fun I've had in a long time."

Carl took a sip of his coffee. "Well, driving them is the rainbow over all the work, about nine months of good hard work to where they'll do that for you. Finding the breeders, raising the pups, feeding and cleaning every day, training every day, building sleds. Then you get to ride and pray to God they don't run into a moose and get themselves killed."

"Does that happen often?"

"Just often enough to remind you it can happen any time."

Bill stuffed his hands into his pockets and looked at the ground.

"Could I run the big team once?" When he looked up Carl was staring hard at him.

Carl threw the last of his coffee out and stuck the cup on a nail driven into the dog-yard post. "Help me unhook these guys," He unhooked the wheel dog's tug line, led it into the yard, and hooked it to a chain. Bill limped around the team with the other wheel dog.

When they got to the lead dogs, Carl said, "I'll get those. Don't want them to be handled by anyone but me for a while yet."

Bill shuffled over to the gate.

"Carl. . . ."

"Look, I don't want you messing with the team. Taking the young dogs out a time or two isn't going to hurt them any, but I just don't want you driving the big team."

He walked to the cabin, his back to Bill.

"WHERE'VE YOU BEEN?" Verda said.

"Over at Carl's."

"I can't be holding meals all hours of the day."

Bill looked around, not wanting to meet her eyes.

"Verda, I—"

"Oh, get in here and eat before it burns to the bottom."

She was filling a bowl with caribou stew when the sound of the airplane engine caught his attention. She slid the bowl in front of him and walked back to the sink. He sat there a moment, looking at the steam rising from the warm surface.

He shoved the chair back and walked over to his bed, pulled the duffel bag out, stuffed the few items he had brought into it and zipped it up.

"What're you doing?" she said.

"Think I'll go back to town."

Verda stared at him, the strand of hair pulled under her nose and a hard look in her eyes.

"How long did you think about it, Bill Williams?"

"About long enough." He set the duffel by the door.

"You gonna run and run and run until you've got no place to go?"

He shook his head. "Why'd you throw that cup at me?"

"You deserved it." Verda moved to the table.

"What did I do?"

"Here you are—in your forties and you're as loose as a caribou. You've got no home, no family, nothing to call your own but you're still thinking about it. Seems to me the thinking time is over. I'm offering you a place here—and you're thinking about it."

"I don't know what you want from me, Verda?"

"Course you don't. You haven't thought about it!"

He didn't have an answer for her. He opened the door and limped out towards the store. The pilot was standing on the porch drinking a coke.

Bill nodded to him. "You got room for me going to Anchorage?"

CHAPTER 21

WHEN HE WALKED OUT on the bowl of stew Verda had set out for him, it hadn't occurred to Bill that he wouldn't eat the rest of the day. As soon as he got out of the plane, he threw his duffel over his shoulder and headed west towards the Salvation Army Corp. Clouds drifted in from the southeast across the Turnagain Arm and covered the sun. The chill made him pick up his pace.

A good feeling pulsed through his body as he walked along 4th Avenue to C Street. His hunger and the absence of alcohol for weeks made him raise his head and swing his arms. He was looking forward to hearing Major Russell expound on the evils of drink, homelessness, and joblessness, and then the sweet offering of stew, fresh vegetables, and hot rolls. Major Russell would be smiling when he greeted him, finding him sober.

He climbed the stairs and walked into the warm food smell. The Jesus clock on the wall told him it was time for vespers. Hoping his stomach would keep quiet through the service, he headed for the chapel.

He eased the door open and slid into a seat. The man next to him didn't look up. He had several days' beard on his face and bags that made three separate folds under his eyes. Major Russell's clear baritone boomed out over the group, and Bill joined in the hymn, "Onward Christian Soldiers."

" . . . With the cross of Jesus, going on before." It was just like Major Russell to try and stir the spirit in these people with a good marching song.

The major missed the final chord on the piano, but his voice was strong enough to drown it out and with a deftness born of practice he quickly removed his hands from the keys. He spun around on the stool and with a smile on his face, looked out over the audience. The major, sensing within him the needs of every soul there, would now say one of three things: 1. "Let's pray." 2. "Let me tell you a story about . . . " or 3. "I believe God's gift of food and drink is ready—are you ready to receive it as the gift it is, the miracle He has made with earth and water and sun?"

It all depended on how he read the audience, the season that was upon them, and the condition of the individual he deemed to be in the worst shape. If he thought the worst of them could hold out a few minutes longer, he chose #2. If he thought there was time for a quick heartfelt prayer, he opted for #1, always in the hope that he might, through Jesus, reach just one soul with that uttering. And if he could see that time had run out and there was the risk of imminent audience collapse, he would chose #3, holding out the concept of God's bounty. Tonight he chose #2 and began to give the details of Bill's relationship with the Salvation Army. He told the story in sequence, right up to his sobering up and cleaning up and being sent back to his village for a funeral.

" . . . And he now has returned to us and is in the audience tonight. When you are getting your heavenly rations, please take a moment and welcome Bill back in his new capacity as community coordinator for this corps." He broke into a wide smile and closed with a prayer thanking God for the food, the warm room they were in, and the healing grace He provided.

"Let's eat," he said.

The congregation filed out, some stopping to say hello to Bill as they passed by. Bill waited for Major Russell, who was herding people down the front aisle and toward the dining room. When he got to the door where Bill was standing, he reached out his arms and gathered him in.

"Bill . . . so good to see you. And look at you—you're looking so good, so clean . . . let me smell your breath." He sniffed and then smiled. "So clear. Good for you, good for you."

Bill nodded and smiled. "I've missed you too."

"How were things in the village?"

"Pretty much the same."

"You look thinner. Didn't they have moose stew and fresh bread?"

"I took a little walk—wore me down some."

"A little walk?"

"About ninety miles."

"Ninety miles! You'll have to tell me about that. You hungry? Let's go eat." He took Bill's arm and guided him toward the dining room.

As they approached the room, Bill heard sounds that resonated with him. At first he couldn't make the connection, then he realized what he was hearing called to mind. The dog yard at feeding time. The only noises in the dining room were the sounds of eating, flatware clinking against dishes, bowls being set down on tables, platters being moved around, feet shuffling underneath the table. No conversation.

Same thing in the dog yard. Barking, tail wagging, rattling of chains, until the food was ladled into their bowls and the sounds changed to lips closing on food, slurping, chewing. Bill wouldn't ever in his life think of these folks as animals—it was just that the way they entered into the eating of free food was remindful of the peace and contentment the dogs got from their food. Being hungry and getting filled and giving your attention to the meal until it was finished. Then you could look around, wipe your mouth with the Salvation Army napkin and, having that need satisfied, consider your next need and where it might be satisfied.

"How was it Bill?" Major Russell asked when they'd carried their casseroles to a table.

"It was okay." He blew on his first bite, sensing the temperature of the bubbling cheese. "I got into a lot of trouble. I flew out to look for gold, spent all of the widow's money to do that, didn't find any gold, and walked back ninety miles. A bear took my food, and I wasn't in the kind of shape you need to be in to do that. I was stove up for a few days. Hobbled around like an old man."

"Hmmm . . ."

"Then I ended up getting everybody mad at me. So I just left."

"Bill, we need to have a serious talk about where you're going, now that you're back. Armand was asking about someone for a night clerk's job at his hotel. I think you could do it."

"What was this about a community coordinator you mentioned? And what about the name change—this is a corps now instead of a post?"

Major Russell beamed. "Tell you the truth, we don't have a position like that, but seeing you sitting there clean and sober, the Lord just created the position in my head and pushed it out of my mouth with details to follow. We need a coordinator to work with the natives. They're a substantial portion of the corps' population. Now that you're sober, you're an ideal candidate for the job."

"I don't know . . . " Bill said.

"Sure you do," Major Russell said. "Bill, life either wears you down or polishes you up, depending on what you're made of. Are you a soapstone or a diamond?" He chewed a mouthful of food while he looked expectantly at Bill.

"What does a coordinator person do?"

"It would only take an hour or so a day, and you're with them at that time anyway. It just makes you more visible in your community; helps identify people who need help before it's too late. Surely it's something you can do for your fellow travelers."

Bill looked at him. "You also said something about a night clerk?"

Major Russell nodded. "I did. You've met Armand, who's on our board. He wonders if there's anyone here who'd like the night clerk job and could be counted on to fulfill it. I nominated you."

"Seems like you've been doing a lot of nominating."

The major held up both hands. "Guilty."

Bill finished eating and pushed the dishes out in front of him. It reminded him of the end of a meal on the *Northland Echo*. He half expected to hear Mike O'Leary's voice.

"I don't even know what a night clerk does," he said.

"I don't either, but it can't be hard to pick up. Armand would like you to come over and see the situation. Could you go after supper?"

"Oh, I don't know. I hadn't planned on anything like that."

The major laid his hand on his wrist. "Bill, you haven't planned anything. This is a chance to get back up—you could start from this point and only look ahead. Forget the past. Work with me on this." He looked around at the people still in the dining room.

"These people, Bill . . . they have so far to go. But you—just a little bit of effort now and you'll be in a new life. You'll be the next commander of this corps."

Bill snorted.

"No, I mean that. You can lead if you try. This is an opening God has provided to you. Showing you His hand. Showing you His love. Take it. I know you can do it. You know it too. You led half a dozen guys out of the biggest battle in Europe, and you can do this." He withdrew his hand. "A corps, by the way, is larger than a post. It shows we've come a long way here."

Bill stared at him for a long moment.

"Okay," he said finally.

"Praise the Lord!"

ARMAND WAS THE FIRST Armenian Bill had ever met. He stuck out his hand and said, "Welcome to the Plaza, Bill. Let me show you around." He started for a small restaurant and bar combination adjacent to the lobby. His movements were quick and fluid, and Bill found he had to walk fast to keep up.

Over two coffees in a deserted corner of the restaurant, Armand outlined the duties of the night clerk.

"Bill, is there anything in the job description you think you'd have any problems with?" he said.

"I don't see any," Bill said.

"Major Russell tells me you were a corporal in the army. You directed men in their duties?"

"Yes."

"How did you feel about that?

Bill twisted in his seat. "Not sure how I felt."

"Did you feel good about it? Did it make you feel strong and reliable? Dependable?" Armand cocked his head waiting for the answer.

"Actually I felt cold and tired and hungry all the time there. I didn't have these feelings you're asking about."

"All the time you were in the Army?"

"No, when we were surrounded and trying to get back to our lines."

Armand looked at him for a long moment.

"All right," he said finally. "I'll get in touch with you at the corps tomorrow."

CHAPTER 22

"How'd it go?" Major Russell asked when Bill got back to the corps.

"Okay, I think. I'll know tomorrow."

"Guess who came in while you were gone?"

Bill squinted his eyes and looked out the window. "I can't guess—you'll have to tell me."

"Wayne Turner. He's in the kitchen."

His head plopped forward and he blurted, "Wayne Turner?"

Bill wasn't sure he would have recognized Wayne. He was huge—had to be 300, 350 pounds.

"Hello, Bill," Wayne said, his smile wide as a river. He was seated, an empty plate in front of him, holding a cup of coffee. The grin on his face was welcoming. "Do I need to stand up and salute?"

"No, we don't salute in here," Bill said reaching down and hugging his gigantic shoulders. My God it's good to see you."

"All of me?"

Bill smiled. "There is a lot of you."

"After the Bulge I never wanted to be without food again. And you know what?

"You haven't," Bill answered. "Bet you're not as fast as you were," Bill said.

His eyes lit up and he smiled. "Faster than you'd think."

"What are you doing here?" Bill said.

"Construction. At least I was until the snow hit. It shut down the asphalt plant, so we're laid off for the winter."

"What brings you in here?"

Wayne gestured at the empty plate. "The food."

Major Russell poured a cup of coffee and set it down on the table. Bill looked around for something to eat and found some sourdough buns in the breadbox.

"Any more of those?" Wayne asked.

"They didn't give you enough supper?"

"I suppose to them it was plenty. I take a lot these days." He buttered the bun. "I've got diabetes. I need something all the time."

"Diabetes?"

Wayne patted his stomach. "Fat. To much fat—to much sugar."

"Why don't you cut down on it?"

"Ah—I like it too much." He bit off half the bun and chased it with a gulp of coffee. "What've you been doing?"

Bill gave him an abbreviated version that left out a lot of his activities with George, but covered his search for gold.

"Where you gonna live?" Wayne asked when he finished.

Bill shrugged. "I just got back."

"You could stay with us. We'll be needing some help on the rent."

"Who's us?"

"Me and a couple of guys from the crew. There's room." Wayne looked at him and smiled. "We'd keep your share low, 'cause you'd be on the couch."

"Sounds cozy," Bill said.

WAYNE OPENED THE DOOR. It wasn't like Ilene's place. Scattered clothing was on the back of the chair and couch, dirty dishes and pizza boxes on the table, newspapers on the floor. Wayne picked up a pair of socks and a shirt in front of the couch, then ran his meaty hand across the back, pushing everything into a pile which he threw on the floor in the hall.

"Sit down," he said with a wave toward the newly cleared couch.

Bill looked at his back walking toward the refrigerator. He was amazed at the thickness of him—twice as wide as he remembered. Wayne popped the caps on two beers and set one in front of

Bill. Then he lifted the bottle and drank half of it in one draught, belched, smiled, and launched himself onto the couch. It tilted toward his end.

"What do you weigh, Wayne?"

"I don't know. Say, 325 pounds . . . on a good day."

"What's a good day?"

"When I've got a case of beer to drink."

"A case?"

"You haven't touched your beer," Wayne gestured with his hand.

"How do you hold twenty-four beers?"

"It's kind of like chain-smoking." He smiled. "You drink one after the other until they're all gone. Drink up."

Bill hesitated. He'd had no alcohol for more than a month. He was clean, sober, working—on top of life for a change. He might just taste the beer. Just put the beer to his lips and take a couple of swallows. They slipped down easily. He ran his tongue around inside his mouth savoring the cold fresh taste. The beer hit his stomach and spread throughout his chest, pushing the gentle warm feeling upward.

God, how he'd missed that feeling.

The door flung open and two guys dressed in dirty Levi's, base-ball hats, and Carhart jackets walked into the room. They took one look at the beer in Wayne's hand and went straight to the refrigerator.

"For crying out loud, Wayne, you drank half of it!"

"And I'm just getting started." Wayne waved his beer at Bill. "Want you to meet Bill Williams. He and I won World War II sin-gle-handed. This is Dan and the ugly one is Chuck."

Dan nodded a greeting. "You order anything yet?"

"No," Wayne said.

Chuck went to the phone and ordered three large pizzas. He went out to the car and came back with two cases of beer.

"Ante-up time, guys. Twenty-five dollars for the beer and pizza divided by four is . . . is $6.25 apiece."

"Bill's my guest," Wayne said.

"Your share is $12.50, then."

Wayne pulled a twenty-dollar bill out of his shirt pocket.

"Ready for another?" he asked Bill.

Bill's bottle wasn't empty. He felt slightly disconnected and woozy. Must be because I'm tired.

"Yeah, I'll have another."

"Guys," Wayne said, "what would you say about Bill shacking up here a few days? He could sleep on the couch. He's getting a job at a hotel plus he's working for the Salvation Army corps."

"Okay by me," Dan said.

Chuck tipped his beer. "Me too."

"What would you say to $50 a month?" Wayne said.

Bill nodded. "That's fine." His eyelids were slowing and he felt good all over. He didn't want to move from the couch. By the time the pizza got there he was on his fourth beer.

THE MAJOR EYED BILL as he walked into the chapel. "Good morning."

"Morning, Major," Bill replied. "Can I get some coffee? Maybe a roll or some oatmeal to go with it?"

"You don't look too good," the Major said, his head tipped back.

"Ate something that didn't agree with me. Didn't sleep too well either."

"I see. Had breakfast?"

"Kinda. Two pieces of cold pizza," Bill said.

"That's not breakfast."

Bill patted his stomach. "Feels like concrete."

The Major poured two cups of coffee. Bill fixed a bowl of oatmeal. "I've got something to tell you," the Major said.

"About what?"

"About what I'm going to tell you about . . . that's what."

"Thanks," Bill said.

"You're welcome. I had a talk with Armand about a job for you at his hotel." He's offered four hours a night, all your meals and $10 a shift until you both see how it is working. If you both like it, he is prepared to give you longer hours and more pay."

"How long would that take?"

The Major shook his head. "Don't know. Depends on how you do."

He tucked his chin into his chest and sorted out his next words. It took him longer because he added a short prayer that what he was about to say would be received in the right way. .

"You've told me about your work on the riverboat and with the packer on the AlCan and the army. You've told me some stories about Arctic Village. What I don't know is . . . what is Bill Williams' plan for the rest of his life? What plans . . . what ideas . . . where is he going . . . and how is he going to get there?"

He scratched his chin. "A reputable businessman is willing to take a chance on you and provide you with some of the basic needs of life. No more scrounging food at various charities. No more sleeping in basements, alleys, or wherever night finds you. We can get you suitable clothes to do your work and after a short time, you will be working forty hours a week, getting decent pay, and be a productive citizen. And . . . you can help me move others along that same path. Once others see you have made it back into the mainstream, they'll be more motivated to try. This is your big chance Bill . . . and one for me too?"

Bill's stomach turned over. If it wasn't Verda wanting him to find the gold or Carl telling him he couldn't drive the dogs it was the major finding him a job. He let out his breath and sat for a moment in complete silence, complete resignation, complete understanding that there was a lot of life ahead of him and he did have a choice. The major was right. Right then, giving up drinking and cold pizza was not that difficult.

"What do I need to do?" Bill said.

The major beamed. "You'll do it?"

Bill nodded. "I hope your faith in me is justified."

"Great Glory in the morning."

"Is this a big deal for you?" Bill asked.

Major Russell put his arm around Bill's shoulder. "Bill, this is one of those days when God is in his heavens and all is right with the world."

"Sounds fair to me," Bill said.

"Indeed it is."

BILL HAD HIS PANTS half on when Wayne opened the door and proceeded to the refrigerator with a case of beer hanging from his right hand.

"New clothes?" he asked.

"Stuff for the hotel work," Bill said.

"Want a beer?"

"Naw . . . I'm headed to work," Bill said.

He tried on the shirts and finally put together a reasonable outfit.

"Hey Wayne, how long do you think it will take me to walk to Fourth and C Street?"

"If you were fast like me, take you fifteen minutes. You . . . maybe a half- hour."

"Did you always win the liar's contest on the reservation?"

"When I was sober." He handed Bill a beer. "One of the five basic food groups."

Bill looked at the beer in Wayne's giant hand. "Around here it sure is."

"If we were in California, returning our empties would be a major source of income. Too bad they don't pay for them up here."

"You didn't hear me. I said no."

"No?"

"I'm going to work."

IT TOOK BILL thirty-five minutes to walk to the Lane Hotel. It was cold, but the snow that had dusted the streets earlier in the week was gone. He reported to the hotel manager, whose nametag identified him as "Rodney, Mgr."

"So you're our new night clerk?" Rodney said.

"Yes, sir."

"Oh, you don't need to 'sir' me. Please call me Rodney, everyone else does. Let me show you your duties and then if you have any questions I'll try and answer them. Goodness knows it doesn't take a college graduate to do this job." When he led Bill behind the counter, he glanced at his clothes.

"You look fine," he said. "Are those clothes new?"

Bill thought a second. "They are to me."

"Well, they look good on you. Clothes make the man, I always say." Rodney took the better part of thirty minutes to explain everything to him. During that time the phone didn't ring and nobody came into the lobby. It looked to Bill like he would have time on his hands.

"I leave at ten and the other night clerk comes in at midnight, when you can leave," Rodney said. "If you need me, just push this button right here, which rings in my office, and I'll come running out. You think you have everything? Good. Nice meeting you, Bill. Welcome to the Lane."

WAYNE WAS ALONE AND had a beer in his hand watching the Tonight Show when Bill got back to the apartment.

Wayne looked up. "How'd it go?"

"Okay. The manager's a little weird."

Wayne grunted and returned to the show. Bill got ready for bed.

"Want a beer?" Wayne asked.

Bill pointed at the beer in Wayne's hand. "That can't be good for your diabetes."

"It isn't."

"Why do you keep drinking them then?"

"I'm gonna die of something, just as well be diabetes as anything else. We could of been killed in Germany but we weren't."

"You take anything for it?" Bill asked.

"I'm supposed to give myself shots every day and check my blood sugar."

"I haven't seen you do that."

"I don't do it very often. It's a pain in the ass to stick a needle in yourself all the time. I don't notice any difference if I do or don't. You want a beer or don't ya?"

Bill knew it wouldn't be just one. "No thanks," he said. "I'm tired, I'm going to bed."

"Will the TV keep you awake?"

"Did the German shelling keep me awake?"

He tried to get comfortable on the couch, but sleep alluded him. It wasn't the TV set, it was the thought of the beer he now wished he hadn't turned down. And Wayne was making strange noises. His breathing was strange—shallow and wheezy. Bill got up and turned on the lamp. Wayne was asleep in the chair. His skin was gray, the breath from his nose and mouth strained, pushed, like air coming out of a bicycle tire.

Bill shook him. "You okay?"

Wayne opened his eyes and nodded. Bill sat down on the couch, hands clenched, and watched him fall back to sleep. He stared at the back of Wayne's head, his eyes following the rolls of fat bulging under his ears reaching down to touch his shoulders. Had it been that long ago they escaped the war and sat on the banks of the Rhine toasting VE day?

Bill listened to his breathing, a raspy gargle followed by an intense effort to bring in air. Bill shook him by the shoulder.

"You're not looking good. I think I should call the doctor."

Wayne shook his head. "I'll be all right. I've been here before."

"Well, holler if you need me." He lay back down on the couch.

At 3:30 Dan and Chuck came in with a woman they were holding up between them. Dan held her while Chuck opened the refrigerator door, took out three beers, and headed for the bedroom. Bill went over to Wayne's chair.

Wayne was ashen gray and wheezing—Bill felt his neck for a pulse. It seemed awfully slow. There was a medical kit on the table Bill hadn't seen before. It contained a hypodermic needle, some vials and some cotton balls. He could see a small puncture in Wayne's left arm.

Bill didn't know what time the girl was ushered out of the apartment, but he heard Chuck telling a taxi driver where to take her. At first light he checked on Wayne. His breaths were shallow and slow, and as far as Bill could tell, he hadn't moved a muscle since 3:30 a.m.

Dan and Chuck were in bed. Bill was too worried about Wayne to sleep, so he dressed and went out for a walk. The dawn air was brisk. In the trickle of traffic making its way into town a police car pulled up next to the sidewalk and stopped.

"Hello, Bill," Patrolman Pat said.

"Hello yourself," Bill said.

"What are you doing out this early?"

Bill shook his head. "Couldn't sleep. Got a sick friend. You know Wayne Turner from the Corps?"

"No."

"He and I were in the war together. He's asleep in a chair, but something's wrong with him and I don't know whether to call the doctor or not."

"You want me to check on him?" Pat said.

"Would you?"

"Tell me where."

When they got to the apartment, Pat squeezed Wayne's arm gently, then shook it. Wayne didn't respond. Pat grabbed his hand and lifted the arm, then let it drop. It flopped and stayed loose. He lifted Wayne's eyelid with his thumb but there was no response.

"This man's got a problem. Call 911."

Pat gave Bill a ride to the hospital. "I gotta finish my shift. I'll be back around 8:30 and see how things are going."

"Thanks, Pat."

A MAN IN GREEN scrubs came out into the waiting room and removed his mask.

"I'm Dr. Bollack. Do you have any idea how much insulin Mr. Turner gave himself?"

"No, I woke up and he was slumped in his chair."

"His sugar count is way off—below thirty—he's in a coma. Right now it's touch and go. We're doing everything we can, but diabetic shock from too much insulin can be fatal. I'll have someone come tell you if there's any change."

"I'll be here."

Bill sat down. He thought not of the 350-pound Wayne, but the strong muscular Shoshone he'd met in basic training whose uniform and shoes didn't fit. The soldier he'd escaped the Snow Eifel with. He should have he'd kept better tabs on him. After the war it seemed like they both were going to live forever.

The clock read 8:00 a.m. Breakfast would be cooking at the corps, and Major Russell would be limbering up his fingers on the piano urging the early stages of arthritis out of them for the morning sing. He'd have his head tilted back, eyes partially closed as he reached for a note that was too high for that early in the morning. A prayer session in song, that's how he'd explained it to Bill.

How was he ever going to justify the major's faith in him?

Dr. Bollack came through the swinging doors, tired, depressed, his forehead wrapped in a frown and stood in front of him.

There was no preamble. "We lost him," he said. "I'm very sorry."

Bill stammered. "What do you mean, lost him?"

"He died."

Bill felt like he had been punched in the stomach. "But there was nothing wrong with him."

"His sugar count was terminally low. His heart stopped in the coma."

Heart stopped. That giant heart that had gotten them off the snowy ridges, across rivers, through towns, back to the Rhine—had stopped.

He sat without moving. The doctor laid a hand on his shoulder. "I'm very sorry." His green covered feet turned and slowly disappeared through the doorway.

The click of boots brought his head up. He saw Patrolman Pat and the clock at the same time. It was 8:35 a.m. Pat juggled his body into the chair next to him.

"He's gone, Pat."

"I heard. I'm really sorry. Didn't know you two had been friends so long."

"Didn't seem like it. Seems like it was just yesterday." Tears welled in his eyes as he turned and looked at Pat. "Were does the time go?"

Pat turned his hat in his hands. "It goes while you're living it."

Bill blinked his eyes. "I need to walk."

"You want a ride back to the apartment?"

"No."

"I'm sure sorry about your friend."

Bill nodded. Seemed to him like he was always nodding. Like he'd been nodding since he was born. Agreeing with anything and everything that happened—good old Bill, you can always get a nod out of him. Pat was going home. Where was he going?

He walked outside. The upper rims of the Chugach Mountains were etched in the early morning light. He stuffed his hands in the pockets of his jacket and walked toward the Corps. Maybe he could help out around the kitchen, sing a song with the major, catch a prayer that would mean something to him. The cold air made his eyes water and he blinked it away. He wanted to remember this day as long as he lived. At the Corps, Bill pitched in setting the morning tables. It was oatmeal and toast to settle down the anxiety that passed for normal in the early morning of a fall day when the autumn sun still radiated enough warmth to let a street person survive in an alley where it shined for a few hours.

Major Russell walked in and put a hand on Bill's shoulder. "I'm very sad about Wayne. Pat phoned me."

Major Russell was struggling for his next words while Bill stood, napkins and flatware in his hands, feeling tears sting his eyes. He had cried at Coric's death somewhere in Belgium in a ditch in the early morning. Now he cried for Wayne's death, as senseless as Coric's.

"Would you like to have the funeral here?" Major Russell said.

Bill nodded. He did not trust his voice.

"I'll make the arrangements."

BACK AT THE APARTMENT, he looked at the refrigerator and thought how it would feel to have a beer—a lot of beers.

He decided against it. He'd lost the best friend he ever had today, and he wanted to be there for the occasion.

CHAPTER 23

BILL WAS FIFTEEN MINUTES early for work. A low level of noise greeted him as he entered the hotel, and a quick glance confirmed that the restaurant was full. He saw Harvey Munn sitting at the bar drinking his usual Southern Comfort and Rumplemintz shooters. He checked in at the desk, then took a quick tour of the restaurant and bar.

Glass in hand, Harvey looked him over. "You look down in the mouth," he said.

"Hello, Mr. Munn." Armand had instructed him how to greet the regulars.

Harvey polished off the drink and set his empty glass down with a satisfied smile.

"Buy you a drink," he said.

"Thank you but I can't drink on duty."

Harvey looked at the clock. "You don't start for another ten minutes. Come on, have a drink with me. You ever tasted one of these shooters?"

"No."

"Then join me. What do you want to celebrate today?"

"We could drink to my friend," Bill said.

"Sure. Who's that?"

"Private Wayne Turner."

The bartender glanced around to see if Armand was in any of the booths, then set up another shooter glass and poured the mix.

"To Private Wayne Turner," Harvey said. "To his good health."

"To his good health." He swallowed quickly, the alcohol warming everything in his body. He shuddered and his eyes closed. When he opened them, Harvey was smiling.

"Have another," he said.

Bill held up his hand. "No. No thank you."

"Did you like that?"

"It's okay."

"Got a kick to it, doesn't it?"

Bill nodded, thanked Harvey, and walked out of the bar. He felt warm and at ease. So he and Harvey had drunk to a dead man's health—well, Wayne would have understood it and joined in if he could have.

AT MIDNIGHT WHEN HIS shift was over Bill walked into the bar and took a stool.

A voice behind him said, "I see you're feeling better."

It was George Norton.

Bill turned. "Better than what?"

"Better than you deserve."

"Since when did you care?"

"Since the day you walked out on me," George said, taking the barstool next to him.

"I walked out on you? You told me to leave."

"I didn't mean forever. You work here?"

"I'm the night clerk."

Harvey Munn slid over one stool.

"Hi, Harvey," George said. "Got a drink for an old buddy?"

"Hullo, George," Harvey said. "You like these?" He held up his shooter.

"Hell, yeah—love 'em."

"You two know each other?" Bill asked.

Harvey smiled and held his glass up. "Do you want to drink to anybody?" "To absent friends," George said.

Harvey turned to Bill. "How about you?"

"Okay—just one more," Bill said.

BILL LOOKED UP AND down the street. It was cold, but there was no snow. He glanced up at the streetlight, almost fell over, and spread his arms out to balance himself.

George started walking, and Bill followed. They weaved their way past Reeves Aleutian Airlines office, where the security lights showed the trophies inside. George stopped and looked at the wolf hide on the wall.

"We could get a lot of money for that wolf," he said.

Bill focused on it.

"What do you think?" George said. "Three hundred dollars—maybe more?"

"All black?" Bill said. "Maybe four hundred."

George walked to the alley. "Get in here." He pulled Bill out of the light. The back door was locked, bars bolted over the glass. George kicked the door. The door didn't give, but his kick knocked him back in the alley. He ran at the door and kicked it again. He stood and looked at the door for a minute, then walked past Bill and into the street.

"I know where there's an easy one," George said. He walked several blocks with Bill trailing behind until they stopped outside a medical clinic.

"There's one on the wall in there," George said.

Bill looked but couldn't see anything. "How do you know?"

"Been in there couple times."

George went to the back of the building and tried the windows. One slid open.

"Bill?" he whispered. "Boost me up."

"What're you going in there for?"

"Get the hide. Boost me up." He lifted one foot.

Bill shoved on his leg and George slid over the sill into the room. The alarm erupted in the freezing night. Lights flashed. In the sporadic light Bill saw George at the window, then a furry hide hit him in the face. He fell to the ground.

George giggled. He wrapped the hide around his middle, zipped his coat, and pulled the wolf tail out under his chin. Then he bent over like a bear and walked down the alley. Bill followed. At the corner they turned around and looked at the lights flashing out of the windows. The alarm was piercing. A police car sped by, lights flashing, and turned into the clinic parking lot.

"YOU SELL THE HIDE," George said the next morning. "Bring back the money and I'll buy the whiskey."

Bill sat up. He felt dizzy. "I don't know where to sell it."

"I took it. You find some place to sell it. If I sell it you ain't getting any of the money or the whiskey."

Bill ran a hand over his head. He squinted at the bare daylight out the dingy windows. George's shack hadn't been cleaned since the last time Bill saw it. He lay back down and held his throbbing head in his hands.

"Get the hell outta that bed and go sell this hide!" George said.

Bill turned his back to him.

George grabbed the hide and lashed it across his back. He took hold of Bill, rolled him on his back, and pressed the hide against his face.

"Damn you—you get up and sell this hide!"

BILL WONDERED IF HE could whip him. He was younger. He was hung over, but George was still drunk. He should be able to do it. The major would be expecting him at the Corps, and he had to get to the hotel later. The way he felt, the last thing he wanted to do was try selling a hide. He got up on his knees, and George kicked him in the shoulder.

"Hey."

"Get up, dammit. Go sell that hide."

Bill threw the blankets in a pile on the bed and jumped up. He swung at George and missed.

"I'm not gonna go peddle that hide. We shouldn't of taken it," Bill said.

"Well—we did take it and I want the money for whiskey." George walked away then turned suddenly. "I want it now."

ANCHORAGE POLICE DEPT. REPORT

Case #73-4501
Name: Bill Williams
Date of Birth: 10/10/25

Date: 10/11/73
Location: 130 W. 4th Ave.
Arresting Officer: Lt. Phil Brender

Officer's Narrative of Event:
David Green Furs called stating an individual was attempting to sell them a black wolf hide that appeared to have been torn from a wall mount. I responded at 1105 hrs. to find suspect with black wolf hide in hand and asking $350 for it. I asked to see it and he handed it to me. I questioned him as to where he got it and he was very vague. I arrested him on suspicion of burglary, impounded the hide, and transported him to Anchorage jail for booking.

Lt. Phil Brender   10/01/73
_____   _____
Officer's Signature   Date

Badge No. 1210
Time: 1152 hrs

Bill jerked the door open with one hand. The other held his shirt and jacket. The cold stabbed his bare torso causing him to shiver. He fumbled with his clothing, turning the shirt over in his hands until he found the buttons.

"I'm not gonna do it!" he yelled.

George stuffed the hide into an old rice sack. "Here," he threw it at him. "And don't by gawd come back until you've got money for it." He slammed the door.

The chill air drove through Bill. He stood like a frozen statue devoid of thought or feeling as he looked at the sack on the ground. He had no idea where to sell a stolen wolf hide.

GEORGE GRABBED HIM FROM behind just as he reached the top step. He put his hands inside Bill's belt and threw him in a crazy arc down the stairs to the sidewalk. Bill's head hit the concrete. He couldn't get his eyes to work right. His head felt like it was on at an angle.

He felt in his jacket for the bottle just as George kicked him in the face. He had never been hit that hard. He knew through the haze that he was busting up. Blood was running down his throat, and George was still kicking him. His chest couldn't expand and take in air.

Christ, oh Lord—George's gonna kill me. Kick me to death.

He covered his face with his hands and felt a kick in his back. He heard the bottle clink on the concrete. He reached inside his coat, found it, and rolled it down the sidewalk toward the building. George grunted and stumbled after the bottle.

In his forty-seven years Bill had never failed to get up when he wanted to. Now everything in him pulsed and ached; his blood and urine were draining on the sidewalk, and he was telling his body to get up, and it couldn't make it.

Bill blinked his eyes but couldn't clear his vision. He could just make out George looming over him when he was kicked again. The blow struck him at the base of the skull. He felt no pain—only the jerk of his head. My God, I'm going to be paralyzed. I'm going to be a damn vegetable.

"DON'T MOVE HIM. Call the paramedics, he's hurt bad. Bill, you dumb shit, how'd you get in a mess like this?"

Inside his head Bill could hear Patrolman Pat talking, but he had trouble making sense of the words. He stared at the uniform and badge and blinked his eyes. At least George hadn't kicked his eyes out; he could still see something.

"You just stay still," Pat said. "Help's on the way."

IT HURT SO MUCH. The paramedics arrived and when they reached to move him he tried to say "don't, don't, don't let them touch me it hurts too much," but no sound fought its way through his spasming lungs and broken ribs. He felt cool just before he passed out—like he used to feel with the first wind off the river signaling the end of summer when he could smell the drying fish.

A man in a white coat with a clipboard reached for Bill's arm.

"Hey, fella . . . ."

Bill opened one eye a little. It was just a slit in the swollen flesh around it.

"Hey fella—uh . . ." The orderly looked down at his clipboard. " . . . Bill Williams. We need to get some info on you. Can you talk to me a minute?"

Bill tried to talk. His lips, his throat, wouldn't let him. He nodded.

"Okay," the guy said, "let's see . . . we got your name—Bill Williams, right?" Bill nodded again.

"This will only take a few minutes," the orderly said. "Let's see . . . mother's name? That's her maiden name."

Bill couldn't nod any more. He took a short breath, let it out, and managed to groan her name. He tried to move. It seemed to him that all of his bones had sunk to the bottom of his body and he was lying on them with the muscle and fat piled on top.

"Ah . . . the last question," the cheery orderly said, "if there should be an untimely demise, what do you wish done with your remains?"

Bill opened and closed his lips to get them flexible enough to talk. "What do you mean?"

The orderly paused a minute and then said, "If you die while you're here, what do you want us to do with your body?" His brow furrowed as he looked out the window. "I'm sorry, but it's something we must know while you're still lucid."

Somehow, through his cracked lips, he smiled. "Well," he started, "I want my head mounted . . . hang it on the wall in the Union Club. The rest . . . feed to the wolves."

The orderly threw his hands up. "I can't make any sense with this guy."

A shadowy figure backed away from the bed, then the overhead lights went out. The figure moved back to the bed.

"Bill? It's Carl."

Bill didn't move but his lips parted.

"Carl?"

Carl nodded. A woman touched him.

"He can't see you nodding," she whispered to Carl.

Bill twisted his head. "Ilene?"

"No . . . ."

Bill opened one eye. "I hate for you . . . see me like this."

The woman nudged Carl.

"How are you, Bill?" he said.

"You see how I am. Drunk. Hurt." He breathed heavily several times, and caught the putrid smell of his lungs and mouth. "What you doing here?"

"Came to see you. We're concerned about all this. This wolf hide business and fighting. It all comes from the drinking . . . doesn't it?"

Bill turned away.

"You like this kinda thing? Drunk. Fights? You think this is some way to live your life?" Carl swallowed. He stared at the figure wrapped in cotton gauze. "What are you going to do with your life?"

Bill wet his lips. "I didn't do so well looking for gold."

Carl shrugged. "There's lots of other things to do besides that."

"I can't seem to get out of this. I try. I get one drink and I can't stop. I just can't stop." He tried to mop his eye where the tears collected.

Carl clung to the side of the bed and looked out the window at the leaves dropping and whirling in the wind. "Bill I'm concerned about you. What can I do?"

"Why're you in town?" Bill said.

"I came in to sell some stuff to pay for dog food. I've got a real good team, Bill. I think it can win the Iditarod."

Bill didn't respond. He tried to focus on the woman with his open eye.

"Who's she?"

Carl looked at her. " Carolee."

The woman moved closed to Bill. "Hi, Bill. I'm a friend of your brothers. I know Patrolman Pat and Major Russell. That's how we tracked you down."

Bill tried to clear his throat. "Give me a sip of water?"

"Sure." Carolee eased the straw into Bill's mouth. He kept his open eye fixed on her while he sucked some water, swallowed, and coughed. She held the straw and he drank again, his eye still on her.

Good-looking lady. Carl always gets the good-looking ones.

Carl turned from the window. "Bill, why don't you come home? You're hurt real bad—I don't know what all you've been doing in here, but it can't have been good. I'm worried about you, little brother. You gotta quit this drinking business and settle down."

"Where's George Norton?" Bill asked.

"I don't know any George Norton," Carl said.

Bill moved his hands, worked his fingers into a fist, then unclenched them and spread them in front of his eyes. He reached for his head, felt the bandage, and traced it to his left ear. He touched his face and his chest and ran his fingers up and down over his ribs.

"I think I'm gonna live," he said. "Didn't think I'd be alive when I woke up." He caught his breath and stiffened. "This is some pain. Carl—remember when your sled hit the tree—knocked you out?"

"Sure."

"Did it hurt when you woke up?"

"I don't remember."

"I remember Dad . . . Uncle Charlie looking down at you like you were dead, and then you came around and everybody laughed"

"Yeah, they did."

"I need somebody laughing now so I can get well."

"I don't feel like laughing," Carl said.

"Ask the lady to laugh for you."

"She doesn't want to laugh either." Carolee looked down at the polished linoleum floor.

Bill took a deep breath and exhaled. "Oh boy, that hurt."

"You're gonna hurt for a while."

"I've hurt before. It'll hurt worse when it's healing. I never felt it when the shrapnel hit me—but I felt it for days after that."

Carl paced around the room. "You want us to stay?"

"I'm tired. I gotta sleep."

"We'll see you in the morning then," Carl said moving toward the door.

Bill looked at Carolee. "Thank you."

Carolee smiled and touched his hand. "You're welcome. Hope you feel better tomorrow. We'll drop in and see you then."

Bill closed his eyes and nodded.

She turned, but Carl wasn't in the room. She walked out into the hall and partially closed the door.

The orderly was passing by. "Mount his head? I swear I never heard such a crazy thing. And feed his body to the wolves—like we've got wolves to feed in Anchorage."

ANCHORAGE POLICE DEPT. REPORT

Case #73-3416
Name: Bill Williams
Date of Birth: 10/10/25

Date: 10/05/73
Location: G St., between 4 & 5th Ave.
Arresting Officer: Sgt. Pat Dugan

Officer's Narrative of Event:
Unidentified caller reported a fight on G Street
between 4th and 5th Avenue. I responded with
my trainee at 1906 hours, to find suspect down
and out on sidewalk. Suspect was injured and
we called for transport to Alaska Native
Hospital. He was transported and checked in
to Dr. Jordan at 1938 hours.

Sgt. Pat Dugan   10/05/73
Officer's Signature   Date

Badge No. 1576
Time: 1945 hrs

CHAPTER 24

BILL WAS ALMOST SOBER. He didn't intend to stay that way. He looked at the people in the room with him—they were all losers. They reeked, some had teeth rotting out of their heads, and the clothes they wore were held together by twine and safety pins with an occasional piece of duct tape covering a hole. He stood up. He wobbled but he could make it up the stairs. This was no place for him to be.

He got a firm hold on the banister and pulled himself up. There was a day when he would have run up the stairs. He could hear voices as he neared the top.

Major Russell was speaking. "They need a place to go, to be safe . . . ."

"Look, Major," another voice said, "feeding them and praying with them is one thing, but putting them up simply prolongs their misery and actually enables them to maintain their life style."

Bill stopped on the landing. They were on the outside of the door.

"They don't have a life style," the major said. "You talk as if they plan their lives. This isn't a plan, this is the failure to plan . . . ."

"I understand your feelings, but big cities have tried it and sleep-off places simply remove the misery from the street life. They eat here, then they go on the street and beg the price of a bottle, get drunk, show up here in a warm place, spend the night, and start out again after breakfast. We think it ought to be closed down."

"Do you think this is a good place to spend a night? Have you ever been down there with them? I can't believe you and the committee think it's enabling them. If you saw it . . . ."

Bill opened the door and they both stared at him. Major Russell looked distressed. The other man in suit and tie had a hand on his hip and was pointing at the major, about to say something.

"Hello Bill," the major said.

Bill nodded, and walked toward the kitchen. There was no food on the tables, and someone he didn't know was putting down paper plates and napkins. He went into the lounge, collapsed into a chair, and stared out the window into the street. He had to get something in his stomach pretty soon.

A woman walked through the door and approached the front counter. She stood with her back to him, but then she turned her head slightly and he could see her profile.

It was Ilene.

Bill got up and ran out the front door. He hit the sidewalk and turned right. His shoes were untied, but he thought they would stay on until he got away. Bile came up in his mouth and he spit it out between breaths. He turned into the alley and slowed to a fast walk. At the other end he crossed the street to the library.

When he got to the back of the stacks he found George asleep with a book under his head. The sound of Bill's rapid breathing woke him.

"What you all heated up about?"

"I need a drink," Bill said.

"Who doesn't?"

"You got any?"

"Would I be here if I had any?"

Bill pulled a chair out and saw the librarian look down the aisle. He grabbed a book off the shelves and opened it.

George sat up. "You sure know how to ruin a man's sleep."

Bill put the book down. "I either need to get a drink or I need to quit drinking."

"Yeah. I've heard that before."

Bill didn't respond. The hotel bar was out. Armand had not allowed him to come back in there after that disastrous night. He could beg for the price of a bottle, but Ilene might see him. His stomach needed whiskey . . . then he'd be okay.

NEXT MORNING BILL STOOD facing Ilene in the hallway of the Salvation Army corps. In the gray light, he looked tall and strong. The light faded his features and softened the effects of whiskey. He was shaved and combed.

Major Russell turned to Ilene. "He came in last night. This morning we helped him a little—he cleans up pretty good, doesn't he?"

Ilene walked over to him. "Bill, will you take a ride with me?"

He nodded and followed her out.

ILENE PARKED THE PICKUP truck and turned to face him.

"Bill, I don't have much time to say this, so I want you to listen real good. I know you're feeling sick—and we both know why. Only you know why you ran from me yesterday." She took a deep breath but it didn't disguise the quiver of her lips. "I came to tell you that Carl is dead." She waited for his reaction.

He felt like he'd been hit in the face.

She continued. "He slammed into a tree while he was training the dogs. I want you to take his team and run the Iditarod."

"Hit a tree? Carl hit a tree?" Bill looked out the pickup window. "He did that once when we were kids." He gripped the handle over the door until his knuckles turned white. He turned to Ilene. "Where? How?"

"At the bend close to the Old Ones cabin. Looked like the sled skidded and launched him into a big cottonwood." She looked down at her hand. "We'll never know for sure, of course—but that's the way it looked to the troopers."

Bill tried to recall every corner of that trail. He had walked it, what now—some thirty years ago. For Carl to die out there alone. . . . He probably froze too.

"The dogs?" he said.

"A trapper heard them howling and picked them up." She had an expectant look on her face.

He shook his head slowly and his shoulders sagged. "My God." He looked at his hands hung on his thighs and moved his eyes along the veins from his wrist to his fingers, like highways to nowhere. He felt exhausted, beaten, robbed of vitality. The unexpected had cleaned him out.

Maybe I can do this for Carl. I don't know if I can remember enough of it to make sense, but I can start the race. Give Carl's dogs a start anyway. If the old Bishop was right, Carl could see that I did that much.

"And you want me to drive his dogs? He wouldn't even let me do that when he was alive."

Ilene sat on the seat with her back against the door and looked across the pickup cab at him.

"Take his team . . . ."

Bill shook his head. "He wouldn't want me to do it." Tears were spilling down his cheeks.

"He would have wanted you to do it—you know he would. He was so happy when you ran the young dogs. He said several times after you left that you were a natural dog driver."

They sat silent for a minute, Bill staring at the second hand on the dashboard clock.

"Ilene . . . the Iditarod's a thousand miles. I can't do that. Look at me! Will you for God's sake look at me?"

She took out a Kleenex and wiped tears from his cheeks. "You walked to Venetie, didn't you? You helped build the AlCan Highway, didn't you? You led your squad out of the war, didn't you?"

"Ilene, Ilene—that was years ago. I can barely stand up. I'm not sure what day it is and I'm sick . . . "

"You're not sick—you're hung over. Hung over will wear off while you're on the trail. You know how Carl trained the dogs and you'll remember how to drive them." She turned the ignition key on. "The race is starting in an hour."

She maneuvered the pickup into the traffic.

Traffic was heavier now, and as they got closer to the stadium they could see the mushers' vehicles backed up and intermingled with the spectators trying to park.

Ilene pulled out the race bib.

"Here, put this on."

It wasn't the kind of thing that came easy right now, but he got the bib over his head with the drawstring dangling and sat humped over, staring at the traffic. There were choices. The pain behind his eyes would go away and then he could decide, but Ilene was asking him to decide right now. He closed his eyes and wished she hadn't asked. He was startled by her voice.

"Bill . . . what's to become of you?"

He stared at her. He didn't know the answer in the sense she meant the question, but he knew what was going to become of him right that moment. He grabbed the door handle and while the pickup was still moving jumped out and swung the door closed. He stumbled, put his hands out in front of him, then caught himself and didn't fall. He straightened up.

A line of pickups a block long was waiting to get in the gate. He stumbled along the snow-covered walk, catching himself several times from falling.

How the hell am I gonna do what Ilene is asking? Yeah . . . I remember dogs but a thousand miles . . . I can hardly walk.

When he looked up he wanted to see Carl standing there. It was a joke, wasn't it? To get him out of the drunk tank. *Carl . . . Carl . . . Carl. You were too good, too strong to die like that.*

He looked back at Ilene. Her eyes followed him and now he was thirty feet from the gate. He could hear conversations, laughter, dogs barking, smell the exhaust.

"Whoa there, fella," the gate guard hollered as he stuck out his arm.

Bill pointed to his bib. "My rig is back there."

"Where are your registration papers?"

"I don't know."

"Get me the papers and your sled and dogs, and you can get right to it."

Bill began walking back. Ilene was still about a block away.

Can I do it for you Carl? Can you see me doing it out there thinking about you, standing on your sled, driving your dogs? Ok… I'll do it for you. It'll be in memory of you. That's all I have to give you.

He started jogging, and the headache moved behind his eyes. He reached the pickup, pulled open the door, and stood on the running board.

"Registration papers?" he panted.

"They're in that folder."

He started jogging back down the sidewalk.

She parked and got out. When he saw her he straightened up and held his hand on his forehead. Each beat of his heart drove a spear through his brain.

She smiled and held out her clenched hand. "Here. Aspirin."

He opened his hand under hers and smiled back. "Got any whiskey to take these with?"

She pulled back her arm and doubled her fist.

"How about some water, then?"

She reached into the equipment bag, took out a bottle of almost frozen water, and handed it to him. It reminded him of the frozen canteens on the Snow Eifel.

The announcer called the first racer to the line.

Someone shouted, "Ilene!"

She turned to see Carolee waving from the mushers' gate. Ilene jogged off, and Bill hooked up the wheel dogs.

He hung the snow hook over the bumper of the pickup, then went to the front and pulled the towline taut. If his stomach would stop turning over and if he could get some food in it and if the aspirin would kill his headache and if he didn't die from the tomato and sauerkraut juice Major Russell had poured down him this morning . . . he just might make it out of this park.

The announcer' had a loud, clear voice.

"Number five, Joe Redington Sr., the Father of the Iditarod. Joe is from Knik and has two sons running the race with him this year. He's starting with a sixteen-dog team and that big black-headed lead dog is Feets. Give him a good round of applause, and Joe—we'll see you in Nome."

Carolee walked up and handed Bill a large bucket of Kentucky Fried Chicken.

"Eat some now, save some for later," she said.

"It'll freeze."

"So? Heat it up when you're cooking the dog food."

The announcer's voice demanded attention again. "Racer number nine, Tim White, hails from Taylor Falls, Minnesota. Tim has fourteen dogs. Tim, are your dogs used to these Alaskan temperatures? Well, he says they are and we wish him well. Tim White on his way to Nome."

Carl's dogs were harnessed, the sled packed. Bill took a look around, then inhaled, tucked his chin against his chest with his arms folded, and held the breath. The queasiness in his stomach and the headache made him weak, and he leaned against the pickup.

I am where I am because of what I am, and everything I've done has led to nothing. I am nothing—I have nothing. Here I am with twenty-five mushers who think they can make it. They don't have any doubts. They aren't sick. When Carl trained the dogs for this he must have thought he could not only make the distance but win the race. I have no hopes of winning—doubt I can make the thousand miles. But I can try.

He exhaled, pulled the hook off the bumper, and let Ilene and Carolee lead the dogs up to the starting point.

He was third in line. He set the snow hook and walked down the line, looking at the dogs. Ilene adjusted a harness on the right swing dog. Bill got back to the sled. They moved up to the on-deck position.

Carolee and Ilene were standing side by side, and Bill reached out his arms and touched each of their hands. There were a lot of unanswered questions in his mind, but these two people believed in him. He blinked several times to clear his eyes. He thought of words to say but nothing came out.

The team in front was tearing down the track, and the announcer's voice boomed out.

"The next racer is a substitute driver for Carl Williams of Arctic Village. Carl was killed in a tragic accident recently, and his brother Bill will be driving his team. Bill is wearing bib number fourteen and is running sixteen dogs. How about it, Bill, are you ready to go? Well, he's nodding. Let's give him a big hand as Bill Williams heads for Nome."

Ilene handed him the snow hook and he stuck it on the bag. He put a chicken leg in his mouth and stuffed the bucket under the tarp.

The announcer counted down. "Five...Four...Three...Two ...One! Bill Williams is on his way to Nome."

Bill whizzed past Carolee and Ilene, standing on either side of the dogs. He had never gone so fast on a dog sled, and his eyes watered so much he could hardly see the track. He tried to take a breath, but the chicken choked him. He spit it out when the lead dog turned on the first curve, and as the sled whipped around the turn, he lost his grip. He hit the ground hard and rolled. The breath was knocked out of him, he struggled to get air.

Major Russell emerged from the crowd along the trail, got his arms under him and helped him up. He was still gasping. A bystander had stopped the team and the Major led him to the sled. He grabbed the drive bow and the Major pulled the snow hook. He could hear the announcer saying ..." but he looks all right."

Major Russell leaned close to his head and whispered, "Good luck Bill and may God be with you."

Bill struggled to look behind him as the team bolted down the trail. The Major was waving.

The team ran hard until they approached the road crossing at Lake Otis Parkway.

"Whoa...whoa!"

He glanced down to find the brake pedal. He pressed it and looked up when the leaders started up the bank. He had his weight full on the brake as it caught a black spruce root. The brake snagged, and as the sled and the team slammed to a halt, Bill's feet flew off the runners, his hands left the drive bow, and he catapulted over the sled.

He lay there for a minute, then lifted his face out of the snow and got up on his hands and knees. The dogs were looking at him.

"Okay. Okay." Bill looked back at the dogs. "Let's pretend I'm just learning."

He pulled the sled back until the brake sprang up.

"Hyaaa!"

Rusty and Napoleon dug in. The sled rose over the edge of the bank, the tow line tightened, and the sled that Carl Williams had built skimmed along behind sixteen dogs going east out of town, heading for Nome, Alaska, 1050 miles to the northwest.

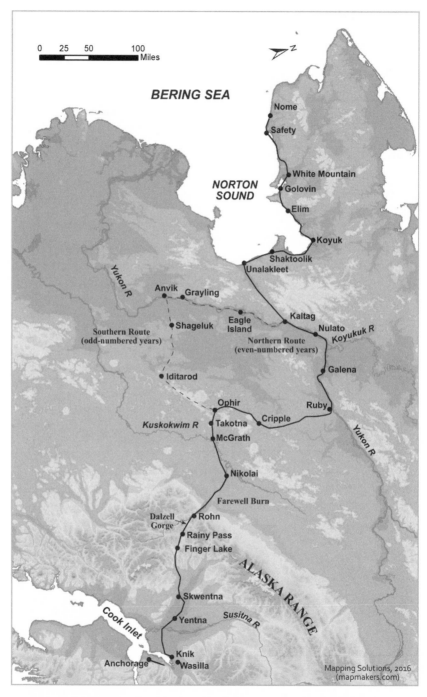

1973 Iditarod trail route from Anchorage to Nome, Alaska.

CHAPTER 25

THE DOGS HAD SLOWED down. They were moving, but the tug line was often slack. If they were his dogs he would know each of them, be able to tell right away which one was causing the problem and figure out how to fix it. But he didn't have enough miles with them to know what trouble they could cause or how to get them out of it.

Carl knew how to train dogs. He and Bill had learned the same things from their dad and Uncle Charlie, so at least these dogs would know what he meant when he spoke to them.

His stomach felt funny. It was always like that after the whiskey wore off. He inhaled and belched. The good feeling lasted a few seconds, then the queasiness started again. He needed whiskey to take care of it.

The leaders at the front of the team were forty feet away and Bill found it hard to concentrate, to keep his eyes focused on the backs of the dogs. He closed his eyes and felt the swampy feeling come over him again. That unglued, unhinged, swimmy feeling he always got.

Why would Ilene think I could do this? I'm gonna have to stop and throw up in a minute. If I make it to Knik it'll be okay—I can tell her I can't do it, it's too much to expect.

He went dog by dog until he found the one who was causing the problem with the tug line. That's what you did when you trained, but he hadn't trained these dogs, he didn't even know most of their names. Their names were on the harnesses—tonight he would look at them and get the names straight so he could talk to them tomorrow. What a hell of a thing to be driving dogs without even knowing all their names. He reached for the whip.

The whip cracked and every dog in the team glanced over its shoulder, tongues flogging the air. The man had made his move. They could ignore the man—they had before and they could again—but when the whip snapped over their heads the second time, the message was clear.

In his present state he couldn't tell which ones buckled down or exactly when, but the sled jerked, then smoothed out, and for the first time the tug line was taut. They pulled like a team. For twenty minutes they ran that way, ran like it was fun, like they enjoyed doing it, like they were bred to do it.

When they got to the Matanuska River, Bill stopped on the bridge and took a pull from his water bottle. When the water hit his stomach he felt woozy and his head pounded. Suddenly he was sick and vomited hard, bent over, hanging on to the drive bow to stay upright. The dogs looked at him. He kicked snow over the vomit and wiped his mouth.

"What're you looking at?"

Most of the dogs turned their heads and looked down trail. Bill wondered if he could stay on the runners if they ran over the bridge. He had to chance it.

"Hyaaa!"

The leaders, more cautious than he thought, took the trail across the bridge at an easy trot. Halfway across he heard a voice and looked behind him. The next two teams were in view, one already onto the bridge. He closed his eyes for a few seconds and a wave of nausea swept over him.

He could hear the dogs panting behind him and the musher's brake dragging, then the musher yelled, "Trail!"

There's no place to pass here. What's got into the guy?

He looked across the bridge. Fifty yards to go. He could make that. He let them run. "Hike!"

Across the bridge he heard it again. "Trail!"

"Gee! Gee!" Bill hollered.

Napoleon leaned to the right and Rusty turned with him. They pulled off the trail into six inches of new snow and slowed down. When the team passed, Bill searched for the face of the musher, but it was hidden in his parka. He looked back to see the second team only fifty yards behind. He kept the team in the soft snow until they passed.

Suddenly Rusty and Napoleon yelped and leapt forward, straining at their harnesses. They pulled the others along, some jerking, some leaning hard into the harness, pulling the towline straight as an arrow. Bill almost fell off the sled as it slipped in beside the passing team.

One of the passing dogs turned her head and nipped at Rusty, and that was all it took. Rusty and Napoleon jumped on her. The dogs tangled and ran into a tight circle that brought both teams to a stop.

The mushers grabbed the tug lines and pulled. Bill lifted a dog in each hand while it snarled and pawed at the power that had taken it out of the fight. The other musher got his whip, and the crack was like nothing Bill had ever heard before. It stopped all the dogs but Rusty and the female. Rusty mounted her, then the other dogs lost interest and spent the time grooming themselves.

Bill looked at the other musher standing by his sled, whip in hand.

"Dammit!" the musher yelled.

Bill just looked at him. Heart pounding, he tried to get enough air in his lungs. He sat down on his sled. It would take twenty minutes for the dogs to uncouple, and he needed the rest. His insides were boiling, and he felt unsteady and irritable.

He got up and walked around his sled.

"Sorry about that," he said to the musher.

"Yeah. She just came in heat this morning and I didn't have another dog to switch with her. She's rejected all my males today, I thought we might make it to Rainy Pass without trouble."

Bill stuck out his hand. "I'm Bill Williams and I'm sicker than a dog."

"Roger Stanley—from Willow. Why're you sick?"

"A touch of the flu, I guess." He bent over, a dry heave following up from his stomach.

"Can I give you anything?"

"Got any whiskey?"

"Don't carry it. You'll dehydrate and die out here on that stuff."

Bill sighed. "There're times when I'm willing to die for it."

"That really why you're sick?"

"Hung over. Hung clear over all the way." Another dry heave hit him.

"Glad you took this so good-natured," Roger said. "You need anything along the way, let me know. Your dogs look better than mine, you'll probably be ahead of me all the way. Anything I can do for you?"

"No," Bill said. "But if you find my team and I'm dead on the sled, kindly bury me along the trail and let the dogs go to Nome."

Roger laughed. "Done deal." He turned to his team. "Hike! Hike!"

Since Bill had arrived first he should have left first, but it didn't bother him. There was more than a thousand miles to go, and he wasn't sure anyone could make it. The last time anybody drove to Nome, twenty-four mushers had met in various places and driven a hundred miles apiece to get the diphtheria serum there. No one had ever done it as a race with every team going the full distance.

He lined out his team.

"Hyaaa!"

He drew in a deep breath and looked down the trail as far as he could see, past Roger Stanley to where the trail bent left toward Goose Bay and Knik.

Once at Knik Lake he stopped to get a snack for the dogs and himself. Roger was stopped at the tree line doing the same.

Stored in the sled bag was a plastic sack labeled DOG and a smaller one labeled CARL. The DOG bag was full of frozen balls, one of which he handed to each of the dogs. Watching them put the balls between their paws and break them apart with their back teeth, he could see this was a snack they were used to and liked.

The CARL bag held pemmican. Chopped up jerky, blueberries, and rose hips blended with rendered fat. The fat melted on his tongue—the taste reminding him of what his Dad used to take along for trail snack. The sweet tang of the blueberry with the pulpy rose hip and the smoky taste of the jerky assaulted his mouth, irritated by whiskey. There were twenty bags. Had Carl thought he was going to make a thousand miles in twenty days?

His hands were cold and he put his gloves on. It had slipped his mind how fast heat leaves exposed skin, and even though it was sunny with no wind, the temperature was ten degrees. He saw Roger lace up his sled cover.

He dropped the bags into the sled, strung the cord over the load, and shook the sled. The dogs stood up, and he spent some time looking at the names on their harnesses. He would need to water them at Skwentna, where he hoped he'd be before dark.

It was easy for Rusty and Napoleon to find the trail through the spruce trees while Bill struggled to hold on and stay upright. The swish of the runners and the blurred trees lulled him into a semi-conscious state.

On the Yentna River, where the trail cut into the lowlands next to the bank, the sled bounced over a sapling and snapped him awake just as it teetered on one runner and fell over. The team towed it on its side for ten yards, then halted. He sat up in the snow and was struck by the quiet, so absolute that not a single sound touched him. His forehead was wet, his breath labored. He blinked several times and looked around. It was as if he had been dropped into the middle of a new world alone and was traveling it with no known boundaries.

It was a struggle, but he stood up. The team straightened themselves out, and the towline was tight. These dogs knew more than he did.

"Hyaaa!"

The lead dogs topped out of the valley and stopped. Forty feet behind them, Bill couldn't see over the bank. As the sled came over the rise he saw the rear end of a moose disappear into the trees, the leaders right on its tail. He jumped on the brake.

"Whoa!"

He threw the snow hook and let it drag like an anchor. It didn't slow the team. He wrenched hard, flipping the sled over on its right side. As it was going down he threw his legs in front of him, stiffened them, and drove his heels into the snow. The sled skidded to a halt.

Rusty was wrapped around a sapling. Napoleon stood and looked at the moose running up the hillside.

He righted the sled and stuck the snow hook. He had to disconnect the towline and thread the team backwards out of the trees, and by now the aspirin had worn off and he had a splitting headache. *What was Carl thinking when he'd trained these dogs? There had to be a plan for running this race. Wait a minute—did he really care? If he made it to McGrath nobody could stop him from having a drink.*

He came to a small frozen lake and halted the team. On the map it looked like Rabbit Lake, about a hundred miles from Anchorage. He mushed the dogs to a flat place off the trail and set the snow hook.

He tied the snub line to a tree, unlaced the tarp, and took the water bucket down to the lake. While he was chipping through the ice he saw another team swing in and stop. He recognized Roger Stanley. Who should have been ahead of him.

He filled the bucket, covered the water hole with a sack, and kicked snow on it to keep it from freezing over.

"Mind if I camp with you?" Roger asked.

"Free country," Bill said. "Fact is, I'd be happy to share the work with you."

"What's for dinner?"

"The dogs are getting the best of it," Bill said. "Beaver stew. I'm on frozen chicken."

Roger had a fire going by the time Bill got the dogs watered and fed. Bill shook out his sleeping bag and threw it on a ground pad between two spruce trees. He took two aspirin and sat on the sled to finish his cup of coffee.

"Just like the boy scouts," Roger said.

"Reminds me of the Snow Eifel. I haven't camped out in the snow since the winter of '44. Didn't want to ever do it again."

"What's the Snow Eifel?" Roger said.

"You ever heard of the Battle of the Bulge?"

"No."

"Well, throw another log on that fire and if you don't fall asleep I'll tell you about the Snow Eifel. Is there any more coffee?"

BILL HEARD ROGER moving around before light. He stuck his head out of the sleeping bag. There was a fire going, and Roger's dogs were eating.

"Roger—how'd I get ahead of you yesterday?"

"I got lost. You will too if you stay in the sack. I'll see you down the trail."

Bill crawled out of the bag. His wool clothing was damp, and steam rose from it as he stood by the fire and looked at the dogs. His headache was gone. And his enthusiasm was up—if he'd ever had any for this trip.

"Your turn to cook breakfast, Napoleon."

At the sound of his name Napoleon looked up. There was sympathy in that dog's eyes that sure beat the looks he'd received from people. He was sorry he'd been away from the animals for so long.

He looked at the tracks other teams had made as they passed through without waking him. He thought about Carl's dream to run this crazy race, then about why in the world he was doing it for him. By the time he was warm he had come up with five reasons to turn around and go back to Anchorage.

The dogs ate and drank while Bill sat on the sled and ate frozen chicken, his feet in the snow and his coat open to the fire. He had never eaten frozen chicken for breakfast before, which made him wonder what would be in his musher bag at the checkpoint. If he was lucky the dogs would get beaver and he'd get bags of frozen moose stew that could be heated up. Now, if Major Russell would get the message and send out a dozen sourdough buns and fireweed honey . . . .

He took a deep breath. The cold killed all of the smells but the spruce trees and the fire. He exhaled. This was the best he had felt for a long time. His headache was gone, and he didn't ache anywhere in particular. He inhaled again and held it.

He heard dogs, and a team came into view. He waved. In a few seconds they were gone. His dogs watched them go, then looked at Bill, their eyes asking if they were going to leave soon.

"You ready?" he said.

They wagged their tails. Rusty jumped up and down and barked. The others stood and shook themselves.

He packed the sled and untied the snub line. The sky in the southeast was beginning to lighten—it would be sunrise in another couple of hours. He stood on the runners and looked around the campsite. The fire had burned itself into the snow and would go out in an hour.

"Hyaaa!"

Napoleon and Rusty snapped the tow line straight, the wheel dogs leaned into the weight of the sled, and the team pulled onto the trail.

CHAPTER 26

THE DOGS SETTLED DOWN after the first mile, and Bill tried to calculate the wind-chill factor. He could not believe how fast they were traveling—had to be between twelve and fifteen miles an hour, and he was cold. He started kicking when they came to a hill, but they were going so fast he couldn't get his foot to bite in before it bounced off.

When they were on the level he practiced bending his knee like he was running with one leg, placing his foot between the runners and kicking. Hard to tell if there was any increase in speed, but it warmed him up.

The sun was just peeking over the mountains when the team came around the trail cut into the side of a hill and Napoleon reached down to take a bite of snow. In that split second, the swing dogs piled into him and the dog was tumbled and wrapped in the harness.

Bill slammed on the brake and ran up to him, traced each line and pulled Napoleon's head and legs out of the harness until he could stand up. He stood erect, had his tail up, and wore that big grin a dog gives a musher when he's healthy and fit.

"Napoleon, when you want a drink just ask. As a matter of fact I'd like a drink myself. You got any whiskey?"

The dog averted his eyes.

Bill looked at him. It was the first time he had taken a moment to really look at one of the dogs. He knew Ilene would have handled these dogs with her hands—they knew her better than they knew him. As he knelt with Napoleon on the trail, the desire for a drink came so fast and strong on him that he tottered.

"We've got to get to McGrath," he said.

The dogs were unimpressed.

The trail was marked with dog-team tracks and old campfires, but as they descended into Moose Creek it split, one fork going across Moose Creek and the other hanging on the bank and then winding out of sight around the corner. Bill made a quick decision and let Rusty lead onto the frozen creek. Rusty and Napoleon were well into the overflow, with the swing dogs dancing to either side of it, before Bill noticed it. He couldn't tell how deep the overflow was or if it was dangerous. The leaders slowed down, the team stopped pulling, and the wheel dogs, who were not yet in the overflow, towed the sled right into it.

"Hyaaa!" he hollered. "Hike! Hike!"

The leaders looked for a way around, but the snow caved off into the water whatever direction they moved. The overflow was now up to their bellies, over the sled runners, and flowing into Bill's boots.

His foot slipped on the ice underneath and he went down on one knee. The sled jerked sideways—he lost his grip and skidded. He tried a one-hand pull up to get back on the runners, but his left arm wouldn't lift him.

"Dammit!"

The leaders made it to the far bank. When the sled hit, it pitched up and a runner slid under his foot. The dogs shook a rainbow of water that froze on contact. He pushed them to run to the top of the rise, then called a stop.

He started for the front, reversed, and planted the snow hook. How many times had Dad said that a man on foot in the backcountry was a man in serious danger? Always plant your snow hook or tie the snub line. It only takes a minute, and it could save your life.

He checked the dog's feet, drove on to a flat place, and stopped. There he built a fire, changed his wet clothing, and gave himself and the dogs a snack. He climbed back on the sled and lifted the snow hook.

"Let's see what Skwentna looks like," he said. "Hyaaa!"

FORTY FEET ABOVE THE Skwentna River, a man who introduced himself as Joe Delay walked out from a log cabin with a big smile on his dark face. Apparently other teams had been there but were long gone.

"I want a drink of whiskey," Bill said. "You have any here?"

Delay's smile vanished. He shook his head. "Let's see your dogs. You check in there by the door—just sign your name and the time you came through."

Bill kicked the snow hook in and walked over to the cabin.

Delay picked up one of Napoleon's legs. "You hit the overflow on Moose Creek?"

"Yeah."

"How bad was it?"

"More than a foot deep," Bill said. "You know what time it is?"

"Ten-thirty." He was looking at Napoleon's feet. "Feet look okay. Did you run them or stop and dry them?"

"I stopped. Is there anyone behind me?"

"You're last on the list. You gonna make it?"

"To McGrath, at least. The tavern there still open?"

"McGuire's? Yes, it's open." He stood up. "Your dogs are looking good. Let me check your equipment."

Bill unlaced the sled bag. The bottom was frozen from the overflow crossing. Delay named each piece off as he saw it. "Sleeping bag, axe, snowshoes, food. What are the caribou hides for?"

"We never trusted a sleeping bag—especially wet."

"Ok. You're good to go," Joe said.

"Think I'll brew up some food for them," Bill said. "You care where I go to do that?"

Delay pointed. "I've got some wood split over there and you can have your back to that drift catching the sun."

"Thanks." Bill started off, then stopped. "What's the next checkpoint?"

"Finger Lake. About thirty miles—on a good day."

"How far if you're nursing the remains of a hangover?"

"About a hundred."

Delay headed for the cabin. The thermometer next to the door registered twenty degrees. Almost balmy.

Bill opened the CARL bag. There had to be something besides pemmican in there. He found some moose and caribou jerky, a sack of raisins, and candy bars. The chicken had ice crystals in it, so he tried a candy bar. He had to thaw the bar under his armpit before he could bite it.

A snow machine driver drove up, cut his engine, and slid to a stop. "You the last one?"

"That's what Delay says."

"Your dogs look good. How you feeling?"

"Guess I'll live to McGrath."

The driver tilted his head. "You might make it. The trail's packed good—to Rohn, at least. If a storm hits, you might have trouble finding it in the Farewell area."

"How far ahead are the others?" Bill asked.

"Stretched out between Finger Lake and Rohn. That's about fifty miles from here."

The dogs stood up. Bill looked at them "You're ready, huh?" He closed up the sled bag and pulled the hook. "Okay, let's do it. Hyaaa!"

The takeoff was so fast his left foot slid off the runner and he had to kick with it to get back on. The trail led over the edge, down the bank, and across the Skwentna River, but they were going so fast when they reached the rim that the sled flew off the edge and landed fifteen feet below. He managed to get both feet on the inside runner and keep the sled upright as the lead dogs raced downhill like they were on a mission.

The sun was out, he was following a well-marked trail, and he could stand upright on the runners. Not a bad way to spend a day. He wondered what George Norton was doing right now. Freezing on the street looking for a drink, or asleep in the library next to the heater? And what would the fine Major Russell be doing mid-morning? Did the major really care about him or had he just been one of his projects? Ilene? His face softened. He had to laugh when he thought about running from her. What would she think if she found out he was the last musher to go through?

"Hike! Hike!"

The dogs moved from a trot into a lope. Bill figured they might be going fifteen miles an hour here on the level, maybe faster. He looked at the tug lines, which were as tight as a bowstring.

Carl had got himself a real dog team.

THEY PULLED INTO FINGER Lake at 2:20PM. A man stepped out on the porch and watched him snub the team to a post. Bill stepped off the runners and saw snow that looked like it had been a staging area for the 106th Infantry. Everything was tromped down; spruce boughs and dog crap littered the landscape. A two-foot-deep trail was driven into the snow from the parking area to the lake, where a sack covered a hole through the ice. It was so warm he unbuttoned his jacket on the short walk to the check-in.

"I'm Jerry Morris." The man held out his hand. "You must be Bill Williams."

Bill shook hands and said hello.

"Come on and sign in." Morris headed inside. "What time did you leave Skwentna?"

"About 10:45, I suppose."

Morris looked at a clipboard and ran his finger down the sheet of paper. "That's the fastest time anyone's made between Skwentna and here. Twelve miles an hour, give or take a little." He smiled. "That's moving."

Bill thought a minute. "What was the next best time?"

"Three hours and thirty-five minutes. By the way, the Iditarod Air force dropped off a bag for you."

He stepped back into the room and handed Bill a gunnysack with his name stenciled on it. Inside the sack Bill found some dried salmon, caribou jerky, a piece of cooked beaver tail, a sack of dried blueberries, a small bucket of KFC chicken, and a note:

Bill,

We got some food together for you because we know by now you're tired of chicken. But just in case you aren't, Major Russell is sending some more. Hope you and the dogs are doing well. We pray for you three times a day and are waiting for the radio to tell us where you are.

All the best,

Ilene, Carolee, Maj. Russell

Bill smiled, stuck a piece of smoked salmon in his mouth like a cigar, and nodded to Morris.

"Thanks. I'm going to feed the dogs and get back on the trail."

He clumped down the steps to the sled, gave each dog a ball from the DOG sack, and went back to Morris's cabin.

"Jerry, who was the last musher through here?"

"Roger Stanley. He's ahead of you maybe three hours."

"How far to the next checkpoint?"

"Rohn? About seventy miles. If it was nice and smooth like what you came over it wouldn't be too bad, but you're headed for Ptarmigan Pass. Then through Hell's Gate and up the Kuskokwim. Those are some of the roughest places on this trail."

Bill nodded. "Any weather coming?"

Jerry tapped the barometer twice with his fingertip and turned the center dial. "It's reading 29.4 right now. That's not good. Down a little from this morning."

Bill thought back to his army training. "What would a good storm read?"

"Oh, going down any further than twenty-nine would be a problem this time of the year."

"Think I'll try and beat the weather to Rohn."

Jerry stepped out on the porch as the team trotted by. "Be careful at Happy River," he said. "It's a steep trail down."

Bill waved. *How bad could a place be called Happy River?* The snow machines and the other dog teams had left a hard-packed trail, a virtual highway for him to follow. Being last had its advantages.

RUSTY BROKE INTO A lope, and Napoleon moved with him. The rest of the team got into the act and the sled moved fast through the buried trail. Here and there tops of spruce trees stuck out, and he guessed the snow depth at more than four feet. It got deeper, and he could see places where teams had hauled off the trail, an occasional hole where a musher had stepped in up to his chest.

After an hour they started off the top, following the steep trail down the side of the bluff to Happy River. He could only see edges of the trail carved out of the snow—where it went beyond that would be a discovery for the lead dogs. They picked up speed, and as the sled crested the hill he spotted the dogs below him heading straight downhill. He slammed his left foot on the brake and threw his weight to the right runner, forcing it into the snow.

"Whoa! Whoa!"

He yelled until they reached the bottom. His left pant leg was full of snow packed in by the brake. When they hit the bottom he pushed the brake with every ounce of his strength. It held, and he jammed the hook in with his foot.

"Whoa!" He jumped off and ran to the front of the team.

Four dogs hung by their harnesses over a cliff a thousand feet above Happy River. Their feet just touched the side of the cliff on each swing, but there was no purchase for them.

He took the tow line with both hands, but it slipped through his mittens. He shook off the mittens, pulled the gloves off with his teeth, and wrapped his bare hands around the line.

"Rusty! Napoleon! Here, boy—here , boy!"

He pulled hard on the two hundred pounds of dead weight. The dogs' back feet touched the wall of the canyon on each swing, and during that brief moment they sunk their toenails in. He had the tow line stretched over his shoulder; each time they touched, he pulled and they gained a foot. He called again and they got all four feet into the side of the cliff and strained, their shoulder muscles flexed like racehorses.

He slid the tow line over his shoulder and took up the slack. His strength alone was holding them up. It was like a tug-of-war with a swinging bag of lead. One dog showed his head above the edge, front paws dug into the snow, toes spread wide, curved toenails gaining inches at a time. The swing dogs were up.

He went further down the tow line and wrapped it over his hands and wrists. He called and pulled. Rusty and Napoleon rose up over the edge, and he fell backwards. He lay there a moment, then sat up, pulled on his mittens and gloves, and slapped them on his knee over and over again. From where he sat the view over Happy River was stunning. He grabbed Napoleon and hugged him.

"Let me know next time you're going to do a high dive."

He could see Rainy Pass Lodge several miles before they reached it, and he had already picked out a place to rest and feed the team. The darkness came on them while they were driving in. All through the feeding process the light had dimmed so that he didn't notice how dark it was until he started looking for his food. He craned his neck up and gazed at the stars. They were going to spend the night here. That changed the whole picture. He ate a few bites, then took the axe and began looking for spruce boughs for dog beds.

Every swing of the axe hurt. He cut eight armloads of boughs, snow-shoeing back and forth. Most of the dogs had lain down on the snow, and he had to get them up to put the boughs under them. He wondered if it was worth it.

He sat on the edge of the sled and ate the warmed-up beaver tail so rich in flavor and tallow, something that would stay with him, and then he stopped chewing. His eyes closed and his head dropped to his chest. The beaver tail didn't make a sound when it slid into the snow.

How long he slept there, Bill didn't know. What he did know is that his hands and face were numb. He tried three times to pick up the beaver tail melted down into the snow, but his fingers were so stiff and unfeeling that he gave it up and stood.

With the darkness had come a slight wind from the northwest over Rainy Pass. He stamped his feet. They were stiff but still responded. He did some knee bends, twists, squats, then put mittens on over the gloves and wrapped a scarf around his face, leaving just his eyes open. Several eyelashes were frozen together, so he covered his face with his hands and blew his breath into them until the frost melted.

Why had he ever agreed to do this?

He lay down on the sled and did pushups. He smiled at the thought that he was doing calisthenics when he and Wayne had done everything possible to avoid them while he was in the army.

He worked the big muscles that gave off more heat. When he was done, he considered building a fire or crawling into the sleeping bag. The bag won. Just before he zipped the outer cover he glanced at the dogs, all wrapped in a ball, their faces tucked under their tails. They would get more sleep than he would this night.

A SMACKING SOUND AWAKENED him. He peered through the sleeping bag opening. One of the dogs was eating something close to the sled, pulling the last piece from the snow and tilting his head to get it into his mouth. It looked like beaver tail to Bill. The other dogs were watching him eat but none were challenging him for it.

Back to chicken. He wondered what time it was. The stars had moved—he'd probably slept five or six hours. Weather looked good. The quicker they got to McGrath the quicker he could get out of this race and get his life settled down again.

Settled down to what? What is there in my life that's settled? What's good about it?

He hadn't thought about his life since he got fired from the hotel job. Well, that wasn't quite true. He had thought about whether he had a life at all. He wanted to stay numb most of the time so life wouldn't interfere with him. He couldn't think of any plans he had. He knew where to go when he was cold, when he was hungry, and where to get enough for a bottle. And clothes . . . they gave him clothes at several places. There was some satisfaction in knowing he had learned the street lessons George taught him. He wasn't dead, like Wayne. Old Wayne, who had dodged more bullets coming out of the Snow Eifel than you could shake a stick at, dying in an easy chair.

Unlike him, Carl had had trappings: house, wife, dogs, truck, gold. No kids, though. Wonder why he and Ilene never had any kids?

What does Ilene want out of me? Why did she pick me to run this team? She could have found someone else. I just want to get to McGrath, buy a drink....

I don't have any money. I'll sell something. A dog or something. I'll need a drink when I get there. Matter of fact I need one now.

He worked his way out of the sleeping bag and threw each dog a ball. He hesitated when he came to the dog that had eaten his beaver tail. The name on the collar read Ned.

"Ned is a dog's name?" he said.

The dog looked him in the eyes.

"You full of my beaver tail?" The dog looked from Bill's eyes to his hand holding the meatball.

"I'll expect a lot of you today. You get me to McGrath, I'll let you have beaver and meatballs too." He threw Ned the ball.

He checked his supplies, repacked the sled, and hitched the dogs, giving each one a pat and a rubdown. He stepped on the sled runners.

"Hyaaa!"

The front teams had marked the trail, and that kept Rusty and Napoleon sniffing the tracks when they turned down into Hell's Gate. As they neared the pass, a flock of Ptarmigan erupted into the air and the team burst forward. Each dog thought he had a bird for sure and leapt at it, snapping his jaws in the empty air.

The sled shot out from under Bill and left him hanging by his arms from the drive bow, his body trolling behind like a rudder. The birds crossed the trail, gaining altitude toward the pass, then the lead dogs made a sharp right turn after them and buried themselves in soft snow up to their necks.

In an instant it was quiet. The birds were out of sight and the dogs, tongues dripping saliva over their jaws, tails wagging, looked back at Bill with innocent eyes. Wasn't that fun, boss? Wasn't that a blast? He laughed for the first time in years. Then he cried.

He was alive. Vitality coursed through his body, alone in the high country with a view from horizon to horizon. He had traveled far enough that morning to forget his pains, and his head felt like it belonged to him again. The sharp air purged old habits. The tears came quickly and at first he was ashamed, his head bowed. Then he lifted his head to the bitter chilled sky and let the tears run down his checks.

The dogs left standing chest-deep in the snow seemed to be figuring a way out, as if just standing there letting their feet ball up didn't make sense to them. They stamped their feet and yelped. Bill did not respond.

The tears stopped and he took a deep breath. At that moment the sun broke the horizon and he turned his face to it. The sun is warmth, the sun is life. You who made the sun and the heavens and earth—help me.

Napoleon yelped. Bill looked at him.

Crazy dogs. You stick us in the snow, then holler about it.

He pulled the sled back onto the trail and set the snow hook.

THE REST INVIGORATED THE team, and they headed down toward Hell's Gate with enthusiasm. The southwesterly wind blowing on top kept the snow from piling; Rusty drove right into the wind but Napoleon turned his face from it. On bare ground Bill got off the runners and jogged to lighten the load. The team picked up the pace, and within fifty yards Bill was running like he did in high school. He couldn't keep it up at 3,200 feet, and he jumped back on the runners, which soon slowed the sled down. He got off and ran again.

In daylight it was simple to see the entry into Hell's Gate. The team turned along the trail, which began to serpentine, and Bill could only see his leaders occasionally since they were around a corner before the sled got to it. The river bank was high, and he could see where other teams had crashed.

Rusty and Napoleon disappeared, and the other dogs followed two by two until the sled zinged over the bank. Bill's heart seemed to jump out of his chest and into his mouth. He stopped breathing and clutched the drive bow as the wheel dogs and the sled became airborne. In that fraction of a second in the air he could see the drop was only ten feet.

"Hell's fire—we're gonna live through this."

He was being pulled down the trail at maybe fourteen miles an hour. There was no time to think. The lead dogs were making most of the decisions, but somebody had to stand on the runners, steady the sled, and stop it if he could.

Ahead he could see parts of trees, blow downs, and sweepers, frozen and sticking up through the snow and ice. They could tear a sled up or impale a dog. He slowed the team down.

"Whoa!"

The leaders slowed from a trot to a walk. Where the canyon narrowed, Bill heard the gurgle of open water just as the leaders hopped over a tree and disappeared. He got off the sled and pushed it over the tree. It smacked into the team, bunched up in front of a crevasse. Each group of two dogs jumped across as they came to it, and finally with all sixteen dogs on the other side, the sled was pulled toward the crack.

Bill jumped off, grabbed a stanchion, and heaved with all his strength to throw the front of the sled over the crevasse. But the brush bow tipped down, caught the ice, and the sled dived into the water. The tow line slid along the face of the ice until it jammed into a crack. The team stopped as if it had hit a stone wall.

He braced his feet and pushed back on the sled. It didn't move, but his feet slipped and he slid into the water up to his knees. He scrambled out of the water and jammed the snow hook into a crack in the ice. He took the axe out of the bag, jumped the crevasse, and tied the snub line to a blow down. By the time he sat down at the water's edge to chop the tow line, his legs were numb.

One clean swing of the axe and the tow line separated, but the sled didn't move. It was caught under the slab of ice. Under the tilted-up back of the sled he chopped two pockets in the ice for his feet, then got under the sled and lifted. The moment the bow scraped free, the sled came down on him. The 200 pounds of sled and gear squeezed him against the ice—then he reached a stanchion and pulled on it. The sled moved a few inches. He tried to get his toes to work, to push him out, but he had no feeling in them. On the next pull he reached the brake. He stopped for breath. Two more pulls, and he was out.

He pushed the sled to the other side of the crevasse, took off his mittens, tied the tow line to the bridle with a double half-hitch and yanked it twice. It would have to hold. With numb hands he gave each leader a pat and rubbed all the dogs on the neck while he untied the snub line.

"You're good dogs—just don't know the sled can't jump."

He stood up straight and stretched his back. It was sore but nothing that getting to McGrath wouldn't cure. He couldn't feel his feet. From the map it was maybe five miles through Hell's Gate, and he looked to see how much daylight he had left. He would have to build a fire and thaw out. The camp would start here.

CHAPTER 27

THERE WAS NO LIGHT except for the stars when Bill awoke. He studied the sky for a minute from the warmth of his sleeping bag, spit out a few loose caribou hairs, then decided it was close enough to the new day to get started. The fire had burned out, and while he chugged around gathering up firewood the dogs opened an eye or two but none of them got up.

The feeling had come back into his feet, but from there up every joint, every muscle, was sore, and his skin felt like it was scraped raw.

A little coffee and food and he'd be okay. Dogs seem subdued.

He cooked a double batch of dog food and stood over the dogs to make sure they drank their water. Then he sat on the sled and dawdled with a breakfast of coffee, dried blueberries, and frozen chicken, reluctant to get started. The horizon was beginning to lighten as he pitched the coffee grounds over the windbreak and got the outfit ready.

The ache in his stomach muscles from hauling, lifting, and pushing the sled yesterday had him feeling dragged out. The dogs were moving but not making great time, the wind in the Kusko canyon partly to blame. It was 10:00 by the time the team pulled into the Rohn Roadhouse. He tied the team off, threw them a snack, watered them, and tried to stand up straight. When he got what he thought was straight he put his arms out like a scarecrow.

Another musher walked over, limping. "Hi, I'm Randy Duncan."

"Hello. Bill Williams."

"How did it go through Hells' Gate?" Randy asked.

"I see how they named it."

"Yeah. Crippled up a couple of my dogs. And me," he added.

"You hurt bad?" Bill asked.

"No. Stove up. Don't think anything's busted. How your dogs doing?"

"They seemed lazy coming up the river," Bill said. "They worked hard yesterday, though."

Randy put his hands on the small of his back and stretched back.

"I don't know. I'm thinking of scratching. The lead teams are in Nikolai and McGrath already, and here I am stove up and two dogs hurt."

"I'd like to at least get to McGrath," Bill said.

"Me too. But I think I'll scratch here. I can't see any reason to keep on pounding down this trail."

Bill rubbed his eyes. The windburn had made them sensitive.

"Your eyes hurt?" Randy asked.

"Yeah. The wind, I think."

"Don't you have any sunglasses?"

"I didn't pack my bag," Bill said, "but I didn't see any."

"Boy, you'll need them to get to McGrath. Across that Farewell the wind blows a hundred miles an hour, they tell me."

Randy limped back to the water hole. Bill sat down on the sled and felt the ache going through each section of his body. He could go back with Randy, the two of them together. That would make a load for a bigger plane, and they could all get back to town today or tomorrow. To hell with McGrath, he could be in Anchorage in half a day.

No. He stood up and headed for the checkpoint. The checker, who introduced himself as Mike, pushed a clipboard at Bill and handed him a pencil. "You're the last signature I need."

Bill took the pencil, but his hand was stiff and he shook it at his side. He looked up at Mike and smiled.

"Easier to hold the drive bow than this pencil." He flexed his hands again and signed.

"A guy can wear out his hands on that grip, can't he?" Mike grabbed his coat and hat, and they walked out to the dogs.

"Your dogs look good," Mike said. "They all drinking? No diarrhea or sickness?"

"Yes and no."

"Okay. I've got some stew cooking. If you'd like a hot meal, come on up."

"Thanks. I'll be there soon as I feed the dogs."

"YOU'D DO OKAY WITH the Salvation Army," Bill said as Mike dished out large bowls of moose stew to him and Randy. "They serve a lot of this."

"How about the quality?" Mike asked.

Bill sipped a spoonful. "I think you've got them beat . . . by a hair." He pulled a moose hair from his mouth.

"That's my secret ingredient," Mike said. "Gives it body. What're you boys figuring to do?"

"I'm going to scratch," Randy said.

"I'm going on," Bill said.

Mike nodded. "Well—just let me know when you're pulling out."

Randy looked up. "Bill, you really going on?"

"I've got to."

"Nobody's got to."

"My brother built that sled by hand," Bill said. "He trained those dogs. Two people I think a lot of put me on this sled when I was in no condition to sit in the sled let alone stand on the runners. We're about a third of the way, and I think I'll just finish it."

"The leaders are at McGrath," Mike said. "You'll never catch 'em."

"Probably not, but I've seen some evidence of sick dogs around, and mine aren't sick and they aren't tired. I'll bet those leaders came through with some tired dogs who weren't eating or drinking."

"True," Mike said.

"I didn't get enough training miles on mine," Randy said. "They're pooped out and broken up. So am I. I'm scratching."

"Maybe you ought to wait until morning to scratch," Bill said. "Your dogs will be rested and so will you. You might feel different about it in the morning."

"I don't think so."

The radio crackled. "Rohn, come in. Over."

Mike backed up his chair and walked to the radio table.

"Rohn. Over."

"Any word of Duncan and Williams yet? Over."

"Both are here. Over."

"They comin on? Over."

"Williams says he's coming and Duncan is thinking of scratching. Over."

"Don't know if it will make any difference to them, but a storm has hit between Nikolai and McGrath and all the leaders are stopped dead in their tracks. They're camped out all over the trail. Let us know when your guys leave or scratch or whatever. Over and out."

"Could I buy some aspirin and a pair of old sunglasses from you?" Bill asked Mike when he'd switched off. "My sponsor will send in the money for them."

"I think I can spare some of both," Mike said.

When he left the room, Randy said, "You're really gonna try it, huh?"

Bill nodded. "You know, it's different for me. I haven't been of any use to myself or anybody else for twenty years. I think I gotta finish this race. I've been thinking . . . I don't see how it could be any harder getting from here to Nome than it was coming through Hell's Gate. The storm has stopped the leaders. We can catch up."

"Their dogs will be rested by the time you get there—they'll leave you in their dust."

Bill smiled. "There won't be any dust that far north."

Mike put a bottle of aspirin and a pair of sunglasses on the table. "Try these on. See if they fit."

They were tight, but Bill felt immediate relief from the light. "You sure you can spare these? I'll see the money gets to you."

"Forget it. The mushers left enough dog food behind to way more than cover the cost of those. I hope they work for you."

"I'm already feeling better. Think I could run behind the sled to Farewell."

"I don't know, a man thinks he can run behind the dogs, but the dogs are going twelve miles an hour and the man is doing six or seven and it doesn't equate unless you're going uphill."

Bill stood up. The pain wasn't as bad. He flexed his back and shoulders, lifted his legs and swung his arms.

"I feel pretty good. Mark me down as leaving, Mike. Randy— you coming?"

"Not me. Good luck, Bill. I'll watch how you do. You need anything I've got?"

Bill shook his head. "Thanks, Mike." A quick image flashed through his head and he added, "And as my friend Major Russell would say, God bless you."

Mike gave him a funny look. "About ten miles you'll hit the Post River coming in on your left. Turn up the Post and around Tunis Mountain. You won't miss that—it's almost 6,000 feet high. Trail should be clear from there to Farewell Landing Strip. Good luck."

Bill nodded. On the porch the sun was clear. A good run, and they could make Big River early tomorrow. He would have to travel during the night, but the trail beyond Post River was off the river and it shouldn't provide many obstacles. And if there was a full moon . . . .

Bill's lead dogs wanted to go, stamping their feet and jumping as his team pulled out. As usual, it took a mile or two for the dogs to become a team, but they were considerate of those who wanted to urinate or look at some piece of equipment dropped along the trail. Bill was considerate too, and for long moments of time he wasn't standing on the runners or seeing the dogs, he was planning the rest of this race.

CHAPTER 28

DOWN THE KUSKOKWIM, THE sled moved faster than Bill could run. He leapt up with his hand on the drive bow to keep his balance and was pulled through the air. By the time they reached the entrance to Post River, he stood on the runners and turned the team. The leaders had just straightened the team out when Rusty jumped straight up and the left swing dog disappeared. The team jerked to a stop. Bill jumped off the sled and inched his way along the tug line to the swings.

The dog was visible under the water, imprisoned in a hole in the ice, his harness pulled hard against the edge of the hole.

He reached in, grabbed the harness, and lifted. Water poured off the dog and into Bill's boots. The dog was shaken but breathing. He scanned the banks for firewood, then remembered what his Dad had taught him about a wet dog. He got the team across the hole, took a towel out of the sled, and rubbed the dog as dry as he could. The dog would have to run to dry off.

Past Tunis Mountain, he followed the trail in a northwesterly direction, hoping to see the Farewell towers soon. If he could make those fifty miles, he'd feed and rest the team there and be ready for the trip through Farewell. The map showed the trail to be level, which could mean a fast run.

They rounded a corner and Bill could not believe what he saw. It looked like a frozen waterfall. The trail went up a hill covered in ice.

Two contradictory possibilities hit him: stop and reconnoiter, or drive hard and fast and see if the team could get up the hill. The team was still moving, their backs rising and falling, and through his wind-burned eyes he could see the leaders had not slackened.

"Hyaaa!"

He opened the sled bag and closed his hand around the whip. Rusty and Napoleon reached the base of the ice hill with their mouths open and their bodies gathered in a magnificent effort. When the whip cracked the dogs jumped forward, heads down, chests close to the ground. Their claws dug furrows in the blue-green ice. The sled skidded, then straightened. In seconds they were up and over the hill.

Once over the icy hill, the trail drifted in and out of the trees. Bill stopped. He didn't intend to run clear to Big River with a quart of water in his boots. He dumped out the water, changed his socks and felt liners, and tied them on the sled to freeze-dry. There was no feeling in his feet, but he could move his toes. He stood on the runner and started kicking with first one leg then the other. With an assist from his kicking, the dogs picked up the pace. He reckoned they were running over fifteen miles an hour.

The difference in speed was noticeable. He kicked for a mile, before stopping. If he could kick all the way, they could catch the other mushers. If he could get off the sled and run up the hills, they could catch the other mushers. He hadn't caught anybody yet, but he hoped to catch them all at McGrath—and come hell or high water, he would make McGrath.

The team made good time toward Farewell, and a hundred thoughts crowded his mind. Thoughts about Carl and Ilene building this team to win and he was only taking it as far as the next drink. But—dammit—she knew what I was the day she put me on this sled. He thought about the cost of flying everything out from McGrath instead of Nome. What he would say to Major Russell and Ilene and Carolee if he didn't finish the race?

What would he say to Carl if he did or didn't finish it? I did the best I could. Would Carl believe that? Could Carl see him now? Could Herb Chulpach and Wayne? Could Major Russell be right about this God business and his ideas about this life and the next one?

Why does he believe in me? I don't believe in myself. So far this life has been little more than pain and disappointment. Wait—I enjoyed myself on the *Northland Echo*, I enjoyed big Mike O'Leary. I enjoyed Corporal Reprise Sims, and oh, I enjoyed Wayne. He smiled. I even enjoyed hunting moose with George.

He recalled Peck Hanley. Working those horses through the bogs was a lot harder work than driving these dogs to Nome. The thoughts kept him alert through the spruce forest and tundra of the Farewell area.

It started snowing. It was the kind of snow he didn't see at first, but knew it was coming down. It was wet on his face just a little at a time and then occasionally it would sting. He didn't look up. He pushed the dogs just the same, just as hard, and they didn't feel it either—at first.

Then the parka felt different. The wolf hide the woman used when she made the ruff matted together. The snow melted on his face.

What did he need to be thinking about? Visibility? It would get worse. Darkness? He had everything in handy places, and the flashlight was okay. Dogs? Food, water? Two of them were getting dehydrated. He would have to get them to drink at the next stop. Feet? Dogs seemed to be holding up well, more than he could say for himself.

A light shone out of the canvas sides of the tent at Big River. Bill was lucky to find it in the gathering darkness. A man emerged from the tent and stood by the trail.

He put out his hand. "Hello. Etu Etu."

Bill sunk the hook and limped over to him. "Hello."

Etu Etu turned and walked into the tent. "Please sign paper."

Bill removed his mittens and gloves and flexed his hand until it was loose enough to hold the pencil and sign his name. Etu Etu looked at the paper.

"You are Bill Williams. The last musher. Good. Good." He smiled. "How are your dogs?"

"Okay. Two of them aren't drinking much, I need to hand-water them. Can I get to McGrath tonight?"

"Better here. You go McGrath tomorrow. Big snow stopped them all in McGrath."

"Everybody's at McGrath?"

Etu Etu nodded. "You rest and get early start. Good for you. Good for dogs."

Bill thought for a moment. "I'll feed the dogs."

He got the food and prepared it all, knowing he would have a new sack in McGrath. He took the two dogs that weren't drinking into the tent and hand-dripped water on their tongues. There was no facility to drop a dog here. If they didn't get better, he would drop them in McGrath. He watered both dogs, saw that they ate most of their food, and re-hooked them to the tug line.

Etu Etu opened the flap of the tent. "Ready?"

Bill looked up. He could see the warm inside of the tent lit against the dark backdrop of the sky, the stars and northern lights fighting each other for light dominance. A man he didn't know was inviting him to share his food.

Inside, the floor was covered with food sacks, smoothed out like a carpet except for the cooking area, where a small Coleman stove sat on short legs and held a pot leaking steam and the delicious scent of stew.

Etu Etu handed Bill a tin cup filled to the brim. It was hot and fragrant. There was a small tin of biscuits, one of which he took and dipped in the thick stew.

He chewed and looked at Etu Etu, who smiled back at him but didn't offer any conversation.

"How far to McGrath?" he asked.

Etu Etu cocked his head. "Oh, fifty miles maybe. Maybe not."

"They have a tavern there, don't they?"

Etu Etu nodded.

A mental picture of sitting at the bar overwhelmed him. He didn't know if Ilene had made arrangements for him to have any money or credit in McGrath. He could beg it off someone, but he wasn't a beggar on the trail, he was a musher. Mushers didn't beg drinks off other mushers. How disappointed the major would be to hear that he had made it to McGrath, taken Carl's and Ilene's dreams to the tavern and washed them down with alcohol.

He licked his fingers, wiped them on his pants, and handed his bowl to Etu Etu.

"Thanks," he said. "Mind if I sleep in here?"

A gentle smile, a nod of the head, and his arm pointed to a place along the sidewall of the tent.

Bill took a quick look at the dogs, then lay down. He tried to program his mind to sleep about four hours. The dogs would be refreshed, and he could get by with that. The plan was forming. Sleep four hours, then run to McGrath, scratch at the tavern, and do some drinking while waiting for the plane to pick them up. He'd be last at that point—no one would expect him to do any better. It was a good try but not the right timing, and timing was everything. If they'd come to him ten years ago . . . yes, he might have made a good job of it. His mind fogged, and the dream was not the same as his plan.

The cold was intense when he awoke. He didn't know how long he'd slept, but Etu Etu was snoring on the other side of the tent. He rolled on his side and felt stiff muscles argue about moving. He got to his elbows and knees and stretched, twisting every joint, ligament, and muscle until he could stand up. His right hand cramped, and he grabbed it and held it straight with his left hand until the cramp abated. He sat up and blinked his wind-burned eyes.

He crept through the tent flap, and Napoleon raised his head. He walked over and put both hands around his muzzle.

"Can we get to McGrath in the dark?" he asked the dog.

Napoleon looked him in the eye. Rusty lifted his head.

"Want a snack?" He turned the sled upright and dug into the dog snacks. As each dog came awake, he downed his snack and then looked to make sure the dog next to him had eaten all of his. Bill got water from the hole in the ice and watched each dog drink. The two dogs that hadn't been drinking last night took on enough water so that he didn't have to hand-water. He checked their harnesses, connected the necklines and tug lines, and straightened up again.

His back reminded him of his age and condition. He stood on the runners and pulled the hook.

"The trail forks up ahead," Etu Etu said with just his head stuck out of the tent. "Take the left fork."

"Thank you for your hospitality," Bill said. He smiled and wondered about the man's life. He seemed content, even happy, living out here with few people around. He shook the sled.

"Hyaaa!"

RUSTY AND NAPOLEON GROWLED loud enough for him to hear over the running sled. They ran on with the dogs lifting and dropping their heads, the hair on their backs sticking straight up.

Then he saw them. A quarter of a mile away on a small rise, traveling at the same speed and in the same direction, was a pack of eight wolves.

"Good dog! Good boy!" Bill called out.

The dogs responded with raised tails and a deep growl. The wolves cast glances at the team but continued running parallel in their general direction. Bill turned away to see what the trail held for the next fifty yards. When he looked back, the wolves had stopped and were sitting at the edge of a wind-blown rise, heads tilted back in a howl that made his neck creep. Another quarter-mile, and the wolves were behind them. When he turned to look again, they were loping off his right side about 100 yards away.

Now he could see why the officials had stopped the race at McGrath. The storm blotted out the entire Kuskokwim valley with a white wall of wind. The front of wind and snow was as visible as a building, and they were headed directly into it.

He halted the team and surveyed what he was about to enter. Having second thoughts, he pulled over and tied the team to a spruce tree. He figured they had come about twenty-five miles and had that much yet to go. He snacked the dogs. It would be good to water them, but he noticed several were eating snow, and the others could make it to McGrath without water.

He'd intended to get going as soon as the last dog finished his snack, but as each dog finished, he looked back in the direction of

the wolves, and an uneasy feeling came over Bill. He could no longer see or hear the wolves. What he knew and felt were two different things. He didn't want to test either of them here and now, so
he walked amongst the upraised hackles and erect heads and tails,
and petted each dog and talked to it, then untied the snub line. He
walked back to the sled, and as he reached for the hook he heard the
howls in the trees—much closer now.

He pulled the hook but didn't have to shake the sled to get the
dogs' attention—they were all standing and looking back in the
direction of the howls.

"Hyaaa!"

Rusty and Napoleon turned their heads and pulled onto the
trail, the swing dogs doing a good job of making the turn and the
wheel dogs pulling to put the sled in the tracks and on the trail to
McGrath.

Bill zipped his parka closed and made sure his scarf was handy
if he needed to cover his nose and mouth. He'd been in Alaskan
storms many times, but this was the first time he'd headed into one
because he wanted a drink more than anything else in the world.
Common sense dictated that he camp and ride out the storm. His
desire for a drink pushed him toward McGrath. Get to where there
was whiskey, then he could scratch the race and end this hardscrab-
ble experiment with his life.

The dogs slowed and almost stopped at the edge of the storm.
Never had Bill seen anything like it. The edges swirled with small
snow particles being driven parallel to the ground. Inside the storm,
the sky was black. And the sound. The sound was like an endless
train coming by just outside his vision, somewhere within that
boiling mass. It blotted out the trail, the sky, and the surroundings.
Rusty looked back at Bill as if to ask, "You want us to go into that?"

Bill could taste the bourbon now, and the inside of his mouth was
wet. He pulled the whip out of the bag and cracked it over their heads.

"Hyaaa!"

The sound of his yell was swallowed up by the roar of the storm,
but the dogs heard it and picked up their pace.

CHAPTER 29

THE WOLVES WATCHED THE team disappear into the storm front. They sat on their haunches for a minute, then the leader stood up, shook himself, and started off at a trot parallel to the storm line.

Inside the storm Bill could not see past the wheel dogs. The sled began to slow. Bill cracked the whip, but the speed did not change.

Okay, take your time—it isn't far.

A wave of dizziness swept over him and he thought he would fall. He tightened his grip on the drive bow and lifted one foot after another to make sure he was on a runner. All boundaries had disappeared. There was no up or down or sideways, and only one color. Somewhere in this whiteout there was a trail, but the dogs would have to find it.

You don't know where you are, do you? Well, at least you know who you are. You're one lost Indian.

A tree became visible on the left side. It looked familiar, and Bill halted the team and set the hook. He walked over and looked at the tree, then around the area. It all seemed familiar.

"We're headed the wrong way," he said. "Napoleon, you got us turned around."

He got back on the sled and turned the team. Napoleon stopped, and the team stopped behind him.

"Hyaaa!"

Nobody moved. He got off the sled and walked to the front. Napoleon looked up at him with a smile on his face.

"Let's go," Bill said.

He pulled the dogs straight and went back to the sled out of sight of the lead dogs again. This time when he yelled the team took off. He closed his eyes to rest them against the driving snow. He wished he could close his ears and rest them from the noise of the storm. When he opened his eyes, he thought he saw the same spruce tree again.

"Whoa!"

He set the hook and looked at the tree. "We've circled—we're headed the wrong way again. You crazy dogs!" He walked over to the leaders, then got down on one knee and took Napoleon's head in his hands. His eyes fell on the outline of a paw track in the snow. The track was bigger and deeper into the snow than any of his dogs would make.

A wolf? He released Napoleon's head and ran his hands over the outline. It was frozen. He walked ahead several yards, checking. The big tracks went straight ahead.

"Okay, I'm crazy. You're right. Let's go."

The wind howled, and he could never see more than fifteen feet ahead of him. He thought at times that he only had two dogs, that the rest of the team had disappeared, run off, joined the wolves. Snow caught in his beard and drove inside the parka hood, the whiteout distorted all balance with the earth, only his feet confirmed the solid substance under them. At times he squeezed the drive bow until his hands were numb so he could feel still attached to the sled.

He was afraid now to think about McGuire's Tavern, afraid the thought would poison his brain and cause him to fail in this storm that could take his life and leave the dogs hooked up to a sled with no driver. He knew the dogs wanted to stop, eat, and curl up. Let the snow blow, they could sleep under it. It was he who wanted the town.

Bill watched the wheel dogs rise in front of him, then felt the sled hit the incline. They came out onto a flat area, and as they whipped by, he could make out the shadowy outlines of airplanes. They were on an airstrip that was also the main street of McGrath. Bill let the dogs run to the edge of the airfield and the lip of the bank going onto the Kuskokwim before he halted them and found a good place to camp. There was another team close by—the weary dogs lifted their heads but did not offer greetings.

The trees close by had all been stripped of their lower branches to provide bedding for dogs. Bill snubbed the team and got out his cooking gear. While the food was warming he dug the sacks out, settled the dogs on them, and covered each of them with a second sack. They started to work on their feet while he cooked and set up the tent.

Set up camp, feed the dogs, then go to McGuire's.

The wind drove down the river and swirled into low-speed whirlwinds at the top of the bank, but the cold was not intense.

A good thing. Water. Got to get them water. He followed a rutted walking trail down to the river and found the mushers' hole in the ice. He filled the buckets and turned to go back. For a moment he had a complete whiteout in front of him. There was no up, no down, no direction, no change of lighting. Everything was flat, and he stood there with the buckets of water dragging on his arms. A whisper of wind cleared the trail, and he trudged back up to find the team mostly covered with snow. Large flakes were falling that would wipe out the trail if it kept up.

Bill smiled. I got here just in time.

He poured water and ladled out the food. Most of the dogs were asleep by the time he headed over to McGuire's Tavern.

He opened the door and stepped in. People were everywhere, with mushers standing at the bar or seated at a table in the back of the room. Several mushers turned and looked at him.

A trapper put his hand on Bill's arm. "I've got beaver. You want to buy some?"

"I don't know if I have any money."

The trapper looked at him like that was something a person should know.

Bill walked up to the bar. He licked his lips and ran his tongue over them.

"What'll you have?" the bartender asked.

Bill looked around, then took a deep breath.

"You the owner?" he asked as he expelled the air.

The man nodded.

Bill ran his hands down the sides of his parka and unzipped it, the cold air trapped inside rising against his face as it escaped from the jacket.

"Did Ilene Williams send any money here for me?"

"You Bill Williams?"

Bill nodded, his tongue folded between his teeth, his eyes searching the owner's face.

"Yeah. You've got a credit. What'll you have?"

Bill let his eyes run over the bottles behind the bar. The warmth was making him drowsy, and his legs felt unstable.

"Do you have any good bourbon? Maker's Mark or Knob Creek?" He swallowed as the saliva built up in his mouth, the anticipated taste of the whiskey activating the soft tissue inside. He could already feel it warming, relaxing, then sending back the fire.

"How about Jim Beam?" the bartender said.

"Do you have Canadian Club?"

"You're pretty choosy for a musher. No. No CC."

"I used to work in a hotel, and we had a good bar. Okay. Jim Beam then. No ice, just in the glass. Half a glass full."

The bartender looked up at him. "That will about use up your credit."

Bill felt a rush of panic. One stiff drink would use up his credit?

"How much more do I have?"

"Enough for four beaver, to only be used for beaver, and about two more ounces of whiskey."

"Two ounces?" Bill said too loudly. He looked around. Several mushers looked at him, drinks in their hands. He rubbed the palms of his hands on the parka. The noise in the back of the room subsided as he stood there, his body weaving slightly.

"Okay," he whispered.

The bartender poured a generous four ounces, and Bill watched him put the cork back in the bottle and return it to the shelf. He reached for the drink and held the glass in his hand. He smelled it first. Maybe he should drink cheaper whiskey. He would get more of it. He smelled it again with his eyes closed.

He set it back on the bar and looked at it. His mind had started a running picture show, and he couldn't stop it. How good he would feel after he had this drink. How many more drinks he would want— would need, would have to have—after he had this drink. This drink wasn't enough, by a long shot. The amount of cheaper whiskey he could have until his credit was used up wouldn't be enough.

He ran his tongue over his teeth, inhaled, and closed his eyes. The smell of the place grew stronger. He put both hands on the bar and took a step back. He opened his eyes and glanced at the people on both sides of him.

Six ounces. That's all? That's not even close.

"You okay?" the bartender asked.

Bill nodded. His mind was racing. If I can get to the Kuskokwim from Anchorage without a drink, I can get from the Kusko to the Yukon and the Yukon to Nome. That's why Ilene only gave me little credit here. She didn't trust me not to get drunk. He took another step backward, then turned around to find the trapper.

"I need some beaver."

The trapper led him outside and pulled the frozen carcasses out of a burlap bag. Bill loaded them in his arms.

"The bartender will pay you. How much are they?"

"Twenty dollars apiece."

"Do you know anything about the trail from here to Gane's Creek?"

"Sure. I trap the Imnoko country. Go there all the time."

"Will you come tell me about it?"

"Can I have your whiskey when I come back?"

"If you go in and save it now."

FOUR HOURS LATER THE trapper lifted the flap of Bill's tent and shook him awake.

"Time to go," he whispered. "I'll give the dogs something."

Bill crawled out of the caribou skins and pulled on his boots. He stuck a piece of jerky in his mouth, thawing and chewing it at the same time, then stepped outside. The snow was still piling up, but the wind wasn't as bad. He didn't like leaving in the dark in country he didn't know, but this was the first day of the rest of the race and he could picture Nome now as a land of golden temples and wide streets.

The trapper had the dogs harnessed, and Bill checked them. Neck line, tug line, harness straight. He offered the trapper a piece of jerky.

The trapper cocked his head in the direction of the Imnoko. "You'll need that out there."

"Thanks for your help."

The trapper nodded, grabbed the lead dogs' harness and started them down the hill and out onto the Kuskokwim River ice. Yelling into the wind, the trapper repeated his instructions. Bill nodded and got the dogs moving. He didn't want to alert the other mushers to his team's leaving McGrath at night.

He was almost to Tatalina when the light began to fill the sky. The swooshing of the runners on the snow gave off a gentle background noise that was amplified in the pre-dawn quiet. Bill felt every surface of the uneven trail as the sled bent and slid over it, driving the vibration through his feet and up his legs.

At Tatalina he turned northwest and crossed the flat country into Ganes Creek. He found the place the trapper had told him about and set the hook. Moving around, chopping the frozen beaver and salmon, and getting water generated enough body heat to keep the cold from bothering him. Their four-hour run had moved them out of the storm and into colder weather.

It had also catapulted them into first place. It was tougher to find the trail now with no previous teams to follow, but they had made good time, and when Bill went to sign in at the check station, it startled him to write his name first on the page.

He signed, then stepped back and looked at the book. It was the first time he had seen his name at the top of anything. He was number one into Ganes Creek and heading for Nome.

"How far behind are the others?" the checker asked.

"I don't know. I left in the dark."

"Left where?"

"McGrath."

The checker scratched his head. "You already here from McGrath? Today?"

Bill nodded.

"Man alive," the checker said. "Who'd want to travel at night?"

Bill shrugged. "It wasn't bad. We had stars, some moonlight."

"Well, that's something. That's something. When you fixin' to leave?"

"Don't know yet."

"Well, come check out when you leave. Need anything?"

Bill pulled on his mittens. "You know the temperature?"

The checker looked through his bifocals and squinted. "Twenty below."

Bill fed the dogs, shook out the sacks, and let the dogs sleep. After he had repacked the sled he crawled on top, covered himself with caribou hides, and fell into a deep sleep. The sled was close enough to the trail that he could hear others if they came by.

Barking dogs awakened him. He pushed the hides back and glanced sideways at the trail. A team was stopped by the cabin. He could see the checker and musher talking, then they both looked over at him. He pulled the hides back in place and a smile crept over his face.

They'll be wondering who this guy is who's sleeping while they're just arriving. Good for them to wonder a little.

BY THE TIME THE third team came through, Bill figured he and the dogs had slept long enough. Besides, they now could follow trail instead of breaking trail. That would make them faster. He shook the sled but he didn't need to. The dogs were all up and alert.

The trail followed the Imnoko River to Cripple Landing, then wound past Hunch Mountain, a 272-foot hump in the middle of the broad flat drainage leading to Poorman. He let the dogs run at their normal pace along the river basin, hoping to catch a glimpse of the leading teams.

He would have to see if running four hours and resting four hours would work. It meant keeping a twenty-four-hour schedule. But that gave him twelve hours on the trail instead of eight. Everyone else stopped at dark. If he didn't get lost or have other night problems, he'd be ahead of the game.

The two teams that had passed him at Ganes Creek were stopped alongside the trail near Placerville. Bill slowed down and waved. They waved back but didn't seem interested in conversation, so he picked up speed and headed for Poorman. He hadn't gone a hundred yards, and he knew why they'd stopped. He would be breaking trail all the way to Ruby. They felt they could catch him when they wanted to.

A slow anger rose inside of him. This wasn't just dogs against dogs. This was also a thinking man's race. They had beaten him to McGrath and were stopped by the storm. Now he was in front, and they were planning on letting him break trail nearly all the way to Nome—then passing him at the last minute with fresher dogs. He would have to review his plans. Get the camping schedule tightened. Lighten his load. Make sure all the dogs were working at the top of their form.

"Hyaaa!" he bellowed. "Move, you huskies! We're on our way to Ruby, come hell or high water."

A PLANE FLEW OVER and the pilot pulled into a stall and threw a bundle out of the window. The lead dogs came to where it lay in the trail looking like a big pineapple with red streamers. Bill set the hook and walked up to it. His name was written on the sack in large black letters.

Inside was some fresh jerky, chocolate, a letter, and a photo. He unwrapped a Hershey bar and bit into the frozen chocolate. It tasted waxy until it warmed up in his mouth. He looked at the photo, still chewing. He smiled, then laughed. There, sitting on the steps of the Salvation Army building in Anchorage, were Patrolman Pat, Major Russell, Ilene, and Carolee. They had smiles on their faces and their arms in the air like they were cheering.

He unfolded the letter.

Dear Bill,

You can't hear us but we got word that you're in the lead out of McGrath and we're cheering our lungs out. Our hopes and prayers are with you always. Love to you from us.

It was signed by each of them.

PS: We also understand you only bought beaver. Your progress is being told at evening vespers and many of the people coming here are cheering also. If you can do it . . . so can they.

God bless you.

Bill blinked several times and his face tightened. He looked at the dogs, all of them wondering if the bag held anything for them.

"Here. Look at this." He showed the photo to each dog. Rusty sniffed the photo, then licked his lips.

"Oh, you smell the jerky, do you? Well, that's for me but I have something for you, too."

He dug out the round balls, held them in his hand and let each dog take one. They begged for the chocolate and jerky but he pocketed those.

He looked at the sky, clear with a few wispy clouds off to the west. He checked the map. They should be able to make the Sulatna River before the next rest.

A north wind was blowing straight into his face. Down in the creek bottoms it was cold, and Bill kicked to keep warm though his energy was flagging. He pulled out some pemmican.

His thoughts drifted, unable to stay on one thought for longer than a moment, then an overwhelming thought settled the confusion. How good he was feeling. How long has it been since I knew

Another team topped the bank and stopped behind John's team.

"Holy Cow," the musher said, "I thought the meeting was gonna be in Nome." He pulled off his glove. "Walt Peski." He stuck out his hand.

"I'm Bill Williams."

"Oh, you're the one Ilene picked up the bib for. Well . . . you're doing good so far." He tugged his glove back on. "Dogs looking good too."

"Yeah . . . I was a little out of it when I started off. Jim Beam took me for a ride."

Walt smiled. "Old Jim knocked out some guys at McGrath, too."

"Two," John said. "They scratched when they couldn't find their team or remember how to get on the sled. Damn shame."

"And a waste," Walt added. "To have come so far."

"You'll be okay?" John said.

Bill nodded. "Good of you to check on me."

Walt turned back. "We're gonna camp up by Long Creek. There's room for your team too if you want to pull in."

"Thanks for the offer."

BILL SMILED WHEN HE went by their camp and didn't awaken a dog, much less a musher. Long Creek was in the middle of his four-hour run, and he was going to work this schedule until he got to the Yukon River.

He had been kicking since they left the Sulatna, and the exertion had kept him from freezing. If he could keep kicking another two hours, he was sure the tingling feeling would be gone and his feet would be warm. It was getting colder, the air was dry and harsh, and the numbness in his face told him that this night was going to be the coldest yet.

Shortly after he made camp the northern lights started, and somehow he felt that was a good omen. This didn't seem like just any night. It had an aurora of its own. It was going to dance and deepen and be very cold, and he knew that intense cold was a taker of life. But he had spruce boughs and food and a good fire going. He and the dogs would be all right.

Nothing moved as he went about fixing the meal for the dogs and himself. He chopped frozen beaver and salmon into the melted snow water and stirred and urged the dogs to eat and drink.

In the bottoms it was searing cold. A tree popped—it sounded like a rifle shot, but it was the cold in the tree. He put four caribou skins over the boughs as far back as he could under the tree drift, tied the sled down, and piled enough wood to feed the fire until they started off again at first light. Had he forgotten anything? He lay down, tucking the skins around him.

He waited for the warmth to begin. It had to be at least thirty below. It had been that cold when he and his dad killed the moose on Trail Creek. The moose had frozen as fast as he cleaned and skinned it, and it was colder here tonight. Maybe it was fifty below. At sixty below your spit freezes before it hits the ground. He almost got up to try it, but the warmth hadn't come yet.

Did I get too cold before I got in? He pinched his butt. Some feeling there. He needed more time.

The lights danced, and he watched them for a while. And then, just when he was thinking he would have to get up and roast himself by the fire, the warmth started coming and he could feel the tips of his fingers. He relaxed, and sleep came.

In the morning, he knew he would have died had there not been coals for a new fire. He had never been so cold in his life. The mucous in his nostrils froze with every breath. His eyes ran and the moisture froze on his eyelashes, freezing the lids shut when he blinked. He had to cup his hands over his mouth and eyes and blow warm air into the pocket to thaw his eyelids, then make sure he blinked his eyes only part way so they wouldn't freeze shut again. He danced around in the partial dawn and slapped himself with his arms, flailed his arms and legs about, did calisthenics, scared the dogs. He would get warm, by God, no matter what it took. A person who's moving around can't freeze.

Dammit—where's my blood gone?

The stillness didn't answer. It absorbed every word he said. He was alone there—and it had to be seventy below zero.

HE APPROACHED RUBY WITH a tired team. John and Walt would surely pass him here, but running four hours and resting four was keeping him in the lead, and he needed the rest.

He checked in amidst a group of the local people, who were happy and proud to see an Indian man leading the race. One young boy took hold of the lead dogs.

"Come to our house," he said with a broad smile.

"How far is it?" Bill asked.

He pointed to a cabin fifty yards away. "Over there."

Bill looked to see if he would be able to tell when other teams went through and decided it didn't make any difference

"Okay," he said, and the boy took off running with Napoleon's tug line in his hand.

At the house, Bill spread the sacks while the boy got water. Two dogs were not drinking.

"You have to hold their mouths open to drink?" the boy asked.

"Just these two. They're too tired to drink."

"Pry these bowls apart and put one in front of each dog," Bill said. The freezing bowls sizzled when Bill ladled the warm food into them.

He had finished feeding the dogs when John and Walt drove into Ruby and greeted him.

"Hey, you didn't camp with us last night," Walt said.

"You guys looked so comfortable I didn't want to wake you up."

"Is that musher talk for I want to stay in the lead?" John said.

"I told you I'd clear the trail for you to Nome," Bill said.

Walt grinned at him. "You and the dogs okay after your bath?"

"Yeah, we're all clean now. We even smell good."

"Okay," John said. "See you down the trail—it'll be faster on the river."

"See you in Nome," Bill said.

He went into the cabin with the boy, who lifted the lid and stirred the pot. The air filled with the pungent smell of meat and fish stew.

The boy led him to a small bedroom.

"This is my room. You can sleep here."

"Thanks. Will you wake me in four hours?"

"Don't you want something to eat?"

"Something besides pemmican and Kentucky fried chicken, maybe?"

"How about stew with fried bannock bread?"

"Okay."

The woman introduced herself as Pauline Mercer. Her husband was away on his trap line, and her son Peter had asked her to invite a musher to their house.

"Where did you camp last night?" Peter said as Bill ate the thick stew.

"The other side of Long Creek."

"Peter," his mother said, "let the man eat."

He did, but not for long.

"Did you drive during the night?"

"Sure did."

"How could you find your way?"

"The moon." Bill patted his pocket. "I have a compass and a map, so I know where I'm going."

"But when it's dark you can't see the trail," Peter said.

"My lead dogs can find the trail."

He was forcing himself to stay awake and knew he would soon lose the struggle.

"I need to go to sleep now. Thank you for the food, it was very good but I'm too sleepy to enjoy any more of it."

He was asleep within moments of lying down on the bed.

PETER SHOOK HIM AWAKE. "It's four hours."

"Okay." He tried to sit up, but the softness of the bed wouldn't let him rise. Peter was sitting in a chair by the bed. "Peter—take my hand."

Peter took both his hands and pulled him to a sitting position. "Hand me my liners."

He bent until he thought he would break, slipped the felt liners onto his feet, and then, holding to the bedpost, stood up.

"Getting old," he said.

"You aren't old," Peter said.

"I'm old and stiff." He ran his hands over his chest and stomach. "But you know something? I'm alive."

He went into the main room, where Pauline sat reading the Bible beside the stove.

"Did Peter watch over me while I slept?" Bill asked.

Pauline nodded and lifted the Bible. "So did this one."

"Well, He has so far. I hope He keeps looking out for us sinners and old fools. In the meantime, thank you for your hospitality. And the good food. I won't forget this."

He went into the arctic entry and put on his outerwear.

"You look a lot bigger when you get your cold clothes on," Peter said.

"That's to scare the bears," Bill said. He rubbed the boy on the head. "I wish I had a son like you."

Peter smiled. "Can I go with you?"

Bill smiled back. "Afraid not. I have to travel light."

"Will you come back?"

"Maybe next year."

"Promise?"

When did I ever promise anybody anything?

"Yes. I promise."

"Can I help you with your dogs?"

"If you do what I say."

"Okay. I will."

They opened the door onto a clear day. The thermometer attached to the unpainted door casing said it was thirty-five degrees below zero.

Bill put on the sunglasses the checker had given him at Rainy Pass Lodge. He couldn't remember his name but he remembered his face, the mustache, his smile—and his kindness in giving him the glasses. He didn't expect them back and he hadn't asked money for them. He'd just given them to him because he needed them.

"First we have to snack the dogs and give them some water," Bill said.

Peter took the bucket in his hand and headed for the water.

Bill looked down the Yukon River. From Ruby to Kaltag they would be on the river. Flat and fast. He could make good time. It was about a hundred miles to Galena—he'd need a stop somewhere along the way, but he might get fifty to sixty miles in before stopping. He wondered where John and Walt were.

Just then three teams came into the checkpoint and stopped. The fast teams were catching him.

CHAPTER 30

ON THE YUKON THE dogs stretched out. He let them run while he watched the riverbank to see if he could determine how fast they were going. The trail hugged the south bank of the river where the snow-machiners had created it. The trees whizzed by, and he judged they were doing maybe twelve miles an hour.

The four-hour run ended about the time the sun began sinking below the tops of the Kaiyuh Mountains. Three of the dogs were slacking on the tug lines, but they all perked up as they came to a pullout where Walt and John must have stopped. Bill sunk the snow hook and stretched his back. He doubted there was another human being within fifty miles. There was an aloneness here that was at once stifling and expanding.

Evening settled in while he cooked the food and checked the dogs. The three slackers seemed okay but wouldn't look him in the face, a sure sign that they were ailing. He hand-watered them, felt their ribs, and gave their legs a massage, then took out a towel and rubbed them all over. It was dark by the time he was through, and most of the dogs were asleep. He tried to stay awake but he nodded, then lay down on the sled and pulled the tarp over him. He would just sleep a couple of hours, and then they'd be off.

His thoughts drifted from Major Russell to Mike O'Leary to Corporal Sims and finally to Ilene. That was the last he remembered until he heard wolves howl. He peeked out of the tarp and realized how stiff and cold he was. The dogs were howling with the wolves.

It was a good time to head towards Galena. He was running more at night now, and he would get a new flashlight there.

The moon illuminated the river trail, and the tracks John and Walt had left were easy to follow. There'd been no storms here since the trail was made, and Napoleon and Rusty didn't even slow down when they struck unbroken trail.

So—Walt and John are camped someplace close by.

They were in the lead again with nothing but white around them, the only sounds the soft whoosh of the runners sliding through the snow and the occasional creak from a wheel-dog harness. The surroundings pulled at Bill's senses, leaving him the distinct impression that the world was made up of a forever flat place in the snow with a few trees in the distance, and that mankind was on a sled being pulled through that flat place with no goal in mind but the running through it. That the beginning was too far back to remember and the end too far ahead to see. His eyes fluttered, his mind drifted, and then he dozed.

The sled veered into deep snow and jolted him awake. The team stopped, and he walked up to the leaders. They were sitting down and looked at him like they expected him to put the sacks out so they could camp. They were five yards off the trail and stuck in the snow.

"Napoleon, you know better than that. We're running four hours, then we'll camp. Okay?" He pulled the dogs back onto the trail. In a few minutes he dozed again, and the leaders pulled off the trail and stopped. The stop awakened him again. He set the hook and walked forward.

"Rusty—you tired? Napoleon—what's the matter, boy? We're running now. We'll camp later. We need to keep moving now." He rubbed the leaders' ears and face. He led them back onto the trail, pulled the hook, and got back on the runners. In a few minutes he was dozing and the team stopped again. He looked around him and took a deep breath.

"So. The driver can't doze if the dogs can't sleep. Is that what you're telling me? I need to stay awake?"

He took out a stick of jerky, then put it back, took out a Hershey bar, peeled back the wrapper, and stuck half the frozen chocolate into his mouth. He couldn't close his lips around it until it melted enough to break up. He chewed on the chocolate, letting the sweet taste stay in his mouth as long as he could before swallowing. Then he put his mind to thinking about something that would keep him awake until they got to Galena.

He traced the arrival of the 106th Infantry Division in the Snow Eifel step by step and arranged it into days. He could remember the cold and the driving rain that turned to snow when they arrived after the long truck ride. He tried to remember each man, each foxhole he dug, the action, how he felt when they surrendered, and their escape. He smiled at the memory of wading the Our River in the dead of winter, and compared it to falling into the Sulatna River a day ago.

It's one thing when you're twenty and another when you're forty-eight. And a foot or two is different from going in up to your armpits.

He caught himself between consciousness and sleep again, and he started to whistle while he pulled out a rope. He tied the rope around the drive bow, took two loops around his waist, and tied the other end to the drive bow on the other side. If he fell asleep, at least he wouldn't lose the sled and team. They would still be a unit even though they might drag him a hundred yards.

THE LATCHSTRING WAS OUT on the Galena check point cabin. Bill pulled it and looked inside. A sleepy voice said, "Yes?"

"I'd like to check in and out," Bill said.

"Just a minute." The checker came out in a bathrobe.

"Sorry," he said. "Didn't know anybody was running at night. And who might you be?"

"Bill Williams. How far you figure it is to Nulato?"

"Fifty . . . sixty miles."

"Is the trail good?"

The checker nodded. "They just cut it yesterday and we haven't had any weather since then. The big one blew through a few days ago when you all were held up in McGrath. Should be clean and fast."

Bill nodded and smiled. As tired and hungry and dirty as he was, he was smiling more on this trip than he had smiled since he could remember. There was a good feeling running through him— smiles had been missing from his life, but here on the Yukon, in this race, he was enjoying himself.

"Thank you," he said.

He drove the team through the village and found a flat space near the trail. He cooked the dogs' food, chopped a hole in the ice and watered them, and made camp with his last energy. He used another flare to start large logs bunched on the riverbank. The fire got so big it melted snow for a radius of ten yards, and he had to move his camp further back.

Getting water, building a fire, tending the dogs, and cooking was taking too much time. If he had to hand-water some dogs or help them with their feet, it ate into his sleep time. If he dozed standing on the runners, the dogs stopped. He would think about that in the daylight when he wasn't so tired.

It was two o'clock in the morning before he went to sleep. Despite his fatigue, he had worked out a routine to speed up the chores. He would try it on the river camps and refine it so when he got into Eskimo country he'd have it down pat.

When he awoke there wasn't a sound. The cold had drifted in and covered the river village. A wisp of smoke rose from two chimneys about four feet above the roof, then flattened out and spread horizontal to the ground. Bill could hardly keep his eyes open. He turned on his side, pulled his legs up against his chest, got to his knees and stayed in that position, trying to stabilize his head. Weariness was jammed into every joint and muscle in his body. He wondered how the dogs felt. He crawled out and stood up. Several dogs raised their heads and looked at him. When they saw he wasn't going to feed them yet, they covered their faces with their tails.

"Let's get out of here," he said. "Let's go downriver." He started to hook them up, then realized they could eat a snack ball while he was getting ready.

The team looked good. There was not a hint of light, but the full moon made travel easy on the river. He could see where moose had crossed the trail, and where they had walked in it for some distance to avoid the deep snow.

The first pink streaks of light broke over the hills near Yistletaw. He stopped and cooked a huge meal for the dogs, feeding the last of the beaver and salmon. *I hope Ilene shipped more to Nulato or Kaltag. I can run to Nulato on this feeding but I don't want to mess with dry dog food.*

Wonder how far I am ahead of John and Walt or the other teams at Ruby? They didn't have to stay the night if they didn't want to.

The routine he had thought of going to sleep last night worked well this morning, and he was sure he had cut time off the camp-and-eat process. He could cut down more—but where? He needed to look at it again.

He passed through Koyukuk like a freight train. Several people shouted when he came through down on the river. He waved but didn't rest there. He'd learned one thing about the villages. Their people were friendly and helpful and at times villages were havens from the cold and dark, but stopping in them took twice as much time. To eat hot stew and mop it up with fresh bread, stretch out on a bed, get really warm all the way through, were treats to a cold, hungry musher, but they were time-consuming treats. You had to be civil, engage in conversation, answer questions.

He heard an airplane and saw it land at Nulato, close to the river. By the time he got there the villagers had gathered at the checkpoint and were calling out to get him to come to their homes. They all had good sales points: hot moose stew, fresh bannock, smoked salmon, a place for the dogs, an available bed. Each proposition was put forward by an energetic youngster with a big smile who imagined himself behind a team of huskies, standing tall, whip in hand. Who also wanted to be able to say that the first musher stayed at his home.

Bill stopped on the side of the runway and looked for his musher's sack. He walked the length of the sacks stacked against the snow berm. None had his name on it. As he shook his head, the checker walked up.

"You must be Bill Williams. I'm George Walton. How're you doing?"

"Can't find my sack."

"Well, let's see." George grabbed a couple of sacks and pulled them forward to look on the backs. "I don't see it either. Tell you what—you can take either of these sacks. These guys scratched at McGrath and I'm sure they won't mind."

"Okay."

The first sack had commercial dog food in cooking-size pouches. There was also a sack for a musher with a card attached to it from his wife. Bill hesitated.

"Go ahead," George said. "He's never gonna see it."

Inside the sack along with chocolate, trail mix, and several small packets of M&M's were three 1.5 ounce bottles of Kentucky Sour Mash Bourbon.

"Well, there's a trail treat," George said. "A wee dram of whiskey to ward off boredom and exhaustion."

Bill clutched the three little bottles in one hand. He didn't have a long argument with himself about them—the decision took only a few seconds. He loosened his grip on the bottles, bounced them in his hand, and handed them to George.

"Not my brand," he said.

George put them in his pocket. "Well, I'm sure I'll find someone who can use them."

Bill swallowed. The saliva had started to flow. He swallowed twice more, then forced his mind to think of the dogs.

"I don't know if they'll eat this stuff," he said.

"What you been feeding them?" George asked.

"Beaver. Beaver and salmon."

"You'll be able to get some beaver in Kaltag. I heard Whitey Simmons came into Kaltag with thirty beaver on his sled."

"Then they can live on this until we get there." He lifted the sack and took it to his sled.

A small boy tugged on his sleeve. "Come to our house—we're ready for you. Come on." He pulled Bill toward his house.

"Wait—wait. I need to bring the team."

At the house, he watered and fed the dogs, hand-watering four of them. He put some Vaseline on an irritation that was developing on Rusty's left front foot, which Rusty proceeded to lick off.

The family fed him plenty and showed him a bed surrounded by hanging blankets that made a womb of darkness. Bill barely noticed—he was asleep as soon as he rolled over. When he told the boy to wake him in four hours, the boy asked if he could do anything else for him.

"Yes—make a list of the mushers that come through while I'm sleeping." The boy nodded, and the last thing Bill remembered was his asking his mother for a pencil and paper.

When he awoke it was dark outside and he tried to recall what time it was when he went to sleep. He sat up on the edge of the bed, a ripe, sweaty smell rising up his shirt.

Either I have to get a bath or take another swim in a river.

He stood up and was unsteady for a moment. He parted the blankets and walked out into the room. The boy's mother was writing in a book.

"Hello," she said.

"Hello. What time is it?"

"Seven."

Bill blinked several times and rubbed his hands on his coveralls. He had been asleep nine hours.

"Where's the boy?" he asked.

She nodded her head in the direction of the checker's cabin. "He's keeping track of who's coming and going."

"I asked him . . . " He stopped and put his tongue between his teeth.

It didn't make any difference now. He felt refreshed and he hoped the dogs did too.

"Would you like some coffee and pancakes?" the woman asked.

"That would be nice. I'll check the dogs."

At the checker station Bill found the boy. He looked up at Bill, smiled, and handed him the small paper pad with the names scrawled in large block letters.

1. John Scribner

2. Walt Peski

3. Joe Branigan

4. Harold Green

5. (the number was waiting for a name)

"Did any of them stop in town for the night?" Bill asked.

The boy looked at the checker.

"No," George said. "They all checked out."

"When?"

"Well, let's see. Scribner and Peski were traveling together and they left at 12:30. Branigan around 1:30 and Green took off at 2:16."

"How did they look?"

"Looked good," George said.

Four teams ahead of me, but they'll be stopping for the night. If I can run four hours, that'll put me in Kaltag about midnight. Then find the guy with the beavers, leave around four in the morning, and be a good way toward Unalakleet by dawn while they're still sleeping.

He walked back to his dogs. At first they were Carl's dogs, and the association between them and his brother was still strong. But since the Sulatna River dunking, he'd come to think of them as his dogs. He liked that thought.

What'll happen to the dogs when the race is over? Would Ilene let me keep them? What would I do with them in Anchorage anyway? Well . . . I don't have to stay in Anchorage. I'm not making much of a life there.

"Can I help feed them?" the boy asked.

Bill shook off his mind games and reached into the bag.

"Here. Give them each one ball."

He checked the snub line and went in for pancakes. By 8:00 he was standing on the runners. The boy was in the sled basket.

"Okay. Who wants to get on with this race? Who wants to go? Hyaaa!"

The team trotted out of village and down onto the Yukon, tails up and wagging. At the edge of the river ice, Bill stopped the team and the boy crawled off.

"Goodbye," Bill said. "Thanks for everything."

The boy hugged him. Even with all the clothes between them Bill could feel his strength and determination. He held the hug long enough that Bill began to feel uncomfortable about it.

"We need to get going," he said, and the boy let go.

"When will you be back?"

"Maybe next year," Bill said.

"I'll wait for you then and I'll do everything for you again."

"Okay. We agree on that."

"Goodbye," the boy said and stood back as the team drove out onto the river ice, following a strong trail made by the preceding teams.

A fair wind blew at his back as they hit the Yukon, and Bill started kicking. It made him warm, got rid of the aches and pains, and speeded up the travel. He'd been traveling about two hours when he saw a camp only five yards off the trail. Their dogs barked and his team responded, but he didn't recognize the teams or the outfit. Had to be Branigan and Green, holed up with a tarp set against the wind coming downriver, their fire almost out. He'd be two hours ahead of them when he got to Kaltag.

He'd forgotten to get a flashlight in Ruby. Somehow he had to remember to get one in Kaltag. Going out onto Norton Sound at night without a flashlight would be foolhardy.

In another hour he passed John and Walt's camp. When morning came they'd be hot on his trail and traveling fast. They were getting a good night's sleep and their dogs would be rested.

Some village dogs barked as he climbed the long bluff into Kaltag, and out of the night villagers began to materialize at the checker's cabin. Didn't these people ever sleep? The village was treating the Iditarod as a vacation from the dreary winter life.

"Anyone know a Whitey Simmons?" Bill asked the checker.

"Right here," a voice said beside him.

"You've got beaver?"

"Yup. Twenty bucks a carcass."

"How many have you got?"

"More'n you'll need."

"Let me check my bag and I'll tell you," Bill said.

Whitey tipped his head. "Okay. But they get more pricey the longer it goes past waking me up."

When the checker brought his bag, Bill opened it to find only one beaver carcass and about a dozen salmon.

"Whitey, I'll take eight beaver. Wait a minute. I'll take them all if you'll accept credit from my sister-in-law."

"Who's she?"

"Carl Williams' widow from Arctic Village," the checker said. "She's good for it."

"I don't know," Whitey said. "I should save some for these other mushers." Bill didn't want to leave beaver behind for other mushers who might have figured out that what they were feeding wasn't doing the job for the dogs. He didn't want to haul all of the carcasses on the sled, either.

He looked at Whitey. "Well?"

"Okay . . . okay. You tell me where to get the money from her and I'll do it."

Bill took eight beaver on his sled, put the other twelve in a bag, and told the checker to have them sent to Shaktoolik with the Iditarod airplane.

"I need to get a flashlight," he said when he signed out.

"I got an extra you can borrow," the checker said. He brought it out from his cabin. "Send it back or send me a new one from Nome. I kinda like having a spare."

"Thanks. I'll be sure and do that."

BILL MUSHED THE TEAM about a mile off the Yukon River. If he could judge a four-hour sleep, he could be out of here and halfway to Unalakleet by dawn.

After feeding the dogs, he built up the fire and moved the sled close to it. He removed his heavy outer clothing, put it under him on the sled, and lay down. Now if the fire would just last about four hours, the cold would wake him up. He crossed his feet and tucked his hands under his armpits. He was hot on the fire side and cold on the other. He went to sleep with some reservations as to whether his plan was going to work or not.

He awoke looking at the stars. He felt like his right kidney had frozen and all of his ribs had fused, and it took him two tries to sit up on the sled and get his feet over the side. He added more driftwood to the fire, which was a circle of coals blinking in the pre-dawn darkness, and danced around to warm up while the fire grew hot enough to cook a meal and melt snow.

While the dog food was cooking he checked the trail. No new tracks beyond where he'd turned off last night. He was still in the lead. Now the dogs. Three didn't get up and respond to the morning call. He checked each of them, running his hand over them, touching all of their bodies where they might have injured themselves. They acted down in the mouth and had runny stools, probably from the brief change in diet. The beaver and salmon would get them back in shape.

There was a hint of daylight in the eastern sky as they drove down the Unalakleet River basin and up and down the Nulato Hills. The constant wind whipped the snow into swirls, and Bill had to focus hard to keep from getting disoriented. With three dogs feeling poorly and the extra beaver weight, the sled slowed down—the ninety-two-mile run would take at least two four-hour stretches—but that didn't bother him as he twisted and bent himself over the drive bow, working the kinks out of his body. Go easy with the stretching. You're almost forty-eight years old. Actually, you feel stronger now than you ever have. If Wayne had lived to see this he wouldn't have believed it.

THE SUN EDGED UP over the Nulato Hills and pushed its way south little by little. At a place where it topped the hills and bathed the trail in sunlight, Bill hauled the team to a stop in a circle made by a snow machine. When he stopped he was amazed at the strength of the wind that had been behind him. With it at his back, he hadn't heard the menacing wail it was making over the whaleback ridges.

The dogs looked at him, expecting a treat. Had they not pulled the heavy sled and him four hours without a stop? He grinned at them.

"You want a snack, don't you?"

He dug in the sled sack. He'd forgotten that he'd let that boy feed them the last balls. There'd be more in the sack at Unalakleet, but the dogs were looking at his hands coming out of the sack right now. They closed their mouths and swallowed. Then they looked at Bill, tails stiff.

"No more. All gone."

The dogs looked at his hands again and then at his face. Some gave up and lay down. Rusty and Napoleon did not. They waited, convinced he was fooling them. At the bottom of the sack, almost forgotten, was a half-bucket of Kentucky Fried Chicken.

"What'll you give for some chicken? Would you like white meat or dark meat?"

Every dog stood erect, tails wagging, mouths clamped shut and ears forward, eyes on the bucket. The man had found something to eat.

"We have a leg?"

He held it up for the dogs to view, and sixteen pairs of eyes followed his hand. He put it back in the bucket and withdrew another piece. "This is a thigh. Dark meat like the leg, but more meat and less sinew." The wheel dogs stamped their feet. They were the closest and they could smell the chicken even though the grease was frozen solid in the crusty covering.

There were not sixteen pieces. He looked at the pemmican and jerky. There was sure to be a re-supply in Unalakleet for man and dog. He handed out the chicken first, then the jerky and pemmican. He ate the last piece of jerky and a hard candy he found in the bottom of the sack. He looked around for wood to build a fire and melt water, but there was none. The dogs would have to grab snow.

He pulled behind an outcropping of rocks, where the force of the wind was blunted. The packed snow made it easy to walk and in minutes he distributed the sacks to the dogs, who curled up on them and cleaned their feet. Some were asleep by the time he dragged three caribou hides over to the edge of the trail. Using his heel, he dug a groove in the snow across the trail as long as his leg. Then he put two hides across the groove, lay down on them, and covered himself with the third hide. There was some warmth in the sun, and he judged the temperature to only be about twenty below zero.

CHAPTER 31

SOME DOGS STEPPED OVER and some around the caribou hide Bill was under, but the sled runner ran over his leg. He sat up. The musher, who hadn't seen the hide until the last moment, looked like he thought Bill was coming out of a grave.

"You scared me half to death," he yelled.

"Thanks for being my alarm clock, John."

"I'm Walt."

By then he was too far away to hear Bill. His team looked strong. Bill wondered if Walt had passed John with speed or because John had stopped longer in Kaltag. He walked back to the dogs, alert now that Walt's team had passed.

He was right. They'd caught him about halfway to Unalakleet. They would stop in Unalakleet for the night, having made about a hundred miles that day. If he kept to his schedule he'd be there too, but he would only have gone fifty miles in the last twelve hours while they'd have done their hundred. Still, if the dogs stayed healthy and there were no more accidents, his team could drive up the coast in a series of four-hour drives and win this race.

Wouldn't that be something? He shook his head. *Wouldn't that be something?*

"Okay, saddle up," he said. He pulled the hook and the team slid onto the trail 100 yards ahead of John Scribner. And behind him, coming over the last rise, were two more mushers. The top end in this race was getting crowded.

"Hyaaa!"

Before they passed over the next rise, Bill looked back. He had widened the distance between the two teams by a quarter of a mile. His fresh dogs made an early difference.

We'll see how it works the last 300 miles to Nome.

Towards sunset he heard a siren. It reminded him of Anchorage, but he couldn't for the life of him think of why a siren would be out here. Then he heard church bells ringing.

Is this Sunday? Come on, pull the day up—what day is this?

The siren and bells quit just before he rounded the corner and saw the lodge, three stories tall, amongst a group of tents. The siren again started its low moan, and the church bells began clanging faster and faster. Bill stopped beside Walt.

"Bill, you scared me to death out there. Took ten years off my life, but it sure made my team go faster."

"I didn't know if I could wake up any other way."

"Where do you drop the dogs?" Walt asked.

"What do you mean drop dogs?"

"The slow ones or sick ones."

"I don't know," Bill said. "I didn't know you dropped dogs."

"You only want the fast ones from here on."

Bill checked in and was grabbed by an Eskimo family who had chosen him to stay with them. A boy and girl, both about eight or nine, guided him to their home and helped him put the dogs up. When they took him into the house, a wave of dizziness hit him. He'd been numbed and invigorated by the cold, had lived in it for days now, but the warmth and the smell of food stopped him. He was unsure of his foot placement.

"I need to sit down," he said.

The two kids took his hands and led him to an overstuffed chair. He collapsed into it.

"This is our Dad's chair," the boy said.

He and the girl each untied one of Bill's boots and helped him off with his parka and coveralls. He felt like a patient. The woman handed him a cup of coffee. He looked up to thank her.

"I'm Ida. My husband is on a trip. He thought he'd be back before you got to town." She smiled, her hands clasped across her apron.

"Thank you."

He looked at the two kids, one standing beside each of his legs. He put the coffee to his lips, and it almost spilled. His eyes closed for a second. He felt someone take the coffee and then he nodded off for a few minutes and dreamed of the passage through Hell's Gate.

When he awoke the kids were sitting in a chair watching him.

"I might as well be awake," he said. "My dreams are harder than running the race."

"We picked you," the girl said. "You want to know why?" She rocked back and forth.

"Sure. Why?"

She pulled up her feet and crossed them under her. "We heard on the radio about you and that you were last. And now you're first."

He sat in the chair and nodded his head. A dozen responses flooded his brain but he couldn't speak while the lump in his throat grew. *These kids . . . these kids. What do they know of my life? I'll be a one-day flash in their memories, today's leader in the Iditarod. Maybe I won't win. Maybe I won't even make it to Nome.*

Ida put food on the table and the kids helped him out of the chair. He picked at the food, trying to get some of the good heavy meal inside him. He needed the fuel, he knew that, it was just that getting it down was a long, tedious process at this moment.

He noticed they'd hung his clothes around the stove to dry, but the slow movement of his eyes caught little else. He answered their questions but he couldn't remember them afterward. The warmth surrounded him, and with his stomach full, he asked if he could sit in the big chair again and would they wake him after three hours.

When they did, a man was there, eating at the table. Bill started to get out of the chair and the man waved him back into it. He was larger than most Eskimos, with broad shoulders and long straight legs.

Bill sat up. "This is a good chair. If I had this chair I'd never leave my house."

"It's easy to nap in, isn't it?" the man said.

"Your kids took off my boots, your wife fed me, and I slept in it. I don't think a man needs any more furniture than this."

"You're probably right. A chair and a snow machine, and a guy could be pretty happy. You going on to Shaktoolik today?"

Bill nodded. "I'm running four hours and resting four hours. Do you know how many teams have come in?"

"Five."

"Five?" Bill sat back. They're all catching me.

The man stood up. "The weather's going to get worse. You should stay. I think a lot of wind and snow."

"Is the weather here now?" Bill asked.

The man shook his head. "No—but I came down in front of it, and you're going into it. It's coming off Norton Sound, so it'll be blowing sideways. Hard going up the hills. The trail might be blown over."

Bill wanted to stay. He wanted to eat good hot food again. He wanted to sleep in the chair.

"I can't stay," he said. "Some good people think I can do this, and for me . . . ," He bit the side of his lip. "I've got to do this for me."

He thanked them, put on his outer clothing in the arctic entry, and inhaled several times to get his lungs ready for the cold air.

Ida came out to the porch. "My man, he's Eskimo. I know there are Eskimo and Indian and white people running this race, and I want you to win it. If I had a gold medal, I'd give it to you now. No matter what, just try and keep going, even if you don't win. You set out to do this thing—now you just keep going. It's not far, and you can do it. My man says your team looks good, and you can do it. When you get to the end of the line, I'll be a real proud person that you were in our house and ate here."

Bill looked at her and smiled. "My mother died when I was born," he said. "I've never had a woman tell me anything good like you did now. Thank you." He zipped his parka. "Can I leave some things here I won't need and you mail them to Arctic Village for me? I'll send you the money when you tell me how much it is."

She smiled and nodded vigorously. "Forget about the money. We'll mail it for you. You just go out there and keep going even if it gets hard."

Bill piled everything except the mandatory equipment in a tarp. She took it. He put out his hand and they shook hands like old friends, Bill holding hers a bit longer than he should have.

WALT HAD GONE AHEAD. Good. He'd have a trail to follow. They side slipped down the bank and onto the trail to Shaktoolik, running sometimes on the ice and sometimes on the shore. The bag had a new supply of treats for the dogs and him, but thinking about food right now didn't set well with him.

He could be in Shaktoolik in four hours if everything went right. It would be deep night by then, but at least he had Walt to follow for a while.

Halfway to Shaktoolik he caught Walt camped where the hills gave way to the frozen marshland. He passed and waved, but he wasn't sure Walt could see him from the tent. Tiny ice crystals hurtled sideways and bit into his face. He pulled the parka hood tight around his head to avoid the sting, which left him with only one eye to see what there was of the trail.

Rusty and Napoleon slowed down. Now that they were in the lead and with the wind drifting snow, it was harder for them to find the trail. Bill stopped the sled and walked up to the dogs, who looked at him with expectant faces.

He rubbed their heads. "We gotta get to Shaktoolik. We'll have a rest there, okay?"

My god—here I am talking to the dogs like I expect an answer. If they answer me I'll know something's wrong.

He looked at each dog as he walked back and spoke to first one, then another. They were tilting their heads away from the searing wind, but they looked good. Looked like they could go all the way.

When they came to Shaktoolik, Bill tried to find a spot to park the dogs out of the wind. A huge snowdrift blocked the only street in town. He found a place that wouldn't require him to walk over that drift every time he went back and forth, then signed in with the checker.

He walked back, dead on his feet. Coming through the wind had shrunk his muscles and pulled the vitality out of him. He fed and checked the dogs like a robot and for the first time worried that he might freeze to death. He couldn't shake the fear. But he tipped the sled on its side and bundled up with the caribou skins, not trusting himself to wake up in a house. Four hours—that was all he could stay here. He would never hear another team come into town unless they drove right over him, so he had to wake up and be ready to go. His sleep was fitful and cold.

When he got up, he didn't see the dogs. He looked and couldn't believe it. He walked up alongside where he had left them.

"Rusty. Napoleon. Come on, boys. Where are you?"

The crust broke, and a dog's nose looked out, then another. Like caribou coming out of a river, the dogs rose out of the snow and shook themselves, then stretched. Bill felt a wave of relief, but only for a moment. A vision of two shadowy figures digging his frozen corpse out of the crusted snow passed before him. He shuddered. He had never thought of his own death, not even during the war.

He fed and watered the dogs, the wind turning the water to a thick icy slush before they even got it down. He looked at their feet, but the poor light made it difficult, and he decided they looked good enough to make the last couple of hundred miles. He walked over to sign out and woke the checker up.

"Anyone come in while I was here?" he asked.

The checker pulled his glasses forward on his nose and tilted his head to look through the bifocals.

"Scribner, Peski, Branigan, and Green. And I thought you were the only one crazy enough to run at night."

Damn. He'd come into the village in first place. Now he was in fifth.

"Thanks," he muttered.

"Watch that you take the right fork out of town and don't run out towards the point," the checker said.

Bill nodded and closed the door. As he neared the sled, he heard sounds that made him run. He vaulted over a small drift and jumped into the middle of the team, where two dogs were in a fight. He grabbed the whip and cracked it over their heads. They paid no attention. He used the heavy handle in his hand like a club and brought it down on the shoulder of the top dog. The dog let go and looked up. The dog under him grabbed him by the neck. Bill swung and hit the lower dog, but he held on. Bill dropped the whip, grabbed the dog, and bit his ear.

Instantly the lower dog released his hold and let out a yelp. Bill could taste the blood in his mouth, and with his heavy clothes and greater weight he held the dog under him.

The fight was over. Bill's heart was thudding in his chest.

Let's see the damage.

He inspected both dogs. The bottom one had a cut on his back leg. Bill unhooked him and walked him around. The dog was limping. No telling how bad he would be on the trail.

The dog looked up with sorrowful eyes. "So you're sorry, huh? Don't you know how much I need you out there? You think you can just fight anywhere and its ok and no one will care? Well—I care damn you. You're gonna be left behind."

He took the dog to the checker's cabin.

"Can I leave a dog here?"

"I need you to fill out a form, but you can put him over in that pen. Has he been fed and watered?"

"Yeah. He got in a fight and lost."

"How's the other one?"

"He can make it, I think," Bill said.

THE WIND HAD DIED down and the howling, pushing snow had stopped. Bill climbed onto the runners and lifted the hook.

CHAPTER 32

"Hyaaa!"

Rusty and Napoleon turned onto the trail, and the swing dogs towed the rest of the team over to it. When one of the wheel dogs reached down for a bite of snow, the sled almost caught him in the back legs. *If it isn't one thing it's another.* He glanced from time to time at the dog that had been in the fight. He didn't appear to be suffering.

When the team got out of town, Bill gave a speech.

"Okay . . . " he began. "We're going to run to Nome and then drop dead. You and me together. I don't want any slackers. If you're not pulling your share, you're gonna get the whip—and I'll give your food to those that are pulling." Some of the dogs looked back at him as he talked, his voice the only sound in the beginning light of the day.

He had at last developed a smooth rhythm with his kicking, and it made him feel good to be a working part of the team.

Fifty-eight miles to Koyuk. I've got four teams to catch and I have to follow my plan. But following my plan has let four teams get ahead. What's wrong with it? Maybe when I get near the end I won't be able to stop for four hours. Maybe I'll have to keep going and kill myself. The dogs can take it or they can quit—but they'll outlast a man.

The tempo of his kicking increased, and the sled picked up speed. He began a mental exercise of putting events in his life in sequence and wondering how his life might have gone had they worked out differently.

What if I'd killed the black bear and the grizzly? Would I have stayed in the village and married Ilene and had a nice place and family now?

What if I'd made sergeant in the army?

What if I'd found Herb's gold? Come back with a pan full of it? Would Verda and I have gotten together or just stayed partners in the gold find?

The sun came over the horizon and created a glare landscape. He stopped, dug out the sunglasses, and snacked the dogs. They looked good except for the fighter. Bill took him off the harness and hooked him in the basket. He would give him a ride to Koyuk, then ship him home. He was now down to fourteen dogs.

One of them wouldn't drink. He tried hand watering, but the dog turned his head. When Bill forced his mouth open and dripped water on his tongue, he moved just enough to eject the water. He looked at Bill with sorrowful eyes and lowered his head when Bill released his jaws. He could not be cajoled or threatened. He had run as much as he could. He joined the other dog in the basket.

One stop and I lose two dogs. Now I'm down to thirteen.

Back on the trail, Bill changed kicking legs. It was difficult to get into the same rhythm with his left leg kicking, and his head dropped far enough over the drive bow that the dogs in the basket tried to lick his face. But after a mile he could kick without changing the course of the sled.

Plans began to fill his head now. He would check in at Koyuk and feed the dogs. Maybe he couldn't afford to rest four hours there, would make a quick start for Elim.

He couldn't believe how far they'd come. It was as if he'd been kicking behind a sled since he was born. The wind rash on his face had become a natural texture, the grit in his eyes, normal. This race was lasting longer than his escape from the Bulge—and it was tougher, too. He'd had friends there. Guys who shared the daily struggle of battle. Here it was Bill Williams against the elements and the other mushers. Or was it? The elements were against everybody. The mushers had been receptive of him, kind and help-ful. They weren't against him—he was in the race of his life with them.

What was it Patrolmen Pat had said when Wayne died? Life either wears you down or polishes you up, depending on what you're made of. Well, we're getting a little polishing up right now.

He saw no mushers on the trail to Koyuk. He thought if he was able to see one it would give him an extra shot of motivation. The dogs, too. They liked it when they could chase someone. They got bored just like people. Run for twenty miles in all the same kind of country, no animals or birds to see, just pulling with your nose to the trail—dogs wore down just like mushers. He sang to them for a while but it didn't seem to help either the dogs or him. He went back to kicking. He knew it moved them faster toward Nome, a good bed, a good meal, and maybe some winnings.

What do I do after this is over?

It was the first time he'd thought about the end of it.

My life won't be the same. What do you do after you've been two weeks on a winter trail with dogs? Who needs a dog musher the rest of the year?

His kicking pace had slowed while he was thinking, and now he tried to kick off every second. The pace was killing, but when the mountains behind Koyuk came into view he figured they'd be in town in half an hour. Several hours went by, and they seemed no closer. He stopped, snacked the dogs, and collapsed on the sled. If he got to Koyuk in a couple of hours he could rest some, find out the weather ahead, and get ready for the last dash.

The guys who passed him had planned this race pretty well. They'd let him lay a trail and followed it, just like he'd done the first half of the race. Only now, they cleared out their weak dogs and got rid of their extra stuff and ran towards Nome without a foot on the brake. Smart guys.

He checked in at Koyuk and dropped the two dogs. They gazed at him and the team as it pulled out, but they didn't try to tear down the fence they were tied to.

He was supposed to stop at a local resident's home for food and rest. He got his drop-off bag of food and backup supplies, threw it on the sled, and ran to a place behind the armory where the wind was not pounding.

There were three teams parked there, the dogs sleeping.

Somebody has a change of plans. They've been running all day. Now they're stopped. The game has changed, and they think they can win.

He calculated the time it would take to run to Elim, some fifty miles down Norton Bay and virtually due west. Maybe he could do it in five to six hours. The wind had come from the west all the way from Unalakleet, and now they might be headed right into it.

Everything within him said go to the house. Eat and drink and rest. But he remembered how it felt when he went into the warm house at Unalakleet. How quickly it drained him of energy and desire. He hadn't had any desire when he started this race two weeks ago, but now there was a small fire in his belly.

He stayed with the team. There were three teams in town. That meant two teams were still ahead of him. Probably John and Walt. He could go in the armory and see who was there, but he didn't. He didn't want to feel warm again just now.

He tore open the bag that had his name written on it. Bill Williams, Arctic Village. He smiled. He hadn't been in Arctic Village for years. He reached into the bag and his hand touched something soft. He pulled it out. It was a mink hat with great soft earflaps and a bill on it that would stop wind and snow from pelting his eyes. The inside was insulated and lined with beaver pelt. He took off his hat and tried it on. It slid down and covered his ears with the luxurious fur. Attached to the earflap was a small envelope. He opened it.

Dear Bill,

You're getting this in Koyuk. We don't know how many dogs you have left, what position you're in, how tough

the race has been, or if you're safe and well. But we don't
doubt that you'll make it. We talked David Green's Furs
into making us a deal on this hat. We want you to wear
it when you cross the finish line in Nome. There will be
a surprise when you get there. We love you.

Ilene, Carolee, Sgt. Pat, Major Russell

There was a frozen five-pound chocolate bar inside. He slammed
it against a post and broke off a section. While he chewed it he read
the note over again and used the back of his glove to wipe his eyes.

In two hours and forty minutes, the Williams team was back
on the trail, bucking into the wind and headed for Elim. He had
counted eight, nine, and eleven dogs in the other teams. Other than
at Koyuk, he hadn't seen any dropped dogs. John and Walt might
still be driving full teams. He started an individual screening of his
dogs. He watched to see if the tug line was taut, if each dog had
his tail up and was trotting, if any looked tired or bored. They all
looked good, and it made sense to him to go with as many dogs as
he could since it would lighten each of their loads.

THEY HAD ONLY BEEN on the trail an hour and a half, but Bill's
eyes would not stay open. He could open them and then struggle
to keep from blinking until he was almost asleep, until his knees
collapsed and he stumbled on the runners. He took out a rope and
tied himself to the sled.

The third time he awoke and found himself being dragged
behind the sled, he came up grinning. His legs were stretched out
behind, chest and arms looped over the drive bow, still tied to the
sled but being dragged down the trail like an anchor. He stopped
the team and got into the sack. Rusty and Napoleon gave him a
look he couldn't interpret. He didn't know if they were thinking
they'd like to stop or that he was crazy or what. When he got in the
sack with his head and arms out, he yelled to the dogs to start up.

At least, in this position, he could sleep and they could keep moving without having to pull him along behind them.

When he woke up, he was disoriented. He couldn't see anything. The team was stopped and the dogs were asleep. He knew he would have to get out of the sled and figure out where they were and where the trail was. He could see a trail directly ahead of the leaders and wondered why they had stopped.

His legs were slow to bend. He figured he'd kicked about fifty miles over the last twenty-four hours. Not bad for a man who hadn't done anything but drink for years.

Maybe I'm not washed up at forty-eight. Stiff but not crippled.

"Let's see where we are here." His voice was hoarse.

He walked to the head of the team. There were signs of sleds and snow machines in the snow. He couldn't see far ahead but he could see the trail out front until it disappeared into the dark. He reached down and petted Rusty, then Napoleon.

"Come on, guys. We gotta get to Nome."

They looked at him but didn't rise.

He walked back to the sled and shook it. The dogs rose, stretched, and shook themselves. It was a slow start in the dark, but they were moving again.

The trail rose up and into trees. Bill remembered the trail was to have been along the coast, going pretty much southwest. It bothered him but he didn't give it a second thought until the trail continued on a gentle rise further and in a direction he took to be more northwest.

"Whoa!"

The team stopped. A cloud of steam rose from the dogs' heads and backs. They had been pulling hard.

He got out his compass and the map. His instincts had been right. They were heading northwest.

Where did we miss the trail? He looked at the map. It had to be Moses Point. The dogs had taken the split to the right while he was asleep.

"Dammit!" he yelled. "Dammit, dammit, dammit!"

His heart was pumping hard. He felt strong enough to lift the sled and turn the team around if the leaders didn't take his instructions.

"Gee, Gee! Come on, you lunkheads, get this outfit turned around. You took the wrong trail." Then he corrected himself. "We took the wrong trail."

It was difficult to turn around, for two reasons. The lead dogs were sure they were on the right trail, and the unpacked snow beside the trail swallowed each dog up to his chest as he tried to turn and walk through it.

"Come on, come on—move it! Gee, dammit! Gee, Rusty! Napoleon, make him turn."

Bill had no idea how much time he'd lost or whether he'd know when to turn southwest again—except that it had to be at the coast. He could tell when they hit the ice, but the trail should angle away to the southwest before the ice. He put the compass and map in his parka pocket and zipped it shut.

The trip back down through the hills was fast. So fast that Bill used the snow hook several times and almost lost the sled on one downhill curve. He felt he wasn't as heavy as when he'd started this race, and it was getting harder to hold the sled on one runner.

When the lights of Moses Point came into view, he knew about where they were. At the intersection of the trails he saw how the dogs had chosen the right turn instead of going straight. It looked like a herd of buffalo had tromped over an area several acres in size, and trails went off in all directions. He drove straight to the ice of Norton Bay, a visible line even in the night, and stopped. He got off to look. There were numerous dog and sled tracks, many headed toward Elim. He couldn't be far from Elim—seven, maybe ten miles. How many were ahead of him because of his nap in the sled?

He jogged back to the sled and kicked off.

"Hyaaa!"

The dogs, who thought they had stopped for a snack, were a little slow in moving into their trail pace. Within half a mile they were a synchronized team again, and Bill was proud of them.

The work Carl must have put into this team to get it to this point. He wished he'd had more time with Ilene. He could have sobered up, been more thoughtful. At first the thought that Carl got killed driving dogs seemed preposterous to him. Looking back now, he could see where a musher could get hurt bad, maybe killed. Hell's Gate was one place. And coming out of the Happy River hills was another. He'd been lucky. He was so hung over coming through there that the thought of injury hadn't occurred to him.

The trail rose off the ice and into the low spruce-covered hills before connecting with a road that led into Elim. The wind had stopped and the fresh smell of the spruce forest was a welcome change from the salty sea wind.

It was easy to find the check station. About fifty people were standing around, and large overhead lights lit up the pre-dawn darkness.

A young man tugged on his sleeve.

"You can stay at our house," he said. "Good breakfast, good bed . . . you come?"

"Sign here," the checker said and put the pen on the line for him.

Bill signed, then turned to the young fellow beside him.

"Can't," he said. "Thank you, but I can't."

"We can feed your dogs while you eat and rest," he said.

The dogs looked at Bill like they understood. They'd come fifty miles plus the detour, and they knew they needed to rest. He did too. He was planning on a four-hour stop anyway.

He looked at the check-in sheet. Scribner, Peski, Branigan, Green, and Dick Wilmarth.

"Who's this Wilmarth?" he said.

"Local musher out of Red Devil."

Bill looked at his time in. Wilmarth was in an hour and twenty minutes before him.

"How many dogs did he have?"

"I think he was down to eight or nine. They looked good."

"Where's he staying?"

The young boy spoke up. "Wilmarth's staying with our neighbors. You can talk to him when we go up there."

Bill took a deep breath and as he exhaled, the bottom dropped out of his stomach. It felt like he hadn't eaten for a week. His eyes closed and he left them shut for a few seconds. A bed and a breakfast while somebody else fed his dogs?

"Let's go," he said. "You win. Grab hold of the harness."

As they approached the house, the family poured out of it. One kid grabbed a bucket of water from the entry and started filling the dogs' water bowls. Bill handed over the beaver carcasses and salmon for the dog feeding with a reminder to call him when they thought they had it right so he could check.

The kids looked at each other. Did this musher think they didn't know how to feed a dog?

In the entry Bill removed his outer gear and walked into the main room, mindful of what the heat and scents of a warm home had done to him in Unalakleet. He wanted to displace the trail air and nervous anticipation a little at a time with the heat and smell of the oil fire, the bacon frying, and the bannock. They pulled up a chair for him.

Bill looked at the clock. It was 7:05 and starting to get light outside.

"I can't stay long. I need to be out in two hours."

What made me say that? I planned on four hours.

He wanted to eat all the food they put on his plate, but his head kept drooping. While he was eating, the kids came in and said the dog food was ready for him to inspect.

"Feed it to them—it'll be all right," he heard himself say, not wanting to put on the heavy clothes.

The last thing he remembered was a boy showing him into the bedroom. He didn't dream and he didn't move until the boy woke him. The sun was up. He tried to sit upright in the bed but had trouble with his back. He stood in a few minutes and walked to the living room. The family looked at him as he stood there, weaving slightly. He smiled.

"That was very nice. Thank you," he said.

"Do you want something to eat?" the woman asked.

Bill patted his stomach. "I have enough here to get to Nome."

She smiled and handed him a sack. "Here's some trail food."

Bill took it and thanked her. He went into the entry, shivering at the change in temperature, and put on his coveralls, boots, and parka. He smiled as he took the mink hat from the peg and pulled it over his head. There was a mirror on the opposite wall and he looked in it.

That's me? That's not how I look. He moved his head from side to side and the reflection moved with him. *That's me.* The beard, the gaunt eyes, the skin cracks, the haggard look like he had seen on the German prisoners, all a part of what he saw. He opened the outside door. The cold air was bitter but invigorating. The snow was dusted off the sled, the dogs harnessed and standing. Bill smiled.

"You guys are good," he said. "You're very good." He reached into the sled sack for a chocolate bar, broke off a corner to take with him and handed the rest of the huge bar to the boy who had awakened him.

"Here," he said. "You might like this."

The boy looked at it. "What do I do with it?"

Bill stuck the corner into his mouth and bit off a piece. "You eat it."

The youth smiled. "I'm Alex. Will you come back?"

"Not likely," Bill said. "But thank you for the food and bed. I sure liked it a lot."

"I hope you win," Alex said.

"I won't if I don't get going," Bill said.

He shook the sled and looked at the boy. "Would you lead us out to the trail?"

Alex handed the chocolate to his sister, ran in front of the dogs down to the ice, and turned the leaders onto the trail to White Mountain.

"How far is it to White Mountain?" Bill said.

"It's about forty-six miles on this trail. Don't forget to turn at Walla Walla. There'll be lots of snow-machine tracks and dog trails there, so make sure you get the right one."

"They'll have it marked, I think. Goodbye."

The dogs pulled the lines tight. Bill was proud of them, starting out again with their tails up on only a couple of hours' rest. Now he had to plan on how to win this thing . . .

Wait. He'd forgotten to check out.

"Whoa . . . whoa! Gee, Rusty, Gee Napoleon! Come on—move it!"

The team turned around and sped back to Elim. They had to backtrack half a mile.

First we take the wrong trail. That's the dog's fault—no, it's my fault for going to sleep. Then I don't check out. That's my fault.

The team came into the checkpoint going full speed. The checker stepped out of his house.

"Thought you'd be back," he said.

Bill started to sign and couldn't believe it. Five teams had left ahead of him. While he was sleeping and eating and enjoying the warmth of the house, they'd gotten up and out of Elim. He doubted he could catch them between here and White Mountain, but from White Mountain to Nome he'd make it a first-class race. He signed and noted that he was an hour and a half behind the first team.

"Hyaaa!"

THE TRAIL LED TO a portage through the Kwiktalik Mountains, rising over a thousand feet above the sea and the ridges blocking the north wind. Bill and the team steered through the portage, then cruised down toward Golovin. A north wind caught them as they left the protection of the ridge and knocked two of the dogs over. They quickly regained their feet, but one came up lame. Bill stopped the sled to examine him. He couldn't find any injury, but the dog limped all the way to Golovin.

At Golovin he handed the dogs snacks and dropped off the injured one. He still had not seen any of the five teams in front of him.

They gonna run all day and all night? They can't do that—can they? What if they can? We're running faster now than we were at the start of this race. But so are they. So where do I catch up?

It was easy to follow the trail across the bay and up the Nudyutok River to White Mountain. The dogs perked up, and their trot became a lope as they rounded a bend in the river and saw the village of White Mountain lying against a hillside in the sunshine.

The checker was laughing when Bill opened the door. The smell of cigarette smoke filled the small room. Bill removed his mink hat and looked at the checker, who was winding down his laugh and looking back at him with smile-crinkled eyes.

"I'm Bill Williams. How am I doing?"

"Walt Peski just left. Said he had a complete conversation with his dogs from Elim to here and wished he'd had a pencil and paper 'cause he'd of written it down. I just can't get over the picture of a guy talking to his dogs and listening while they tell him something." He chuckled and shook his head. "You're doing okay. You're in fifth place right now, 'course you've got another eighty miles to go. How many dogs you got left?"

"Thirteen."

"You want to drop any?"

Bill shook his head. "Think I'll keep them all at this point."

"Some of the guys are dropping their slow ones on the theory that the team can only move at the top speed of the slowest dog."

Bill shrugged. He understood the theory but didn't want to leave healthy dogs behind. There was some serious going ahead in the Topkok Hills. He might leave some in Safety, but not here.

"Sign here," the checker said. He scratched his large stomach as Bill signed, then inspected his signature through the glasses that sat low on his nose above a mustache that never stopped moving.

"What's the weather toward Safety?" Bill asked.

"The Air Force tells me there's a hellacious wind coming out of the north in the Topkok funnel. Maybe sixty to eighty-mile-an-hour gusts with a steady fifty miles per hour. Could catch the whole bunch right there and freeze them up. Damnedest place for wind you ever saw. Makes Norton Sound wind seem like the air coming out of a kid's balloon."

Outside, Bill drew in a lungful of fresh air. The cigarette smoke had made him woozy. He took several deep breaths. He remembered being immune to the smoke when he worked at the Lane Hotel and would stop for drinks in the bar after his shift was over. *When was that—a hundred years ago?*

He snacked the dogs. He had to plan on at least one good feeding between here and Nome. He could cull out some of the weighty items in his sled bag, lighten the load. He had what—about a seven to twelve hour run to get to Nome? He could cook a double batch of food right now, feed half and take half with him—feed it on the trail. He wasn't sure he had it right and he went over the plan again, but parts got left out. The grogginess was returning. He needed some sleep.

He shook the sled, but the dogs were slow rising. He wanted to cruise White Mountain and see where the mushers were. He found Scribner's and Peski's sleds parked beside the school, the dogs curled up, the mushers nowhere in sight. He turned down another street and found Branigan and Green beside a large house. Wilmarth's team was stashed behind the checker's house in the sun and close to the checkout. He would know it when anybody left for Safety and Nome. His team was still in harness. They could be on the trail in minutes. He thought he saw a window drape being pulled aside as he drove by. Maybe Wilmarth was awake and about to head out.

Didn't make any difference. He needed to rest, if only for an hour. He found a place where the sun would catch them for a while before it went behind a hill, and then maybe the cold would wake him. It was also close enough to Wilmarth's team that he might hear him leave. He buried the hook in the snow, turned the sled on its side and put the caribou hides down, then pulled three on top and buried himself in them. He was asleep instantly.

It seemed like just minutes before he awoke with cramps in his legs and a sore hip. He straightened his legs and yelled, which woke the dogs. He grabbed his legs. They felt like tree trunks. The muscles were knotted into a tight ball, the pain almost more than he could handle. He stood up and limped around. The dogs raised their heads. When they saw him limping in a circle and yelling, they knew they weren't going anywhere and they lay their heads down and closed their eyes.

"When you guys are hurting, I help you. I rub your legs, give you water, give you a sack to sleep on. When I'm hurting, what do I get? A sorrowful look. That's it." Bill looked around to see if anyone had seen him talking to his dogs. People were all over the village, but no one seemed to think it strange that a musher would talk to his dogs. If the dogs talked back, then they'd be interested.

The sun hadn't set, but Bill didn't want to risk going back to sleep and letting the cramps take him again. He cooked a double batch of food while the dogs slept. The dog food he wouldn't need he put in a sack and dropped off at the checker's along with camping equipment he no longer needed. He noted the checkout times for the teams ahead of him. He hoped they'd camp between White Mountain and Safety for the night, then get an early start and sprint to Nome. Of course, he couldn't count on that.

If he could hold up, he felt sure the dogs could do it. They could go harder than a man could. He dug the flashlight out of the sled bag and stuck it in his parka.

He shook the sled but didn't shout to the dogs. Wanting to leave White Mountain as quietly as he had entered it, he rolled the sled down the bank to the icy muskeg. The sled felt wonderfully light. With the beaver carcasses and salmon out and the extra equipment left behind, Bill was the weight for the team now and not the gear.

He kicked hard down the icy trail and when they reached the Topkok hills he got off and ran, and the dogs, released from the weight, charged the hill. He could see a musher on the next hill when they got to the top. The dogs saw him too. It gave them something to chase, and when they started downhill Bill had to stand on the uphill runner and pull and jerk to keep the sled in the trail—at one point it almost overran the wheel dogs. He was forced to push it into the wind. On the curve he dug the brake into the snow and threw his weight to the uphill side, his breath coming heavy now and sweat trickling down his back. At the next crest the musher was two-thirds up the hill. They had gained on him.

There was no time to plan the final run. Going up the hills and sliding down took all of his concentration. His clothes were sweat-soaked and he worried about coming into the funnel, where the high winds would cut right through him.

"Haw, Rusty—come on, pull! Napoleon . . . haw, haw!"

The leaders listened and turned and the sled angled off, then righted and caught the edge of the trail.

He could hear the wind before he felt it. Coming over the hill it sounded like a flood coming down a canyon. The dogs cocked their ears and kept moving, their eyes fastened on the two teams now in view from the top of the hill.

"Perk up, you buggers—we're going into it."

The dogs didn't hesitate. The wind funnel was like a car wash. Blown snow and dried particles of leaves and bark whipped across his face. Then the wind caught him and tipped the sled over on its side like an empty garbage can. Bill hung onto the drive bow with one hand, his body stretched out behind the sled. The packed snow made it easy going for the dogs, and when he tried to stick the snow hook it bounced and jerked.

He had to get a leg up where he could catch a runner. The heavy clothing slowed him, stalled him—he swung his right leg up in an arc over and over. At last he caught his heel on a stanchion, pulled up enough to reach the hook, and jammed it in, holding it firm with his body weight. The forward momentum ripped up the wind-packed snow until the drag forced the team to give up.

Bill stood up. "Damn you guys, anyway. Can't you hear anything?"

They looked at him, but the gusts were pushing them around on the snow pack and they skidded when they weren't running. The dogs wanted out of there. He lifted the hook and righted the sled. It seemed to him that they were in the middle of the valley about halfway through the funnel. If they could get out of it, they'd be on the sea ice again.

Bill tied himself on the sled. The wind gusts hit hard and frequent with no warning, and staying ready for them all the time was exhausting. Three dogs to windward were knocked over but got back on their feet in the blink of an eye.

A trail marker. It was the first Bill had seen since leaving the hills, and he had to lean uphill hard to avoid hitting it. The wind noise dominated all other sensory perceptions. The wind tugged at his clothes and tried to get past the fur and leather. Bill pulled the parka closer to his face. He didn't know where the others were but he had a good idea where he was. The marker made it clear but it was at the edge of the funnel, where snow-machine trails and dog sled tracks went everywhere.

He stuck the hook and walked ahead with the flashlight. Rusty and Napoleon wanted to turn right and follow the spider web of trails. The snow forced him to half-shut his eyes and he couldn't see well with the batteries so low, but he could see enough to read that most of the tracks led northwest off the ice. He thought he remembered the trail should run southwest on the ice. There were no markers out front in sight, and Bill didn't want to leave the team. He wasn't sure he could find them again if he left. There was no way he could look at the map in that wind, but the compass confirmed the direction.

Whoever had taken the right-hand turn first had led the other four mushers on the wrong trail. They'd probably gone to Solomon by mistake. This was his chance.

He shuddered. The wind had reached inside him, stealing his body heat, and as he turned back to the sled he saw three dogs on the windward side shivering, their hair standing out. They all needed to get out of the wind, get a fire going, eat, and get some rest. They were maybe twenty miles from Safety, the last checkpoint before Nome. He made a mental list: run out of the wind; find some bunched-up logs for a fire, feed the rest of the food and get rid of the weight, sleep for the last push.

I don't want to be buried in a windy place. I wonder if anybody who might be burying me would know that? And I told that hospital attendant to mount my head and put it in the Union Club Bar and feed my body to the wolves. Half of that might happen on this trail if I don't do this right.

He pulled the hook. "Hyaaa! Haw . . . haw!" Rusty and Napoleon looked at him. They had to find and follow the trail. The other teams had turned right. That's where the trail was. They had turned right either by mistake or to get shelter. He wanted neither.

"Come on! Haw . . . haw!"

The leaders heard him and moved to the left. The team followed. If the shivering dogs didn't have food in them it wouldn't make any difference how long he ran them, they wouldn't build up enough body heat. He jumped off and started running beside the sled, hoping to find a bunch of beached logs out of the wind.

He came upon a pile of logs from sweepers, trees that hang over a riverbank. They were frozen hard, every crack and crevice filled with snow and ice.

He set the hook in the packed snow and fumbled at the zipper on the sled bag. It was frozen. Every zipper joint glistened with ice crystals. He removed his glove and put his bare hand on it. The cold metal burned and stuck to his skin, but the zipper moved an inch. He used his other hand. This time he could get a hand in the bag, and he pulled out the dog sacks, Blazo, and the last flare. He shoved the sacks like caulking between the logs and poured the Blazo on them. Then he ripped the cap off the flare and struck it. It sparked. He blew on it and held it away from the wind.

Maybe it's wet. Maybe it will never light.

He blew on it again, lined the two pieces up, and pulled the striker fast across the flare tip. Sparks erupted into a shooting red flame. He closed his eyes for a moment, then aimed the flare at a sack. There was a whump as it exploded and burst into flame. It scared the dogs and singed off Bill's eyebrows but oh, was it warm. It took a few minutes for the frozen logs to catch fire. By then Bill had the food out and a stick of jerky in his mouth.

In five minutes the flames were twenty-five feet high, the frozen logs cracking and popping and the snow melting in puddles around it. The dogs ate and curled for a nap while Bill lay on the sled and let the fire toast him one side at a time. He would only sleep a few minutes. The mushers would have realized their mistake by now and be headed for Safety, and they could surely see this fire rising like a beacon in the wilderness.

The freezing side of Bill woke him up and he started to turn over. The fire was so big that the sled was sitting in melted snow water. There was nothing to put back in the bag, but he zipped it to cut down on wind resistance, pulled the hook, and moved out.

FOR SEVERAL MILES THE lights of the Safety Roadhouse were visible as Bill urged the team on. The lights didn't seem to be getting any closer—in fact, they appeared to be fading in the distance.

How could that be?

Then buildings began to take form, and lights with the distinctive arctic halos shone from prominent points. He stopped the team at the roadhouse. The checker and several townspeople gathered in the surrounding light, the sight and sound of them almost outside of his senses. He signed in and out at the same time and got back on the runners. He was number one and Nome was twenty-two miles away. It had taken him almost twenty days to get here, but he spent only three and a half minutes in Safety.

He didn't trust himself to talk. He could hardly even think. Best to take the team out of there and get into high gear. They could be in Nome in two hours—or maybe five hours. But from here and now, we run all-out. We don't sleep, we don't eat, we run.

Out on the ice a dog wavered, then fell. Before Bill could stop the team the dog had skidded on his nose, then he jumped back up and took off. In a minute he fell again. Bill stopped the team and went up to him. He petted him and roughed him up, and the dog fell asleep. Bill shook him and stood him up. Before he got back to the sled, the dog was down. He unhooked him and brought him back to the sled. As soon as he put him on the sled, he fell asleep.

"Hyaaa!"

The team started off at a trot.

"No—run Hyaaa! . . . Hyaaa!"

He shouted the dogs into a lope. They held it for a short distance, then fell back into a trot. Bill thought that would be all right until he looked behind him and saw flashlights. Other mushers had discovered their mistake and were coming on hard.

"Hyaaa!"

The frame of the Fort Davis Roadhouse was just visible amongst the fish- camp structures, and he strained to see the point where he would leave the Bering Sea and head into Nome up Front Street. He wanted to have the finish line in sight before he took the last remaining strength from his dogs. He heard a musher behind him yell "Trail!"

Bill moved to the right, close up to the snow bank that defined the street. He could feel the electricity of the other team and hear their dogs panting, their harness creaking, and now his dogs went into a lope, their tongues flipping from side to side, saliva dripping, tails like batons in the air, snatching glances at the passing team.

The team pulled even with him, but he didn't recognize the driver. It had to be Wilmarth. They edged past little by little, passed one dog and then another, then the sled eased by in slow motion. It took the heart out of Bill's dogs. They had been passed. Bill held off until he could see the finish line. He wanted to make sure that when he took the next step he had a minute left.

He reached into the sled bag and pulled out the whip. Wilmarth was a hundred feet in front of him when he cracked it. The dogs leapt forward, their feet pounding the snow like someone had forced energy into their lagging bodies.

Wilmarth glanced over his shoulder and saw Rusty and Napoleon narrow the gap between them. He reached into his bag. The crack of his whip sounded like a pistol shot, and his team burst forward.

Bill's elbow was beside his head when he swung the whip again, the crack so loud it hurt his ears. One of the swing dogs stumbled, then gained his feet, but the team had slowed. The gap between the teams was less than sixty feet. The people lining the streets jumped and shouted and the town siren wailed, but Bill was deaf to anything but his heartbeat in his ears. He jumped off the runners and lost his footing. They were going too fast. He made it back onto the runners and kicked with his right leg.

Wilmarth's team pulled ahead. Bill looked behind him. Scribner and Peski were twenty yards back. He could see the whips in their hands, snapping the leather ends in the air. He turned back.

Wilmarth's team veered and then plunged into a group of people on the left side of the street. He jumped off the sled, grabbed the lead dog, and dragged him back into the street, pulling the team behind him. Then he spun around, took the harness in his left hand, and sprinted up the street.

Bill's team was now twenty feet behind him. He dropped his whip and kicked hard with his right leg.

Bill's team closed the gap—almost.

Napoleon had his nose between Wilmarth's legs when they crossed the finish line. Wilmarth fell on the street, his team coming to a halt halfway across the line. Rusty and Napoleon looked back at Bill, their chests heaving and their tongues hanging out.

Bill stumbled down the team line, spoke to each dog and rubbed and petted it. When he got to Napoleon he fell on his knees and hugged him with his eyes closed, tears running down his face. Rusty nudged with his nose and licked him. He reached out and brought Rusty into the hug.

He felt a hand on his shoulder and looked up. He tried to stand, his knees stiff and unbending, and then she was in his arms. He reached around her and brought her to him. Even through his thick parka, he thrilled to the touch of her. When at last he released his grip on her, the flowered scent of her hair lingered on his chest.

"Ilene . . . "

"Hello, Bill."

He hugged her again and smiled at the people standing behind the berm.

"Who's the guy who took second?" he heard one of them ask.

"That's Bill Williams."

"Where's he from?"

"It says Arctic Village. Where's that?"

"Somewhere in the interior."

"I thought they all drove snow machines up there. I didn't know they had any dog drivers."

"Looks like they've got one."

Ilene broke loose and took his hand. "I'll help you with the dogs."

"Good. I'd like your help with the dogs."

She smiled at him. "For how long?"

She took Napoleon's harness in hand and Bill stepped on the runners.

"From now on!" he shouted.

She reached up and put a soft hand over his mouth.

"Shhh . . . you'll wake the neighbors."

Bill kissed her fingers. "By God . . . it feels good to be in Nome."

THE END

Other Square One Titles of Interest

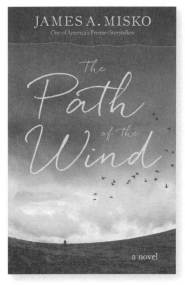

The Path of the Wind
James A. Misko

When Miles Foster received his teaching degree, he dreamed of obtaining a position in the highly respected and financially stable Portland, Oregon school system. Portland was where he and his wife called home—a place where everything a person could want or need was available. Soon, Miles had to face the unwelcomed reality that there were no job openings in Portland. Even worse, the closest available position was in a remote lumber mill town nearly two hundred miles away in central Oregon. Far from the dream job he had anticipated, Miles took the position, which was in an impoverished school with forty students—students who had been passed along despite the sub-par education they had received. Adding to his challenge was a school board with a controlling superintendent—a jealous man who was intolerant of any teaching outside the box, and who became intent on destroying Miles and his teaching career. In *The Path of the Wind*, Miles must find a way to effectively educate his students and defeat the damaging control of the superintendent without losing his job, his marriage, or both.

$17.95 • 320 pages • 5.5 x 8.5-inch paperback
ISBN 978-0-7570-0444-5 • February 2017

As All My Fathers Were
James A. Misko

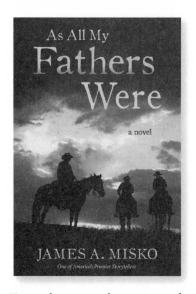

Ranchers, Richard and Seth Barrett, are devoted to running the family ranch on Nebraska's Platte River. It is their intent to keep doing so the rest of their lives; however, the terms of their mother's will requires them to travel by horse and canoe along the Platte River, to understand why their maternal grandfather homesteaded the ranch three generations earlier. From the grave, she commands them to observe industrial farming's harm to the land, air, and water.

A 90-old bachelor farmer, with a game plan of his own, butts in and threatens to disrupt and delay the will's mandatory expedition. While a conniving, wealthy neighbor, seeking to seize the property using a gullible hometown sheriff and a corrupt local politician thwarts their struggle to keep their ranch and meet the will's terms.

The Platte River, "A mile wide and an inch deep," becomes its own character in this turbulent novel and lives up to its legend as being "too thick to drink and too thin to plow."

$19.95 • 416 pages • 6 x 9-inch paperback
ISBN 978-096408264-97

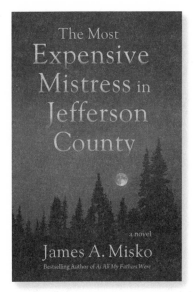

The Most Expensive Mistress in Jefferson County
James A. Misko

What would you do to earn ten million dollars? Would you be willing to compromise your principles? Hawkins "Hawk" Neilson is about to find out in *The Most Expensive Mistress in Jefferson County*.

The United States Forest Service, Fish and Wildlife Service, and Bureau of Land Management and other government agencies have signed a contract—along with 130 ranchers, farmers, and the Nez Pearce Indian Nation—to exchange over $400 million of property in the largest land deal in Idaho history. Hawk has drained his bank account and borrowed more money to close this transaction. Can he make it through the last week before closing? When the Indians suddenly demand an additional million dollars for one of their properties, Hawk explodes. Now he must deal with a situation that could change his life forever.

$15.95 • 208 pages • 5.5 x 8.5-inch paperback
ISBN 978-096408262-5 • December 2016

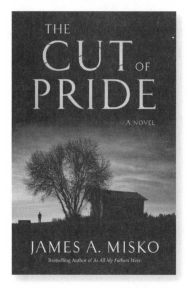

The Cut of Pride
James A. Misko

"In his novel *The Cut of Pride*, Jim Misko does something that is rare in modern literature: He writes about hard, brutal, unpleasant physical labor. And he does so with such vivid detail that the labor itself becomes one of the story's major entities. His cast of complex, dysfunctional characters—owners and employees of a mink-raising farm in coastal Oregon—is nearly destroyed by the seemingly endless toil. Maintaining a sense of human worth is a constant struggle. The brotherhood of men who work well together, like the brotherhood of fellow soldiers, is shown through the friendship of old West Helner and Jeff Baker, a young hired hand. Slaving alongside each other, both are nearly unmanned by Rose—West's domineering wife and owner of the mink enterprise. Here is a story with unforgettable characters, whose pride, distrust, and bitterness make for grim yet gripping drama." —James Alexander Thom, author of *Follow The River*

$15.95 • 208 pages • 5.5 x 8.5-inch paperback
ISBN 978-096408262-5 • December 2016

For more information about our books, visit our website at www.squareonepublishers.com